Sky Dancer

by Midge Bailey

TO MIRANDA

HOPE YOU ENJOY MY BOOK!

Midge x

Dedicated to M, P and E with love, always.

Acknowledgements

Something writers don't often admit to and that's the daily rollercoaster of emotion from crippling self-doubt to glowing pride and back again. Being creative, whether its with words, paint, music, dance - whatever your medium - is empowering and exhausting in equal measure. Each finished work is heavily layered with hours, days, months and, quite often, years of blood, sweat and whittling to the bone.

The burnished gleam of a story ready to be released has been brought about not just by the writer, but also through the invaluable help of others who so very generously give of their time, enthusiasm and friendship. Thank you all so very much for being there for me and for not making me feel like the nuisance I almost certainly was.

To Martin, Poppy, Lily, Sue and Felicity for your love, unwavering support and for being such an important part of this story and the others to come.

To Karen Cox RGN BSc (Hons) for technical medical advice as well as for reading and to Rory Brown for technical HGV advice. To Kate Nash of Kate Nash Literary Agency for guiding me in the right direction and to Jilly Cooper CBE for encouragement and for, rather delightfully, making a 2018 wish come true. I am also indebted to Dawn Cunningham-Read, Sharon Symonds and Sarah Scania for reading Sky Dancer as it grew.

Most of all to my Mum, who is no longer here in a real sense but never far away. Thank you for showing me the power braided into stories and storytelling. Thank you for revealing that which often lies hidden but shimmering with potent magic behind the words.   MB

EAGLES & WILD BOAR

Chapter One

Secrets, we all have them. Stories we'd rather the world didn't know. Past faces, past places, things we've done... or not done. Starvelings in cupboards who hang silent but watchful. Starvelings waiting for that one careless moment when the secret escapes; when it bounds away with manic glee, flinging open doors and unleashing a cacophony of bone on stone rattling which is impossible to stem.

They've got value. Secrets. People are prepared to die for them. Secrets and death.

But it isn't always the one prepared to die for silence that matters. It is the one prepared to kill.

****

Mountain summits in the Scottish Highlands are never the most comfortable places to be in late December but that's where I was, on a mountain, with Gwil. Not quite a ben, more of a corbett, Suilven is an iconic mountain that stands above a wide expanse of barren moor. We'd visited so many times that coming back, even now, still felt like a homecoming. No party hats this time though. This time I was only there because once, a lifetime ago, I'd given my word that I would be.

Through the bitter cold we'd climbed, from relative civilisation to bleak summit, arriving just in time to see the winter sun set. A time for Suilven to become a moon dial, shadowing the land below with its pillar shape ink-black against ice covered bog. Beside the moon, impossibly bright, another big astral player gleamed in; the Plough, semi-inverted as if priest penitent to the North star. There was profound beauty in all that emptiness.

From a backpack, I took out wrapped items: a glass tumbler, opaque with age and a matt black set of nunchaku. Then a thin metal flask from which I poured enough malt whisky to constitute a healthy dram before placing both items, the black and the gold, on a flat stone at the summit cairn.

Contrary to how it looked, the malt and the nunchaku were more totemic than to service any immediate need. In a way they represented a bridge, a bridge between life and death, between this world and the next. Two items, which couldn't have been more diverse, now represented all that had been lost. Even in the peace of that moment, it was impossible to ignore the constant keening around us both - *why, how, what now?* Words to be repeated over and over until they burst out at a roar. A retched hairball of anger, guilt and, ultimately, grief. I was feeling it. The dense weight. The raw, savage slash of it. I swallowed hard and was once again stone. Impervious, cold, emotionless granite like the mountain.

'Well, this is it then,' I said, my voice sounding harsh after so long in silence. Focussing on the distance, I tried to think what else to say whilst we were there. 'Thank you,' ultimately it was all I could find, 'Gwil, thank you so very much for it all.'

I stood beside him, both of us silver shadowed by the moonlight, then lifted him up. I held him high for a brief moment as if to seek a lunar blessing, then removed the lid from the cremation box and released the ash of him into the wind.

Gwilym Collins, mentor and closest of close friends. I'd thought him indestructible, unstoppable and, for a long time, he had been. The loss of him was like a knife wound.

****

A week after the Suilven visit, I spent a fair weather afternoon hanging around at home and thinking, up a mountain again, but this time with ropes. Home was a remote bothy in central Scotland and whilst it had more than a whiff of austere simplicity, it did manage a passable phone signal if I didn't mind climbing four hundred feet up above it. I had wondered if the isolation, let alone the brutal lack of facilities, might turn out to be a problem over time but, even after years, its location remained a constant joy.

Earlier I'd driven for supplies, a not so local shopping trip that took about four hours. I'd also made free with the library wifi connection, downloading messages that had been obligingly piling up since my last visit. Friends and family were well used to such intermittent pickups indulging, mostly without question, my somewhat arcane lifestyle.

At the post office I collected two uninteresting letters and a single neat parcel on which Gwil's handwriting leapt in vibrant and still so alive felt-tipped capitals. Like the messages, it had been waiting. Turning it over and over in my hands, I examined it carefully almost as if Gwil himself might jump out from the taped down wrapping. My hands were stilled by the printed barcode stuck on with the courier label...

...tArvOs, it said, printed below the assorted black lines, preceded and followed by some random numerals.

Tarvos. A word which meant that the neat little package would be work.

Take it or leave it, as always, but that single word was a request for my immediate attention nonetheless.

Inside the mystery package was a book, The Brothers Karamazov by Dostoyevsky which, it had to be said, was an odd choice of text to send at anytime. On the flyleaf was the inscription *To Spider, Happy Christmas* and, tucked between the pages, a single sheet of handwritten codes had been concealed. I almost laughed. It was so Gwil. He'd always had a taste for melodrama. A Russian classic and a page of codes - neither would ever be easy reading.

I put aside the book and studied the codes: A5 in size, a printed copy of a single page on which coloured inks spidered in an abstract artwork of letters and symbols. The codes weren't Gwil's design which probably meant that he'd sent them purely because he'd failed to crack them himself.

Timing, they say, is everything and I had one immediate problem which was that I'd promised myself, during the small hours of a long and bitterly cold night in a bothy at the base of Suilven, that I'd have nothing more to do with that kind of work. I was done. It was over. I'd had my fill of all the death.

Gwil had clearly thought something similar but more literally (if you'd excuse the irony) and he'd sent the package then, rather abruptly, died. His death had left me as the only one currently on staff who could decipher those codes but, perhaps more importantly, it also left me with an understanding. I understood. Finally. I truly did. That frozen night on Suilven gifted that understanding, or perhaps acceptance might be a better term.

The coroner had ruled misadventure. He was wrong. Gwil was an irrepressible, irresponsible risk taker but misadventure, no, that wasn't right. Climbing ropes didn't shear and knots didn't come undone for someone like Gwil.

I studied the package again. The absolute futility of his death had shaken me more than I'd ever admit. But, now, with this work - his work - in my hands perhaps it wouldn't end. Perhaps it should carry on in some form. A re-birth perhaps: to die and so to grow.

Chapter Two - Alyosha

And I will flay the flesh from their bones and strip them bare for angels to eat.

I've done what I've done because of you, Zosima. The dakini have guided well, but I've really done it for you. To keep you safe. It's why I wanted to tell you this, though not like this obviously, this has all gone beyond what I planned. I read somewhere that if you open the window to let in a little fresh air, you have to expect a few flies. Perhaps my illness is the equivalent of a few flies.

And I will flay the flesh from their bones and strip them bare for angels to eat.

You're all that I have that is true; everything else was false. I don't like that. Lies and double dealing, back handers and blackmail. To me, you see, you've got to tell it like it is, keep true to the truth, you're a long time dead, best keep it clean.

And I will flay the flesh from their bones and strip them bare for angels to eat.

Alyosha. The name alone is distinctive. A spiritual man carrying an air of not being entirely in this world. He's become adept at dealing with the roller coaster of his illness and can sense impending shifts in his psyche in the same way that an epileptic might foresee a seizure. The changes come softly in with padded feet and then the distant whispers, like a faraway waterfall, become more audible, more distinct. When that happens he tries to head them off, to get somewhere safe. Just in case.

He's searching on his mobile, scrolling through the contacts list for one number that he always means to memorise but never actually does. Time can slow when he's heading into this frame of mind, movement treacle like, his surroundings blurring until people become trees and he's a forest.

'Hello? Hello Zosima!' he shouts into the phone when she answers on the second ring, relief clear in his tone. 'Thank you! Thank you for picking up.'

'Alyosha? Long time and all that, yes, you can come and stay,' she knows exactly what to say, she always does. 'Where are you?'

'Sutherland, Scotland.'

'Bloody hell! Nice and local!'

'I wasn't planning on getting sick,' there's a background whine in his voice, defensive and childish. It still annoys him that he has to be the weak one.

'Of course not,' her words conciliatory, soothing away the forest gloom like the sun burning away morning mist. 'You'll need to fly down, I expect. Stay exactly where you are, two minutes most and I'll call you back. Ok?'

He waits, staring at the phone screen throughout, chewing at the side of his lip until he can taste iron. He only ever calls now when he needs help. She's ended up reduced to a storm port; better than nothing but a long way from enough.

'Ok, we've a few flights, one leaving Inverness at two today... mmm... nope, that's no good, only goes to Bristol...'

She's talking constantly, nonsense words mixed in with organising a flight. He breathes through it all, edging back from somewhere manic he didn't want to go.

Within ten minutes, she's booked the flight, emailed the details to his phone and arranged to pick him up herself. The relief is monumental. Panic is the enemy of the psychologically challenged, it can gather him up and catapult him somewhere with a speed that defies physics. What he needs now is order. Routine and order.

He's holding a running commentary in his head. Taxi to the airport, pay the driver, check in, smile-don't-forget-to-smile-otherwise-they'll-think-you're-an-arsehole. By the time he's in departures there's sweat on his forehead, little beads of moisture that ball and run. Don't wipe your head, don't wipe your mind, smile-don't-forget-to-smile-otherwise-they'll-think-you're-an-arsehole...

The concourse is almost empty and he starts thinking about flights. Not flights like these. Not flights like the one he's waiting for, where the biggest issue for most will be whether or not there'll be a good film to watch. Military flights, so many of them. All smells and noise, hard benches and middle distance stares. Its much more comfortable hanging out with the bucket and spade, dash and pack, slip, slap, slop brigade. Stop! There he goes again, coupling words, stringing phrases; oral tics. That's how it begins. Panic rushes back, snapping at heels, chewing at fingers and grinding teeth set in rigid jaws.

Brittle. Snip, snap. Splinter. Fracture.

Crack.

Love! Don't love, Zosima, don't ever love. If you're like me, you'll be another who has no idea. Love has screwed my life, in every way. Love and loyalty, oh yes, those bastards, love and loyalty, watch out for them, they carry big knives with sharp blades. They're the ones who sneak in when you're asleep, put hands over your mouth so no one else can hear you scream, they use their words of love as weapons to make you do things you know are wrong. But if you say no, if you stand tall and say no, shout it even -

there's no one to listen, no one can hear you - even if you are right beside them and screaming...

And I will flay the flesh from their bones and strip them bare for angels to eat.

By the time the plane landed, Aloysha was ready to curl up on the floor. It took everything he had left to get through arrivals, the whispering was deafening throughout. One foot in front of the other. One step then one step more.

Here she was, waiting to gather him up and take him somewhere safe.

'You look terrible. When did you last get some sleep?'

He shook his head, words weren't available, at least none that he could ever let out.

She gathered him close and together they shuffled along to the outside. A man with a suitcase on wheels, florid red skin and inappropriate clothing, held the door wide.

'Flying used to do that to me,' he said, looking kindly at Alyosha leaning heavily against her arm. 'Is he ok? Your brother?' Side by side there was no question that they were related. 'Can I help?'

She smiled and said, 'no, thank you, we're fine.' Alyosha just stared, all his strength gone, he'd got lost in the whispers.

She helped him into the car, fastening the seat belt as if he was a small child. Perhaps he was. Some days he wished he still was. His eyelids were heavy, his head lolled on his neck, he no longer had the power to hold it up.

'Sleep,' she'd said. 'Alyosha, go to sleep. Soon be home. Alyosha, go to sleep, soon be home.'

And he was, even before she'd paid the parking fee.

Chapter Three

The first section of Gwil's codes had taken three days to translate and still made little sense. But, then again, anything to do with this sort of work rarely did at first glance.

One had a secret
He hid it in numbers and gold,
Two had a secret
He hid it in Uncle Sam and straw,
But then the strange one found the secret
And it made him yellow and cold,
So he gave it to the red dwarf to help him thaw
But yellow tore the heart and flesh from it
And slew it dead with silvered hooves.

'Is that it?' she asked, with the unmistakeable tone of someone who suspects they're being short changed.

'Yes,' I said, 'that's it so far.'

'All of the original text? You've translated it all ?'

'Not all but I think I've got the bones of it, translated from a form of Tibetan Sanskrit. I have just one paragraph, a rhyme or riddle perhaps. I'm not convinced that it was ever meant to be anything other than an abstract.'

She paced the room and read the passage aloud several times in a breathy whisper, as if clarity could be found purely by speaking the words.

'Don't suppose you've any ideas? Hazard a guess at all? Mmm? Could you?' Suspicion was immediately thrown out the window by the swift arrival of ingratiation. 'Nobody, absolutely nobody else, not even Gwil at his very best, darling, could have done this so quickly. Although I'd give anything to know where he got it from in the first place.'

I felt the same way. It seemed Gwil had sent the package on the morning of his death and no doubt planned to have time to tell me all about it.

She moved closer as she was speaking. I stepped back and stared at her. Why did she need to be so predictable?

'Chuck in as many 'darlings' as you like,' I said slowly, as if to an idiot, 'but you'll still get that translation and nothing more. If you want to me to decode it as well, you're going to have to give me a lot more time and an awful lot more information.'

'Ten days,' she said, 'I'll give you ten days more and all the background I have.'

I shook my head, 'Not enough.'

She hissed out a breath, 'Tarvos, will you remember that this has now turned out to be part of a fucking murder case and not simply a bit of cash in hand!' Her voice rose an octave in frustration.

'Of course!' a surge of red hot fury caught me by surprise. I was only there because of Gwil and now wasn't the time for letting her get under my skin.

'Ok, ok, I'll do what I can.'

She exhaled loudly, 'At last! Darling, why do you always have to be so fucking difficult?'

She went back to her desk and typed furiously on a laptop.

'I've authorised access. Usual terms. You'll go to Dartmoor and don't argue, you will go. Work from there now. I've notified the local police, a DCI Moore is heading the new case. He'll be expecting you tomorrow at 10am,' she waved a hand dismissively. 'Go and dig for connections but, darling please, don't forget there's probably another bomb ticking so try to be nice and don't deliberately make it go off. You're one I'd be very upset to lose.'

Her office was the entire third floor of a building that had once seen more slaves through the back door than most in the vicinity. Occupying a warehouse right in the centre of Bristol docks, the place was made of old oak and now needed holding together, rather appropriately, by a lot of old money. A little spilt blood and sweat between friends of the right sort still oiled the wheels of commerce in the 21st century. Covert security for the oldest of old school organisations, the British Jockey Club, was no exception. As a job, it had its perks for someone like me even if this new posting was unlikely to be one of them.

So, without arguing, I went to a town called Ashfield on the southern edge of Dartmoor. When I arrived the place looked empty, as if it had shuffled into a form of hibernation rigor mortis and then forgotten what to do next. I drove straight to the police station. Inside, behind a glass window, sat a bored looking constable, squinting at a computer screen.

'Can I help?' his accent broad, he glanced up without interest. He had a bland face that could have been twelve or twenty-five.

'Jacob Steel for DCI Moore.'

I waited for the reassessing to occur and, right on cue, it was as if a light had been switched on in a dark room. I rarely looked like a man who might come to such a place willingly and definitely not one who might want anything from the business side of a CID desk.

Without looking away, he pressed a few buttons on the desk phone and said, 'Dr Jacob Steel is here, Sir,' he paused for longer than was necessary and then added, 'I have double checked ID.'

'My word, Dr Steel,' DCI Moore said without any preamble as he walked in, smiling broadly and holding out his hand, 'you don't look anything like I thought you would.'

I shook the offered hand, 'If its any consolation, you do and its Jake. Just Jake, please.'

DCI Moore did indeed look exactly like he should: solid with rugby ears. He had grey flecked hair, military cut; mud brown eyes and a suit.

'Right, Jake, let's go up to my office, talk on the way.'

He led me along corridors and through several doorways.

'I'm unsure how much background you've had so I'll risk a quick brief but with apologies as a given if I'm repeating.'

I'd had minimal background which wasn't unusual so I simply nodded in agreement.

'I've been in the force here for thirty years, grew up in the town and, although its quiet, we do have our fair share of all the usual. Half eaten bodies, however, aren't an everyday occurrence,' he didn't try to hide the fact that he was quite pleased one had finally turned up, 'but that's what we have - the partially consumed remains of a recently deceased male.'

'Consumed?' I asked. 'By what?'

'Boar. Wild boar to be precise. They appear to have found the body first, in what state we don't yet know but they've been dining on it. Thankfully we've recovered most of it, albeit well gnawed and rearranged, with the notable exception, so far, of the skull.'

He held open his office door, ushering me through to a seat in front of the desk; then pushed over a large file and flicked open the cover to reveal several photographic prints of scattered bones in a wooded area. I shuffled them out like a card deck and examined them closely. Only fragments of flesh clung to the soiled remains. There was something immediately familiar about those bones... Hmm. Interesting.

'These are the items that we hope you can help with,' he produced four plastic covered stained sheets of paper and placed them with the photographs. 'These were found in the immediate area of the remains, rolled up around some sort of incense stick.'

I studied each sheet. Notebook sized and stained dark in places, the paper was covered almost entirely in symbols. Intricate symbols that intertwined into a complicated web of several different colour inks. They looked identical to the ones Gwil had sent.

'I understand that you may have already decoded something similar?'

'Translated only.' I shook my head, thinking more about the incense sticks than the writing.

After several minutes of silence Moore interrupted my train of thought,' Are you always this verbose?' A prod to remind me where I was.

I slid the sheets back into the file with the photographs.

'The writing is a form of Sanskrit, I've translated a similar piece of text into English but that was, in essence, a code within a code and, therefore, extremely difficult to decipher. I can confirm that this,' I gestured to the sheets, 'looks like its more of the same.'

'Do you do this full-time?' he rubbed at his lips with the fingertips of one hand, narrowing his eyes.

'If you mean translation then, no, I think even I would find that a little too tedious.'

'How did you get involved this time then?'

'By putting on the shoes of a dead man.'

'Eh? What?'

'Our expert died somewhat unexpectedly and I'm standing in, so to speak. Tibetan translators are, surprisingly, not that common so sometimes it is necessary to scrape a barrel bottom.'

'I was told that you were an authority on ancient languages which, to my uncultured mind, is not exactly the bottom of anything.'

'Ah, well, I suppose that depends on how you set your standards.'

There was a long moment of awkward silence.

'Right, no doubt, you want to get on. Whilst you're here I'll personally authorise and provide any additional support that you require. In return, I expect to be kept fully informed of any and all developments. Agreed?'

'Agreed. I'll expect the same.'

'Of course, we're all on the same side.'

I'd heard that before and, right now, any trust extended about as far as I could spit a rat. He shifted the conversation, such as it was, to practicalities.

'We've arranged accommodation for you in town and there's a desk you can use through there,' he gestured to a side door, 'you also have the services of Constable Brunning - Trev. He's a little unorthodox but absolutely reliable so I hope you'll get on. He'll be back in shortly but, whilst we wait, do you have any further questions?'

'I'd like to go to the scene right now. Assess the amount of boar activity in the area for a start. Its possible they've eaten sections of the notes that were left with the remains.'

'Agreed, I'll get Trev to take you but, a word of warning, the land owner, David Flint, is both obstructive and volatile. Please be careful not to tread unnecessarily on sensitive toes.'

A noise from the side office interrupted us and a face appeared around the door.

'There you are, Trev. This is Dr Jake Steel. I want you to take him up to Flint's place as soon as, pass on any up to date relevant details as you go, ok?'

Short, soft and, with the start of a paunch, Trevor Brunning's appearance didn't fill me with confidence. Perhaps the feeling was mutual as, arms folded, he checked me out down to my shoes for a painful few minutes.

'I have to confess that I was expecting more of your traditional professor. Why the hell did you end up choosing such a career path when you look like you do?'

I replied with silence. I'd no time for dickheads, especially dickheads in uniform.

He was right though. My face gives me choices. I accept that. Take it for what it is, pretty much in the same way that someone with a birthmark or scar accepts, eventually, that its part of them and impossible to change. In my youth, I used to wish for accidents, seems juvenile now, but I wanted to damage this perceived perfection in some way. Break it, destroy it, so I no longer had to be disabled by it. However, I found a way to channel my energies into something much more worthwhile and now, when I look in the mirror, I no longer see demons.

Chapter Four

Trev talked as he drove, filling in gaps. The remains were, in many ways, straightforward and, aside from the notes that I'd already seen, a wallet had been recovered from the disturbed soil which meant that identification might also soon be forthcoming.

We drove up an impressive drive, to park near to an even more impressive stable yard. A man appeared, pointing us back to an all-weather gallop track where David Flint, racehorse trainer, stood next to his four by four on the brow of the hill, watching racehorses being exercised.

Waiting a short distance away, I watched Flint. An ex-jockey himself, he was expensively dressed in an expanse of tweed and had clearly more than made up for any dietary restrictions earlier in his career. In his late fifties, he was almost the complete caricature with a beaked nose and square jaw hinting at well connected bloodlines; his complexion a pebble dashed red. It was the telltale branding of either weather or gin, quite often both. Eventually he looked in our direction.

'Dr Steel, I presume?' he remarked to the air in general, then turned back to watch the next group of horses come galloping from the bottom of the hill; his expression fixed as if he couldn't quite believe what academia let in these days.

He turned again momentarily and stared at Trev. 'Why have you asked to see me again? Isn't it about time you left the rest of us to get on with earning a living?'

It was the usual statement and one even I had heard many times; no one wanted to have the police picking, asking endless questions and, in an already busy day, they could be a right pain in the arse. But that was the job; to ask the questions, to dig, to find the answers that were usually tucked a long way away from the obvious.

Two horses, a bay and a chestnut, thundered past at the gallop, matching stride for stride. Two more followed but the horse nearest to the rail, a grey, fought for its head all the way with the rider sawing ineffectually at its open mouth. Flint cursed loudly as he watched, radiating anger. As soon as they came walking back he let rip at the rider.

'Steph! What the fuck were you doing! That wasn't a piece of work that was a fucking disaster! Swop with Sid and take Drifter back to the yard!' he roared across the open land, his face puce.

The girl paled and walked her horse down to the lad on the bay.

'Useless! Such a fucking stupid girl!' Flint was still ranting. 'She's as windy as they come and has that effect on just about everything she sits on. I shouldn't let her ride but I need the sodding horses to work, don't I? Christ, what I wouldn't give for half a dozen more like Sid. Sid gets the bloody job done without any dramatics.'

Being nervous wasn't a heinous crime as far as I knew but, to Flint, it was clearly one short of homicide. He boiled with tension and bad temper; I wondered if Steph was going to get another torrent when he got back to the yard.

The grey came up the gallops again with Sid on board and, instead of the wide eyed leaping and plunging, it now cruised effortlessly with the rider crouched, almost motionless, over it's withers.

Flint uttered a grunt of satisfaction as the horses passed then turned to face us. 'That's the lot so what is it that you actually need to know, Dr Steel? What can I tell you that I've not already said to the police?'

'I understand that there are wild boar here. Don't they trouble the horses?' I kept my voice light and ignored his tone. A stupid question, perhaps, but somewhere to start nonetheless.

'No, they don't hang around, contrary to popular belief they're actually rather shy. I've probably only seen one or two close to the yard in years. They sometimes forage in the woods and I presume that was where they found the body or whatever it is. All this nonsense and it'll probably turn out to be a sheep.'

'Mr Flint, with due respect, please drop the attitude.' Trev sighed as if Flint was the one being a pain in the arse. 'No-one has time to cover old ground but we've still got unanswered questions. Dr Steel's presence here is vital as he's been specifically requested to survey the area on our behalf.'

I let that little fabrication go by without a flicker.

'Either way, I don't want you lot churning up any more of my land and, as you have no vehicle, I'll have to get someone from my staff to take you. You'll need a four by four and someone who actually knows where to go. How long do you need?'

'An hour maybe, I'm not completely certain but not much longer than that.' The likelihood of finding anything of interest was remote but at least this meeting had given chance for a look around.

'I'll ask Sid to take you up in that case, local knowledge and all that.

21

Come on, get in, I'll run you back to the yard,' he marched to the Land Rover and swung himself in.

Typical of most farm vehicles, the inside was layered liberally with mud and dog hair. On the dashboard broken bits of leather held in empty crisp packets and a large uncapped hypodermic syringe, the tube crusty with age, wedged upright into the screen vent. I was grateful that there wasn't a territorial terrier in situ as well.

Into the yard, Flint dragged up the handbrake and jumped out roaring for Sid. Trev muttered something derogatory as we, once again, also got out to wait.

Flint's shout had found Sid washing down a steaming horse and he was now very obviously spelling out our inconvenient request. It was hard to tell what Sid thought of it all as he still had on black tinted racing goggles, the Dettori look obviously; black skull cap and black neck tube, there wasn't much visible of his face at all. With black jacket and breeches, Sid didn't give much away. I waited and wondered if he was actually old enough to drive.

The racing yard was large for this part of the country, many of the residents now staring at me over smart half doors. A radio played quietly and lads laughed with one another; aside from Steph's roasting it appeared, on the outside, that all was well working for David Flint. To one side of the stables, about six feet from where we waited, a large Scania horse lorry was parked. A pair of anonymous legs poked out from underneath covered by oily blue trousers which had hitched up to reveal hairy ankles above work boots. There was a loud metallic bang from the lorry's underbelly combined with a volley of swearing which was immediately followed by the rolling arrival of a grease can towards my feet. The ankles shifted to one side.

'Pass that back, would you?' a man's voice called out. 'Save me getting up, though only the guvnor knows why I'm having to do this again today!'

I rolled the can back towards the outstretched hand with my boot.

'Cheers,' the hand and the can disappeared once more along with the ankles and the banging began again.

David Flint returned, hands still deep in his pockets. 'Sid can take you up now but don't hang around as we all have work to do.'

He turned away, stepping closer to the Scania.

'Get a bloody move on, John, you're blocking the yard,' he addressed the side of the lorry receiving an answering grunt from underneath. With a silent gesture of annoyance he got back into his vehicle and drove off.

Trev's radio squeaked into life and, after a brief conversation, he said, 'Apologies, I'm wanted elsewhere. I'll send a car for you if I'm likely to be delayed. Would an hour be ok?'

'An hour is probably more than enough but, no hurry, as and when.'

Trev left as Sid arrived, lifting up goggles as he walked towards me. It was only when he removed his skull cap that I realised that Sid wasn't a lad after all. Sid was very definitely female. Maybe mid-twenties, blonde hair and sea blue eyes that made me think instantly of waves and mountain sky. It took longer than it should have done for me to re-order my thoughts.

Chapter Five

We'd met before. Twice in fact. I never forget a face.

On the first occasion I'd been a woman, or more precisely dressed as one, at a black tie charity dinner for horseracing's elite. It's a long story that probably warrants further explanation at another time. I remembered her eyes most of all as they'd been arresting; ocean blue darkened by some internal pain that she obviously believed hidden. The second time had been, somewhat obscurely, at a famous Scottish monolith. I'd spent most of the day free climbing its less friendly side and, at the summit, she'd been there, expensive camera covering those troubled eyes.

And here we stood once more, the third time. Inevitable if sequence is your thing and probably just as inevitable if its more about fates. Despite our previous, she clearly didn't remember me. Nothing at all, not even a well hidden flicker of recognition. But I remembered and now I also remembered her name: Sidra Fielding, professional jockey. Clearly I'd spent too long recently up a mountain as I had known that she lived nearby, riding out for several west country trainers but probably more regularly for Flint as he was the closest.

'I understand you're looking for the boar. I can show you where they hang out but I can't be certain that they'll actually be there. Is that ok as a start?' A smile flashed high speed across her face, gone again in an instant.

It did make me wonder if she'd made the transformation from lad to girl so dramatically with the sole intent to off balance but, silently berating myself some more, I nodded, forcing my thoughts back to codes and bones.

Her Land Rover was ancient, a classic she said; it was basic but spotless inside. No snarling terrier but a large lurcher slept, curled in a dormouse ball on a quilt in the back, it didn't even open an eye as she started the engine. Up across the tracks, slowing through potholes and ruts, she stopped by a locked gate and passed me a key.

'We need to go through there, would you mind?' She gave me another one of those light speed smiles.

I stepped from grass tuft to grass tuft to avoid the liquid mud in the gateway, Converse weren't practical footwear and yet another thing I should have thought about today. Through the gate and on over another field to a dense mass of broad leaved trees that sat, like a bowler hat, on the top of the hill. She drove to one side towards a hunting gate, then stopped, turning off the engine. It's odd how sometimes silence can seem deafening.

'Is this boar central?' I asked.

'They're often here, doubt we'll see them but you can sometimes hear them. They rarely come any closer to the yard, just staying on the boundaries of the estate as far as I'm aware. That wood' she pointed over to a line of trees, 'links with the place where the body, or whatever it turns out to be, was found.'

'If you could show me any actual tracks it'd be really helpful. I'm hoping to get an overview now as the police will probably get a specialist team in later.'

She hesitated momentarily, as if undecided as to whether to say something or not.

'Ask away, what do you want to know?'

'Am I that transparent?' she laughed.

'No, not at all. Academic's mind,' I touched a finger to my forehead, 'pathologically inclined to being one step ahead.'

She laughed again, eyes sparkling. 'Why do you want to find the boar? Are they… going to be charged?'

'If only it were that easy. Unfortunately they appear to have taken some of the remains with them - a porcine packed lunch, perhaps. The police are attempting to get what's missing back again.'

'Oh. Bloody hell. I hadn't thought of that. Not pleasant, is it?'

'No, not really. Will we go?'

She nodded, hauling at the handle to open the door. With hindsight, it would have been better to find my own way, or have waited for Trev. Too late, it was done now.

We walked through the narrow gate under the trees. The ground deep with layers of leaves; a few obvious and well used footpaths led on in either direction. Aside from us, the only other noise was the cawing of rooks; staccato pulses of bird speak that sounded like Morse code as we walked beneath their roost. The air smelt heavily of bird, wet leaves and rot.

'There's a track just up there,' she pointed vaguely in the direction we were heading, 'they do seem to stick to the same paths, a bit like badgers. I don't know if it will make a difference to what you need but this place is full of rights of way. The world and his dog will have been through since yesterday.'

'That's ok, it's a bit of a longshot but every possibility is worth exploring.' I looked around, trying to form an impression of the whole wooded area.

'You're new to Ashfield?' she glanced over and then turned away quickly.

Why was she finding this uncomfortable; either being here with me, or was it the actual place that we were in? Tension radiated from her. Why was that?

'New to the area, I arrived this morning.'

'Don't mind David, he's a good trainer and a relatively good boss, just fairly inept at being human. I blame it on public school floggings myself,' she smiled broadly.

Humour and that smile. A breath of fresh air compared to the usual belligerence. But where was she coming from? One minute high alert, next minute humour? I couldn't quite work her out. She took out her phone, looking at the screen but also watching me from the corner of her eye as if to be ready to run if I morphed into a monster.I knew a little about her because of other work I'd been involved in and because she was a popular jockey, the pretty ones always seem to be (both the boys and the girls), but she was still hard to place.

Crouching down to look at an animal track that skirted the gate and disappeared through a large hole at the base of a hedge, I spotted a tuft of thick coarse hair caught on a bramble. Taking a pen and small torch out of my pocket, I collected it in a folded plastic bag, marking the bag with reference and location. There was sadly no sign of anything like more notes or the missing skull. I spent another twenty minutes looking, but found absolutely nothing except a recent, and very large, pile of boar faeces which I collected too because you can get good DNA from shit.

What puzzled me most was that the estate was surrounded by wild places and yet a murderer, if it was murder, chose a place where discovery was almost a dead cert. He or she either didn't care or had planned it that way.

'Sid, thanks again for your help,' I hoped she wouldn't mind the informality. 'I've seen enough for now and don't want to hold you up from your day any longer.'

'It's no problem; I'd nothing left to ride this morning in any case,' she turned and walked back towards the narrow gate.

'Must be handy to have this yard so close to home. Do you ride for Mr

Flint often?' I sought an easy topic of conversation. Jockeys often travelled hundreds of miles a year to ride horses at exercise for their owners and trainers, it was an important part of the PR of the job if nothing else.

She turned and stared; something was there, defence possibly, or surprise - I couldn't be sure.

'How do you know where I live?' Her tone guarded as if I'd said something very personal or made an accusation.

'You gave a statement to the police, as did everyone else; its part of my job to read them,' I lied easily. I hadn't read her statement but if she was bothered by me knowing her address, she'd be horrified at just how much else I knew.

'Of course. Sorry,' she waited as I followed her through the gate. 'Are you interested in racing?'

'In a way; I'm Irish which means that horses are probably part of my DNA and, politically, it always pays to know the headlines at least. However, there's a good chance that I'm the milkman's by blow as, being staunchly Catholic, it was a bit of a free for all in my home town.'

She smiled easily at my levity, if I'd said something earlier that raised hackles then it appeared forgiven. But there was definitely something about her and I was beginning to feel like I was missing the point, as if there was some undercurrent here that I wasn't seeing.

****

The rest of the day was interesting in its own way, but revolved purely around trying to concentrate at the police station. Trev was proving useful in both his coffee making abilities and in knowing all the details, but the office was noisy with constant interruptions. I'd give it one more day and then find somewhere else to work from.

Out of necessity that evening I went, reluctantly, to the local supermarket for basic supplies. I was once told that shopping can shrink your soul and, wandering down the aisles, I still believed it. Settling on essentials and deciding to eat out a lot, I walked back to the tills, stopping to look at the rack of newspapers. From the corner of my eye I saw someone I recognised – Sid.

She pushed a small trolley, head on one side holding a mobile phone with her shoulder, quietly having a conversation and shopping with none of my soul shrinking drama. I found that I was already trying to make a further assessment about Sid, the rider of racehorses, purely by what she put in her trolley. The minute that realisation hit me I turned and went to pay. That was definitely not a place to go.

There is a universal law that cites that whatever pocket your car keys are in, the hand on that side will be fully occupied with holding a lot of other stuff. In order to reach those keys, all of those things will have to be carefully balanced and, of course, this almost always results in a lot of that same stuff, usually the breakable bits, ending up all over the floor. As I attempted this delicate manoeuvre, Sid walked past and, inevitably, I caught her eye.

'Hello, fancy seeing you again and in a place like this! Umm...sorry...we're practically neighbours and I don't even remember your name. Its Dr...um...?' she stumbled over her words and stuttered to a halt.

'The hard realities of life are centred in places like this, Sid,' I gave up on the key retrieval, 'and as we're being neighbourly, I'm Jake.'

'Jake,' the smile put in a brief appearance, 'you should use the bags, it's so much easier and don't lock your car – I never do.'

'Be embarrassing to this nicked, especially as it isn't actually mine.' I went on with the ineffective juggling. She came closer, lifted purchases from my hands and waited whilst I retrieved my keys, handing it all back as soon as I had the door open.

'Nice to see you again, Jake.'

She was gone, off with her neatly packed bags. I watched her drive away, wondering why she was nothing like the person I'd been told she was.

Then it hit me. Tibet. Of course. I got back into the car and went straight to the police station in search of Moore.

Chapter Six

'Sky burial? Never heard of it. Are you sure?' He wasn't impressed when I rang him, but he came back anyway. 'Ok, let's have your thoughts.'

'Sky burials are common in remote areas which are predominantly buddhist - Tibet being just one. Any death requires disposal of the body, burial or cremation usually. But what happens in a place where, geographically, such disposals would be either impossible or impractical?'

'Why impractical?'

'Most of the topography is mountainous so no topsoil and there aren't enough trees to make cremation routine.'

'Ok, I'll take that. So what happens in a sky burial and what makes you think that Flint's is one?'

'I'll can give you more detail later but, in brief, this is a form of burial where the body is taken to the top of a mountain or high slope...'

He interrupted, 'Flint's woodland is neither of those.'

'It isn't the *where*, it is the *how* that's pointing me towards a sky burial ceremony.'

'All right, carry on then.'

I pulled out the photograph folder again, slid out the prints and arranged them on the desk.

'See here, those incense sticks pushed into the ground? There's a pattern to them. I'd put money on the fact that those will be juniper incense and, if they are, that would be enough for me to want to assess whether this is actually an attempt at a sky burial.'

He squinted at the print and said, 'I'm still not getting this, Jake. We've a scattered set of human bones, partially eaten, some missing altogether and you're telling me that some hippy sticks define it not as a murder but as a buddhist ceremony,' he shook his head with a sigh. 'I'm not dismissing you completely, but if it doesn't make sense to me it won't proceed with the team either.'

'You'd definitely define it as a crime especially as disposal of a body in this way is, like fly tipping, rather frowned on in the western world. With a bit more time, your forensic team will be able to confirm when death occurred and that will help to take this further. But, right now, it's a sound theory to explain why you've got dismembered and stripped body parts, regardless of the post-mortem boar damage.'

'Ok, I'll try to remain open minded. Tell me what you know.'

I opened a digital photographic file of a series of sky burials on my laptop. 'Following a death, the body is put into a sitting position, wrapped in cloth and treated with a great deal of ceremony. Note, please, that I'm summarising, this ceremony is a big deal and takes place over a number of days.'

I paused and he gestured me to continue with the wave of one hand.

'The families of the deceased make offerings at the monastery, prayers will be said. The body is then carried on the back of either a close friend of the deceased or a family member. It will be carried in this way to the burial site. They fracture the spine and limbs of the corpse so that it can be easily folded up into a bundle.'

He widened his eyes but remained silent.

'The journey begins at dawn, family members and friends walk with the corpse all the way to the site, but the actual ritual is carried out by a rogyapa who is a kind of priest or perhaps, more precisely, an undertaker. It is his duty to perform the last rituals on the body.

'The family generally leave allowing the rogyapa to continue unobserved. He'll unwrap the body, position it face down on the ground, burn juniper incense to attract the vultures and the cut the body up into small sections. There's a ritual associated with the order in which this is done, but it usually begins with cutting off the hair, amputation of the limbs, evisceration and slicing up the body parts. He'll flay the meat from the bones and spread it out over the burial site for the vultures to eat. These birds are the key to the whole ceremony, if they don't eat the body quickly then it'll hang around causing all sorts of problems. The rogyapa may also pulverise the bone and mix it with barley flour to ensure easier consumption. A proportion of this pulverised bone may be kept by the deceased's family to enable continued communication or assistance from the ancestor.'

'And all that is still practised?' Moore didn't look convinced.

'Look it up, it has been for millennia. One has to remember that, from a Buddhist point of view, the real trials of death are the inner ones. The sky burial is just a means of passing on nutrients to another, the physical body becomes a vessel that is no longer required.'

'So the boar were Devon's version of this rogyapa?'

'No,' I shook my head, 'if I'm right, the boar were the dakini; a kind of holy angel. In Tibet vultures are often called dakini. They're revered as angels or holy birds, sometimes called holy eagles; they come in large numbers to eat every human scrap. My favourite vulture name in this context is sky dancer; however, in this case, I can't see a Devonian boar being that light on its feet.'

Moore laughed, 'Ok, I'll buy it. Talk to forensics in the morning, pass the theory past them and see what they think.'

Chapter Seven - Alyosha

And I will flay the flesh from their bones and strip them bare for angels to eat.

Brothers. They are love and loyalty. Because of love and loyalty they made me what I have become. Evil bastards, they would do anything. So don't ever love, love is the worst kind of evil I know and, trust me, I know a lot of evil. I've seen the worst of it; it colours my world from the minute I open my eyes to the minute I fall asleep. I fight those times, Zosima, fight waking up and I fight going to sleep. If I could stay in one state, I might cope. But when you sleep you dream and you wake up and it's just as gut-wrenchingly awful as when you went to sleep, worse each day perhaps. So then you go on once more through the hours knowing that at some point you will fall asleep again, you can't stop it forever, can't hold it back forever, I've tried. Most I managed was three days and then I fell asleep whilst I was fighting it, couldn't stop it. Like a lot in my life, I just have to be the one to see it, to experience it, can't stop it. So don't, Zosima, don't ever love. Love is the reason that all of this madness, all of this insanity began, a perverse sense of loyalty and a belief in the purity of love.

I'm mad, I know that, Zosima, quite mad. But there are degrees of madness, I dip in and out, it depends. I can give you gibbering insanity to cold psychosis, I can do it all because I've had to. But yes, I'm quite barking. If you take a plant, a plant that is delicate because that is the way it was made. If you take that plant and stress it, force it to grow a certain way, tie it down with wires, it will always end up one of two ways - dead or twisted. I'm still here, so that makes me twisted. I'm still here because of you. I've stayed on because of you. Because I knew, if I tried hard enough, I'd be able to right the wrongs. Right the wrongs for you.

Best I start at the beginning. Best I tell you it all because then you'll see, I know you will. It took far too long to bring it all together, but I've nearly finished.

And I will flay the flesh from the their bones and strip them bare for angels to eat.

Alyosha slept for three days without apparently waking. When he was ill the medication he needed sedated him into submission. Zosima cancelled her work and stayed with him, sleeping curled up at the foot of the bed, tiptoeing and shuffling around her house, waiting for him to return.

Alyosha, poor Alyosha with his badly wired mind. He hadn't always been like this. Once, lifetimes ago it seemed to Zosima, he'd been just like she was. A bit more sensitive perhaps but he'd appeared to have the whole world waiting for him. Handsome, clever, energetic; he'd been more fun that she could keep up with.

There were five years between them, Alyosha older and then there were two further siblings, older again. A larger age gap meant that the older ones were rarely around as playmates and, perhaps, it was just that which had drawn Alyosha and Zosima together.

A treehouse in the garden became mission control, Alyosha assuming the role of big brother, teacher, parent and soul friend. They spent hours in the treehouse, Zosima listening with rapt attention to Alyosha reading stories of magical places where all the endings had a smile, where everyone lived happily after. It wasn't to be the same for them but that just made the stories all the more important. Alyosha was always her hero, as a child she'd worshipped him but life moved on, things happened, words were voiced that couldn't be taken back - ever. Alyosha was hard to love now, but she tried just the same.

'What's the time?' he mumbled as he lifted a tousled head off the pillow and finally opened his eyes. 'Or should it be what day?'

'Tuesday, nearly one as in lunchtime.' Zosima smiled, the lack of tension in his face was a good sign. A good indication that he'd mentally climbed back out of the forest pit once more.

'I'm starving? Got any grub?'

'What do you want? I can do toast, or an omelette, how about an omelette to start with?'

'Mmm, potato. Jacket potato with tuna. Mayo. Tuna mayo and sweetcorn!' He was abruptly sitting up, grinning and stretching.

'Ok, little Lyosha, I'll make it whilst you have a shower. Phew! You smell worse than the dog when he's indulged in fox.'

She could tease him, safe in the knowledge now that he would take it for what it was, a sign of affection and nothing more.

They spent the rest of the day together idly heckling the television, drinking tea and eating quite a bit of toast. Zosima took a moment to thank the gods that he'd come down, or up, from wherever it was that he went. She loved him but, however calm she'd sounded, he was terrifying when he was ill. He became someone else then, someone she couldn't reach and couldn't understand.

'I'll make a move tomorrow,' he said quietly, knowing she wouldn't want him to go.

'No, not yet. You've only just woken up. Come on, stay for a few more days.'

'You've work and so have I. I left it all in a mess this time, just dumped my stuff and ran.'

'Are you eating properly? Sleeping properly? You don't look after yourself, Alyosha and if you don't you'll just get sick again.'

'I promise I'll do everything properly. I take my meds, eat, sleep and say my prayers every night, cross my heart and hope to ride winner in the Grand National.' He dissolved into laughter, delighted that he'd remembered the promise they used to make to each other. At three and eight it had been the pinnacle of their aspirations, although Alyosha also had a thing about being an astronaut for a month or so.

'Will you do something for me?' Zosima sat directly in front of him, taking hold of both his hands.

'If I can.'

'Come and visit me when you're well. Come and visit me often just because, don't wait until I have to hold you together to get you through the door.' She held on tighter to his hands as he tried to pull away. 'Promise me, promise me that, Alyosha.'

'I promise,' he said, but it was an empty promise and they both knew it.

In the morning, when she woke at five, he'd already gone.

Chapter Eight

It was dark with a damp mist forming but I decided on impulse to go for a late run. Listening to music through earbuds, my thoughts shifted to the bones and their secrets, I was still no further forward with how they'd come to end up where they did, or what story the codes had to tell.

In the gloom, I came across a barn with lights on at the end of a long track. It seemed remote from the town, a second home barn conversion perhaps, it was hard to make it out completely in the mist and darkness. Running past, following the track up and above the lit structure, I stopped briefly and looked down. It was my kind of place; away from other houses, outbuildings huddled next to it, something that looked like balcony on one side, the vague reflection of a large window that might have run the whole width. I could imagine the view from there across the moor, knew it would be worth seeing.

I ran on for about half an hour more and then turned back, retracing my path in the darkness following the light of the head-torch. Back to the town, I glanced at my watch, it was nearly eight; a quick decision, drop into the pub and check out who was there or stay home? I looked down at my muddy clothes, not great evening out attire, but then again the perfect excuse to leave early.

'I thought you weren't coming! Where have you been?' Trev spotted me straight away.

'I didn't know that I was expected,' I stared at him blankly and shrugged. 'No matter, got here in the end. What're you drinking?'

'Just got one in thanks, but come and sit with us when you've found your way through.' Trev gestured to a group of tables close to the bar, which seemed to be seating only people from the police station.

The Fox and Hounds wasn't a sleepy little pub; every table was full, people waited at the bar. Friday evenings were clearly a good time for business here. I ignored the frank unfettered appraisal from most corners, never had any interest in any of that social form filling; the hidden, or not so hidden moves that people make. The new boy here, I could almost hear the speculations lining up around me as I stood waiting at the bar.

I listened to the conversation as it drifted around. Trev, ever the raconteur, started to tell a convoluted story that took ages to get out in its entirety and then resulted in punch line that no one got. He tried to re-explain it but the others jumped in offering ridiculous suggestions and, between them and the beer they'd all had, there wasn't much chance of him reaching a conclusion quickly.

Turning away from the bar finally with a pint in my hand, I heard the outside door bang and arriving with a blast of cold, wet winter air, was Sid. This time she had her dog by her side and without looking around, she wound her way through to the far end of the bar, the dog followed and then lay down at her feet. Dripping wet, they'd clearly both been caught in rain that I'd avoided.

As I watched Sid, another racing yard employee stood and came to sit on an empty stool nearby, effectively blocked my escape route.

'Hi, Jake, isn't it? I'm Katie.' A girl, probably early twenties; petite, pretty in an elfin sort of way.

I really didn't want to be to drawn into a conversation with anyone. This Katie had purpose written all over her and easy options were never my style, however they were offered. Trev appeared, as if by magic, elbowed me theatrically and then laughed raucously, looking at me like I was the evening's entertainment.

'Is that the time? Time I was going then.' I took a mouthful from my pint and turned away. There was a limit, especially here, to what I'd put up with.

'Don't go, stay a bit longer,' he backed up immediately and turned on the charm, such as he had, to hold me.

I thought about Sid at the bar. 'Ten minutes, that's it.'

He grinned and emptied his glass in one long swallow. 'Good man, right choice, mine's a pint. I might even pull as all the girls want to talk to me, trouble is that they only want to talk about you.'

I didn't bother with a response but took his glass, completely ignored Katie and turned back to the bar, finding myself next to Sid.

'Hello Jake, out with the boys?' she asked but didn't look up from where she going through her coat, eventually pulling out a folded note from a zip pocket with a small noise of triumph.

'Mmmm, something like that, I'm planning on bolting shortly.' I looked away trying to catch the attention of the bar staff.

'I'd make an informed guess that you've been running,' she gestured to her muddy trainers, 'me too.'

'Quite the detective, I'm impressed.' I was pushed closer to her, edged out of range of the bar by a group of lads. 'Is it the mud splatter or the smell that gives me away?'

'I can hardly comment, glass houses and all that. Seriously though, this is a great area for running, especially as you don't seem to mind the dirt.'

'The route I found this evening worked well but I expect there are better.' Back in the queue again for being served, unless I paid attention I was going to be there all night.

'I'll mark some good ones on a map if you like, drop it by your work.'

She turned slightly and, quite out of the blue, I felt as if she'd reached out and physically touched me. She blinked and stared, wide eyed, as if she'd felt it too.

'Great, that would be great.' I struggled for words, finally got served and stumbled off to find Trev again. It had been a very long time since I'd reacted like that, my guard was usually impenetrable.

Katie had another friend now; they sat either side of Trev. He was clearly delighted but I wasn't, surrounded by inane conversations that did nothing more than irritate. I remained silent and Trev made up answers but then, when Katie's leg skimmed mine, I stood and abruptly left wishing I'd never gone, cross with myself that I'd even considered it.

Outside the rain was a soft and steady patter, puddling on the road and making the pavement area shiny under the pub lights. The mist pervaded, pressing low against the houses. It suited my mood, even if it made it a little claustrophobic. I walked slowly back to the flat, hands in pockets, head down and dampness seeping in. Lost in thought, I didn't pay much attention to the footsteps until she was almost next to me.

'Jake?'

She was smaller in the dark somehow, perhaps because of her clothing, perhaps because of the insulating effect of the mist.

'Lousy weather,' she said with a shrug; her dog shook in a rolling wave, spraying an arc of raindrops around itself. 'About those running routes, take my mobile number, I could talk you through some good ones on the map or text me if you prefer,' she paused as if now doubting her decision to have come after me. 'I'm sensing that wasn't your kind of fun tonight.'

'Was it that obvious?' I pushed my hair back from where it was dripping into my eyes and shoved my hands deeply back into my pockets.

'No, not really, you did look slightly cornered but I think you handled it well for a new boy. The locals aren't the shy and retiring sort.'

There was that attempt at teasing again; good try Sid, but I really wasn't in the mood for any of it now.

'Not a great evening for running either, but at least I managed to miss the rain.' The words came out heavily weighted with my irritation. I took her number but more to get rid than to encourage.

'I, however, appear to have timed it badly,' she said quietly. 'See you around, text if you want routes.'

She was gone, running off into the darkness with the dog loping easily at her side but she refused to stay out of my head that night, she even haunted my dreams. What was that moment in the pub, that feeling that passed between us? I thought about that a lot over the next few days, even brought up her number on my phone and stared at it once or twice, but I didn't call. Aside from this job, I'd other things on my mind.

****

Trev slunk in late with a monster hangover as his lingering companion, his planned day off cancelled at the last minute due to a roster shift. I took a sadistic delight in helping him to suffer. However, he did tell me a lot more about Sid, the fact that we'd been talking hadn't passed him by, although he actually warned me off. Told me that her local nickname was Sid Vicious, that she was untouchable, unapproachable and generally best left well alone. I'd heard similar about her before. But I didn't need warning off, I'd decided that all by myself a long time ago.

The next week passed with the early and positive identification of what was left of the bones. Sally North, the police pathologist, had done her stuff forensically and come out with a result that opened a whole new can of worms.

'The chewed bones are a Marcus Williams, which you may or may not already know,' Trev was first with an update. 'Mr Williams had been listed as a *misper,* reported by his wife just over two months ago now. Spookily enough, we continue with the racing connection as Mr Williams was a racehorse owner and just before he went missing he had been warned off by the racing authorities. Although we still don't have his complete skull, you were the one to bring in the golden egg.'

I raised my eyebrows, wondering what that meant.

'Teeth are fairly indigestible for boar apparently and the poop sample you lovingly brought back was full of Mr Williams' dentistry. Good call, Jake, but whether they crunched up the rest of his head is anyone's guess;

we still have no recognisable skull bones, just cervical vertebrae. Anyway, excuse the pun, but that's enough for someone like you to get your teeth into. It's all in the file so go, do your thing and see if helps with the decoding. Oh, and the incense was juniper so the ritual idea might not be beyond possible. Forensics are keeping an open mind, as am I.'

I read through the reports. I'd heard that the Jockey Club had begun investigating Marcus Williams because low level blackmail and dodgy runners were allegedly top of his list of daily pursuits. But he'd been small-time, nothing involving large sums or significant people but then, nine months ago, he'd started to move in much bigger and darker circles. Gwil had been sent to sniff around as it had been hoped that Marcus, a weak link in every way, would quickly incriminate himself in such a shark filled pool where he didn't speak the language or have the right branding.

And Gwil died whilst sniffing around. Or, most probably, Gwil had been identified and executed. Game over.

Gwil had found Tibetan cryptograms and now, here, there were more... Was there a connection?

Everyone had been looking for Marcus overseas but if Flint's yard opened up as an angle that might put a different look on it. Flint, for all his old boy do-you-know-who-I-am impatience, had been deemed clean by preliminary covert investigations. Perhaps, with bits of Marcus turning up on his doorstep, it was time for someone to dig a little further into his affairs.

Off my remit but for interest, I reviewed the list of horses I knew Marcus had in training, when they raced and where. He'd been quite successful as an owner over the last ten years, about ten to fifteen horses on average, buying and selling each year, all over the country with various trainers including a D. Flint. Was that the reason he'd come here, perhaps simply to see his racehorses?

But what did ignite another spark was that his regular jockey had been out of action with a nasty fracture for almost all of the last six months before the racing authorities had taken action. Marcus' replacement for that period had been Sid Fielding. With the bones here and Sid here, that had to be a connection worth a second look.

I had full access and authority. It wasn't exactly just translating the notes that littered my desk, but in a roundabout way, it might be the background I needed.

I decided to track down Gwil's dodgy informant first, the one that had told him that, regardless that he was laying low from his wife, Marcus was very much alive when in truth the boar were gnawing on him. Although extreme care would be needed to avoid stirring up unpleasant repercussions as that particular informant was buried deep within some very unpleasant friends and their relations. They weren't people I wanted to stumble upon unprepared or, to inadvertently allow to stumble upon me. Gwil, ever the risk taker, had done that and it hadn't ended well.

So for speed, and just because I could, I sent a little mole of my own to sniff around and see what was going on. Sitting in front of my laptop, silently wishing my mole *bon voyage* I clicked send and off it went. A cyber-mole, my favourite kind, pretending to be something it wasn't.

Quite a lot like me in fact.

Chapter Nine

My phone rang almost as soon as I got into the car the next morning. I checked the screen before I answered it, most calls were coded but this one wasn't.

'Dr Steel?'

'Who is this?' I didn't recognise the woman's voice at the end of the line.

'Sorry to call out of the blue but I was given your number by Sergeant Campbell. He said you needed information quickly so I hope you don't mind me calling you direct.'

'I didn't catch your name?' I hadn't a clue who this woman was but I'd swing for Tommy Campbell when I'd got rid of her.

Sergeant Campbell was the officer in charge of a very small police station in the Highlands. He was really a friend of a friend, but he was also an information magnet. He knew facts that no-one else did, how he found out I never knew but he wasn't often wrong. Tommy's greatest loves were single malt, salmon fishing and munro bagging, although not necessarily in that order. He'd neatly side stepped any promotion to stay exactly where he wanted to be; in charge of a very small police station in a very small Scottish town.

'Och, sorry, Dr Steel, I'm Polly, Polly McDonald. Tommy told me that you were looking to find out about any recent buddhist sky burial ceremonies.'

'Did he now...'

'Yes, yes, he was quite clear about it. Anyway, I won't keep you, I'm sure you're busy but I just wanted to let you know that we found a sky burial here just recently.'

'Ms McDonald...'

'Polly, please, just Polly.'

'Polly, a sky burial? Where and when?'

'A corbett not far from where I live and just over three weeks ago, give or take a day. I'll have to look it up if you want the exact date.'

Thank the gods for someone who answered questions properly. 'Polly, where do you live and what was the name of the corbett?' If she was as good as she sounded, I should be able to get some valuable information.

'I live in Lochinver and it was on Suilven where we found what we think was the remains of a sky burial.'

41

Her words froze me. Suilven. Same place and at about the same time that I'd climbed with Gwil's ashes. No-one else had been about for the whole of the climb but there had been a man, in the early hours of that night, who had come into the same bothy I'd camped in. I hadn't paid much attention, assuming he was a climber too, going up as I was coming down. In any case, sleep had evaded me so I'd moved on in the darkness and not given him a second thought.

'Polly, will you be at home later today?'

'Yes, Dr Steel, I'm at home all day. Why do you ask?'

'May I come and see you? Could I talk to you about what you found?'

'Of course, it'd be a pleasure. I'm a keen, although very amateur, photographer so I also have some stills from that day, doubt they'll be any good but you're welcome to have a look. I've never seen anything like it before.'

Halle-bloody-lujah, it got better and better.

As soon as I finished talking to Polly I rang Moore and told him I'd be away for two days, then after securing a seat on a plane, I rang Tommy and called him everything but a Christian for giving out my number to a nutter. I didn't let on that I was both delighted and on the way to have a look at her snaps.

Scotland was as gorgeous as usual and it was pleasing to have such an excuse to pop back for a sniff of mountain air. Polly, true to her word, had taken some excellent photographs of what did actually look like a sky burial.

'Dr Steel?' she'd opened the front door of her mid-terrace house and looked quizzically from behind half moon specs, as if she'd been expecting someone else.

'Hello, Polly. I'm Jake, Jake Steel.'

'Gosh, you *are* frighteningly good-looking, aren't you?' she shoved her glasses back up her nose with one finger and stared intently at me again. 'Tommy told me that you were so that I wasn't caught out, so to speak.' I sensed granite behind her sensible appearance, she'd never be one to be caught out easily. 'You've the eyes of a faerie, do you know that?'

'Ah, yes, I've been told before... Sorry I'm late but I've had quite a bit of a journey to get here.' I was hoping she might offer to put the kettle on but mostly that I might get in off the doorstep. 'May I come in? Its cold and we've a lot to talk about.' I tried switching to Gaelic and the result was dramatic, I shifted from being stranger to friend in a heartbeat.

'Come in, come in! Where are my manners? Tommy has told me so much about you, he'll be popping by in a while, I expect. I did tell him you were coming for tea.' Polly was much easier to talk to in Gaelic, some Scots were. Having found the key, I stayed with it.

She pulled a packet of photographic prints from a drawer in the kitchen, placing them, almost reverently, on the table next to a slumbering tabby cat. I opened the packet and scanned through what she'd recorded.

'This was exactly how you found it?'

'Yes,' she nodded, 'I was first up Suilven that morning, I got quite a surprise I can tell you. Have you ever been there?'

'Yes, many times. In fact I was there just a few days before you found this.'

'It is a truly amazing place - very spiritual. I can understand why someone might want to perform such a ritual on the summit, can't you?'

Of course I understood. Gwil had felt exactly the same but I didn't pass on that fact. The immediate problem that I had now was that the sky burial which Polly had so extensively photographed was that of a dog.

It had been beautifully done from a ritualistic point of view but it wasn't quite what I'd been expecting. She told me that the police had arranged a postmortem which revealed that the dog had died of completely natural causes a few days prior to its discovery at Suilven. That neatly explained why I'd found no investigative reports about it on the police database.

It was disappointing in a way that it hadn't turned out to be a human burial, but time spent in the Highlands is never wasted. When I returned to Devon, I had Polly's photographs as well as a bottle of Edradour whisky that she'd insistently pressed into my hands on the doorstep.

Tommy had arrived after an hour, walking straight in as if it was his house and engulfing me in a back slapping bear hug.

'How long are you back for?' he asked, stepping back and looking at me intently. It was his version of a visual frisk, I could hear cogs turning. 'You don't look well.'

'Cut it out, Tommy. I'm working and I've not the time for playing fly fishing with PC Plod.'

Tommy turned his attention to Polly. 'Bet you never thought you could still drag a man seven hundred miles in a day, Pol! But you did it with this one and that'd make you one of the very few. They've named him after the mist you know, because we can never get a clear grip on him!' He dissolved into laughter at his own cleverness.

'Seven hundred miles?' Polly was looking confused. 'Seven hundred miles from where?'

'Ignore him,' I said and explained, 'I was in Devon this morning when we spoke, I'm going back there again later tonight or in the morning, whenever I can get a flight.'

And that's probably how I ended up with the bottle of Edradour.

****

Staring blankly out of the window on the flight home, I tried to remember the man who'd come into the bothy that night. Shadows, that's all I could remember, I hadn't exactly gone out of my way to be sociable, in fact I'd barely looked his way at all. Gwil would have kicked my arse for the omission, '*you never know who or what will walk through the door, Spider, keep your eye off your dick and on the ball at all times. Zenshin, it is a way of life not a weekend pleasure....*'

Chapter Ten

The following Sunday was one of those winter days that promised of better weather to come. It was dry and bright, the trees in the town square charcoal stick stark against a pale blue sky. I'd given myself a day off and now had a perfect running opportunity as, to be frank, I was more than a little bored and running would mean not staring at the walls.

Updated instructions had shifted the emphasis of the investigation without me having to ask. Perhaps I'd be moved from Dartmoor early to dig deeper into Marcus Williams' more personal affairs, as Gwil had been trying to do. It was frustrating, but more interesting than simply translating, to have to work backwards with a high level of threat but no clear direction to head in. Rather than brood, I got changed and was out the door within five minutes, headphones on, another world in my head.

The air had that slightly seductive freshness, laced with wood smoke and open fire winter friendliness; right now it was a day for going out and breathing it in. Pulling up the zip on my jacket, I shut out the increasing chill and ran up to higher ground. I found myself eventually on a parallel track to the remote barn, coming at it from the other way, stopping up on top of a small rise and looking down on the courtyard, I was interested to see it again in the daylight.

The barn was enclosed by the moor with three large trees around it, clearly positioned in the lee of the wind. A motorbike distracted as it roared up the long driveway, a diminutive rider standing up on the foot pegs as the bike leapt the ruts of the stony track at speed. It arrived in front of the house skidding to a semi-circular halt. The rider kicked down the side stand and jumped off, pulling off a black helmet.

It was Sid. Of course it was. Shit. Not just a rider of racehorses, clearly also a rider of motorbikes.

She walked into the house and disappeared from view. So this was where she lived. I'd known the address, not the actual location. I turned and immediately ran on, trying the rough sheep track that led away from the house, back in the direction of the town, but it was too late, she was now firmly in my thoughts again. And this time I distinctly heard Fate sniggering as I ran away.

From my pocket, I pulled out my phone, skipped to the album list, shuffling to some early Rolling Stones and turned up the volume so that it was far too loud and disruptive for me to think about anything else. Lengthened my stride and upped my pace, shutting out everything but the music.

I was almost off the track when she reappeared, pulling up behind me on her bike. I wondered if I could just carry on and ignore her, perhaps she wouldn't recognise me, perhaps she'd just ride on by. But, of course, she slowed and there was nothing for it, I had to stop, even if just to give her passing room. Pushing up the visor with a gloved hand, her blue eyes danced in the bright, flat light, she was clearly speaking to me. Berating myself for not staying the hell out of her way, I pulled the headphones, letting them hang against my zip as she pressed the kill switch to silence the roar of the bike.

'Nice day for it,' her eyes creased at the edges, a black scarf over her mouth and nose underneath her helmet.

'Mmm…and for bikes?' The bike was a grunty trail bike, a big four stroke Honda, not typically a girl's first choice. But, then again what else should I expect, this Sid really was turning out to be anything but typical.

'Bikes rock!' she was definitely smiling now I could hear it in her voice. 'Are you coming or going?'

'Going, as in going back, I'm done for today.' I looked away towards the town, willed her to just go on her way again.

'Would you like a coffee? My place is just down there, you can take the short cut across the field. A map opportunity perhaps? However, if you're busy, it can be another time,' she spoke as if she didn't mind either way.

I stood for a moment, found I was saying yes and then wishing instantly that I hadn't. This was not a place to explore; Sid was proving to be someone so much more than she should be and I'd vowed not to mess around in those circles. Moths and flames – I could smell burning wings. She directed me back to the house with the courtyard and then, with several slow kicks to align the piston, produced an athletic little leap to kick start the big bike, turning it around slowly in the track and charging off. I waited for a moment, very badly needing not to be intrigued by her but that little display was just making her more interesting not less.

The outbuildings turned out to house the Land Rover and the bike, with a cobbled courtyard in front. Up close, it was all subtly but expensively designed, green oak and glass, unobtrusive in its location almost as if it'd grown there all by itself. It made my place look a lot like a shed.

She was sitting on the step as I approached, hands hugging her knees, black Hein Gericke jacket open at the zip, black jeans and black boots. Her lurcher bounded around, big laughing face, no barking; either he liked strangers or I'd managed an effective disguise.

'Great location.' I said.

'It is. It's far enough away from people to feel remote, surrounded by all this beauty and wildness and yet, easy to live with. Want to come in?' she looked at me steadily as if once again she didn't mind whether I did or not. And once again I wanted to say no, to make some plausible excuse and bolt. Stupid, I'd said yes to coffee…

The interior was as good as the outside. It seemed to consist mainly of glass and bare wood, a natural New England vibe. She told me that the glass was treated so that it retained heat, all very eco, but that it was also reflective at night so no loss of privacy in the dark hours, you could see out but not in. That explained why I could only see a dull reflective surface when I'd run past the first time. Dominating the main room were two huge oil paintings on the walls, expensive and stylish abstract seascapes, one hanging dramatically double height.

A coffee pot already bubbling on the top of a wood burner filled the space with evocative aromas. She poured some into two cups, pushed the lurcher out of the way on the sofa and gestured to me to sit. I sat, still running an internal dialogue as to what the hell I was doing there, but then found that, actually, all that didn't matter.

Almost immediately we were talking. Conversation that was easy. Conversation that skipped along bringing with it the calming comfort of good company with a like mind. Good craic, oh how I'd missed it. Frankly charmed by her and the way that she was, my carefully contained manner slunk off leaving simply Jake and, what was even more astounding, Jake was really enjoying himself.

'So is your policeman's lot a happy one?' she was sitting cross-legged on the rug by the wood burner; one elbow on her knee, chin resting on her hand. 'With understanding significant others?'

'I'm not a policeman, just simple translator but my lot, as you put it, is almost always a happy one. As for significant others - I gave everything up for Lent.' Surprising myself that I'd even answered that one. 'What about you?'

She snorted laughter. 'You clearly know that I'm supposedly the world's most ferocious female. I expect that you know more about me than I do as Trevor Brunning's tongue is reputed to talk all by itself! No, there's no significant or any kind of other in my world; I gave them up for life, not just for Lent.'

The lurcher, whose name was Finn, stretched and produced an enormous yawn that sounded like speech, making us both stare at him. I caught sight of the time; I'd sat and talked and laughed with this woman for well over two hours, yet it felt like a quarter of that.

'I'd better go, time has flown.' It was easy to smile at her, easier to find words.

'Jake, thank you. I can't remember when I've listened to such silliness and laughed so much.'

'I'm not generally known for my ability to entertain but there is, of course, a first time for everything. But it should be me that's thanking you - great coffee, good company, you rescued me from a very dull Sunday.'

'We've not even looked at the maps! Bugger…sorry… all that and you still have no new routes to run.'

'Tell you what, would you like to go for a drink, show me a pub that's halfway decent here, bring the maps and I'll buy a round?' I kept my expression light so that she took this for exactly what it was and nothing more. I wasn't looking for anything other than friendship, hadn't even been looking for that from someone like her. But here I was.

'You bring the craic again and you're on,' it seemed she knew where I was at. Arms-length, barriers in place, she was there too.

Chapter Eleven - Alyosha

And I will flay the flesh from their bones and strip them bare for angels to eat

Remember the colt that I watched being born with Father, Zosima? He told me, when the colt became so good he had to be syndicated, he told me that he would give me shares, give us all shares and it would be our future fund; for our education, for a house, business, who knows? We were children, who knew what our dreams might be.

The oldest brother was showing a head for investments so Father gave the shares to him to manage. The colt had a very bright future; he was going to make a lot of people a lot of money. The brother, ever the chancer, thought he knew better, be years before we needed those shares, you and me, we were too young. So he pawned them, pawned them for their value. He could never have imagined that the colt would be quite so successful. He struggled, really struggled to buy them back, had to borrow again to make that happen. He did it and then immediately pawned them once more. The younger brother knew all about it because he was involved too. And the colt, so successful, was making money hand over fist; he couldn't step out of the way of the money pouring in for him. Everyone was so pleased, this would put the stud on the map; increase the value of the mare and the colt's siblings. But not the brothers, they could no longer afford to buy back the shares, like some rare Rembrandt, the colt was worth millions now. Of course, they hadn't pawned them to just anyone, they'd chosen the big boys, the people who killed if you didn't pay back.

The brothers had lifestyles, we had school and packed lunches, they had status and front and face, all so very expensive to maintain. The colt went to race, it was to be his last before retiring to stud, remember that, the parents went on the plane, hired a plane to see him run? He would be worth even more then, if he won, he'd be retired to stud, those shares would be even more valuable. The parents were so pleased, they'd set us up for the future, we'd have millions each. But they didn't know what the brothers had done, didn't know the kind of men they had become. The brothers weren't pleased. They had to force the sale of part of the horse to be able to pay for it all, in order to get the money now. The only way the parents would agree to that was if they were no longer around to agree or disagree. The brothers pleaded with the parents to sell but they said, no, over their dead bodies, the horse would be for all, for the future, as such a horse comes along only once in a lifetime. Maybe that is when the brothers got the idea.

Alyosha had gone back to work, managing a few days before the cracks began to show once more. He put it down to the stress of his job but, deep down, he knew it was part of the holy work he now had to do.

When he'd read up about being born again, about being received by the eternal one, most reports had told of it being a truly joyful and wondrous event. There wasn't much that was wondrous about the way he was feeling. So, just in case the fault lay with him, he decided to meditate and pray hourly, then half-hourly, until soon he was doing nothing but praying.

Alyosha, we have work for you. Eagles woke him in the early hours. They often did, it was their favourite time of day.

You have family to make safe. Storms are coming, you need to get the precious cargo into the hold and get rid of the bad apples.

They spoke in riddles so he took it upon himself to decipher the meaning because they never repeated instructions. As always he wrote it all in his moleskine notebook using coloured pens to underline and circle important words.

And six is the number. Six is the number of what? Six is the number that will die. Alyosha. Six is the number.

The shaking began shortly after the eagles had left. Limbs shaking so hard that his teeth rattled in their sockets, he crawled to the bathroom and vomited into the basin, retching bile until he had nothing left but air to gag. He lay on the cold floor, curled himself into a ball and began to pray again.

Zosima... He needed Zosima...

No, Alyosha. No Zosima. Not this time. This time Alyosha will be strong. Alyosha must be strong for Zosima this time. He will be so strong he will show them all.

And with those words, the eagles picked up his mobile phone using his fingers and flushed it down the toilet.

Chapter Twelve

So that was it, as nothing more than friends we got on like good friends should; easy, no sides, no obvious undercurrents. Over the course of the next week or so I saw quite a bit of her; she showed me pubs I'd never have found by myself and, with Finn, we walked routes I couldn't wait to run. We talked superficially about everything and anything, made up ridiculous stories to laugh like children about and she told me some of the most shockingly obscene jokes I'd ever heard. Purely platonic without obvious agenda, I carried on enjoying her company immensely.

'I'm racing on Friday for David, may even ride a winner, it is good enough.'

We were discussing the coming weekend sitting in a rural pub with yet another OS map on the table. Sitting side by side, looking at the tracks on the map, she was pointing out a new route. She knew the whole moor; where there were bogs, where there were boar, where you might get shot by the military, where you might get flashed by strange men, where loose dogs were an issue; she seemed to know it all. As she pointed out a track our fingers met accidentally, it was like static shock, just like the moment before, there was something, some weird connection every now and then. We looked at each other and laughed it off.

'So what are you doing after the races?' I sought normality again, pushing away unwanted thoughts.

'Oh, hanging out with you I expect, boring you with the minutiae of my day, jump by jump. That's if you're free and don't get a better offer in the meantime.' Her eyes flashed, she was teasing again, something she was relentless at.

'Right you're on. You buy the meal if you win and I'll chauffeur.' Bluff called, I waited as she sought a quick response and added, 'but if you lose it's a burger and I'll pay.'

'No! Not a burger, yuck! Never! They might say they're one hundred per cent beef but they don't tell you which bit of the cow it came from – its all foreskin and testicles!'

We agreed in the end on a non-burger evening and, for ease of a daytime winning or not update, I finally gave her my mobile number. Secrecy, an intrinsic part of me, came with the nature of the places that I hung out in. Releasing the number was a massive statement of trust, of friendship and of the simple enjoyment of being around her.

On Friday afternoon at work, my winning or not update came.

Buried two from home. Bruised and battered. R u still up for burger? 😞 *S*

She'd fallen, as had the horse, with two fences to jump before the race finish. I typed a reply.

Do pub. I'll drive

Gd, suits black & blue walking wounded. Time 4 pickup?

7.30? From yours?

Gr8. C u then.

She was waiting, black skinny jeans, black boots, black fleece jacket; always black. Long blonde hair loose around her shoulders, sea blue eyes bright in contrast, leaning against the oak beam upright to the porch with obvious discomfort. She got into the car and proceeded to tell me how much she'd gone off horses as this one had delivered a few kicks on its way back to its feet. I was amazed that she'd walked away from it so easily, jockeys were made of tough stuff I knew, but there was very little of her to lessen the impact. By the time we got to the pub of her choice, I felt like I'd been racing too. I was getting dangerously used to being around her. Steady on, Jake, keep it tight.

As we were leaving at the end of the evening, with a sudden whimper she leaned against me, a cramp from seized and bruised muscles in her shoulder.

'Oh! Fuck! That hurts!' she hissed, grabbed my arm and tried to straighten her shoulder by pulling against me. 'Fuck! Fuck!'

She was bent double almost sobbing with pain as she tried to stretch out the cramp. I held her arm, slipped my hand just under her jacket and massaged the tight knot of hard muscle on her shoulder and bicep, succeeding in releasing the spasm. My fingers against her muscle, almost against her skin and immediately I was monumentally overcome with physical need for her. I'd never experienced anything so instant, so intense before, it coursed violently through making me tight chested and short of breath. Cramp released, she stared at me as surprised as I was by the ferocity of that sudden flare between us.

'Crikey... Are you carrying a Taser or something?' Eyes wide, her voice no more than a whisper.

'Nope, sorry I left it with Finn; he said he'd some rabbits to subdue later.' I camouflaged over my turmoil. No, this wasn't happening. Not to me.

Driving her home, she returned to her usual good humour, more stories, mostly made up but very entertaining nonetheless. I tried not to think too hard about the feeling that had roared through us both, thinking about those sorts of feelings was always trouble.

As I turned off the road onto the stone track to her home, the change in atmosphere within the car was immediate as if she'd suddenly become someone else. Slowing to avoid the first pot hole I glanced over at her, sitting so silent; she was looking away, out the window into the darkness. Her face reflected back from the dashboard light looked haunted. From the stereo speakers, Tom Petty was singing quietly about Mary Jane. *'...one more drink to ease the pain... too cold to cry when I woke alone...'*

A premonition, was that what it was? That sixth sense thing, whatever you might call it, something had shifted here. The lightness and laughter gone to be replaced by an undercurrent of something else. Something strong and black and bleak, an emotional representation of the winter moor outside.

****

Driving up to the front of the house the security lights flicked on, I pulled the car around in a circle so that it was facing back down the drive again. No point in making any assumptions from her point of view, or mine. We often had coffee and it'd been easy to do so until tonight. Right now, I was ready to leave.

I turned off the engine and Tom was halted midsentence. Aside from the wind wailing outside, there was no sound until she sighed deeply, a profound weighted exhale which did nothing to release the tension. I got out and went around to open her door, she looked up and there was a flicker of something within her eyes that could have been pain. What could I say? She'd have to work this out for herself, decide what she wanted to do next. Torn now, I wanted to go and, just as much, wanted to stay. Bollocks. This wasn't where I wanted to be.

Leave and leave now, my decision was made. I stepped away, half a stride to give her space, to take the pressure off. I tried a smile, just a little 'it's ok' smile of reassurance. I didn't expect her eyes to fill with tears. Fat, heavy tears that spilled silently over her lashes. This was yet another person. The woman I'd got to know over the last few weeks was hard as nails, super confident, composed and feisty. That woman had an answer for everything, laser sharp retorts that could slay at ten paces.

'Are you ok?' I held out my hand, open palm to reassure, a gesture as old as time of honest intent, no hidden weapons.

'I simply don't know,' her voice a whisper against the wind.

'Look... let's save coffee for another time.'

I was still trying to process what was happening here, the turning into the track to her house and suddenly we'd shifted emotional continents from the easy warmth of a Caribbean sun to blasted tundra of arctic waste.

She looked so lost for a moment but then with a small movement she straightened her shoulders, reached for my hand and led me to the front door. At that moment it would have been trite of me to have pulled away but the feel of her hand in mine... that didn't help... that didn't help at all.

'Sid,' I stopped her at the door, 'please understand that I'm really not here for any reason other than I enjoy your company. It isn't actually my style to have a hidden agenda, what you see is what you get. Talk to me if you want to, or not, there's no requirement either way.'

Lies, now every word seemed like a lie.

She turned away unlocking the door and pushing it open, greeting Finn who lay upside down on the sofa with his legs in the air. Only a lurcher could remain in such a ridiculous position; he was such a bloke, all beer cans and boxer shorts in front of the football. He wagged his skinny tail vaguely and went straight back to sleep - some guard dog.

'Can you check on the wood burner while I make some coffee?' she called and went through into the kitchen.

I was sitting cross legged in front of it, lost for a moment in more of those unwanted thoughts when she came back, putting a tray on the stone hearth.

'Thank you for this evening, it was another memorable one.' Looking at me from out of the corner of her eye, I watched the edge of her smile work its way right up with her glance. So trusting, she was covering over something enormous and simply trusting me. I should have left there and then.

Why had this become suddenly so volatile? I could sense determination from her, as if she had decided to see this through no matter what, even if what she really wanted to do was run away too. Oh! Sudden realisation thundered in. She was afraid of me. As if by a simple touch on her shoulder *I* had become someone to fear. Why? I tried to work out if it was fear of me personally or of who she thought I represented. Police? Was that it? In too deep perhaps, does she think she's gone too far? More thoughts reeling around and nothing joining up. Why?

Fingertips tingling, I could still feel her skin; feel her as if she was now touching me, my heart beat faster with that thought alone. Jake, come on, pull out mate, get out. Job's blown. Go home.

'Coffee?' she held out a cup, her hand steady now. I knew mine wouldn't be so I placed the cup immediately down on the small trivet beside stacked logs.

'I seem to have managed to knock the stuffing out of this evening, haven't I?' she moved away, sat down on the floor and crossed her legs elegantly. Behind the casual tone, fear remained. She was hiding something. I could see it now. And I could also see it was something that she was absolutely terrified of.

'One must have the courage to dare', a Dostoevsky quote slipped into my thoughts and, with it, I remembered the package Gwil sent to Scotland when all of this began. Coincidence or fate? Who could know. Funny thing courage, it can get too big for its boots sometimes and fling you further than is truly safe. I was here, in this moment and, as I was, it was as good a time as any to try and find out if either one of us had the courage to dare.

'Is it something that was said, or not said? Sometimes it is the unsaid words that are the worst.' I tried to keep it light but there I was, a school boy again, all dry mouth and tight trousers.

She said nothing more for a long time, just sipped coffee and so I waited, forcing myself to think of something else, something less intense.

'It isn't words, unsaid or not, that are the problem. It's the potential that's freaking me out.'

'The potential of what?'

'Us, Jake, us,' she turned, sea blue drew me inextricably in. 'I know that you can feel it. I know that was us back there in the car park. I barely know the real you but I simply don't behave like this. I'm really struggling here.'

She smiled; a small helpless smile that made her more beautiful, not because it revealed her vulnerability but because it revealed her strength.

'I don't do relationships, don't do close. I hate gossip and guard my privacy much better than Finn does this house. I've had so much fun, being friends and I really don't want anything to change that.'

'There's not much else to me, Sid. Shallow and superficial all the way.'

Lacing my voice with humour and hoping it would help. I also wanted what we had before this tension began, needed the distance I'd maintained before.

'That perhaps is another issue,' she said, 'because you're anything but. It's a while since I met anyone like you, if I ever have.'

I held her gaze and felt the truth of her. She was unique, mercurial, captivating and I was bound by nothing more than the soft curve of her cheek bone framed by strands of golden hair. Perhaps it was simply the firelight, but an inner strength shone out from her, as if she had made a life changing decision and was empowered by it. And in that moment I realised that I hadn't even begun to know her.

'Why do you not do relationships?' The words came out unbidden. 'You don't have to tell me. My mouth has broken my nose more than once.'

'No, I should explain,' she wound her arms around her legs, renewing her defences. 'I was with someone a long time ago. I thought it was love. It wasn't. It took me a long time to work it out. After that I promised myself that I'd no longer be available. Call it self-preservation or call it cowardliness; I simply won't willingly take that kind of pain again. Do you know, for a while back then, I wondered if I'd survive it,' she laughed dryly, as if she was berating herself for some small act of silliness. 'So now, I get my kicks from horses, if you'll excuse the irony, and riding motorbikes far too fast.' She gave a small, self-effacing smile. 'Perhaps I misplaced my sanity at the same time as I broke my heart.'

'And is your heart still broken?'

'No, not anymore, amazingly it did heal. But now I keep it chained up out the back and don't look at it too often.'

'I should do that perhaps, mine sits here on my sleeve and it often gets me into trouble.'

I could feel my just about clinging to the rock face grip slipping. I was going to be headlong into this if I didn't start backing out. She simply kept looking at me. We had arrived at the moment, I could sense it clearly. She fought with whatever her decision was, one minute certain, the next not.

'Stay. Please? Will you stay with me tonight?' without dropping her gaze, she asked in a whisper. 'I know I shouldn't ask you but I really don't want to be a coward for the rest of my life and it can't rain all the time, can it?' Her eyes, now so dark and haunted; that final decision hadn't come lightly.

If she could find that level of courage, then so could I.

'This is holiday land, Sid. There are supposed to be more days of sunshine than there are of rain,' I held out my hand and let go of the rock face.

Chapter Thirteen

On that wild night, there on the rug in the warm glow of the fire, she was momentarily hesitant as if she was once again unsure of where we were heading. I stilled, waited, seeking her eyes.

'Are you ok?' I had to ask, she was trembling.

'Yes, I … I really want this… want you… It's just...' she looked away, her voice a whisper '…it's been a long time… I'm a little scared.'

'Sid, don't be. This stops now or whenever you want it to. You just need to say.' I stroked away a strand of hair and kissed her.

Tears again. Glistening tears silently slipped down her face as she dropped her head onto my shoulder and cried without making a sound.

'Sid? Please, Sid, tell me what's wrong.'

Something much more complicated than the oldest of pleasures was going on here and, blinded by desire, I was missing it. It seemed her projected determination had come undone with her shirt buttons.

'I can't...so sorry...I'm so sorry but I can't put it into words.' She spoke into my neck, clinging to me so that it felt like I was the only thing that would stop her from falling.

'I know that you're afraid. What are you afraid of? Is it me?'

She sat up quickly, looking at me fiercely. 'No, Jake, no, it isn't you at all. I wouldn't - couldn't be here if I was afraid of you.'

'Then, if you can't tell me what the problem is, can I do something to help make it right?' Touching her lips with my fingertips, she closed her eyes as if I was doing nothing more than making it worse. Whatever *it* was.

'You're right, I'm afraid but not of you, I'm afraid of this,' she gestured with one hand as if to indicate how close we were physically. 'I'm very afraid of what might happen. Of what does happen. I was sure I could do this, wanted to do this, especially with you, but now...'

'Ok, ok,' I moved her away and slowly re-buttoned her shirt, she stopped my hand and shook her head.

'Don't, please. Don't give up on me just yet.'

'It isn't about giving up, quite the opposite, but you shouldn't feel like this, not even slightly. Wait, don't rush, you'll know when it's the right time.' Not knowing what the problem was meant it was hard to say anything sensible. 'Sometimes, when I have something on my mind, I find a mountain and climb it.'

She stared at me as if I'd grown an extra head, 'Metaphorically or actually?'

'Actually, with ropes and, sometimes, even without.' I winked at her and was rewarded with one of her dazzling smiles.

'How do you do that?'

'What climb mountains? Well, once you get past putting one foot in front of the other, it gets a bit complicated to explain,' I feigned puzzlement, sliding into a soft Irish accent. 'First, you need a mountain...'

'No! Not how you climb, silly! How do you shift my mood from dark to light with just one sentence?'

'It's a skill not many of us have, I admit,' I replied, sticking with the Irish. 'But then, to be sure, I never imagined having such a discussion with someone whilst they had their legs wrapped around me.'

'Oh, you really are something else,' she wrapped her legs tighter and kissed me for a long time. Now that was much better. 'I've waited so long for this moment, forgive me but I can't tell you why, I simply don't have the words. But, here and now, if you wouldn't mind taking this really, really slowly, please could we start all over again?'

Holding her close, slowing everything down and softening every movement, I backed up a hundred miles and let her lead. Without moving away she tugged at my t-shirt dropping it casually on the floor beside us. She was kissing me again, moving her hands across my chest, splaying out her touch and then outlining with one fingertip the words of the tattoo etched on the inside of my right arm.

I held her, hands on her waist and up her sides, skimming the edge of her, making my touch a suggestion and nothing more. Her eyes blue fire into mine, her fingers feather touching, tentatively stroking the lines of muscle across my stomach, down scuffing the waistband of my jeans, making nerve endings reach out in searing desperation for more. What was she thinking at that moment? I'd little left in the way of ordered thought. I was somewhere else, heavily clouded with profound desire for this woman.

Traitor. I felt like a traitor...or worse... There was still time, I could stop this...no...don't stop this...

Very slowly she undid the rest of her shirt, letting it slip from her shoulders. Lowering herself down, giving me her weight but not for one moment letting me out of her gaze. There was no fear now, but I was still waiting and following her lead as she gradually, with each ragged breath, became someone else in my arms. Someone who wanted. Someone who was in the thrall of this roaring need just as I was.

Our bodies wound together, entwined as one, time slowed or ceased to exist as I held the naked curve of her. All that tension, all that heat. It surged and boiled, until it was all just sensation, fanned and concentrated by a tremendous passion, wave after wave of hunger and need. We were lost into it. Moulded to me, the feel of her every movement sang of an exquisite sensuality, there was no room for detachment, it was, she was, all-consuming in that moment.

Bastard. Jake. You really are a bastard now.

But a profound discovery was made in those dark hours. Profound and unexpected in that I experienced something I didn't know existed. Perhaps it was because it had been a while, perhaps it was because of the way she was, or the way I was. The specifics don't matter but I've never experienced anything quite so intense. Felt it build, generating an improbable tension and then, at its peak, power out through me like a divine force, locking us hard together as she cried out to me, to the gods, to the stars... to anyone who might have been listening. I'd no breath left when she finally lay still against my shoulder.

Floored by such an unexpected experience, reeling in some strange and alien no man's land, I struggled for clarity, struggled to make sense of what had just happened. To have gone through with this was now shocking me. I am distant and controlled and defended. I don't do this. But... Something new was here. Something I didn't know. What was it? Something I thought might have been missing from inside of me stretched and looked around as if it had simply been waiting for this very moment.

'Oh my... Thank you,' she whispered after a long silence, her breath warm against slick skin. 'I never knew such a thing could happen, never knew that this was possible. That was... I don't have words... something else...'

Sitting up, she gave me the most beautiful smile and then it hit home. I could no longer pretend to berate myself for a dishonourable act. I could no longer fool myself. I was here all along because I wanted to be, spending time with her had never really been anything to do with the job. I was here and I was feeling like this because of her.

'I'm so very pleased that I didn't stay home because of the rain again,' easing away, putting back on her shirt, she stood and held out her hand. 'If

I'm going to be fit to ride in the morning, I've got to soak these bruises. So as I'm apparently much, much braver than I thought, I'm going to really push my luck and ask would you... please... oh fuck it... would you please come and share a bath with me?'

Flicking off the lights as we passed, we went upstairs and into an enormous bathroom.

'Put some music on, just through there, you choose. It's connected to speakers here so just choose what you like.'

Through there turned out to be her bedroom. A brass bed and bleached oak chests, pale purple and cream throughout. On the floor beside one chest was a canvas holdall, on its side and open at the zip. Spilling out from inside was a pair of mens boots, an electric shaver and a telephoto lens for a Nikon camera. I glanced around the rest of the room but nothing else looked as out of place as that bag did.

I decided to ignore it for now and, searching through the eclectic selection of music, settled with a mix from her recently played list. Outside the wind was still lashing the moor, dragging the trees into a reluctant dance; the very last vestiges of their autumn leaf dresses, kept as if in memory of a previous summer, now stripped away by violent gusts. I looked out, my reflection caught and held, as I was, in the unexpected wonder of this night. Soft hands around my waist and she was there, I turned in her arms lifting her chin so as to meet her mouth. She was all need again, her kiss fierce and wanton, she clung and made me burn for her once more.

In the warm embrace of the water, gently lit by candles, we talked quietly about somethings and nothings, she was laid warm against me, her hair spread in wet tendrils over my shoulder. For a long time we stayed there, until the candles flickered and one went out.

'Blimey, what are we like! I've no idea what the time is and I've got to leave at six. We must need at least some sleep.'

She stood and, for a brief moment, there was her back completely exposed in the candlelight as she pulled a big towel around herself. The new born bruises from her fall were shocking enough, but I'd not expected the scars. They were not the kind of scars that you got from falling off racehorses.

Letting out the water, stepping out of the bath to take her proffered towel, she smiled at me.

'That's quite a body you have, Jake, a beautiful sight to behold.'

'Now, Sid, that isn't fair, you're taking all my best lines.' I eased her wet hair back over her shoulders and said nothing about bags or scars.

Sinking together into the bed, sleep was found to be really not that important after all. At some point my phone rang, I ignored it at first but when it immediately rang again, I couldn't pretend any longer.

'Are you on call for the police?' she was sitting astride me, looking like an angel in the semi-darkness, her hair tousled by my hands. She was almost more irresistible like that.

'Not officially,' holding her tight with one arm so as not to let her move from where she was, I reached down over the side of the bed, pulling out the phone from my jeans thrown in a heap on the floor. No message but two missed calls and both police. Shit. I groaned under my breath.

'Sadly, I'm going to need to ring in.'

I pulled her close kissing her for far too long, momentarily torn but then reluctantly sliding away. I found clothes as those missed calls would mean that my night was over for certain. Pressing the redial I waited as it rang twice and was answered with a bark.

'Where the hell are you? Why don't you ever answer the sodding phone?' It was Trev and he was a little cross. 'Moore's having a melt down here because he can't find you. I assume that you're in the arms of some delicious piece so, as I've had to put up with the ranting, I'm now delighted to pull you away from whoever and tell you, and I quote, 'tell Steel to put it back in his trousers and shift his arse in here now, immediately, if not sooner.' Ok, so can you do that? And now, mate?'

'What's going on?' I spoke quietly into the phone, turned and looked at Sid laying there, all eyes and silence.

'Murder.' Trev said it with a mock Glaswegian accent and laughed. Taggart had a lot to answer for. 'Seriously Jake, it's a messy one and, for some reason, Moore wants you on site. Shift your arse there's a good chap.'

I disconnected and sat back on the bed. 'Its work, I have to go.'

She tilted her face and kissed me lightly which rapidly became something more. I could so easily have stayed but sense prevailed and she let me go, sitting back, easing up the quilt under her arms.

'I'll call you later, ok? Take it easy, no flinging yourself off any more horses.' I touched her lips with my fingertips and turned to leave. 'Thank you, Sid, for a wonderful night. I'll call you later.'

Chapter Fourteen

My name was mud in the office. Moore was seemingly on the verge of apoplexy and he roared for a good five minutes about newly arrived dickheads, whoever they were, who didn't answer their phones on the first ring. I stood there and took it until, spleen vented, he got down to the serious work. Trev drove us both out to the scene, working the car through police tapes and road closed signs, we stopped and walked to a lay-by, artificially lit now with portable lights through the freezing early morning gloom. Moore updated as we walked.

'Preliminary reports are that it will be hard to ID this body, but as a first step, we're working with identifying documents from the wallet in the clothing. They belong to a John Wozniak, forty-nine, married with three kids, local resident and horse-box driver for David Flint. Yes, that's right, *the* David Flint. Funny how he's becoming a household name around here this month but for all the wrong reasons. Anyway, back to the body that may or may not be John Wozniak, found in a pull in here, the B436, with his head smashed in. No buddhist ceremony this time, Jake; no witnesses, no murder weapon as yet. Reported by passing motorist at four fifteen am; Alan Cooper, sales rep, not local, who'd got himself very lost following his sat nav and stopped to check the map, although why anyone relies on sat nav's around here beggars belief.' Moore looked over to Trev. 'When we're done here, go back up to Flint's – give them all chance to get into work first. Find out what everyone was doing yesterday afternoon and evening. All teams are already on scene and, when they're done, I want the body to go back to the morgue. Usual form, you know the score.'

Trev nodded, pulling up the collar on his jacket to ward off the cold. Moore looked thoughtful again, thick fingers tapping on his chin.

'Walk with me a moment, Jake,' he turned away so I followed him until we were out of earshot of anyone else. 'I have to do this, I have to ask where you were?' He fixed me with a searching stare, 'You're clearly a lot more than just a translator, professor or not. Did you know anything about this? Are you investigating separately?'

I said nothing so he carried on. 'Additionally, I'm wondering whether you may find this professionally difficult and the only reason I'm asking you to tell me is that there may be a conflict of interests. This is the second issue concerning that racing yard and almost certainly a second murder.

Jake, I have to tell you that I saw you last night in the car park of the Fat Friar in the company of someone connected to the yard. Don't worry, it isn't common knowledge but it will probably become such even though I don't talk out of class. I'm going to be blunt and ask what is the nature of your involvement with Sid Fielding?'

I thought over what he was saying. The timing couldn't have been worse.

'I'm not currently at liberty to say anything concerning any external investigation. However, as it appears that you already know, yes, I was with Sid Fielding, I came from her house this morning.'

I kept my face impassive, might as well get it out into the open now before it came back to bite me. That might hold it at bay for a while so that I could work out my own game plan. I hoped that I wasn't denying or admitting personal involvement specifically. At this stage and with the amount of sleep I hadn't had, it was all too confusing.

Moore stared for far too long. 'I'm sure I don't need to mention proper procedures. I know you aren't strictly police payroll but, whatever your own game plan, there are certain lines that aren't crossed.'

I smiled at his words, so diplomatically put. If only he knew.

'Those lines haven't been crossed,' I said truthfully. What had gone down between Sid and I had nothing to do with any investigation that may or may not be happening.

Trev appeared at my shoulder as if by magic, his face told me he'd heard just enough. He'd never make a poker player.

'Right, thank you, you'd better keep your head down for now.' Moore turned and walked away, displeasure radiating from him.

Trev let out a low whistle, staring at me with utter disbelief. 'Well, bugger me sideways! Jake, you're either very good or very stupid. Sid Vicious! I don't believe it! There's many a man who's tried and been knocked back, how on earth did you get in? And, more to the point, how did I not know but the DCI did?' Trev was clearly both shocked and delighted with such a tasty morsel of gossip. It would be common knowledge within half an hour of our return to the station. 'There was me thinking you were out running and yet it was obviously a very different kind of exercise that you've been getting!'

I stared back at him. 'Discretion, Trev, please? It may not be what it seems.' He simply shook his head, a broad grin from ear to ear.

I turned away with a sigh, reaching in my pocket for gloves. Almost next to me the someone the DCI thought was John Wozniak, his face now unrecognisable as anything human. It had been battered into a soft pile of hair, brains and bone shards. Trev had been right in more ways than one. The whole job was becoming very messy.

Chapter Fifteen

As I'd been asked to attend, I wasn't going to waste the opportunity to be polite and study what the police had found. My mind started to run through possibilities, questions appeared and scenarios played out. The way he was lying, and that was a definite, it was a man; on his back, the knees of his jeans thick with mud, spoke of him probably being hit first from behind. Dropped to his knees with the force of an initial blow, it probably killed him outright; subsequent blows appeared to have been delivered in a killing frenzy as the stalky grass was liberally coated but the rest of his body appeared to be untouched. Thankfully the scene was sheltered from the wind which had torn at Sid's house last night and there had been no rain, but it was clearly several hours since death had occurred. This man had lain here kept as a secret by the quiet road and winter darkness.

I studied his shoes, cheap leather lace-ups speckled with condensation, heels worn down on one side, nylon socks covering skinny ankles, the coarse hair on his leg curling around the top of his left sock. His jeans stained now, the stench from a dead body was never easy to be around. I heard someone gag and retch behind me. I looked on up the body; a bloated, flaccid stomach bulged to either side of his waistband restrained by the fabric of his shirt; a drinker perhaps, a lover of junk food, certainly not someone who cared for himself very well. His hands clean, open and empty, fingers curled up towards the sky, nicotine staining on two fingers of his left hand, a plain wedding band with a small callus below it, frayed cuffs poked out from the sleeves of a black blouson jacket with the racing yard's logo on the left of the zip. Splattered with the sprayed contents of the inside of his skull but otherwise untouched. The murderer had battered the man's head in and left the rest alone. I wondered about that, not so frenzied after all perhaps.

As it was being fully tented, I examined the immediate area around the body carefully with my pocket torch without moving from where I stood. There on the grass of the verge, close enough to have come from the body, was a piece of paper, no bigger than half a credit card, marked into small squares with emoticons printed on it. Acid, LSD probably; little squares of mind trips for the user. I looked for Trev, he was throwing up into the hedge some distance away – I let him be. Moore walked back towards me coming away from the officers he'd been talking to.

'Well, what are your thoughts, Jake?' he thrust his hands into overcoat pockets, buried his chin into his collar to either keep out the smell or the cold, or both. 'Sometimes an outside opinion can be helpful.'

He wasn't going to let it lie then, I was an outsider and should not forget it.

'A moment?' I held up one hand to stop him. 'There are drugs — there on the verge, may or may not be connected with this body.' I turned looking for one of the forensic team who came over efficiently photographed and collected the squared paper into an evidence bag, marking it with content and location.

'Ok, I can make a few preliminary suggestions based on what's here; firstly, I don't think this body is the John Wozniak who works for David Flint. Secondly, I think this man was killed in situ and that he was hit from behind, mud on his knees as he dropped; he's now on his back but there's no sign of a struggle. The killer worked around him perhaps, hit him from the front when he was on his knees otherwise he'd probably have fallen forward, maybe the killer wanted to be seen by his victim. His hands are clean and, aside from the splatter, he appears to be unmarked elsewhere from what I can see here and now.

'Initially, my thoughts were frenzied attack, now I'm thinking the murderer specifically pulped his face as a deliberate act rather than due to some uncontrolled fury. He stinks of spirits, he has the appearance of a drinker but he may have been forced to drink. Or perhaps drugs brought him here or, perhaps, he was just passing and got lucky. He's been cleaned up, or he washed himself before he came here, his hands are too clean to have come straight from work and/or he may have had his hands tied or held — he doesn't appear to have put them out as he fell. Perhaps there was more than one assailant.

'The murderer must have been absolutely covered in what was once this man's head so there has to be a good chance of a forensic trace here from whoever he or she was. Any sign of a weapon? Has to be hefty and blunt to cause the mashed effect. I wouldn't be thinking blade.'

Moore shook his head and stared at the body thoughtfully. 'Why are you so certain that this isn't John Wozniak?'

'I saw someone I was told was John at David Flint's yard the day I arrived, he was working under the horse-box at the time. To be honest I didn't see his face but we can't see it now either. The lower body of the

John Wozniak I saw on that day had a small star tattoo, looked old and amateur, blue ink slightly smudged, above his left ankle at the lateral base of his calf muscle, I could see it clearly as his sock had slipped down and there's no tattoo in the same place on this body. Secondly, the John Wozniak I met on that day was right handed and this man here is left handed. See the nicotine staining on the left hand; it's unusual for a left hander to smoke with the right or vice versa. The first John Wozniak was also a smoker and had staining on two fingers of his right hand.' I stopped, thinking hard. Something clicked into place.

'Looking at this body, I'm thinking this isn't an isolated murder. If we go back to Marcus Williams and the peculiar absence of a complete skull, you still have only fragments, imagine this body if it had got as far as getting the same burial/boar treatment. I'd have to say that there is every indication that you might be dealing with a second murder by the same person or people. It's too similar to ignore.'

Moore stared at me. 'Who are you really, Dr Steel? I'm beginning to wonder about you... I've met Wozniak quite a few times and probably wouldn't have spotted those facts straight away. Right, good stuff, let's get back, pass on your thoughts to forensics before we go.' He turned on his heel and walked briskly back to the car.

Once back at the station I drove to the flat for a change of clothes and sent a quick text. *Not from me but word is out. Hope this doesn't make it difficult at work.*

Almost immediately a message pinged back. *Don't worry. Who cares anyway? Want to bring an umbrella again tonight?*

Despite myself, I laughed. *This is holiday land so no umbrella required and it has now stopped raining! Where and when?*

I changed whilst I was waiting for her reply. My phone pinged. *Mine. When u like — run til 7. Don't eat.*

I smiled, that thought would keep me going throughout today which was just as well as not one person at the police station was going to let the gossip pass by as my personal life and none of their business. I'd so many renditions of Lou Reed's song that I thought I might be forced to thump someone. Within an hour, I took Trev to one side against a wall and placed one hand loosely around his throat. Whatever happened to professional confidentiality?

'Cool it a bit, Trev. I know you're bored to tears most days and this is a bit of excitement for you. But remember this actually is my bit of excitement and none of your business. Also, have you thought that you may be jumping to conclusions and making assumptions that are simply not true?'

Trev was grinning. 'You're a good sport, Jake; I didn't think you'd last this long before having a go,' he punched my arm lightly, 'all the stuff they say about you clearly isn't true.'

I let that quip lie as reputations have a tendency to stalk, popping up at odd moments with a banana skin unless you're very careful.

'I'm going with my first assumption whatever you say, mainly because it's so much more fun! How is she by the way? Good as everyone thought?' He said it quickly and made a run out of the door. I heard his laughter all the way down the corridor.

Working through what I had access to, the most obvious question hadn't been asked yet: where was *the* John Wozniak? He hadn't turned up for work and I had to wonder what he was up to. In my eyes, he was a suspect. Did he know who our pulped man in lookalike clothes was? Discreetly logging on to another system, I started digging for him myself. Half an hour later, Mrs Wozniak suddenly reported him missing. Now that was enlightening. Thankfully no-one had yet trotted along to ask her to ID the roadside body, so she had no cause to think the police might have been already looking for him.

I wondered if my little mole could have had any part in this man's death, whoever he turned out to be; sometimes moles could cause no end of trouble if you sent them off in the right direction. The next few hours would probably be even more revealing if my mole was strutting his stuff with the right company. Working in ever decreasing circles, the epicentre of this puzzle was getting closer and I wanted to be there with a clear view when it arrived.

****

Forensics finished at the scene and the body made its way back to the morgue. I wandered down to find out what was known whilst I waited for some other answers to find their way to me.

'Jake, good to see you on this finest of fine days, how are you finding our sleepy little town now? Is it as much fun as the dusty halls of academia?' Sally twinkled. Short, stocky and easy going; when not in scrubs, she wore jeans and t-shirts with bone close political slogans. I'd been surprised to find out that she'd a young family and a husband, I'd had her down as a woman in comfortable shoes.

'Not so sleepy, Sally, I came here for peace and quiet — yet to find it.'

'Ah! But I hear that you've been riding out as well,' she glanced up and whistled out a breath.

'Does everyone think they know my business? Perhaps I ought to tweet updates so you all get the facts straight.'

'They'll get bored soon, don't worry. Ten years or so and you'll be old news.'

'Come on, I'm not that interesting surely?'

'Oh, but you are! The DCI has today given you full access to all my records and that strikes me as odd for someone who's supposedly here just to translate some writing,' she winked. 'All that smouldering brilliance and now you're bedding Ashfield's most delicious, and usually unavailable, lady jockey! You're going to be hot news for a while.'

'Let's move on, shall we?' I tried firmness. 'Come on, Sally, talk shop — what do you know?'

She shifted immediately into work mode, full of long words and complicated descriptions. Boiled down to the fact that the man had probably died sometime between 7.30pm and 1.30am the night before. As I'd thought, he more than likely died from a heavy blow to the back of the head, something metal and long, possibly a tyre lever or similar, he had bruising down one shoulder ending in a v-shaped depressed fracture possibly from the end of the weapon. His skull was then battered until it looked not unlike ratatouille for whatever reason, he wouldn't have been alive for the following blows. There were flakes of chrome plating in the pulp. He had taken LSD but it was only partially metabolised, he probably ingested it shortly before he was killed. Perhaps the killer was his supplier or, perhaps, he'd been drugged in order to subdue. It was, she said, her remit to speculate. Gut contents and further path tests were still being worked on. The sample I'd spotted on the grass verge was indeed LSD. Beside the drugs another find - three joss stick stubs and guess what - they were juniper. Too early she said to comment on the likelihood of a connection between this murder and the boar bones. I took her provisional report and went back to see Moore.

'I've asked David Flint to try for an identification as the body was wearing his yard's jacket. John Wozniak is still awol at the moment and it's going to be too harsh on Wozniak's wife to expect that of her in the circumstances, especially with the fact that this may not be him, but Trev will interview her formally later. Uniform have already taken her statement with regard to her missing husband.' Moore was working through the routine. 'Any further ideas about a possible identity?'

I shrugged, all I knew was that I'd not met him before. John Wozniak – where was he? It was starting to irritate now. Apparently he'd not gone home last night, or turned up for work in the morning. I got the feeling we were being led, being led to think, if only for a short while, that the roadside body was John Wozniak. Was that why his face had been removed? But if that was the case, joss sticks or no, then that would that mean that my theory about the connection with Marcus Williams was false. I wanted to know more, something was missing here.

'It seems that our friendly box driver was a right sleaze.' Trev had gleaned some further gems from the yard. 'He was known to be a bit mouthy with the younger girls, if you know what I mean, and partial to lay-bys. No one wants to take it any further though which seems a bit odd as some of them are very young. His status at the yard is just missing at the moment, no-one aside from Flint is aware that anything else might be the case and I haven't let it be known that we already think the body isn't Wozniak. Unfortunately it is well and truly out that we've had a murder. They'll probably add two and two and get eleven as usual.'

'What did Flint think about what the girls said?' Moore asked.

'He denied all knowledge, said that his driver was above reproach in all ways. He's clearly lying. I pushed, he got shirty and asked me to leave.'

'Ok, what about Alan Cooper?'

Alan Cooper, the passing motorist who found the body, had hung around the station as he was very shocked. I could understand that as it wasn't every day you stumble upon what he had. But he gave a clear, concise statement, didn't argue about giving his prints, a DNA sample and, surprisingly, still shook Trev's hand as he left. Sadly, he said nothing that connected him to the murder at the moment or that seemed likely to assist in anyway.

'Right, Trev go to the Wozniak's house. Talk to the family, but for pity's sake be sensitive. PC Jones will be there still so work with her. Find out if the wife knows anything out of the ordinary. Jake, while you're working from here stay clear of the racing yard please.' Moore held my gaze.

I'd been expecting it and probably would have initiated it if he hadn't. Everyone was going with the assumption that I was definitely personally involved with Sid, hadn't come from me but I went with it. I was employed to work with the police here, no-one else was aware of any other aspect of my professional life and Moore needed to play this out semi-publicly otherwise questions would be asked.

'Are you asking me to avoid Miss Fielding?' I asked as if to clarify.

'I would tell you to leave it if I could, but I can't. You'll have to be discreet, it goes without saying that nothing is discussed but you know that already. If she becomes a suspect it may be different though.'

'I hardly think she can be. She had a fall yesterday, racing. The horse fell and kicked the breath out of her. I was with her from 7.30pm until you called me in, I didn't notice her leave to carry out a murder and I'm sure I would've done.' I dropped in a little belligerence.

'All right, don't get smart. As it is now, I've had to ask for additional support from Exeter. We're expecting a DS tomorrow but no-one ask me for anymore, I don't know who or when.' Moore turned away and went back into his office. I wondered why they needed that additional support; surely they could manage both cases without too much trouble?

I stood for a moment, thinking and then followed him into his room.

'May I have a moment?' I closed the door behind me. 'How thoroughly has the yard been checked? I know John Wozniak has been missing officially only overnight and I know you wouldn't be worrying about him usually, but that body was made to look like him a bit too much for me to just walk away. I'd like to check the yard myself, to rule out the obvious locations for him to be hiding out. Hopefully we can assume he's not at his home for now.'

Moore said nothing for a long moment and then nodded. 'Ok, go alone though. You're not supposed to be around that place. David Flint is obstructive and if he gets a sniff of anything, he'll go off the deep end. I'm going to say I don't know anything about what you're up to, which, to be frank, isn't actually that far from the truth. So, ok, go but try and follow police procedures.'

'I'll think of a reason why I need to have a look if I'm asked. He must have a workshop or something similar at the yard, and there's the horse-box he drove to the races yesterday. Flint has no declared runners today so it's unlikely that the box has been moved since Wozniak left it. '

'David knows John has been reported missing, but he should know nothing in detail about the body on the roadside yet. He may be thinking what everyone else is in that it has to be Wozniak purely because the two things have happened together.'

'Understood. But I don't like the fact that Wozniak's wife has come forward in the way that she has. Granted her husband hasn't been home since last night but, from what you know, that isn't so unusual. Why is it so important you know about it now? I believe you're being pushed to follow a certain path by her contact and by the fact that the body has been dressed as if it was her husband.' All sorts of ideas were presenting themselves now. This was much more than it seemed and I hated to feel even a hint of manipulation.

'Right, go then. Be as quick as you can, I'll hold onto Trev. I want keeping up to speed on everything,' he sat heavily behind his desk. 'No withholding Jake, regardless of your own agenda, this new murder means the rules have shifted.'

I nodded. 'Of course.'

We really were on the same team, maybe coming at it from different angles but we both needed the same answers.

The farm entrance of Flint's yard was roughly gravelled with patchy hard-core unlike the smooth tarmac of the main drive. Tradesman's entrance it was in every way. Parking the car, I wandered over to the barn that housed the horse lorry finding my way blocked by two solid doors hung with professional looking padlocks. Without more than a quick glance around, I picked the locks and was inside almost immediately, I'd soon know if I was being watched on CCTV. The lorry stood facing out towards the yard; a Scania, silent and proud, royal blue livery, sign written with D. Flint, Racehorses, in large black lettering on all four sides.

Not a soul was around as I walked around, climbing up the three steps towards the cab. I didn't try the door in case of alarms but simply peered in; digital tacho reader empty, everything tidy awaiting the next trip. There was nothing unusual to be seen from where I stood. Stepping down, I walked around again and tried the jockey door, the small door to one side to allow access to the horses from outside, it was locked. I continued checking for anything obvious, around to the rear and back up the other side. Nothing looked out of place and the box was spotless which meant it had been cleaned as usual after racing. John Wozniak might be an unpleasant bloke but he knew how to look after his lorry.

I walked round again, looking down this time, checking underneath the box. The barn was concreted and dry, swept clean of any mud. I saw something, a shadow maybe, underneath the body of the lorry and crouched down to see it better. An oil leak perhaps; a small puddle of something wet or staining under the box. I took a pen torch from my pocket and shone it towards the patch. Straightening immediately, I walked back to my car and drove just outside to the public road.

'Get me DCI Moore quick as.' I speed dialled the number as I was leaving. The shadow under the lorry, the dark stain that might have been an oil leak — it was blood, fairly fresh and far too much of it to be anything other than something nasty.

Chapter Sixteen

Moore had the honour of David Flint this time so Trev and I drove back in through the farm entrance with SOCO and Sally's team on their way. The horse-box barn was cordoned off and with the keys now, we had a look inside.

Into the rear of the horse-box, where the horses travelled in comfort: rubber floor, padded walls, cushioned partitions to separate them from each other, this horse-box carried six horses in thoroughbred luxury. Three stalls facing front with access for a groom to their heads from the cab through a sliding door. Behind that three more front facing stalls with a similar groom's aisle that was accessed through a small door. All the partitions folded back to one side to allow for whatever was needed on the next trip. Side and rear unloading ramps, all hydraulically controlled for ease of use, air conditioning for people and horses, CCTV both inside and out; it was spotless first class travel. Probably wasn't the worst place to meet your end if that was how it was going to be.

Suspended from a metal roof runner, designed to house a partition, hanging from a leadrope of the type commonly used to guide a horse from its headcollar to wherever you wanted it to go, was John Wozniak. Dead. Very dead.

He'd dripped his life onto the floor and, because this was luxury travel and no sordid waste should collect in such an environment, he'd leaked slowly out through the passive drains to the concrete outside. Unlike our mystery man, John Wozniak still had his face, but in the loosest of terms. He'd been hung by his feet using the leadrope, his throat had been cut along with his wrists and he'd dripped from that position for several hours. Bled like an animal carcass in the butcher's shop. His face, even dark, bloated and swollen by gravity and death, was probably still recognisable. His expression indicated that he hadn't skipped easily over the rainbow bridge.

What was that saying about it not raining but pouring?

It takes a while to sort through a situation like that. Positive ID was a relative formality in the circumstances. If Mr Flint thought the police had been a pain in the arse before, it was nothing to what they were to him now.

Back at the police station, my phone vibrated silently with a text from Sid. *Jungle drums r sounding. Big brother coming tonight — won't stay but b prepared or come later. S*

A small note of something still to be looked forward to in a chaotic day, but I wondered about big brother; George Orwell slipped into my mind. Also, what did she mean by come prepared?

****

As Trev was typing up his preliminary report Lisa, PC Jones, rang in from the Wozniak's house asking for a translator and additional support.

'You don't by any chance speak Polish, do you?' Trev asked as he picked up his jacket.

'I can get by, why?'

'There's a bit of a language barrier with Mrs Wozniak, could you come with me and see if you can help?'

The house was on an ex-local authority estate on the wrong side of town. Lisa had been kind about Mrs Wozniak, I wouldn't have given her the time of day. Even when informed of her husband's untimely demise, she'd been aggressive and defensive, Lisa struggled to get a straight answer from her. I didn't fare much better and, although no previous, it was patently obvious that she knew about her husband's outside interests.

Surprise, anger, horror, shock, disbelief; any and all common reactions to receiving the kind of news she'd just had. I saw nothing except defence, the 'don't blame me', 'it's not my fault' knee jerk that could have meant many things. It made me think that she already knew, or at the very least, had been expecting this to happen sometime soon. How she was really going to feel about it, when it sunk in, was another matter. She never asked how or even why.

'What is it with you?' Trev said as we went back to the car. 'Wish I'd a touch of what you have. Even in the middle of a murder investigation, one look, that all-American-boy smile of yours and suddenly everything remotely female is panting at your feet. Lisa was blushing like a school girl even though it annoyed the hell out of her.'

'Just ignore it, Trev, I do. It is just a face. Anyway Wozniak's wife has already proved your theory wrong, she wasn't exactly helpful.'

Trev started the engine. A movement behind the car made me glance in the side mirror and there was Mrs Wozniak, walking quickly around to the house next door, disappearing behind the hedge and out of sight.

'Has anyone been around to the neighbours yet?'

'I don't know. Why?'

'Mrs Wozniak has just gone next door, in a hurry too.'

He turned the ignition off again. 'I think we should give her five minutes and then go and make sure that she's ok, don't you?'

I knocked at the door, there was no answer. We waited a while, knocking again, still no answer. Trev went down beside the house, along the narrow passageway to the back, reappearing with a look of surprise on his face.

'She's there, in the kitchen at the back. She's… what you might say… receiving comfort in her time of need…' he stopped, waiting for me to ask, I just waited. 'She's with a lad so we'd better get the door answered before it gets any more…'

'What! Already! She's only just gone in the door! I take it she's willing?'

'Oh yes, mate, most definitely from what I saw. Oh, and as another issue, the greenhouse in the garden is full of weed. I'm thinking that this is turning out to be a cracking day!'

'I'll lean on the doorbell then, distract them for you.'

Trev called Drugs to ask them to assess the greenery in the neighbour's garden as we waited, with zero result, for someone to come to the door. I stood to one side, leant down and opened the letterbox, checking carefully for safety's sake. I'd once had a syringe through a letterbox, not something I wanted to repeat in a hurry.

'Mrs Wozniak,' I called through the letterbox in Polish, 'you have thirty seconds to open the door. If you don't we will arrange for forced entry which will mean search warrants, squad cars and lots of police in uniform. Your neighbour's plant collection is already of interest.'

I stood back and counted out loud. I'd reached twenty when the door opened, a young lad stood there; late teens, primate bloodlines. A fetid stench of dirt and drugs wafted out with him.

'What?' he said, in Polish, all attitude and feral stupidity.

'You are?' I was no longer in the mood to indulge any of them.

'I don't have to answer you, you're just a pig,' he glared back.

'No, you don't. But then we'll just arrest you on suspicion of cultivation and possession of a controlled drug.' I went for intimidating, said it quickly, made it sound like I could just drag him off if I felt like it. Another time and place and I'd have had him whimpering on the floor for even thinking those words, but not now with Trev so close on my heels.

'Not my plants, they're the old man's.' He was immediately back pedalling, not as brave as he thought he was.

'Where is he?'

'Not here.'

'Where's your father?' I asked again, patience wearing thin.

'Away, so you can piss off,' he quickly pushed the door closed. I stopped it easily and stepped into the hall. I really didn't want this to take all day. Trev went on ahead of me.

'Where's Mrs Wozniak?'

Having both of us in the house was clearly more than the lad could handle and he backed quickly in the direction of the kitchen. Trev checked out the other rooms downstairs as we followed, all empty of life forms but full of junk and landfill.

I watched the lad twitching, wondered if he was rattling, hoped not as that would make him unpredictable. Trev had confirmation that Drugs were on the way and, from the smell of the place, I imagined that upstairs was likely to be a rainforest. Mrs Wozniak was now sitting on a tall stool, leaning against a sink full of unwashed dishes; she lit a cigarette and inhaled to her ankles. Grieving widow she still wasn't. Had she come around here so swiftly to pass on information or had she come around here for 'comfort' as Trev had put it?

She slowly dragged her eyes over us, reminding me of a reptile exhibit I'd once seen in a Chinese backstreet. The possibility of sex obviously hadn't sweetened her up in anyway.

'I understand that this must be a difficult time for you...' Trev began, the twitching lad butted in.

'Ha! That's what you think! John was a twat, always had been. No-one liked him, quite a few will be glad he's been done over.' So he could understand English if he wanted to. Even though he'd answered in Polish, that was interesting.

He went and stood beside Mrs Wozniak, putting his hand on her shoulder. She froze and picked it off distastefully as if it was a slug.

I stood looking at them and wondered what kind of a life she'd had with Wozniak, wondered how it began with this lad. IQ of an ESN goldfish, trousers under his arse, piercings and tattoos, living proof that the evolutionary process was constant as someone once said and, if he was already an addict, what a waste of a life.

'How old are you?' I asked him softly.

'Fifteen…seventeen…' he answered before he thought about it, correcting himself instantly.

Much younger than I'd thought, it was often hard to tell, some were shaving at nine. Drugs arrived and it all happened a bit quickly after that. Trev ended up arresting Mrs Wozniak and detaining the lad, who turned out to be not quite sixteen and epileptic rather than an addict. Uniform went to the pub or somewhere similar to find a parent.

Trev was still smiling broadly. There had to be drugs upstairs, nothing else seemed to make him smile like that.

'Weed growing everywhere, reckon the loft space will be full too. Lights and automatic watering in the bedrooms; it's quite a set up,' he was delighted. 'Got to be a factory, Moore will be made up. I really do like days like this!'

It was nearly six by the time we got back to the office. So much for dull and boring. Now there were two murders in addition to Marcus; alleged underage sex, Class A drugs, a cannabis factory and a pack of neglected kids. Yawning, I wondered if I'd jinxed the place by calling it holiday land.

Chapter Seventeen

It was gone eight when I left, yawning again. Back at the police flat, I stood under a hot shower and tried to summon some residual energy, it was somewhere far away and the water made me feel only marginally better. Putting a towel around my waist and lying back on the bed, I reached for the phone and sent a text: *R u free 2 spk?*

Instant reply. *Yes.* I pressed call and she answered before the second ring.

'Jake.' I heard the smile in her voice. 'Good day at the office?'

'Not bad, how about the fast lane and the bruises?'

'The fast lane is still a blast. I'm very black and blue, but no more fallers. Are you coming out to play?'

'How's your brother?'

'Still here, dealing with some big m and a.'

'M and a?'

'Mergers and acquisitions which is tech speak for legally screwing some poor guy out of his business and life's savings, then selling it on, almost immediately, for squillions to some else. No common old dirtying of hands and money rolling in to swell the already morbidly obese coffers. Top job, all round top man, pour another g & t.'

'I take it that you are full of admiration for such a strong work ethic?' Her quick summary made me smile.

'Oh yeah, he's my inspiration. I, a mere mortal, fawn at his feet and bow down as he walks on water,' she giggled.

'When are you expecting him to leave for Moneyville?'

'Don't know... look... you've probably had a very long and hard day, but you could come anyway, it's not like he's really here for me. I think he's come because of John - he's sniffing out details. Think bloodhound, he looks like one too.'

'How does he know about that?' It always amazed me how quickly this kind of information went viral and, for that matter, why would a horse-box driver be of interest?

'Friends in high places I expect. Do policeman have high places? Anyway those kind of high places.'

'Nice to know corruption and back scratching are still alive and kicking.'

'Oh yes, against the wall and kicking very hard from what I heard.'

'Ah, that's coercion, that's different.'

'Is it? I thought the ability to deliver a good kicking was a standard issue requirement for all the boys and girls in blue. Yourself excluded, of course. I'm hesitant to tar you with that assumption.'

'I'm not police, Sid, but tar away, I'm not averse to a good kicking. In fact I do it quite often in my spare time.'

'Jake!' she squealed down the phone. 'Be serious or is it more of that coercion?'

'The police are cutting down these days, sad but true. No, this is karate, different kind of kicking.'

'Karate, as in the martial art?' she breathed the words, like I'd said I was away to the moon.

'The very thing.'

'How good are you? No, let me guess, you're either teaching it or you're some mega Dan black belt.' She was teasing, laying a trap and I wasn't about to walk into it.

'Hmm.'

'What is hmm?'

'It's the noise bees make when they're happy.' I answered flippantly.

'Jake! Now you're just being silly. Come on, come and play. Finn likes silly and he can do silly at one hundred miles an hour for all of a minute before the sofa misses him.'

'Does big brother know of me?'

'No, but I'll rectify that right now. He's an arse, just to forewarn, you may need to adopt the patent policeman-down-the-nose attitude with him if he's still here. He's all fat boy bluster; admittedly brain the size of a planet, but dick the size of a tadpole.'

'Sid! Such words out of the mouths of babes. If I meet him now I'm going to have that disturbing visual in my thoughts.'

'Go on, come – I'm still cooking.'

'Have you done with running?' I looked across at my watch, trying not to think how late it was already.

'Didn't go because of my unexpected visitor, will you come over?'

'Um, only just got out of the shower, need to get dressed.'

'Mmm, now… Jake... Now that's an interesting and delicious visual for me, I'll hold that very close in my thoughts.'

'Are you flirting with me, Miss Fielding?'

'Heavens no, of course not. It seems that I'm far too easy to bother with anything as complicated as that.'

I sat and thought for a long moment. It's strange how one night can change so much. Two murders in one day wasn't exactly what I'd expected from this job either, but it could be like that. Feast or Famine. I should be working. I knew that. I shouldn't be charging back to the jockey. I knew that too. I still smiled to myself - feast or famine...

In a way I was still working. Sid's brother might be worth getting a look at, especially as he appeared to know a whole lot more than he should. Yeah right, Jake, good show of pretending that you're thinking with your head.

Chapter Eighteen

In a show of solidarity against the Brother, I put on black jeans and a black t-shirt. Sid was easy to predict as she never seemed to wear anything that wasn't black.

She opened the door, in black, looking gorgeous and launched into a kiss that almost knocked me off my feet. Then, with a broad smile, took my hand and led me into the room. Her brother was sitting on the sofa looking like he owned the place, he probably did.

'Seb, this is Dr Jake Steel. Jake, Seb Fielding – short for Sebastian, my eldest brother.' She melted away into the kitchen and I felt as if I'd been thrown to the lions.

Sebastian Fielding: late forties or early fifties, pin stripe city suit, overweight, receding and greying hair, a complexion that shrieked of high blood pressure. In fact, he reminded me very much of bottom dwelling fish, something that lay in the mud with a lure to draw in its prey. He launched straight into an intense inspection. I stared back but kept it semi-friendly; I wasn't going to be easy to intimidate and he looked like he might have been a bit disappointed about that.

'So… Jake Steel,' he sneered in a ridiculously pompous voice, enunciating my name so slowly I wondered if maybe his real accent was something embarrassingly regional. I felt my hackles rising and forced myself to think nice thoughts, he was Sid's brother after all.

'I understand that you're in finance.'

'Yes, merchant banking. Sid told me you work for the police,' his tone dripped with condescension.

'That's right, how very clever of you to remember.' Two could play at being an arsehole.

First impressions: arrogant, obnoxious, a lover of status and all its symbols, all paper front and no spine. A flicker of insecurity visible in an almost imperceptible muscle tic by his left eye. But insecurity that would make him more bully than victim. Chalk and cheese from his little sister.

Sid swanned back in, handed me a glass of red and sat on the arm of the sofa. She grinned at me and then at her brother. 'I smell cat's pee. Who's winning?'

I laughed and the brother looked like she was something unpleasant. She tutted.

'Oh, why don't you go, Seb, if you can't be nice. I've stuff to do.'

'I came to check you were ok,' he looked like that meant a lot more than it should. 'All this going on right here on your doorstep.'

'And I have a friend right here to call on,' she grinned again, ignoring his obvious expression of distaste. 'I'm safe enough.'

'You aren't involved with the police investigation, are you? How can you be if you're seeing my sister?' He appeared worried all of a sudden and it seemed not for Sid's safety.

'Not directly.' I smiled without meaning it, wondering why he thought there was a connection between Sid and the dead men, aside from the racing yard.

Sebastian Fielding really did seem to know more than he should, the details of the murders weren't common knowledge, statements had been taken but kept tight. Seb must have a direct line to someone as he seemed to have been told at almost the same time as I'd found the body in the lorry. That was too much of a coincidence and I felt the immediate urge to do some digging. As for the roadside body, well, that was something else entirely.

Seb stared pointedly at Sid, she glared back which made me wonder what else was going down. He seemed uncertain for a split second but stood, gathering up brief case and suit jacket.

'I'll ring, Sid. Keep in touch; let me know if you need any help.'

He put a hand on her shoulder, like a claw, kissed her on one cheek, staring at me as he did so almost as if he was staking a claim. I couldn't help but notice that she cringed from him, her body rigid until he moved away.

'Look after her, Jake Steel, she deserves so much better than you.'

The Brother was clearly not cool about boyfriends. But then again, what brother was.

She saw him to the door, holding it open as if to hurry him out, face down, impatient.

'Sorry about him, he's always been rude but thankfully he's an infrequent visitor,' she wound her hands around my shoulders. 'So, after all today's events, would it be inappropriate to ask if you've brought your umbrella?'

'Not inappropriate at all but actually, work besides, the sun has shone all day. It seems we really don't need umbrellas here after all.'

'Funny that, I thought it was unseasonably sunny too for the time of year. Are you hungry?'

'That would depend.' I said. Her eyes were immediately speaking of a different kind of hunger.

'On what?'

'If its ready or if it will be ruined if it waits for a little while longer.'

'Do you know what? I think this particular meal would be better for two things.'

'Oh… and what are they?'

'I think it needs to stand for a while and I always find it is so much better to begin with a starter.'

The meal was all the better for being left to stand, quite a long while as it turned out and the starter was exquisite. Back sitting in front of the fire together, she asked about work.

'I can't talk about it. I'm sure that you understand why.'

'Of course, I expect that it's hard for you, with knowing me and everything. But John murdered and the other… before… was that a murder too? None of this is an everyday occurrence in my ordinary life. It's way too scary and way too close.'

'Yes, it was. And, yes, it's complicated,' I shrugged. 'It doesn't matter at the moment; this kind of thing does happen. By that I mean you and me, murder, whatever you read about in the papers, is a rare event. You don't really need to be afraid. This all seems bigger than it would if it was happening, say, in Exeter or had happened to people you didn't know.'

'What is you and me, Jake?'

Now that was a loaded question.

'What do you want us to be?'

'Something more than just a passing through, something more than a one night stand.'

'This, I believe, could be classed as a second night so we've already dealt with the latter. I'm not just passing through, but let's just see how the days fall for a while. Are you ok with that?'

'Yes. Crikey, I've held off this long and I can always go back to racing bikes! With no disrespect to poor John and whoever the other person was, life is simply too much fun now and I'm all for making the most of it.'

She settled back. I liked the feel of her against me; she fitted well, it felt right to be here with her. The situation with the driver and the mystery man seemed to have not affected her but then she wasn't privy, as yet, to the fact that I'd got another dead and known to her, on my hands, let alone a load of text I couldn't yet decode.

****

I didn't stay, slipping away into the cold, dark night just before one. She stood outside, waiting on the doorstep and watching me leave before turning back into the house. I didn't want to go. The flat was cold in comparison. I put on a side light, stared around the box that it was, wondering what would make it feel more like a place I wanted to be. On impulse I sent a text. *Thank u, another fine sunny night. It's raining here.*

She didn't answer. I put the kettle on and made a cup of coffee, knowing I'd regret the caffeine but sleep was somewhere else.

What on earth was I doing messing about with Sid? It didn't fit my life to have any tethers. I was caught and held by her but, in reality, I'd no experience of what to do next, I'd never let anyone this close before. And what was all the more astounding was that I was comfortable with her. Me - the stone hearted loner. Bloody hell, on occasion, I almost didn't recognise myself.

For distraction, I went back to work and began to sift through the mess of loose ends that currently formed the basis of my job. Numbers and gold, uncle Sam and straw... I was still a long, long way from discovering the meaning of that first paragraph. Marcus. Let's go back to Marcus. But before I got any further there was a noise outside, followed by another and then something rattled lightly against the window.

I stood up slowly and went to one side of the window frame, holding the curtain away with fingertips to see out. An umbrella; a great big, colourful, golfing umbrella was hiding someone down in the street. I waited and the umbrella moved as a hand came out to pick up another pebble from the ground.

Sid. Of course, it was Sid.

I went down the stairs to let her in, wondering how she knew which window was mine. Another loose thought was that not many women would have felt safe out alone at night even somewhere like here, after the events of the last twenty-four hours. Should I think about that? But, then again, Sid had always been way too complex, shifting from one state to another seamlessly and always leaving me feeling like I might have to up my game.

'Couldn't have you getting wet so I brought an umbrella,' she grinned sheepishly.

'You should be asleep.' Back in the flat, I took the umbrella from her and let it slip to the floor.

'So should you. At least I'm not working tomorrow.'

It had been less than two hours since I'd left her, why was it, now she was here, that I felt like it had been far too long?

'These flats have rules that are never to be broken, stray mollies visiting at night are against those rules,' my disappointed face, 'people will talk.'

'You're already the talk of the town, they'll let you off.'

'Actually *we* are the talk of the town. Strange bloke gets Ashfield's most eligible and usually unavailable molly,' I kept my face deadpan, 'so I was told. Words out, are you ready for the fame?'

'Are we talking front page?' She was pressed so close. Blue fire smouldered.

'Possibly, with glossy pics from the paps; look out for them, they may spook the horses.'

She stepped back for a moment and let the long drover's coat that drowned her slide to the floor, I inhaled sharply; she was almost completely naked underneath.

'We could go for page three,' she whispered.

'Sid…' I groaned. There wasn't going to be much sleep again tonight.

****

I was wrong, I did get some sleep. When the alarm buzzed, I was alone again, half wondered if I'd dreamt her, but there propped by the door was the umbrella. Strangely, I felt like I'd slept for hours.

'Someone's happy today. You see working on a Sunday doesn't do it for me but then to each their own.' Trev was grumpy, shuffling papers, cursing at the computer with loud exclamations as if it was being deliberately slow to annoy him personally.

Moore stuck his head out of his office.

'The roadside body is still to be identified forensically but I'm going with you, Jake, in that it isn't anyone known locally. Flint ID'd the body from the horse-box as John Wozniak, he also confirmed that Wozniak had a tattoo. Trev, run another check on missing persons and see what comes up, Sally is prepping a DNA profile.' Moore yawned and rubbed his face with both hands. 'The new DS is coming about three, sort a place at a desk for him please.'

'Do we have a name for this new DS yet?' Trev asked.

'Somewhere,' he yawned cavernously again and flicked through messages on his computer screen. 'Yes, a Tom Sorrell. Hails from your area, Jake, do you know him?'

My mood plummeted instantly to my boots. Oh yes, I knew Tom. This could go either way now. Tom and I had done basic military training together before he'd decided on joining the police; he was hard as nails, straight down the line and we either got on really well or nearly killed each other, there was no middle ground. Why him? Why did it have to be him?

'Yes, I know Tom.' I kept it brief.

'Is that good or bad?' Moore asked.

'It's a while since I've seen him. He's supposed to be good at his job though, very good. You'll just have to see what you make of the rest of him.' I left it hanging, best case scenario, he might provide sport for a while. Maybe even take the spotlight off me.

'Better hope that he's still good then, Jake. We're not usually so busy.' Moore snapped as if I'd been the one to bring in the murders.

Everyone was grumpy it seemed. Ah, but there is something perversely satisfying about being the one with the smug, impossibly cheerful air. Try as I might, I couldn't suppress it. Though, as a dead cert, I knew that also made me the really irritating one today.

Chapter Nineteen

An hour or so later my phone rang, I checked the screen - Tommy Campbell from Scotland.

'Hey, Tommy, what's up?'

'Something and nothing, Jake. Probably something and nothing, but Paul called a little while ago and told me that he'd seen a bloke hanging around your place earlier today.'

'I take it that means it wasn't anyone he knew?'

'Aye, that's correct. Expecting visitors?'

'Nope.'

'I thought not. What would you like to do about it?'

'No worries, Tommy, I'll send Paul a message but, just in case it takes a day or so to get to him, you can tell him to check for vermin up there as often as he likes.' I paused then added, 'tell him some of them are big bastards.'

Paul Oliver was my nearest neighbour in Scotland. He was ghillie to several small estates in the locality; mid-forties, fully paid up, tartan wearing, single malt drinking, ten generation Scot. We'd met because he'd passed close enough to my place when I was rebuilding it to take an interest and, probably just because he'd felt like it, he'd returned with a bottle of malt to make an introduction. He drank me under the table that day and became a firm friend from then on.

I took Polly's bottle of Edradour from my car, packaged it up and left it at the post office to be sent to him together with written permission to carry out any pest control on my land that he saw fit. If I had a vermin problem at home, Paul would know just how to sort it.

****

Tom Sorrell walked into the office at just after three thirty, a duffle bag over his shoulder. I looked up at him and my first thought was that he hadn't changed a bit. Tall and lean with black, scruffy hair and blue eyes; a combination that always seemed to attract the girls. Most people reacted to him the same as I did, love him or hate him, never much in between. Mostly I think you had to be female to really like him.

'Jake,' he held out his hand. 'Its been a while.'

My presence was no surprise to him which was actually reassuring. It confirmed my feeling that this police station was more than a little leaky.

'Seems that way. Tom, Trevor Brunning, Trev, Tom Sorrell.'

Brief introductions done, he dropped his bag on the floor by an empty desk and Moore appeared as if by magic.

'Right, Tom, good to have you on the team here. You know Jake already I understand and you've no doubt met Trev,' he nodded to himself as if ticking boxes on some mental list he held. 'He'll fill you in on what has been going on. You'll be working with Trev and leading a surveillance team at David Flint's yard, in place from tomorrow. There's a whole load of stuff going on there and I'd very much like to get to the bottom of it. We're doing the usual house to house, known contacts etc and I'm dealing with the press. Find somewhere to stay for tonight and I'll have admin sort something more permanent for you tomorrow. We'll meet again in the morning and discuss how this is to be approached. All right?'

I was surprised about the team surveillance, not only a really expensive operation to put together but hugely labour intensive. In this small town there were only very few attached to CID, team surveillance would mean that uniform officers would have to be drafted in. But what was really intriguing me was what Moore knew, or thought he knew, to warrant such an operation. I waited to see if there was going to be any more information forthcoming. It wasn't. Moore swiftly dismissed us as if we were kids at school with the bell just rung.

'Coffee? Jake? Tom?' Trev asked and disappeared out the door to fetch it.

'How are you, Jake? You're looking like life is treating you well.' Tom sat easily, crossed his legs, resting an ankle on his knee. 'What are you doing here?'

Typical Tom, at home anywhere, designer scruff clothes where even the rips were expensive and strategic. It was a good job his work ethic wasn't so superficial. He looked casual, but he was as far from that state as the Queen is from a benefit cheque. He was manufactured in every sense, always had a plan and the core of all his arranging was always what was best for him personally. He could be an unreasonable, aggressive bastard on occasion but I tried not to hold that particular flaw against him; the same had been said about me. As a police detective though, he was one of the best at his level.

'Translating mainly. I've only been here a few weeks so early days but a murder or two does seem to concentrate the work load,' I tried to establish where he was at now. 'Did you ask to come or were you sent?'

'Sent. I'd rather have stayed where I was but shit happens and here I am,' his voice had a slight edge. 'Surprised to find someone like you here, I'd have thought this would be too mundane. I had heard you were permanently overseas but it seems that was wrong. You still with Fran?'

I looked up sharply. He was the main cause of me not seeing Fran anymore, I wondered why he asked. I could work with him but I'd never forget that incident. As for any other background details, I ignored them on the neither confirm or deny basis that the police adopted so often.

'She said that you were getting back together. It was a while back but she seemed pretty certain.' He wasn't backing down, as far as Fran was concerned, he really wanted to know.

'Well, that would be news to me. I've not seen her for years.'

'So you didn't go back?'

'No.' Not that it is any of your business, I thought.

He surprised me by laughing. 'I expect it was her way of dumping me then! I haven't seen her for a couple of months and she doesn't return my calls.'

Well, that was interesting, not. Fran had become consigned to history because of Tom Sorrell and his charms. She fell catastrophically head over heels for him and I rapidly paled into insignificance in her life, I didn't hold it against her, Tom had that effect on some women. It was as if they couldn't help themselves. She'd tried several times to force me to be more the man she wanted me to be; told me often that I had a dead heart, no soul and a vicious streak.

I understood where it came from, knew she wanted to wound and shock me from my sound proofed life where everything was kept at arms-length. But, for whatever reason, I didn't see the point in even trying to prove her wrong. In fact, right up to now, I really didn't give a shit for what any woman thought, none of them could reach the real me, that was hidden so deep as to be invisible. I liked it to be so.

It has taken me a long time to insulate myself that well. I don't form permanent relationships at any level. Fran I'd been with casually, on and off, for about six months which was an exception. She'd always wanted more than I had to give. In the end it had been easy to walk away leaving her with someone like Tom, knowing that I'd have gone for good at some point soon anyway. But when he made some stupid squaddie comment one night in a city pub six months later, both of us a bit drunk, both of us far too short on sleep, it escalated and very badly. It was the only serious formal warning I'd ever had and it shook me from the place where I'd ended up. I requested immediate transfer and got it, hoping never to see Tom again.

Here and now, Tom held no demons. I'd since found other ways to tame the fire that usually burned me more than it did anyone who crossed my path.

****

Later we drove in separate cars to the Fox and Hounds and, leaving him at the bar sorting out a drink and some lodgings, I sat down at one of the tables and pulled out my phone to text Sid.

Have u had a lazy day off?

Yes went back to bed

I smiled and sent a reply. *Good job 2. Umbrellas r tiring to carry about.*

Where r u? U done 4 today?

Fox & Hounds. New staff member.

Liquid t?

No B & B (him not me). Done 4 today.

Meet u there in 10-20. K?

K.

The beauty of text messages, all sorted in less than two minutes. Tom came and sat down to the far side of the table.

'Room ok?' I asked but really didn't care if it was a rat infested pit. Knowing Tom he'd probably have somewhere else to lay his head by midnight.

'Fine,' he said and looked around. The pub was quiet, a few couples in and a big lad playing the slot machine. 'Where's the best place for food around here?'

'This is it, unless you want a drive.' I sat back and sipped at my drink, orange juice to his pint.

'What are you about tonight?'

I don't know what shocked me more, the fact that he asked or the fact that he thought he could.

'Being busy, I expect.'

'On a Sunday? Still martial arts? Or is there something new?'

I wished I hadn't said yes to a drink, suddenly I'd no interest in sitting there with him asking questions. There was an awkward silence between us, the noise of the slot machine paying out the big lad, loud and immediately irritating. Maybe it wasn't the slot machine, maybe it was just my reaction to Tom.

'I'm sorry,' he spoke first, looking down at the table as he did so, twisting a paper beer mat with long fingers. 'It's been on my mind for a long time. I was a shit and you didn't deserve the fallout.'

I must have just sat there staring at him. Never, in my wildest dreams, had I ever expected to hear those words from him.

'Well, just so as you know. I am sorry.'

I could think of nothing at all to say in response but just then the outside door opened and we both looked up as Sid walked in. She scanned the room with a half-smile on her face and then caught sight of Tom. She immediately turned around on her heel and walked straight back out again without acknowledging either of us.

'What a bloody small world,' Tom inhaled loudly and spoke almost to himself. 'Sid Fielding and all the way down here in darkest Devon.'

'Do you know her?' My voice sounded hollow.

'Of course, I do,' he replied. 'Well, to be honest, I've only ever got as far as trying to know her as so many have done both before and since no doubt. Know her brother better, we were at school together. I can't believe she's here though. Bloody hell, talk about coincidence. Wonder what she's doing now? Last I heard she was in Newmarket riding racehorses. Is she involved at the place that was discussed earlier?'

I nodded vaguely and tried hard to think of something to say that was going to remain neutral. 'What do you mean tried to know her?'

'Oh fuck! Jake! Look at her! What do you think I mean? She's one of a kind gorgeous,' he stared with widening eyes as if I was the muppet for not seeing the glaringly obvious. 'But she's quirky as hell; she knocked me and many more back so many times we were breathless. I don't know of anyone who got in there, except for a jockey once, years ago. Maybe she's just not interested in blokes,' he turned towards the window to watch her go back into the car park, lit in the dusk now by the pub's floodlights. 'What I wouldn't still give for her to say yes. She does it for me in a big way.'

I don't know what I'd have done if I'd found out that they had history but I ignored his final comments, spoken so softly into the air, perhaps he didn't realise he was thinking out loud.

'Well you'd be right that she's known to be a bit quirky. But she's interested in blokes, I know that for sure.'

He turned quickly, 'So? Spill? Who's she seeing? Who finally got into her bed? Bet it's a jockey or trainer. That would be her style. Has to be someone with money and influence in her world,' there was a bitter edge to his voice. Being spurned by her had obviously left a scar.

I finished my drink and stood. 'No, it seems someone much more ordinary did it for her.' I gave him a quick smile, feeling that I could afford to be generous now. 'I'm off, see you tomorrow.'

I walked out into the car park and there she was, sitting on the bonnet of her Land Rover with her hands in the pockets of a padded coat, right by the pub window. I wrapped my fingers around her scarf and gently pulled her forward to kiss her but didn't give in to the temptation to see if we were being watched.

Chapter Twenty - Alyosha

And I will flay the flesh from their bones and strip them bare for angels to eat.

Don't fret, Zosima, you're all that matters now. They tried to involve me. They wanted me to become part of their twisted world, I said no. Brother One said I must, he was head of the family, I must do it, he'd looked after us, you and me, and now I must help him. I reached out to anything that spoke of love, I needed that so badly then, perhaps I still do. My mind was different; you know that, even then, I struggled sometimes when others did not. They said that they had something to make me feel better, they gave it to me, made me take it first and then after, I wanted it, very badly. They made me an addict, Zosima. For a long time that is what I was, all that I was, all that I could be. I did the things they wanted. I didn't care just so long as I got the drugs. It took me a long time to get out from that hole.

I found out then that the colt was having a problem at stud. Now the brothers had borrowed millions against those share values and they had prestigious mares booked to visit the horse. If he failed to get them in foal he would lose value, if he failed to get them in foal they would lose it all. That couldn't happen. And it didn't. I did what they asked me; there were lots of people like me, doing what we were told, afraid or dependent, or both. I was both. They hurt me, one day, when I dared to stand up against them, took me years to try again and the same thing happened. But now, this time, I will be strong and I will be prepared.

Alyosha woke feeling good for the first time in what felt like weeks, he sat up in bed and stretched his arms high above his head. The clock said nine in the morning but he hadn't got a clue what day it was. He looked around, his good humour changed to horror as he saw just how much of a mess his place was in. But then, that was something he could sort out today, he smiled to himself, he'd definitely sort it out today.

The fridge was empty, as were the cupboards. Alyosha couldn't quite remember when he'd last eaten but that wasn't unusual when he'd been ill. No matter, he'd shave, have a shower and then go shopping.

He was dancing along to the radio by late morning, three bin bags in the middle of the kitchen now full of the detritus of the previous weeks when he couldn't quite remember what had gone on. He'd message Zosima, she'd know. If only he could remember what he'd done with his phone. So, whilst he tried to remember, he cleaned the flat, scrubbed the floors, walls, even pulled out the cooker and cleaned behind it. The eagles must have had a party again because there was blood on his clothes, it was in the bathroom sink and even in the bath. He'd have to mention it next time they came round, they were such messy eaters.

That night he had a strong urge to speak to Zosima again but he still hadn't found his mobile. If she knew he'd lost it then she'd come to him. Of course, how stupid not to have thought of that sooner. He found an old padded envelope and wrote her address on the front of it in long elegant script, sticking a selection of stamps carefully with a ruler to make sure that they were exactly, precisely, without a shadow of a doubt, straight as a die. Straight as a die, blind as a bat, sly as a fox.

But it was no good having an envelope with nothing inside, however would she know it was from him? He laughed at that. Laughed and laughed. He laughed so much he became afraid that maybe he wouldn't be able to stop. But he did stop. After a while.

He looked around for something he could send... aha... his notebook, his special moleskine notebook, she'd know then that it was from him. Without a doubt. Without a clue. Without a leg to stand on. Wing and a prayer. Bat and a ball...

Chapter Twenty-One

'Sid, remember we were talking about karate last night? I promised to go and meet someone who might be able to help me do some training, its just up at sports centre, do you want to come?'

'Of course, that sounds like it might be fun if you don't mind me tagging along?'

'Not at all, if you drive I'll buy you a drink afterwards at the pub of your choice - so long as its still within the county.' I caught a flash of mischief in her eyes and thought I'd preempt any plotting.

Stopping only to drop off my car and collect my kit bag, we made our way to a building that looked, from the outside, very uninspiring. I'd often found a half-decent dojo whenever I working away, however this looked like it might be the exception to the rule. Worth a quick look though, I pushed open the door and walked in.

I hated parading in public like this but two days ago I had been specifically requested to do so. It seemed traps were being baited in readiness which would also mean that someone was taking the time to sniff me out down here as well as in Scotland.

There were only six other people there, five men, all a little younger and one woman. I found my way to a changing room, leaving Sid to find somewhere to be. There was a small seating area, currently inhabited by a group of parents with a writhing pack of noisy children who had just finished a class with a startled looking instructor. Sid had looked at them and then back to me with sad eyes as if she was pleading with me not to walk off and leave her at their mercy which, of course, I did.

A small, elderly Japanese man came shuffling in as we waited, he could have been anyone. But the way he walked, the way he carried himself spoke volumes; he was no doddering old man. This dojo with its unprepossessing building suddenly became something else, something special. He came over, introduced himself, quietly asking about my previous experience and observing all the time with bright bead eyes. He set the other six warming up and gestured for me to follow him, leading the way to back of the hall.

'Mr Steel, it is a pleasure to have you here tonight. Please indulge an old man and work with me, it has been too long. This evening I find I have a yearning for Silat,' he stepped back and bowed.

It wouldn't have been my first guess as Silat has really only one aim, to kill before you get killed. Its Malaysian but, like many others, draws on a variety of influences from other countries, perhaps none more so than China who traded through Malaysia leaving a legacy behind of something more than silk.

He was supersonically quick, launching from one offensive move to another and his blows, when they connected, really stung. He fired a punch, so fast it was a blur, I side-stepped, counter striking his elbow to block his fist, locked his wrist and used an elbow strike to his face, combining it with a knee to his belly as I dropped him to the ground. Done properly it was a single movement, you just had to be bold enough to try it.

I stood back, holding out a hand to help him up but he sprang to his feet and bowed again.

'Good, very good. I hurt now and a little hurt like this, it makes me feel alive again.' He was grinning as if we'd exchanged gifts rather than just pain.

'That looked like fun, although a bit noisy with all that yelling.' Sid said, when the class was over.

Others in the class had been learning how to use the kiai with varying degrees of success. Was one of them my watcher? Who could tell, I couldn't. We walked back to the Land Rover and as I dumped my kit bag in the back she stepped in close.

'It's always very pleasing to see a man who knows how to use himself.'

'Is that so?' I held her gaze. 'So I was right then? You do only want me for my body.'

'What have I found in you?' she stroked my face with soft fingers.'What can a small town girl do when her head is so dramatically turned?' She moved away, opened the driver's door and then, with a broad Scouse accent shouted, 'You comin or what?'

It was impossible to hear over the roar of the aged engine but she wouldn't hear a word said against it. A classic she would repeatedly enthuse, personality and style; I could see little of either in the freezing interior. She parked outside a pub, it wasn't somewhere I'd been before and, once we went in, I thought it wasn't a place I'd go to again. A proper drinking man's pub, that is if you liked whippets and racing pigeons.

'This place is always busy as there's a great folk group who play here often. I think they're local and some nights here even the spiders are dancing,' she grabbed my hand and hauled me towards the bar. 'I'll let you know next time as I'm sure its time you were educated properly.'

'Are we talking folk as in Morris dancers? I don't do bells and ribbons,' I said, 'not even for dancing spiders.'

Drinks in hand we went to sit beside the fire, the woody embers lit her face with a soft glow. She was laughing at me again as if surprised at my ignorance.

'No, no bells and ribbons. This is proper folk music and these guys are really good, I'm sure I have some of their stuff at home somewhere. I'll try to find it later - that's if you're coming back?' she glanced up, uncertain. That sudden shift again. It was a feat of agility to stay on track with her. She leapt between confidence and vulnerability so fast sometimes she blurred.

'If I had proper manners, I'd answer that question by asking another. So, just to ensure that you think of me as well-bred; would you like me to?'

'Of course! God yes! Hell yes! How can you ask that?' She stared at me, stunned for a second and then looked down, 'But that doesn't mean that you have to...'

It was time for a subject change.

'Why did you go back outside when you came to the pub? I saw you come in and go out again.' I had to ask; it'd sat for long enough.

'I wasn't keen on the company you were keeping,' she frowned a little, narrowed her eyes. 'I never expected to see him, Tom, I mean.'

Just at that moment, I faltered in her gaze. She really was so beautiful it made the breath catch in my throat. I saw the smile in her eyes and wondered if it was written all over me. I sat back and sighed, tried to reduce the intensity of the moment. Infatuation? Was that it? Was I infatuated with her? Nah, not me, that didn't sound like me at all.

'Tom and I have a bit of history which I won't taint this evening with. We did work together a long time ago and, at one point, I did very nearly kill him.' I tried to be loose with the details. 'Now I think I can be trusted to be left in the same room.'

She widened her eyes but didn't ask me to expand. 'Well, my knowledge of him isn't nearly so dramatic. He went to school with my brother, not Seb, my middle brother, Josh, who now lives in the States. They were best mates for a long time, probably still are; Josh and I aren't exactly close,' she sipped her drink and seemed to be lost in her thoughts. After a long time, she spoke again.

'To be honest, I got fed up with telling him to bugger off. He got Josh to ask me if I was gay once. It probably never occurred to him that he was the problem, not my orientation.'

'He did say something about it. I think he was keen to know who you might be hanging out with these days.'

'You bad man, that was the Land Rover kiss wasn't it? Was he looking?' she seemed delighted.

'I couldn't possibly say... but I sincerely hope so.'

She giggled, sliding her hand onto my thigh under the table. 'So how long have you been the martial arts king?'

'Hardly! I'm not as good as some, but I've been learning for a while, fifteen years maybe, since I was a lad. I enjoy it. It suits me and it's also very useful at times.'

'I'd have to agree, it definitely does suit you.' Her hand was relentless, her eyes gleaming fire glow.

I blinked slowly, leaned closer and whispered, 'you'll have to stop with the hand otherwise you may not make it out of the room.'

She turned her face slightly to one side, her hair slipping forward over one shoulder in a blonde curtain.

'What right here and now on the floor? Jake, you shock me, who'd have thought it? Right here, amongst the whippets and pigeons? You sure do know how to treat a girl don't you?' she whispered.

I rolled my eyes, stood and said, 'Do you want another drink?'

'Won't work but, yes, please. Water with ice and lemon.'

At that moment a group of walkers came in, the bar, and me, were engulfed by a tide of early evening cagoules and muddy boots. It took ages but I made it back to the table and immediately noticed a massive change in atmosphere. Sid was positively glacial.

'I've just remembered that I need to book some rides tonight. Its time to go.' Tight and hard, her body language was anything but open, her voice clipped and precise.

'Ok... Do you want this drink or just to leave?' I dug around for a possible explanation for this sudden change. No one had come close to the table, but then I hadn't been looking all the time.

'Actually, I want to go now,' she pulled her jacket around her as if suddenly cold.

'Sid, what's happened?' I'd no idea what was going on.

'Nothing. Actually not nothing, just the 'to be expected',' she avoided my eyes, looked down. I was shocked to see that she was shaking, 'I should've known.'

'What is to be expected?' I was still searching for answers. 'What should you have known?'

'Look, Jake, if you want a lift come and get in the car, if not, right now I'll happily let you walk back,' she stalked off out the door. Bloody hell, here we go again.

Picking up my phone from the table I went after her. Outside, in the dark shadow beside the Land Rover, I found her crouching, hands on her knees and tears streaming down her face.

'You have to tell me what's wrong?' I crouched with her, put my hands on her arms tried to lift her chin a little. She resisted.

'Get in the car and fucking shut up would you!' Her voice was like ice. She stood quickly, moving away.

'Before we go anywhere please talk to me. What is going on?' I had to know now, through that anger she sounded hurt, devastated even.

She wiped furiously at her face. This could go either way now and I still had no idea what was wrong.

'I thought you were different,' she hissed. 'I really did. But what a stupid bitch I am, yet again. Seb was so right when he said I shouldn't be with anyone. Shit! This really hurts, Jake! Have you any idea what I went through, no you don't, do you? For fuck's sake, no one does. But you...' huge tears flowed down her face. 'I thought... No! I was sure, so sure that you were different. Yet here I am again, hurting... really fucking hurting because of a man!'

She slumped back against the side of the Land Rover; I approached her carefully, eased my arms around her and pulled her close. She fought for a second and then let me hold her, breaking her heart against me so I waited until she'd calmed a little.

'I've no idea what this is all about but how the hell can I put it right if you won't tell me?'

She made a noise like I'd punched her and pulled away with a torrent of swearing. 'Your phone! Why don't you take a look at the messages on your fucking phone? You had a text whilst you were at the bar, from some woman, it just appeared on the screen, it wasn't like I could avoid seeing it. I can't do this Jake - just can't. Not for you, not for anyone. I can't. I won't put myself there again.'

She pulled at the driver's door. I blocked her gently, she was nowhere near calm enough to drive anywhere and I still needed to look at my phone. Pulled it out of my pocket, keeping my eyes on her as I did so, glancing down quickly as I scrolled through the messages. It would have to be a personal message to have come through onto the screen like that, work was always coded and, even then, I only changed the personal to visible when I was off duty. Looking through the list, all the recent ones were from her and then one new one. Luci, Luci Pasun...for fuck's sake! Who thought of that one?

Luci Pasun; an anagram a child would have spotted. Luci Pasun - canis lupus - wolf.

Jake baby! I'm back – can I come and stay this weekend? Missed you soooo much! Brought you a present but best present of all is me! Love you, sis xxxx

Sniffer dogs had clearly been unchained; watch your back, Jake, wolves circling the building. I re-read the text and, of course, it looked exactly like it was meant to. I breathed again.

'I take it that you didn't read the whole message. Luci is my sister. She's been overseas. I can now understand why that message freaked you out.' It was true, in part, Luci aka Sophie, had been in Australia. 'I'm so sorry, if I'd known I could've told you straight away.' I lifted her chin with one finger, 'I don't do games, Sid, I'm not interested in sharing, there's only you.' There was way too much pain in her face yet again.

'It should be me that's sorry,' she shook her head. 'God, what an idiot I am - always thinking the worst.'

'Give me the keys, let's get you home. We need to talk. Ok?'

'I can't let you drive.'

'You're far too unhappy right now and besides I'm qualified you know. I might show you my certificates sometime if you're really lucky.' I tried for humour and got a small smile.

She was silent most of the way home, not a good sign, but held my hand as I took her to the door.

'Do you want me to stay or leave?'

'I don't know. What a disaster! You probably want to bolt.'

'No, that's actually the last thing I want to do. I think we need to talk; something a whole lot more than my text message is causing you a problem. We need to talk about that.'

'Jake… I can't. It's not that I don't want to talk. I just can't. Not even to you.' She dropped her face, pain coated her words.

'Ok, don't then. We can just do coffee and you can talk to me about something really silly, like Finn.' I lifted her chin once again to catch her eyes. 'I'm here for you, Sid. Trust me. Please trust me.'

Chapter Twenty-Two

Into the house, I got her to sit on the sofa with Finn; he consented to share a corner, just this once. I opened up the wood burner, put on some logs and left the vents open to increase the heat. I went into the kitchen, kettle on, hunting through cupboards for cups and found, treasure, a half bottle of Courvoisier. Coffee made, brandy bottle tucked under one arm, I went back into the sitting room. She was where I'd left her and still unravelling. I needed to put the brakes on. Something as innocent as a misunderstood text had tapped, once again, into something much, much bigger. Maybe now she would tell me.

I poured out the coffee, put a generous slug of brandy in it and passed her a cup. She took it with shaking hands and immediately put it down again. I picked it up and gave it back to her. Finn lay down again, delighted that I'd taken the pressure off him. He liked his attention, but right now, he'd warm fire and sofa and it was late for lurchers - enough said.

I shuffled myself beside her. Cup down again, she stiffened.

'No, please don't. Don't be nice to me, Jake. I can't cope with sympathy right now.'

'It isn't sympathy, I'm not good at sympathy.' I held the mug in front of her once more. 'Somebody once told me that you find that word in the dictionary somewhere between shit and suicide. I just want you to feel better. Drink some of that, please. It might help.'

She took a small sip and then another. 'I'm so sorry, so sorry.'

'You keep saying that. I can't see that you've done anything to apologise for.'

'What a mess. I'm such a mess. Fuck! I can't do this.'

'What can you not do?'

'I can't do this again. I'm not capable. I'm not right for all of this. Oh for fuck's sake, why am I so messed up?'

'You really need to stop that. There's something going on here and blaming yourself isn't going to make it right.'

'Nothing will make this right. Nothing ever does.'

'What is 'this'? I can't understand 'this', talk to me, Sid. Tell me what 'this' is.'

'I can't. I'm not going to relive it. I'm not going there ever again,' her voice rigid, as if she was forcing some terror back into a box.

'Why? This will keep happening until it's resolved. Look at me.'

She lifted her face slightly and then dropped her head again, resting it against my shoulder.

'Come on, girl. The Sid I know is beautiful, strong, reckless, sexy, funny, quirky. Will I go on? I like quirky, quirky is good. Did I say strong? What about sexy? Did I say sexy?' I let my voice change into a soft Irish brogue, lifted her chin again and tried for her eyes. 'Besides, what happened to the pub floor?'

She laughed, a small noise through the pain, but it was there. I exhaled softly and reached for my coffee, at last something positive. I wondered why I was sitting there, dealing with it, wondered why it mattered so much. She was right, I could not, *should not*, base anything important simply on an extraordinary connection and exceptional sex. But she drew me, held me, I couldn't quantify it, she just did. With everything else that was going on right now, the one thing I didn't need was any further complications, but this with her - it was critical, somehow - it was critical to me.

'Whippets and pigeon poo,' she whispered.

'Exactly. You said you'd never accuse me of not knowing how to show you a good time.'

'Jake. Oh, Jake. Here I am in pieces and you, you can still make me laugh. You appear to have the ability to pull me back from the abyss.'

'Abyss! Crikey that's deep - I'm not so good with heights.'

'Oh Jake...'

Suddenly she's kissing me, kissing me like this may never happen again. She wants this, I want this. But. Why is there always a 'but'? It is there, a massive 'but' with big neon arrows pointing at it. Back off Steel; vulnerable, emotional, keep it clean.

'Sid. Stop. I want nothing more than what you want. But this, what has gone on tonight, means that we need to back up a bit. Let's just get through this right now. Are you ok with that?' I spoke to her softly, kissed her, tried to keep it light. Time and place and all that.

She exhaled loudly, pulling herself back from where she'd been heading with obvious effort. 'Why didn't I meet you before this all got so complicated? You're the voice of reason in all this insanity.'

I ignored the significance of that statement, didn't ask the question that was so clearly there. I went with distraction, it always worked well for me.

'Have you eaten? Fancy letting me loose in your tidy kitchen, that is if it's not yet too late to eat? I'm so starving, I could eat a horse.' I found a smile as she looked up.

'Ok, but only cos it's you. I'll accompany you into my kitchen and instruct, but we have no horse in today.'

'Instruct! I can operate a microwave with one finger I'll have you know. Did I mention my certificates?' Silliness, that always eased one back from the edge. 'If I get to cook, I get to choose the music. Is that a deal?'

'Ok, you win. Go cook and educate me with your music tastes.'

'It'll be an education I can assure you,' I pulled out my phone. 'So are you paying attention, Miss Fielding?' I held up both hands, wriggling my fingers like I was preparing to carry out surgery. 'Now to introduce you to some proper music, none of this woolly jumpers, ribbons and bells, mind you. Are you ready to be enlightened?'

She was smiling. I took heart in that.

Connecting my phone to her sound system via bluetooth, I scrolled through the list of artists, so many good ones but which to choose? Ska - any Ska would have done it but, then again, it does take a certain time and place to really be appreciated so maybe not. I got to the 'T's, Tom Petty and T-Rex, also favourites of mine and either could have done it but I settled for T-Rex's *I Love to Boogie* and *Jeepster*, (surely no one on the planet can listen to those particular tracks and not be moved), followed by a whole load of Tom.

In the kitchen, pasta and chicken, all there for the taking and easy stuff to cook. Not too heavy on the calories for those whose weight was critical, loads of mayo for me, whose weight was not. T-Rex finished and Tom began. She sat, her hands hugging drawn up knees as I made a mess doing nothing more than stir frying chicken and vegetables. Tom was loud and, I thought, instructive.

Scooping it all into two bowls, we made our way back to the fire, sitting cross legged with brandy and pasta. What's not to like? Brandy, pasta, T-Rex and Tom Petty - can't be beaten. It seemed to work on her too. She was visibly calmer, visibly more herself. She ate everything I'd thrown into her bowl.

She placed her head against my shoulder then lay so still I began to wonder if she'd fallen asleep. There was something so right about this very moment, almost as if this had been before and was meant to be. I kissed her hair and wandered off into myself, into thoughts of the moor, pulped heads, sky burials and bones.

Shadows. Abruptly, I wondered how I'd manage my work if Sid was going to be around on a regular basis.

Then yet another heart stopping moment, none of that mattered anymore, I was here and this was now. She was here and now. Patently messed up and damaged but so beautiful to me. It was one of those moments. A re-evaluation. I'd known her for no time at all, yet it felt easy, like it had been a lifetime.

Something had shifted tonight, a tectonic slide from what was to what had come to be. That shift was as much about me as it was Sid.

When she turned in my arms and kissed me again, I let her. It really was as much about me as her now. And that was a life changing revelation. At some point we went upstairs and that had an almost life changing quality about it too.

Chapter Twenty-Three

'Jake?'

I was somewhere else, somewhere warm and comfortable, I wanted to stay there.

'Jake, wake up! It's late! Crikey, you sleep like the dead!'

I opened my eyes slowly, it was still dark outside. 'What time is it?'

'Five thirty.'

'Shit, that's the middle of the night. Not time to get up at all.' I pulled the duvet back over my head.

'Maybe not for you, but it is for me. I've to be at David's for six-thirty today,' she pulled the duvet right back off me in a swift tug. 'He's trying to keep the yard working as normal so it'll be a black mark against me if I'm late.'

I opened my eyes again. She was dressed, black jodhpurs, black sweatshirt – Sid's uniform. I reached up and pulled her back into the bed.

'What time are you working today?'

She laid full length on top of me and my thoughts immediately excluded anything sensible.

'Hmm, don't know… do you have to go? Few more minutes… come back in here for a few more minutes…'

'Jake, all this pleasure isn't good for you. You should pace yourself,' she giggled.

'Pace myself mmm… good thought Sid, but no. I'm far too much into hedonism for such self-sacrifice.' I buried myself into her neck, inhaling soft skin.

'Seriously, when are you working?'

'I was being serious - about the hedonism,' I let her go and moved to sit up, yawning. 'Start at eight today, quite civilised.'

'Ok, you'd better borrow the Land Rover and I'll take the bike to the yard. Unless you can get sorted in no more than ten minutes?'

I struggled to order my thoughts and realised that it would be much easier if I got up.

'I can do ten minutes.'

'Ok, shower is through there. If you can be quick, I'll make you some coffee,' she leaned forward and kissed me, skipping away as I caught her around the waist. 'Ten minutes, that's all.'

I stood, reached for my clothes and made my way to the bathroom, she watched me so I took my time.

'You could join me? We could be really quick?' One last try.

'No, Jake, it is more than tempting but I've three to ride for owners and I need a clear head.' She went out the door and down the stairs.

The Land Rover roared down the lane to the town, it was still pitch dark as we pulled up right outside the path to my flat.

'Thank you, for last night, for cooking, for T-Rex and Tom Petty, for looking after me and basically just being you. I don't often lose the plot like that so it isn't something you'll need to put up with often if you choose to hang around with me.'

She reached over, placed her hands soft and cool against my face, pulling me into a kiss. A kiss that was ferociously deep and loaded with her passion. It was a kiss that went all the way to the soles of my feet.

'And thank you, for just being you and for not disliking T-Rex and Tom Petty.' Looking into her eyes, shining at me in the half darkness of a distant streetlamp, I found that I was speaking aloud thoughts. 'Anyway, I'm not certain that I've a choice anymore about whether or not I hang around with you. You've become compelling for a great many reasons.'

Her eyes filled with unexpected tears, she quickly looked away, shook her head.

'You sure know all the right things to say to a small town girl. I'm pleased to accept the role of being your compulsion for as long as you need it.' Another kiss, more shining eyes. 'Now can you go because I need to concentrate on how I'm going to make those horses look good so that I can get the rides.'

'Good luck then.' I said and she was gone, a cloud of diesel fumes slowly dispersed in her wake.

****

Much later I was sitting at my desk staring at nothing, lost into trying to solve the Sid mystery; the reason why she'd overreacted so badly, why there was something she couldn't talk about but obviously still burned within her. Trev placed a mug of coffee down on the desk and made me jump.

'Steady on!' Trev laughed. 'You were somewhere else then, actually you've been there most of the morning.'

'Working, just working,' I tapped my head with one finger, 'you know that thing that you don't do much of.'

'Yeah, right! Pull the other one. If you had your mind on work, I'm a monkey's uncle,' he laughed loudly.

'So that's why you're known as the missing link here, Trev, I did wonder.' I caught the file that was launched in my direction.

He'd spent a few earlier hours interviewing an aggressive David Flint and achieving nothing for his efforts. He either knew nothing or was very good at hiding it. It was getting frustrating for all.

'Jake, Trev.' Tom greeted us as he walked back in, jacket over his shoulder. He'd been up to the yard and elsewhere, checking out the lay of the land.

'You could have told me, Jake. Why did you let me come out with all that stuff and not say anything?' he asked and sat casually on the corner of my desk.

'Nothing to do with you, Tom.' I stared at him and with my eyes gestured that he moved. This wasn't a topic for the office.

'What's all this? What have I missed? Come on you two; let me in on the gossip.' Trev was instantly all ears.

Tom and I were locked into a silent staring contest, I refused to back down and he seemed to want to challenge me. I could sense the raising of hackles, the slow circling and posturing. There was no way I was letting him gain ground. After an age, he sighed and averted his eyes to the window behind me.

'Trev, it's nothing at all. Jake's just keeping his cards close to his chest. After all these years, usual story, the enigmatic Irishman who's still too cool to talk to us mere mortals.' Tom was clearly wanting the last word.

'A fuck tú, Tom.' I was definitely not in the mood to be nice to him.

'Oh… now…I sense an atmosphere and I thought you two were friends. Hey, this isn't to do with the delightful Sid, is it?' Trev bumbled in, both feet into his mouth at once.

I'd no interest in continuing, wasn't sure if I could anyway without the risk of dropping someone so I went to return some archive files. When I got back Tom had disappeared again.

'So what went down, Trev, what did you tell him?' I knew that he'd have brought him up to speed on station gossip.

'Who me? Soul of discretion me,' he grinned; however much of a gossip he was I couldn't help liking him; he was just that sort of bloke. 'He actually guarded your corner, he didn't say anything about anything, all very disappointing, but he was surprised that it was you who got into her pants.'

'You have such a way with words.' I shook my head.

'Not just me, mate, they're running a book on you in uniform, on how long it's going to last.' He was delighted with this piece of information. I was mortified.

'Do you lot have nothing better to do? I know that this is a small town but that's both sad and juvenile.'

'Whatever. It has proven to be very popular and replaced the book that was running on who would be the first to score with you.'

'Where have I ended up? Is this a parallel universe? Are you people for real? Get out more Trev, get a life and leave mine alone,' I went to the door. 'I'm going to see Sally if anyone wants me.'

I sent a text as I went down the stairs. *Is the sun shining still?*

I'd made it all the way to the morgue before she answered.

Brightly, I hv 3 new rides. Free tonight? S x

I found I liked the addition of the x.

7ish?

Ab fab Mine?

I thought for a moment, the residual animosity I felt, albeit irrationally, about Tom still clung along with rising frustration about this investigation. To many dickheads and dead ends. I wanted all that exorcised and I knew how to clear it from my mind - running.

Plan 2 run o'er then – k?

K will cook.

Lk frwd 2 it.

Me 2. x

I swung the door open and went in search of Sally, the smell of chemicals instantly stinging my eyes and nose.

'Jake, my favourite incomer!' Sally was radiant. 'How are you?'

'Fine and dandy. How's my favourite grave robber?'

She laughed. 'Gosh, so it's true, you really do have all the best chat up lines!' she went to the sink and washed her hands, 'Have you come just to flirt with me or do you want something boring like reports?'

'I'd love to say that I'm here just for you, especially as you're such a temptress in scrubs, but it's work, I'm afraid. Got any news?' I liked Sally, mainly because she never seemed to have an off day.

'Oh, you are so dull these days,' she passed me a buff folder. 'Right, the

PM of roadside man is almost complete, my reports are in there and they're also on the system. Our roadside man was in an appalling state, he was drinking himself to death, he was also drunk and had taken, or been given, drugs when he was killed. LSD specifically as we thought. Blood alcohol levels indicate that he'd had quite a bit to drink shortly before he was killed; peeking at his liver, I suspect it was something he did a lot. One other aspect of interest in his toxicology was the additional presence of markers for ketamine. DNA prelim profile will be ready later,' she grinned broadly. 'The provisional report for John Wozniak is also on the system. Might make interesting reading.'

I went back with coffee and logged myself in to read Sally's reports. Roadside body wasn't top of my list at the moment. John Wozniak was though. Let's find out some more about him. Translating was going to have to wait once again.

****

Brief synopsis: scene of crime, a Scania HGV horse lorry at David Flint's racing yard, body found hanging by its feet inside the area designed for carrying the horses. John Wozniak had died from blood loss following deep wounds to both wrists and throat, the latter severing carotid artery, couple of tendons and the trachea. Risk of suicide? Were these wounds self-inflicted? Wrists first then throat? Doable if he was quick and in the right frame of mind. Nope, not likely. Sally's reports revealed the wrist wounds could have been self-inflicted, but not the throat as he was almost gone from the wrists before the throat wound occurred and the angle of the second was wrong. Now, here's a strange fact. The body had been hung post-mortem, hour or so after death had occurred, why? Did the murderer or murderers hang around? Unlikely, but possible. There is the voyeur, the person who gets their rocks off watching someone go but, even with a sick mind, that was pushing it. What did they do in the meantime? Hard to get a clean print off the lead rope that he'd been hung by, but there was a partial one on the metal clasp, no positive on that one as yet. No other clear trace found.

So let's move on with more knowns and leave the unknowns for a moment. Clothing: supermarket jeans, cotton shirt, racing yard's jacket with zipped pockets, underwear, socks, no shoes. Where were the shoes? No watch. Pocket contents…bloody hell…five grand in twenty pound notes, an iPhone full of foreign porn (no children, thank the gods), text messages wiped by someone who knew what they were doing. Who was that…John himself or John's murderer/s? Some cable ties, wallet, driver's licence, snooker club membership card, a disposable lighter and recently opened fifty gram packet of tobacco with green Rizlas, to be precise. The tattoo was still there, where expected, along with the nicotine stained fingers.

Five grand? A win on the horses from racing that day, or something else? I went down to have another look at the lorry, now sitting on site at the station and being examined in the minute and more than slightly anal way the police were so fond of. En route, a quick phone call to someone who squeaked if I looked their way and tried to scamper off before I caught them.

A grass, a snout, there are many words for it. I had a few pet ones of my own, most people in my line of work do. It works on payment usually, I pay them or they pay me. The difference is I pay with money and they pay me with information. Those that pay me are generally working off some form of debt. It isn't bent, not really and definitely not corrupt but, admittedly, slightly left of centre. Whatever. As a system it works. News, I reassured my squeaker, all I want is news.

Apparently, John Wozniak did have the odd flutter but that was it. He tended to spend his waiting time when at the races either in his cab asleep or, in the staff canteen, showing off whilst filling his belly with fried delights and quantities of tea. Word was that John Wozniak was all talk and no trousers. No mention of drugs at all, not a whisper. It seemed he wasn't a man to either sit next to or take seriously. But someone had. Someone had taken him seriously enough to put five grand in his pocket and someone had thought him serious enough to take the time to kill him. All that squeaking and I could still smell a rat.

The lorry, all as it should be apparently, right down to the vehicle detect reports, dutifully filled in daily and logged in David's office. I read the printout from the digital tacho; mileage, speed, hours and rest periods, all by the book correct. Skip back in the RHA Driver's Daily Vehicle Report book that was in the lorry, to the report from the day I'd arrived, when I'd seen John Wozniak's legs and hands sticking out from underneath. A note recording that the kingpins on the front axle had been greased, this was routine maintenance, nothing out of the ordinary. John legitimately could have been under the lorry with the grease gun on the day that I saw him, why he was complaining about it was a question but then again, it seemed he complained about everything anyway.

I had a chat to Mick, the head man when it came to anything that was both mechanical and forensic. Debris, he told me, under the lorry he'd found debris. Debris? Bits of rope and or packaging tape, caught around an axle, he was thinking rubbish picked up from the motorway, not enough to cause a problem or, as a long shot, something more sinister. He spent a happy fifteen minutes showing me the location of the 'debris' including before and after photos of the axle in question.

'Mick, with your expert knowledge, will you be looking at it from a different angle?' I had to ask it, careful not to tread on sensitive toes.

Mick Salter: mid-fifties, skinny, oil coloured hair and skin which may or may not have been what he was born with. Oily blue boiler suit and similarly oily, blue baseball cap, which was probably surgically attached as I'd not yet seen him without it. Reported to be frighteningly easy to upset with a loose word in the wrong place. Mick had a jobs worth hat in his pocket that he got out if he thought any member of CID was getting above their station. He could switch from nice guy to shop steward with militant attitude in a heartbeat. Someone like me was virtually bound to rub him up the wrong way.

'Fire away, what are you thinking?'

'Illegals.'

'What immigrants?' he physically stepped back as if I'd said plague.

'Yep, illegal immigrants, you'd know better than me but could the rope on the axles be ties from a hanger-on.'

It happened all too often. Desperate people will do desperate things to get deep enough into the country to disappear without a trace. Not just England, it happened everywhere. I'd seen three men, tied by their wrists and feet to the axle of such a lorry. The lorry had been stopped on the M25 for a routine check; it had been happily trundling along at fifty miles an hour, oblivious to the men clinging to its undercarriage. If those ropes had broken…come loose…best not to go there. But now, with this lorry and its murdered driver with five grand in his pocket, just the right kind of pay out for looking the other way at the right moment. Immigrants probably hadn't murdered though as they usually had somewhere else to be in a hurry, but the people who made their arrangements, they might have done. Such people aren't renowned for their compassion and empathy. Trafficking. Nasty for all concerned whatever the reason and no matter how desperate the motivation.

'Possible, Jake, I give you that, it is possible but, I'd have to ask myself, would he be out often enough to make it worthwhile?' he pushed himself back under the lorry on the slider board. 'Leave it with me for a bit, will you?'

Later that day Trev's phone rang and, as no-one else was about, I answered it. It was Sally.

'Trev, the DNA prelim profile on roadside male body has come up with a match.'

'Its Jake, Sally, Trev's out. Can I leave a message for him?' I asked, switching screens so that I could see her report. I stared at it for a moment, it made no immediate sense. John Wozniak and roadside man shared the same profile.

'Tell him my report is on the system and that I can confirm that there's no contamination. John Wozniak was a twin; he has an identical twin.'

The DNA profile matched John Wozniak even though we knew it wasn't him, but his twin, being genetically identical, would have profile matched too.

'Roadside man is likely to be John Wozniak's twin brother, Alan. The answers have to be in the fingerprints, so I'm running them again.'

Although the DNA profile would have matched on Sally's equipment, fingerprints were unique regardless of genes. Even so, a definitive result would take time. A lot more time than we could afford. Made me all the more certain that the head pulping thing was for another reason than to make identification difficult. Any lunatic worth his salt would have pulped the hands as well if that was the case.

I sat back, thinking through everything I knew. Marcus Williams, the boar bones and Gwil's marked man. With him came my first problem, the person, another squeaker, but a professional squeaker this time, who'd passed incorrect information either deliberately, or because he or she believed it to be correct, which would imply that they trusted their source completely. On top of all of that, we had John Wozniak's identical twin brother, dressed as if to confuse and that begged the next question, was John in on his brother's murder? Had he got his brother to dress as him? To pass himself off as John? Why? Why might he do that? Then there was the matter of why and how John Wozniak had been killed. Far too many loose ends. I could feel them all but reaching out and trying to grab them wasn't going to work. I had to be a lot smarter than that. The pieces would only fit one way.

The phone rang again, interrupting my train of thought abruptly.

'Jake, can you tell Trev there's no record of these prints. Bloody typical!' Sally wasn't happy, so close and yet so far. 'I'm going to widen the search for a match but it'll take time.'

Sometimes the police just had to let the stones grind, often painfully slowly but it gave them time to grind exceedingly fine. They'd get those answers, eventually; they could identify him now, they could give him a name. But they also needed to be able to prove that it was him, beyond doubt. Perhaps I'd go visiting myself, visit the last known address for the roadside man and find out a little more about those who knew him - the man who was listed as John Wozniak's twin.

I updated DCI Moore with all that I had, asked him to call me if anything else came in. Time to go, glad now, in more ways than one that I was going to run; it would clear my head and give me some thinking time.

Chapter Twenty-Four

I sat on the edge of the bed, shoved police as far from my thoughts as possible and wondered how I was going to deal with this evening.

It had been as if I was caught up in someone else's plan. I'd wanted a relationship about as much as I'd wanted an offer from Vogue. But Sid, this whole Sid thing had just happened, as if some other part of me was calling the shots and now, now I was here, it was extraordinary. That was it, she was simply extraordinary.

My defences were lulled, she'd simply walked on in and, before I'd realised it, she was there. I was beginning to understand, to accept, that I liked her being there. Granted it was probably going to be painful when she left, but she'd opened me up in some obscure way, found her way to part of me that even I hadn't known.

I wasn't ignoring the secret spectre that she couldn't talk about, it loomed large every now and then, colouring who and what she was. But the hard fact was that all these feelings and all these realities were alien. I'd not previously given any thought to such matters being of concern to me, to what I did, or how I lived my life. Now they'd grown large enough to be waving subconscious flags and that alone carried with it a cartload of other issues. Like Luci.

I wished I hadn't started this train of thought because it was literally the tip of the iceberg. I had neither the energy nor the inclination right then to be hauling it all out to examine in detail, so instead I checked in with my messages. Updated those who needed to be kept up to speed and then took the time to give my cyber-mole a quick pat before I sent it off again.

Knowing I couldn't delay any longer, I also send a reply to Luci. *Thx 4 txt. Expect u whenever.* Not exactly expansive but she'd come anyway. I checked my watch, it was gone six already, I was going to be late if I didn't get a move on. I stuffed a change of clothes into a rucksack and sent a message to Sid, *just leaving route via tor.*

Hat and head torch on, I ran down the stairs and was off down the street within minutes. Adjusting the beam from the torch so that it shone about six foot in front, I settled into listening to the music. Joe Satriani tonight, bit of Talking Heads and Queen to follow, concentrated on the rhythm as I warmed up, off the road and onto the moor. Focusing on nothing more than breathing, I tried to shut out random thoughts about codes and bones, but they reared up, large and unshakeable, in the yellow pool of light I ran towards.

I ran up the side of the tor, the outline of its stone cap visible in the shadowy darkness, stopping at the top to look across to the lights of the distant town below. Above, the sky stretched out, pinned with silver stars in the blackness. It was vast and all-embracing. I heard Gwil's voice clearly in my thoughts *'sometimes the smallest step in the right direction ends up being the biggest step of your life. Tip toe if you must, Spider, but, for fuck's sake, take that step...'*

I checked my phone, *No bog snorkelling on the way S x*. I sent a reply, *On tor, big sky. B there in 10*.

The security lights flicked on as soon as I stepped into the courtyard. I blinked away the sudden brightness and sat on the step to take off my filthy trainers; headphones still in my ears, Freddie singing at the top of his voice. Suddenly there were hands from behind, evoking from me an instinctive defensive reaction. I was on my feet and turning in one movement, those hands held tight in mine, wrists flexed ready to instantly twist to the point of fracture…. Stop! Steady on…calm down….

These were soft hands that now pulled easily away and those were her shining eyes that fixed to mine. Heart pounding, I tugged out the headphones, left Freddie hissing and tinny now against my shirt.

'Hey, good run?' she was instantly scorching.

She picked up my trainers and I followed trying to calm jangling nerves. She pushed the door closed behind us and waited whilst I took off the rucksack, holding my gaze constantly. Those eyes of hers were like a physical force, I felt them as if she was inside me; hypnotic, mesmerising. She stepped forward, slowly unzipped my fleece jacket and put her hands, palms flat, on either side of my chest. I had to close my eyes and swallow hard. This incredible intensity from her, I was never prepared. I tried to breathe through it, to contain my response; she stepped closer still, kissed me as though the world was ending and that was it.

I succumbed.

I hadn't spoken at all, had no ability to speak now. Now was roaring need, now was no patience wanting, instinctive, impossible to refuse. She pulled me into the wet room near the kitchen, kicked the door closed and literally wrapped herself around me, reaching over to switch on a torrent of hot water from the shower at the same time. Holding on to her tightly, I let myself become what she wanted me to be.

This was a different kind of hunger, this had no soft edges, no quiet words; it was full on, hard, urgent, right here and now under the deafening torrent of the shower. Somehow clothing was shed; she clung to me, moulded herself hard against my skin, fingers dug into my back and shoulders, she plunged us into yet another loaded kiss. All that passion. All that desire.

Hot water powered down, blurring shapes and movement. She was sinuous, writhing, skin to skin, every movement an intimate touch, heat inside and out. The taste of her, mouth to mouth…the feel of her…all of her… Captured and held, imprisoned. My senses condensed into a focal point of something akin to pure brilliant white light. Brilliant white touch. Brilliant white behind my eyes. And all the while we had the constant pounding of the water to insulate and deafen. Like shamanic drumming it was lifting me out of myself, making me something more or something less than I'd been before.

Locked to her, tense muscle spasmed and arched, flooding in heat, wave after tsunami wave generating such power. After a lifetime or two somewhere else, it exploded within us and hurled its way through and out like a train. Quite literally I saw stars, bright kaleidoscope flashes of light in this surreal place that we'd made. It left me totally wiped out, sagging involuntarily to my knees, no breath left, heart thumping, blood roaring with her clinging on, held by my body still. Unable to do anything more than simply just be for a while, I held onto her whilst the universe returned to some sort of normality.

She lifted her head, her face just wonderment. Mine might have been the same if I could've organised the jumbled incoherence that used to be my mind.

'Sid… Jaysus…' It was inelegant but it was all that I could manage. I closed my eyes.

'It was wasn't it?' She was equally stunned it seemed. Then she laughed, 'just look at the state of this place!'

I looked. There was a trail of muddy clothes that had obviously just been flung in every direction, spraying half the moor up the walls, over the sink and door. My headphones and head torch were sitting in a puddle of mud close to radiator. I'd no idea where my phone was. It looked very much like we'd entertained a post match rugby team.

Eventually we emerged, the room returned to its pre-passion normality, muddy gear in the wet sack in my backpack. I was so glad I'd thought to pack a change of clothes, especially now when I felt like I'd been run over by an express. No train, just Sid. I could barely walk. She was still laughing at me, stretched out now on the rug in front of the wood burner.

'You look totally wiped out!'

'Funny you should say that, I feel like I've been trampled. I've never been jumped in quite such a spectacular fashion before.' I settled back against the sofa, trying to ease out aching legs in the warmth from the fire.

'I suppose we ought to be fed now, don't go to sleep, back in a minute.'

I stared at the flames behind the glass and then checked on my phone, drying out now on the trivet near the logs. It was flashing a message. Luci.

Jake baby — Ring u thurs to arrange/confirm. In bog land, flying in fri. Get lots of sleep — u r taking me partying!!! xx

Luci obviously didn't know how slow it was here in the winter and I hadn't forgotten how tiring she was even when I was fully charged. She'd need careful handling whichever way it went.

Sid reappeared with something that looked deliciously like homemade chow-mien which we ate companionably in front of the fire.

At hopefully the right time I said, 'I have to talk to you about something. It is police stuff and it's awkward. But before I start, I should tell you that what I need to say is highly confidential. I trust you implicitly but you need to know how sensitive it is.'

'This sounds ominous. Why do I suddenly feel afraid?'

'Don't be afraid, but this is serious. I wouldn't normally discuss any of this, but now, because of us, this is different.' I kissed her softly. 'Sid, the bones in the wood have turned out to be a missing person. That missing person was Marcus Williams.'

She inhaled sharply.

'The police know that you rode for him, that you were probably retained to ride, certainly for last season. Then there was a murder, a body left in a lay-by, it is what took me away from here. It wasn't John Wozniak but it was made to look like him. John Wozniak was the body in the horse-box and he'd been murdered too. Both of them were brutally and violently dealt with. Everything the police know so far points to Marcus suffering similar treatment when he met his end. You are one of only two people here with a known connection to them and possibly you're the last person to see John and that makes you of interest. It means that you have to be questioned again, that you'll need to give a statement about your connection to them.'

'Jake! Why? Why are you doing this? What you're saying is that I'm a possible suspect in a murder case and yet you're still here. I don't understand that,' she dropped her head into her hands. 'Last night, oh fuck, last night you knew all of this and yet you still stayed with me. Why?'

'I don't think that you're personally implicated in any of this, its coincidence, but you have to be ruled out and you may know facts that could help. You ride for lots of people, Marcus was just one. It's a small world, this kind of connection happens. It has to be investigated.'

'Jake, you're still not answering my question. Why?' she leaned forward; doubt, confusion, probably both, written on her face. 'Please tell me why you aren't backing off? Or are you? Is that what this is?'

'No, I'm not backing off. I don't know what was behind the way you were last night and I'm not going to push you to tell me. You will if you want to, won't if you don't.' I took her hands. 'Sid, understand this, rightly or wrongly, I'm not working for the police when I come here; I'm just Jake, slightly barking Irish bloke, who's into obscure martial arts. I meant what I said in that I've no hidden agenda as far as you are concerned, no cunning plan – I just like being with you. It isn't straightforward for me either, I've my own demons, just as you clearly do. I have to confront some of them by being with you. But I think its worth the risk, don't you?'

She lay against me for a long time saying nothing; I felt the rise and fall of her chest against mine. Then she sat up suddenly as if something important had just occurred to her.

'I don't know quite how to say this but I do know now that I should,' she blinked slowly a few times, as if forming her thoughts into something she felt able to voice aloud. When she started speaking again, her voice was a whisper. What had I done to the woman who had just taken me apart in the shower?

****

'I was until recently someone else. But, because you were doing my head in by just being you, I could no longer pretend to ignore what was so clearly there.' She pushed away from me, 'Do you have any idea what you are? The way we get along together - I feel like I've known you for forever, not just a few weeks.'

She sat back, agitated now as if she had to find a more straight forward way to say these words.

'And... And then there is the obvious. You're so physical, you have presence... you radiate,' she gestured wide with both hands, 'this intense physicality. It's impossible not to be captivated by it and, as if that wasn't enough, you're also the most incredibly beautiful man that I've ever seen. I can't understand this, you could take your pick from anywhere, so why me?'

'Who knows why such chemistry works with some people and not with others,' I shrugged. 'Just think about tonight, for example, in the shower, I've never been there before, have you? We could never have planned that. It came from somewhere else, somewhere that is, it seems, the combination of you and me. So, I could also ask you the why me question. You've kept yourself away from having a relationship with anyone for so long and yet, here we are, you and me: why me?'

She kept her gaze locked on as if trying to see through, to see through me to the truth.

'No, I've never experienced anything like that before. Not ever,' she laughed softly, dropped her eyes as if a little embarrassed. 'To be completely truthful, I didn't even know it could be like this, not a clue.'

She put her head back onto my shoulder and sighed deeply, speaking into my neck.

'So what happens next? With the police thing?'

'You've already given a statement way back when this began so it'll be along similar lines, I expect. Murder is about as serious as it gets, whoever killed those men needs to be found.' I thought for a moment and then just knew I had to add something. 'There is another matter, something I should tell you now but, if I do, I have to ask you to keep it absolutely to yourself for all time, wherever we personally end up.'

I struggled, this wasn't something I'd talked about before. I didn't know where to begin, how to word it, my secretive side almost lost its nerve but I had to go with instinct. I had to tell her.

'I'm actually involved in highly sensitive covert work. That's what I really do, the translation work I'm doing here is, in part, a cover to enable me to investigate something else. I can't say any more than that at the moment, have probably said more than I should. This work can take me away without warning and it often makes life very complicated. It's important to me that you don't think that there's something else going on, there really is only you. I simply want you to know, to trust me as I trust you. This Jake, the me that comes here to you is the real me, no disguise, this is who I am.

But a change in profile may mean disappearing for a while, it's unlikely at the moment but it's happened before.'

'So you really aren't a policeman?'

I shook my head. 'No, at least not the kind that you mean.'

She exhaled heavily, a range of thoughts seemed to flit across her face.

'If I ask you something will you promise to tell me the absolute truth?'

I nodded, hoping that I could.

'Are you investigating me?'

If she'd worded that question differently, I might have had trouble answering it but as it was, I could say, no. 'No, Sid, I'm not investigating you. I'm here with you because I want to be.'

THE WOLF AND THE PHOENIX

Chapter Twenty-Five

She sat for a long time, twisting the fabric of my shirt around in her fingers and then breathed out a weighted sigh that came from somewhere deep within.

'Why is life so fucking hard sometimes? This is so much more than I'd ever imagined. You're so much more than I could ever have imagined. But, with all this about to happen, maybe I should show you the same level of trust and openness… oh God, this is so hard... But I should tell you,' she pushed away and stood. 'If I'm going to be able to talk, I'm afraid that I'm going to need a drink. You talked about demons, Jake, well these are my demons and, even now, they still truly terrify me.'

Didn't take a genius to realise that this was one of those moments, the sitting ready to go moments when one false move can blow it. But I didn't want her to feel like that. I didn't want her to open that secret box just for me.

'I'm not trying to back you into a corner, please don't feel that stuff has to be aired just because of what I've said. Tell me if you want but not because you feel forced.' I looked up at her, standing there trembling like a lamped rabbit. 'It changes nothing for me.'

'It may do, that's my risk I know, it may change everything. But I would much rather you heard it first from me, especially after tonight,' she turned and went to the kitchen coming back with the brandy. 'Will it be Tom who takes my statement?'

'Maybe, but the DCI is aware that he's known to you through your brother. Tom and I don't have much time for each other personally but he's a good detective, straight down the line, he'll do a good job.' I wanted to offer some reassurance; I wanted to take the pressure off. 'You can ask for it to be someone else, for someone other than Tom if it's an issue. Either way it'll not just be him alone.'

She poured brandy into two glasses, two very generous measures. I watched her hand shake as she did so.

'Jake, you need to be patient with me once again. This is hard, so very hard. I haven't done it before, not ever. I may not actually manage to get it out and you may not want to hear it, so please, feel free to leave whenever you want or simply tell me to stop.'

She passed me a glass and kissed me just once, so gently, almost as if she was already saying goodbye.

She went back to sitting cross legged to one side of the wood burner. Distant, isolating herself as if trying to withdraw from what she had to say.

'Sid, please, if this is…' I started to say but she stopped me with nothing more than a look.

Face back down towards her hands, with hesitant words she began.

'Ok. So where to start? Firstly, I should repeat that I haven't talked about this part of my life to anyone, ever. I've tried to ignore it, black it out and pretend it never happened. Of course that doesn't work because it's always in my head and it's still present on my body. I know you've noticed the scars and I'm so very grateful that you haven't asked about them. Those scars are one of the reasons that I do the crazy stuff; riding the way I do, bikes, the works. I do that stuff to take away some of the memories; the rush, the buzz makes me feel better for a while. Adrenalin, it's a drug, but it doesn't work as well as it did, in many ways I've become numb even to that.'

She gave a dry laugh, a hollow sound edged with ice cold pain. I sat very still, listened and said nothing.

'I stay in the racing world because I've clearly got a masochistic streak. It started as a fuck you world gesture and then it became something I just did, something I was good at. I held my head up and kept everyone at arm's length. That's how the Sid Vicious nickname started, because no one could get near me, I'd built a barrier a million miles high. I took no chances and suffered no fools. I liked that, I liked that very much.'

She dropped her head back into her hands, breathing through whatever this was bringing to the surface and then drank another mouthful of brandy. I watched her wince as she forced herself to swallow.

'Once upon a time, not so long ago, there was a girl who loved riding horses. Her parents had money and interest, a Thoroughbred stud farm in fact. They are producing the very things this girl likes to ride. The girl has three older brothers who all look after her and make sure she has all that she wants. It's idyllic until one day, disaster, the parents are killed in a plane crash on the way back from seeing one of the horses they bred racing in France.

'It'd been a great day, the horse had run its heart out, won doing handsprings and made everyone happy. A shed load of money changed hands as well. That made everyone even happier. Then, quite suddenly, all that happiness crashed back to earth, it ditched into the sea along with the plane and the parents. There were no survivors. The happiness went that day and I don't think it ever came back.'

She took another huge gulp at the brandy.

'Now the not-so-young girl leaves school, she's sixteen and gets a job riding out for a trainer. She wants to be a jockey, that's her dream, always had been and now she clings to it. She wants to be a professional jockey. Great. All is going well. Trainer is pleased, the horses go well for her so the owners are pleased too. She's apparently a pretty girl and soon the boys are asking her out. She's flattered but says no, she's horses to ride and a career to forge. She's such a silly girl, she thought she could get that career by simply being good at what she did, by working hard. Silly, silly girl that wasn't the way at all.

'Then one day, one fateful day, a well-known jockey comes to the yard, he's going to ride for a new owner and luckily, it doesn't always happen, he has free time to come and ride one or two before he races them. Everyone is happy again. This jockey is very special, the best of the best they keep saying, what a triumph that he's coming here, we must really be going places. He turns up on the first morning, flash car and flash gear, such presence; our not-so-young girl is quite taken aback. This is her teenage hero, she'd avidly watched recordings of every race he'd ever ridden and she still had posters of him on her bedroom wall. It got even better when the trainer comes and asks her to ride on the gallops with this horse god; she's beside herself with excitement.'

I watch her as she talks, taking gulps of brandy and picking at a loose thread on the rug. The pain she's reliving is very visible and I'm suddenly finding this hard to hear. I hope this isn't going where I think it might be.

'The well-known jockey is quite charming; day by day, he offers little insights to the not-so-young girl. He helps her hone her skill at race riding, he even gets her a first ride on a racecourse. She's a good girl and the horse wins the race. Everyone is happy, especially the not-so-young girl who is on top of the world. The well-known jockey is so handsome and so lovely to her. He offers to take her home in his car, offers to take her out after the races and tells her, over and over, how special, how talented she is. She's delighted and already a little in love. So naïve and innocent, she thinks he means what he says.'

She stood and slowly walked over to the window, staring out into the darkness. She begins to talk again, very quietly.

'He takes her home to his house, gives her champagne and takes her to his bed. She was just sixteen...'

She stops. Simply stands there with her back to me, facing the blackness outside. I go to her then, padding over on bare feet and fold her into my arms. Tears start, along with this terrible keening that comes from somewhere deep and dark. I simply pick her up and carry her back to the sofa, sitting with her cradled in my arms as if she was a child.

Of course, so obvious now, it is that kind of story. I've heard this kind of story before and I know what this pain means. Right now, I'd sell my soul for this not to be Sid's story.

'He did simply dreadful things to the girl that night and over many more nights. The girl, who knew nothing, was innocent of such matters. He did things that hurt... so much... in every way. He said that if she told anyone she'd never ride again, that he'd tell lies about her, tell them that she did drugs and screwed the owners. That if she ever left him, he'd hunt her down and hurt her again, maybe even get his friends round for a piece of her too. He told her that he'd hurt her, badly hurt her, not just by doing the things that no one could see. He said that this was what it was all about, this was what everyone really liked and the fact that she didn't made her the strange one. The utter insanity in all of this was that she believed him. A part of her thought she loved him, thought that if she stayed she could show him what love really meant and he'd be glad and would love her too.'

I listened, empty now, adopted that insulated approach, not because what she said made me feel like that, but purely because I couldn't bear to equate this to her.

'Then her brothers got to know him. They still had horses in training and interests in horses at stud. Oh, they were so pleased, two of the brothers, that the not-so-young-at-all-anymore girl had found such a man, they didn't seem to mind that she was different, they didn't seem to mind that he was known to have several other girls as well as her. They began to make money on their horses again. Everyone was happy, everyone that is except the not-so-young-at-all-anymore girl. The horses didn't do well for her now, confused by the way she rode, all contradictions and stiffness. But she couldn't say anything, had no one to tell even if she'd been able to. The brothers invited him round to stay, he was always there....'

She stopped, almost panting with the strain of getting these next words to come out.

'Do you know… he raped her … in the kitchen… when the brothers were just in the other room... they could have walked in at any time? He… raped her …there in the kitchen, the safe room... the room where good food and good conversations had been made…fuck… for fuck's sake…the room where she'd made cake with her mother… and he beat her because she tried to stop him. He did that simply because he could.'

I knew that she'd never reported any of this; I also knew who this man was and knew that he walked free, his life unaffected by what he'd done. A very large part of me wanted to go and change that for him. In that brief moment of silence I began to plan how I could make that happen. Softly, she began to speak again.

'She did get more rides because of the company she had to keep. There were people, there still are, who wish to trade a little on that bright light. If only they had known. So she put up with it, she did ok, not as good as before but ok. Everyone told her how lucky she was to have well-known jockey to help her along. Jealous ones said that she was sleeping her way into rides like this was something she'd gone out to do deliberately, nothing more than a silk chaser. Others said she deserved whatever trouble she got, spoiled little rich girl with friends in all the right places. None of them knew — none of them had half a clue about what was going on.

'Then the one day that probably saved her. A known difficult horse, rated with a warning flag and Timeform squiggle, you name it and it had it, form that would have you in hysterics but she's given the ride. Some horses go better for tits rather than balls, you go and ask, they'll tell you, just like that. It's statements like this, so commonplace in the racing world, this is how we know that chivalry isn't yet dead.'

She gave a sick little laugh, a brittle sound like the snapping of sticks.

'The not-so-young-at-all-anymore girl goes into the stalls on this horse and its fine for a few moments and then it goes ballistic. The stall handlers are there trying to keep it still long enough to start the race. Somewhere in the middle is the not-so-young-at-all-anymore girl. But the horse doesn't stand still, it has a blindfold over its head; it panics, rears, front legs catch on the frame of the stalls and then it is down.

'The stupid and slow not-so-young-at-all-anymore girl is dragged down with it. She lies underneath, pinned by legs and aluminium edged hooves. The race is delayed and the other horses released from the stalls. The difficult horse has broken its shoulder and its shot there, right in front of the not-so-young-at-all-anymore girl, she can't get up because its on her and she has broken bones too. She wonders if it might be kinder if she was shot there as well. But eventually an ambulance comes to take her away.'

She looks at me directly for the first time in all of this, her eyes dark, shining with tears. I lean forward and kiss her gently. Just simply to say, I'm still here, I won't leave.

'The well-known jockey comes to the hospital much later, all concern and charm. A doctor takes him to one side, he's known to be connected with her, society media and all that, everyone knows him, he's a household name. The doctor, one sane voice in all this, he asks well-known jockey why the girl's attack hadn't been reported. Says that he's examined her and the injuries she's suffered would indicate brutal and sustained sexual attacks. He says that if jockey boyfriend does nothing then he will. Jockey is all concern, says he's been away, (a clear lie and the doctor probably knows it), he asks are these injuries not just to do with the racing accident? No, says the doctor, absolutely not, these are much, much worse than broken bones and hoof prints on flesh. Well-known jockey is all shock and horror, poor girlfriend, of course he knew nothing, but can he just talk to her, make sure that she's ok? Strangely, the doctor thinks this is a good idea. So of course, of course he can talk to her and take as long as he needs to sort this out.

'But now, for the first time, well-known jockey is on the back foot, he can no longer take the risk, so he threatens me with the whole of Hades and then, a day or so later, very publicly, dumps me. For a long time I looked over my shoulder, for a long time I lived in fear, jumping at every creaking floorboard. My brothers were pissed. What had I done to lose such a good catch? I think Seb has yet to forgive me for such girlie stupidity. They were glad when I wanted to move out of the limelight of Newmarket, down here to the sticks, released some money from my trust fund to set this place up. Perhaps they hoped I'd quietly behave myself now. Seb has an interest in some horses with David, so everyone is happy again and he gets to keep an eye on me.'

She cried again, silent tears. I held her and said nothing at all.

'I've never talked about the rapes and the beatings, I think he really enjoyed it, I think it was what turned him on. He was vicious, so brutal. And he never stopped, even when there was blood... Jake... He never stopped. I was sixteen, turning seventeen when he was through with me. It has taken me eleven years to stop waking up screaming at night, to stop wishing I'd killed him, to stop wanting to challenge my suicidal urge by doing insane things. My body healed eventually but the rest of me may never recover.'

She pressed her forehead softly to mine.

'And it's taken eleven years to let anyone to touch me again; a hug, a kiss, I could bear nothing. Told myself I'd kill anyone who came near me like that again. Then you came by and you changed my world. You took me from my quiet hiding corner, picked me up and simply held on tight. You've opened me up again with your affection, humour and tremendous passion,' she smiled, the warmth returning to her voice.

'I want you to know that I've never been held the way that you hold me, never been kissed the way that you kiss me and, when you and I were together here the first time… I really, really wanted you and yet… I was absolutely terrified. But you, the way that you were, what you showed me that night, I'd literally no idea that such extraordinary feelings were possible. Jake, you've opened me to the beauty that is present within that act, shown me that it's ok, that its safe to let that kind of emotion take charge for a while. So, even if you were to walk out right now, I know that because of you I've been brought back. You've truly shown me that it really doesn't rain all the time.'

What could I say? There was nothing I could find in that moment that would be right to say in response to all of that. I simply wrapped her tighter in my arms and kissed her, tried to pour into that kiss everything that was right about her, everything that made her strong and beautiful and so very special. Then without words, we'd both said enough, I carried her up the stairs.

What happened next in that still dark night was just for her alone. Infinitely slow and tender, every movement controlled and gentle, snowflake touch, softly sensual as simple as an exhaled breath on hot skin. A feather-light skim to steadily flare a molten furnace, surfing on the profound intensity that such a union can generate, until the wave crested and powerfully broke, to plunge us, free falling, onto a pillowed shore.

Chapter Twenty-Six

I lay there as she slept and part of me actually felt a little afraid. Afraid of where this was going, afraid of the feelings that laughed and danced around very quietly, as if they too were being careful not to alert me to their presence. This whole evening had sung to its own tune, it had simply happened and dragged me along on its riotous party. But it wasn't just this evening. Since I'd first set eyes on her, it had been someone or something else pushing me along.

So the question now, the question is… what's the answer? Hmm? Hmm? Come on, Mr Kick Ass Confident… what is the answer to the question?

Sighing, I turned my face towards the ceiling trying to silence those thoughts. I wished that there were guarantees. I wished I had that crystal ball app on my phone, the one that would show me how this would turn out. I wished I could make a factual informed choice, rather than one based on some unfathomable chemistry, some weird genetic coding, that made the simple sight and smell of this woman impossible to resist. Some pheromone she had that rewarded with previously unknown but exquisite pleasure. Could I base such a monumental decision on those facts alone? Was it enough? Could I put myself on the line for her? I hadn't come here to be looking. I'd come here to remain blind. How can this be then, how can she be so much and more?

Like her, I had darkness within me. For years I'd made it infinitely worse by living a dehumanised existence, dehumanised by the constant camouflage, by being someone I wasn't. I'd become an inflated spectre, more terrifying because no-one could see me clearly. Not even myself.

I'm the one who's been labelled vicious, brutal or worse. It was all true too, I absolutely was each of those things. But, this now, all of this, scared the hell out of me. In truth, she was the only one - ever - with whom I dared to be me. The childish me, the silly me, the touch-me-often intimate me. The me that I was only just getting to know. For the first time, I was looking in rather than out without the blinkers, understanding emotion rather than just building thicker walls and protections; touching softly instead of kicking the shit out of it.

They do say that the profoundest gifts are those not explicitly given and she had, perhaps unintentionally, given me the greatest gift of all. Quite simply, she'd given me back a sense of my humanity.

Ha! So, it is becoming clear. Mr Kick Ass Confident… you are… you know you are…. No rhyme or reason to it, shit happens and that's just the way it is. The question, the answer and the problem. Love dude! That's the word! Four little letters that make the whole world turn.

Guess what?

That voice was victorious now, cackling insanely.

You're in love with her.

I slipped out from her arms, pulled on jeans and padded back down the stairs to consult the fire and Finn, as a canine Yoda, he might provide useful insight; if he could stay awake long enough.

Finn rested his head companionably in my lap and the fire flickered in a friendly sort of way. It was a good place to be with those kinds of thoughts. I questioned if I was having this inner turmoil because of what she'd told me tonight. Was this some sort of sick sympathy recoil?

No… No… you were at this place days ago… you've been running from this reality long before you knew all of that black stuff.

That inner voice was beside itself with the certainty of this new revelation. And it was right. This was the reason that I'd burned at the mere mention of her name, why the thought of her made my pulse sing. Why she reduced me to an incoherent idiot on occasion.

Of course, the next problem was what was I going to do about it?

I exhaled slowly. That was an even bigger issue. I played back her words, 'eleven years… it has taken eleven years to allow anyone to touch me again…'

If someone else had said those words to me I might have thought them trite and overly sentimental. But from Sid this was as pivotal as the Magna Carta. She'd come all that way, from a place that was more dangerous and bleak than I could ever really begin to understand and she'd come all that way just to say those words to me. That thought hit like a slap in the face. She was impossibly strong and there I was, whining like a spoilt child, worrying about going with something that must have been as obvious as the fact that the sky was often blue.

I rubbed Finn's ears as he thumped a skinny tail on the rug, his amber eyes, deep and sentient. I was still immersed in thought staring into the fire, when his extra thumping tail alerted me to her. She'd slipped down the stairs to sit beside us, wearing nothing more than my t-shirt. I lifted my arm to let her move closer and placed a kiss on her hair as she curled herself into my side.

'Penny for them?'

'Finn and I have been comparing sofas,' I laughed. 'You know, which are best for crashing on, that sort of thing, boys stuff. He said he prefers cushions but I said a futon was best. But then he told me he isn't bothered about smells and wet patches, I said that I didn't think I wanted to go there.'

I lifted her chin and kissed her simply because I couldn't help myself in that moment. She looked a little stunned.

'Are you ok? You didn't leave and you didn't ask me to stop. But that was a tremendously big baggage dump this evening.'

'I'm ok. I'm pleased, honoured in fact, that you talked, finally let some of that out. You showed phenomenal strength, I'm somewhat in awe of you.'

'Half a bottle of brandy and a gallon of tears isn't exactly a show of strength,' she shook her head, dismissing herself.

I tutted. 'Don't. Don't ignore what I'm saying here. Time you realised who you really are, what you've become. How you've risen, phoenix like, from the ashes of such brutality. Many would have let themselves go, I know this, I see it far too often. It's the dark side of my job.'

'Jake, don't. You'll make me cry again.'

The intense enormity of the moment was a visible presence. Those words, those recently revealed words sat heavy, loaded now and ready to roll. I had a small moment of panic, that just about to jump off a cliff moment, then just shut my eyes and let them out.

'Finn and I haven't just been discussing life, the universe and sofas here tonight and we've come to a fairly monumental conclusion. However, it is something I've never had to think about before. Not ever.'

I opened my eyes and looked at her, waiting there for what I would say next. I locked onto the shine from those blue ocean depths.

'We've come to the conclusion that we're both more than a little in love with you.'

She sat still and silent, taking this new declaration in.

'Right or wrong, Sid, it is how it is. Of course, one of the turning points was finding out that you quite liked Tom Petty.'

Finn grumbled and returned to the sofa. He was in the way and he didn't like being shoved, not by anyone. I sensed I may have to bring humble rabbit pie next time I needed his Yoda insights.

Chapter Twenty-Seven

'Is your work dangerous?' she asked, out the blue, early the next morning.

I laughed. 'Asks the girl who rides racehorses!'

'Ok, I'm being absurd I know! I've not really thought about it like that before,' she looked a little embarrassed.

'Sid. Silly Sid. I'll be fine. This is sleepy Dartmoor after all. Holiday land remember? And…'

'I know! I know you've got certificates!' she interrupted, lightening the moment instantly.

'Come on, time for you to go and ride big horses at speed. I've dull stuff to do like laundry.'

'Would you come racing this weekend? Your sister too, if she wants.'

'Maybe, she's supposed to be here for the weekend and I know, categorically, she's going to be beside herself until she's checked you out. Be ready though, she's barking.'

'I'm sure I can manage.'

'Come on then, take me home before you're late for work.'

Picking up my backpack and trainers, I almost forgot my phone which was still drying by the fire. A message flashed.

Non-urgent – ring in 9am. DCI Moore. What was that about?

Back in the flat, I checked in with the darker side of my life. Revelations; my mole was running rampant and, although he wasn't responsible for all of it, as a catalyst, he was certainly digging up treasure. Then something that stopped me dead. Fucking hell, it had happened! Now that was going to cause seismic activity within the on-going investigation. I hauled myself back from my cyberscape and rang in.

'Jake, come in, I need to talk to you about something.'

I wondered why he hadn't simply sent a text with that request but then I already knew what he was going to say. This was the seismic activity that was now being felt on the police Richter scale.

Moore was at his desk staring into space when I knocked on the already open door.

'Come in, shut the door. I've just had some news that has made my plans change a little,' he passed me a print out with a bold heading at the top which read Suffolk Constabulary, it was an information request. The person they were looking for information on was Sidra Fielding. Expected, but not quite so soon.

'There was another murder last night. Not here, in Newmarket thankfully, we've enough on our plate at the moment,' he rubbed tired eyes with thick fingers. 'The victim was a Gabriel Wallace, yes, *the* Gabriel Wallace. Same method as John Wozniak's brother and possibly the same as Marcus Williams, several blows to the head with something hard. No hint of any buddhist rituals but I have to say that I agree with your theory that there has to be a connection. He was thoroughly pulped too.'

I said nothing. Gabriel Wallace was the well-known shit head jockey Sid had told me all about last night. I was actually quite glad someone had bashed his head in, although it was about twelve years too late.

What the police had now was a probable serial killer. The press would have to be bound and gagged pronto as this was the biggest of all big news stories for some time.

'Thankfully we can be pretty precise; he was on a racing yard with a trainer leaving at 7.30pm. His body was found by his car at 9.15pm, still warm,' he looked up, gaze like a laser. 'I take it that you can vouch for Miss Fielding?'

'Yep, she was with me.'

'Thank you,' he almost smiled. 'I'm getting the feeling that we're looking in the wrong place. So, whilst I still don't wish to compromise your own work in anyway, I'm now a little more up to speed on who you actually work for. I need you to help me find out the connection, aside from racing, with all these people. The connection must be someone other than Sidra Fielding as she isn't the one committing the murders.'

Unspoken words hung in the air. Now for the next stage.

'Do you think Sid is at any risk? She seems to be at the centre of all of this.' I asked.

'No reason to think that at the moment from our point of view. But I'll alert the team so they'll be aware. I've asked for her to come in here at eleven to give a statement in relation to Mr Wallace, I'll try and find out more before then. It has become rapidly apparent that you've more specialist knowledge than anyone else here and that is why I'm seeking authority, Jake, to enable you to go on our behalf to Newmarket tomorrow. Suffolk and Cambridge have been accommodating, they'll assist you in any event. I'm aware about the sensitivity of your profile and I'm not making any of these decisions lightly.'

I didn't mind as I needed to relocate myself and DCI Moore was just making that easier.

'Do you still want me about today?'

'Not if you've got other stuff to do but could you ring me at three, I'll know more then. This is strictly between you and I at the moment, ok?'

It was like chess, sliding players into position and planning tactically for a variety of moves from the opposition. Trouble was, I might know a lot more than the police did but I still didn't know for certain who the opposition was.

'Gabriel Wallace is significant to Sid. I'd like to be able to tell her that he's dead, his name is likely to cause her considerable distress.' I waited as he chewed it over.

'Why? As far as I'm aware they had a relationship some years ago, why would this affect her now?'

'It's extremely delicate. The situation wasn't ever reported but can we just say that, during the time of their personal relationship, Mr Wallace liked it rough; extremely rough. Do I need to say anymore?' I hoped that was enough.

'Ah, ok, understood. I'm afraid I'm going to need to know about that, but let's just see what else comes out,' he sat thinking for a moment. 'Ok, you track her down but be discreet. Perhaps you ought to hang about. How fragile is she?'

'She's stronger than she thinks but I'd say whoever conducts the interview needs to be very sensitive.' I wished I could be the one to do it; this was going to be very hard for her.

'Right, hang about then and pick up the pieces as needed,' he waved one hand, dismissing me and went back to his computer. Trev and Tom were in the outer office now, so I went straight out the door and down to the car park, pulling out my phone as I walked.

Chapter Twenty-Eight -Alyosha

And I will flay the flesh from their bones and strip them bare for angels to eat.

I went away, you remember that I expect, Zosima. I went away and when I came back they had Gabriel Wallace in tow, except it wasn't like that, they were being towed by him. The dog was being wagged by the tail. Now he was an evil bastard if ever there was one. I killed him. You know that, don't you? I hoped he'd be the first but he wasn't, that was just how it happened. I wanted Gabriel to be first and I wanted him to suffer. Didn't quite work out that way but at least he died.

He knew, Gabriel did, all sorts about the brothers. He used that knowledge in all sorts of ways; they were like cowering pups in front of him. I came back and told them to get rid of him, I worked so hard to get clean, to get strong enough to come back. I knew that Gabriel would want more and more, the deeper they involved themselves with him, he would always want more and more. And he did. And they gave it to him, free and gratis. Just like that. Guess what they gave him, Zosima? Do you know? Can you guess?

You, Zosima, they gave him you; bastards. They gave you to someone like Gabriel Wallace, as if you were a piece of meat. You were still a child.

It's been hard for me to carry that all these years. I had no one to tell. You'd talk to me a bit, but never enough and where would I have begun with all of this? Smile. Remember? Don't-forget-to-smile-else-they'll-think-you're-an-arsehole.

The eagles kept him from sleeping. The time was right, they insisted, time to show what was inside him. Three and three make six. Three down, three across. Three down, three to go.

Alyosha was finding it hard to focus, the packet of pills he took was empty. Prayer, the eagles said, prayer is all you need now, you're changing, you don't need the bonds of medication to still your thoughts.

He couldn't challenge them, he couldn't tell them that he wasn't ready. They didn't give him a minute's peace, didn't allow him to sleep. He paced round and round his home, catching a glimpse of himself in the long mirror in the hall. Unkempt, unshaven, his skin looked grey. He looked like an old man. An old tramp of a man in shabby stained clothes. A tremor of fear ran through him.

Beside the mirror was a huge gilt picture frame stuffed full with photographs. He stared at the faces smiling out, snapshots in time from all around the world. He could no longer equate that life to now. He'd risen above all that now. He'd been reborn to act, not just to record.

Slowly he removed one photograph and smoothed the bent corners out. Zosima was smiling back at him from it, she would have been about ten when the photograph was taken, her hair spilling out from a blue baseball cap, the sun catching it and make her shine. Zosima. Why had she abandoned him? She never called. She never came round. She had become just like the others. He'd been left once again. Derelict inside and out now.

Chapter Twenty-Nine

'Jake?' she was riding, I could hear a horse's shod hooves on a tarmac road. 'Are you ok?'

'I'm fine, but I need to speak to you as soon as. When can you meet me?'

'I'm assuming this is very urgent?' her voice was tinged with humour.

'Yes, sadly it is. I'm afraid it's to do with work.'

'Ok,' I heard her click to the horse she was riding and then heard the four time sound of its shoes on the road change into two, trotting now. 'Back at the yard in ten minutes, I can talk then.'

'I'm on the way. Get yourself time away from work.' I didn't want to say anymore.

I arrived there before she did and watched her come up the road on a bright bay horse that skipped sideways, standing in the stirrups as the horse spooked and fly kicked. Black goggles, black jacket, just like the first time I'd met her, she still looked like a boy as she came past. I leant against the bonnet of the car and waited for her to return without the horse.

'What's on? I'm supposed to be at your office for eleven. What couldn't wait?'

'Let's go somewhere else for a bit. Are you ok to leave?'

'Yes, that's fine.'

She walked around to the passenger side and got in. I started the engine and pulled out of the drive.

'What's going on? I'm not liking this one little bit, something tells me there's trouble.'

'I've some news I'd rather came from me than anyone else, rather you were told somewhere other than the police station. Can you handle coming to my flat or do you want to go home?' I turned and glanced at her briefly, I didn't know where was best or how she would cope with this.

'Of course, your flat's fine. What is it…is it anything to do with my brothers? Has something happened to them?' She was getting paler.

'Sid, slow down. It isn't anything to do with your family. I don't want to talk about this in the car, please, you'll understand in a minute.' I stopped at the junction, scanning the traffic, waiting to pull into the square.

'Jake, the suspense is killing me. Please tell me what's going on?'

I pulled over outside the flat.

'Gabriel Wallace was killed last night in Newmarket. He was murdered in a similar way to what we've seen down here. I do know that Gabriel Wallace was the well-known jockey.'

She sat, white faced, taking in that piece of knowledge.

'Jake...' Head in her hands, the shaking began again. 'No. No. No. I can't go through this again. Can't talk about this again. No… Oh no…'

With those words she fainted, simply sagged to one side, falling against the car door in a crumpled heap. I hadn't expected such a severe reaction I must admit. She was unconscious for about five minutes and then slowly returned. I sat beside her as she cried with shock or relief; it was hard to say which was forefront in her mind. So thankful that she hadn't been hit with this in the sterility of an interview room. For a long time that was how we stayed until my phone rang, it was Moore.

'How's it gone?'

'It hasn't gone well. Can we change the interview time?'

'Take her to her home; I'll come there with Sorrell. Do you need any other backup?'

'No, that won't be necessary as I'm not going to leave. I won't interfere but I'll be staying with her.'

'Understood. One hour, Jake. One hour. This cannot wait now.' Moore disconnected abruptly as soon as he'd finished speaking.

'I'm going to take you home, ok? I'll stay with you. The police interview can be done at your house. Are you ok?' I lifted her chin, looked into her tight eyes full of the realisation that she was going to have to tell her story all over again.

'Stay with me. Don't leave,' she clung to my jacket, wound her fingers into my collar.

'I'm not going anywhere, I'll stay with you.'

We drove to her house. I listened to her speaking to David Flint on her mobile, telling him she was going to give a statement to the police; she was so calm, so detached, almost as if she was speaking about someone else. I could hear him blustering on the other end telling her that this wasn't convenient and couldn't she organise her time better, like she'd some choice. If she had, it wouldn't be happening at all.

Back at the house, she went to get changed out of her riding clothes and I made coffee for want of anything better to do.

'Do I have to tell them about Gabriel? Surely it doesn't matter now, it's been so long, I never said anything then, surely it's too late now?'

She sat, pale and small, on the stool in the kitchen, the same place where, just a few hours ago, we'd sat together and laughed.

'I don't know what Moore will want to know, I may not be privy to all the information that he has at the moment. Suffolk Police have requested information about you, probably because of your connection to Gabriel, I think that's really why this is kicking off now.'

Finn heard the car coming up the drive first and barked loudly. A deep noise that barrelled out of him, he even got off the sofa and stalked stiff legged to the door. It's strange how dogs can tell a squad car at fifty paces. I went and opened it to Tom and Moore.

'Are we ok to proceed?' Moore asked.

'She's dealing with it but you ought to know that she passed out when I told her. I'm just here, I've told her very little of the actual detail.' I let him go in with Tom.

I sat a little distance from them, there was an odd atmosphere; the whole dynamic changed by the presence of these men. I listened to Moore's introduction, he spoke gently, with compassion; I watched Tom, studied his face as he concentrated on trying to read Sid.

She talked about when she'd last seen Gabriel Wallace, at the races it seemed, but only in passing. Then she was asked to confirm her relationship with him all those years ago and the fact that, an unnamed witness had given a statement to the effect that, fairly recently, at Ascot racecourse, she'd said that she'd like him dead.

'Of course I wanted the bastard dead, that doesn't mean that I'm capable of actually doing it. No-one ever knew what happened all those years ago except me and him, but the man still terrified me and I wouldn't have willingly gone within miles of him. Our paths rarely crossed, he rode on the flat and he rode in much more prestigious races than I do. I was unlikely to see him at Newton Abbot on a Friday night riding in a novice chase.'

I watched her hands, could see her pain just by looking at them. Then, because it had to be asked, the nature of the relationship she'd had with the dead man came out. She froze, shutting down, breathing slow and shallow. Moore asked again, she didn't respond. Tom sat silently poised with his pad and pen, waiting to continue writing. I moved closer.

'Sid?' I said. She was almost catatonic. 'Sid, you need to answer these questions. I'm sorry but you must answer.'

Moore looked at her intently. 'I'd like to pause this and get a doctor here. I don't want to push it.'

Yet another stranger would make this even worse, but I couldn't overrule Moore in front of Tom.

'What if she'll talk to me? She's already told me about Gabriel and she may find it easier to do so again.'

I knelt on the floor in front of her, took hold of both her hands. 'Can you look at me, Sid?'

She lifted her chin slightly, but her eyes were still fixed.

'These are just questions and you're completely safe. DCI Moore and DS Sorrell need to know what sort of man Gabriel was; they need to find out what happened,' I said quietly. 'Do you understand why I'm asking this? Are you able to continue?'

She nodded and Moore began again with his questions; she answered them all as if she was talking only to me. Amongst other incidents, she described the rape in the kitchen. She must have relived that often in the dark nights when she was alone, her eyes on me continuously, hands wound around mine so tightly that her knuckles were white. She talked about the beatings and about how those scars that sat like frozen silvered serpents across her back had been inflicted. She talked about having to take herself to the doctors to make sure his attacks hadn't given her anything more than pain and bruises.

She stopped mid-sentence, her face beaded with sweat and said. 'Oh, I'm going to be sick.' She got unsteadily to her feet and ran.

'Shitty deal, Jake,' said Moore. 'She's had a rough time.'

'Seems that way.'

'I think we've enough for now. Hang around, pick up pieces and ring in later this afternoon.' He stood with Tom. 'We'll see ourselves out.'

****

She was sitting on the floor of the wet room, a small cloth dripping in her hands, her forearms resting on her knees, head down.

I held the hair back from her face, eased the cloth from her grip to rinse it under the tap and passed it back. She just let it drop, her hand held out, no movement in the fingers. I rinsed it once more and gently wiped her forehead. Her eyes, dead looking, a glassy shine from them — come on, you can do this, you've come through much worse than this.

I helped her through to the sofa, lying her down against the cushions and, moments later, she appeared to be asleep. I folded a blanket across her as Finn stretched himself and settled in, resting his head on her legs. Returning with coffee, I sat on the rug and simply waited for her to wake up again. She slept restlessly, talking out loud, saying whole sentences that were sharp and clear and then just mumbling words. I stayed there, staring into the fire, lost in thought about how she might be connected to these murders. I tried not to think too hard about my cyber-mole, sent before all this began.

In the afternoon my phone vibrated quietly, I went into the hallway to answer it.

'Jake, how is she?' It was Tom.

'Asleep, has been so since you left.' I rubbed my face; the tension was exhausting.

'What a mess, I'd no idea; she's some girl to have kept that lot inside her all this time. I knew the guy, Gabriel was a friend of Josh's. I thought he was a good bloke. Shows how wrong you can be.'

'Did you want anything else or just an update on her?'

'No, nothing else. Are you ok, Jake? It must be a hard job to deal with.'

'Fine. I'm fine.'

There was a moment of silence on the line.

'Tell you something for nothing, mate, she's so in love with you its almost painful to watch. I've known her since she was a kid remember, never seen her the way she is with you. Hook and line I'd say.' His voice was still low, as if he was trying not to be overheard.

'If there's nothing else…?' I wanted to end this conversation now.

'No. That's it.'

There was an undertone to his voice, a sincerity I hadn't noticed before; I wondered if I ought to have been a bit more civil but then, right now, I wasn't in the frame of mind for being nice to anyone but Sid.

She slept on and at around 3.30pm I rang in, asked for Moore.

'How is she?'

'Sleeping, she has been since you left.'

'Bloody mess this is. I've had phone calls from high places this afternoon, just to forewarn you may expect a royal visit from her brother, he's ranting.'

'Which one, she has three?'

'Sebastian. Have you met him?'

'Yes. Banker. Not easy company or easy on the eye.'

'He's been throwing his not inconsiderable self about well above us. There's been a rattling of bones on high. Though how the fuck he knows anything is a mystery.'

'He appears to have a direct line as he knew about John Wozniak almost as quickly as we did. I checked him out and he's all super squeaky clean on the surface but what that's hiding I have yet to discover. How would you like me to proceed?'

'I now have police authority for you to go to Newmarket. From what I saw earlier, I suggest, note that word, Jake, I *suggest* that you try to take her with you. Keep her safe from prying eyes and do some digging. I'm going to say that you're on another case, which in a way you are. Without meaning to cause offence, I'm also going to ask that you proceed cautiously; I believe there's a lot more to this than meets the eye. To add weight to her statement, if it was necessary, I've just seen a copy of her medical records from when she was treated after the racing accident. In all honesty, it must have been touch and go whether she'd survive it and I mean the assaults allegedly inflicted by Mr Wallace, nothing to do with the fall from the horse. It's no wonder the doctor was so concerned. I just wish he'd reported it but times were different then, I suppose; hence why I'm going against all my own proper procedures now. So don't get into bother, it will make me look bad and I don't like to look bad ever. Am I clear?'

'Crystal.'

'Keep me informed of all developments and keep the expenses down; I'll be hung on high if this is questioned.'

He disconnected immediately and I gave a sigh of relief. From the moment Gabriel Wallace was found, possibly from the moment he was killed, Sid was in danger. Now, without having to break cover here, DCI Moore had sorted it in one go. But, then again, as I'd possibly precipitated some of it, it was time I proved my worth.

About an hour or so later Sid woke up, bleary eyed and blinking from where she'd taken herself, probably somewhere a million miles away. She sat up quickly, knocking Finn onto the floor where he landed in a heap with a grunt.

'What time is it?' she looked disorientated.

'Five-ish. You've slept away most of the day.' I tucked a strand of hair behind her ear. 'Bad as Finn.'

'Bloody hell!' she said as she struggled to free herself from both blanket and the returning lurcher.

'No, sit and stay. Work is off for a few days. Let's call it compassionate leave. Its arranged and passed by official channels. David Flint is no doubt still pacing up and down as we speak but DCI Moore is a force to reckon with when he's got a head on him.'

'What about you? Have you got to go?'

'I'm suddenly on a sort of leave as well and, as it happens, I was thinking about asking you to come away with me for a few days. Do you want to come?'

'Where?'

'Newmarket. I've heard it can be bloody freezing at this time of the year. Apparently there's nothing between it and Siberia when the wind blows. Sounds idyllic, don't you think? Nothing like a bit of the freezing flat lands to clear out cobwebs.'

'Nothing sexier than thermals,' she gave me a hooded smile.

'Thermals! I didn't take you for a lightweight.'

She sighed, closed her eyes and shook her head slowly. 'I'm so glad you're here.I really mean that.'

'So am I.'

'You make this mad world manageable,' she blinked slowly, as if trying to orientate herself to a new state of mind.

'Ah, yes, but I rely on guidance from my new friend, Yoda the lurcher. You may only know him as Finn but he's marvellous for life's greatest questions. His sage advice usually involves sleeping in strange positions and farting a lot.'

'Jake, box of frogs, I think.'

'Mad as, definitely. Right, can't stand here gossiping all day. I'm giving you advance warning that I'm about to indulge in a culinary creation in your kitchen, don your stab vest and you can come. Be prepared to be amazed again,' I said. 'Only one slight note of potential normality, Mr Banker the Brother has been rattling his feed bowl at the bars of his cage. The noise has filtered down through police royalty and I'm informed that a visit may be imminent. Best we make preparations. I suggest barricades, but what would be your plan?'

She laughed easily. 'A delightful visual image. I find a straightforward foxtrot oscar often works a treat with overly pretentious relations, it's so subtle, don't you think? Of course, others may prefer a sound kick in the downstairs departments. But, with that particular brother, I fear such action would result in minimal damage.'

Chapter Thirty - Alyosha

And I will flay the flesh from their bones and strip them bare for angels to eat.
'Alyosha? Alyosha? Where are you?'

He could hear her calling. He was back in the treehouse, Zosima was outside in the garden. He peeped out through a gap in the boarding. He could see her now, standing there in bright red wellingtons. She lived in those wellingtons.

Zosima, his Zosima.

But then he remembered. Zosima had abandoned him just when he'd nearly made her safe. She'd left him without a word and now he was alone.

Another noise from behind and, abruptly, he was no longer in the treehouse in the garden of his childhood home; he was hiding behind the rubble of a bombed out building with a camera in his hands. A massive explosion ripped through the air, the sound wave like a monstrous fist, knocking him flat and taking the camera out of his hands. Coughing and wheezing he stood again, blinking away the dust from his eyes.

No more war zone rubble, he was standing alone in the centre of a maypole of prayer flags. The colourful flags fluttered around him, buddhist wind horse flags to protect and guide. The shrine was directly in front, the eagles, six of them, sitting in a majestic line and all of them staring at him with eyes that drilled and pinned.

One by one they moved closer, half flying, half walking. They looked a little ridiculous moving in this way and he so wanted to smile, to show that he appreciated their little pantomime. Ingrained though was the need to show respect, even if they were doing this to make him feel better, he had to show respect. He knelt on the ground as they got closer and held out his hands for their blessings.

Two of them, may have been more, began to circle him and alternately press their raptors' beaks onto his upturned palms. He watched their gestures with wonder, they were almost affectionate, as if they wished to show how much he was loved. Tears formed in his eyes, squeezed through dust clogged ducts by a feeling of ecstasy that bubbled up inside him. A feeling which rapidly changed to horror as, one by one, they opened their beaks and began to tear at his flesh. Unable to move away, he screamed in pain and shock, louder and louder until he slumped, face first and unconscious onto the hard ground.

When he woke again he looked down at his bloodied hands.

The next step had been taken.

He was getting closer because now, on both hands, he was marked with unmistakeable sign of the stigmata.

Chapter Thirty-One

Sid's mobile rang interrupting the cooking, or lack of it. Glancing down at the screen, she rolled her eyes.

'The middle man has obviously been informed. This is Josh,' she touched the screen and lifted the phone to her ear. 'Josh, how are you? Long-time no see. Right... when? Yeah, that's good news, it's been too long,' she sounded like it was anything but good news that she was hearing. 'Thing is, Josh, I'm going to be away for a few days, you know work and all that.'

She held her finger over the phone, 'He wants to know where I'm going, do I tell him?'

I shook my head.

'Look, Josh, I'm about to burn my supper. Can I give you a call in the morning and let you know what my plans are, I'll know then where I'll be and when?'

I moved the timer on the microwave so that it pinged loudly.

'Yeah, you too, Josh. Until the morning then? Have a good one,' she disconnected and exhaled loudly. 'Bloody hell, he's over from the States and wants to come to see me. Apparently he's in London at the moment but I suspect Seb has been frothing at the mouth to him. Your DCI Moore may find he has an ear bashing from brother two as well. Josh never comes to see me — ever. Something is obviously up for him to have got on a plane and come. Nothing like the boys in blue to cause a gathering of the clan, is there? If Alex turns up as well, I'll be forced to go with your barricade plan.'

'Where is Alexander usually?'

'Oh, who knows. At the moment I believe he's one of life's drifters. Both Seb and Josh are driven money makers but, these days, Alex spends his time hugging trees and wallowing in a delayed 1960s haze of love and hash man,' she held up two fingers in the peace sign. 'I love him the most but he's rarely on this planet.'

'Are you going to come to Newmarket then? Will you come with me for a day or so?' I had yet to get that question answered.

'Of course! What an offer! I don't even have to think about it as aside from the chaos of today, I'm having a ball.'

It was my phone that interrupted next. It was Moore.

'Jake, Tom's on his way to you for a quick bit of paperwork. Are you still where you were?'

That was it, there was definitely something going down.

'Should I be concerned?'

'You asked me something earlier, about a possible threat? Do you recall who that was but don't say the name just now if you can be overheard.'

'Yes.'

What the hell was my mole doing?

'It is fact. Sorrell will inform. Ensure that she isn't out of sight, not even for a moment,' he laughed unexpectedly, 'don't expect that will be much of a hardship.'

I don't know what was worse, Sid being a definite known target or Moore trying to be funny. He disconnected in his usual immediate way and I was left staring at the phone.

'What's on?' Sid was asking, not worried, now chopping carrots into impossibly thin strips with a huge knife.

'Something and nothing. Tom is on the way back with some information for me. Won't take long, is it ok that he's coming here again?'

'Of course.'

Finn informed us of an arrival. I went to open the door and found not Tom but someone unknown; a suit, brief case and a 'get out of the way' demeanour.

'Who the fuck are you?' a loud voice barked.

'Could ask you the same,' I blocked the door with my foot as he tried to push through.

'Get out of the way and let me in!' he pushed even harder.

'Not if you can't be nice, whoever you are.' I hauled the door closed and locked it, narrowly missing his fingers as he attempted to prise his way around.

'Who is it?' Sid called from the kitchen. 'Is it Tom?'

'No, some bloke I don't know,' I called back to her as the door was being loudly pounded by a fist accompanied by lots of shouting. I reached for the phone, probably time the cavalry were requested to assist. Sid appeared, wiping her hands on a towel.

'What does...' she stopped in mid-sentence and listened to the torrent of abuse from outside the door, 'Jake, that's Josh. He was obviously not in London when he called even though he said he was. He doesn't sound happy, does he?'

'I did shut the door on him so perhaps he has reason to be pissed.' I put the phone away again.

'Actually with Josh, he doesn't always need a reason. He's used to barking and people jumping. Best let him in, I suppose. Are you and I going to be away together if he asks?'

'You're good, aren't you? Wasted riding horses. You make it up, I'll go along.'

She opened the door to a roaring wall of pissed off CEO hotshot brother.

'SID, OPEN THE FUCKING DOOR!' He was shouting so loud and didn't lower the volume as she did so. 'Who the fuck is this and why is he answering your door? Actually don't answer that, I expect this is the yokel boyfriend Seb has told me all about!'

'Josh! This is my house so don't come here roaring and shouting! What right do you have to tell me who I can have here? Get a grip, shithead or you'll go straight back out again!' She threw words back at him, a furious pixie compared to his city suit and LA tan.

'Some welcome, sister, when I've come all this way!' he was still shouting like a child having a tantrum.

'You came for your own reasons! So back up, find your manners and be nice; your shit has never worked with me. Take off the intimidation face and find the remnant of human being you must keep pickled somewhere about your person,' she hissed at him and turned, stalking away, her body radiating fury.

'Jake, this dickhead is my brother Josh. When he remembers where he is, I expect that he'll be polite and introduce himself properly. In the meantime I'll not be at all offended if you wish to completely ignore him, I often do,' she said and went back into the kitchen.

Josh stood, anger seeping from every pore. I had to look away as I seriously thought I might laugh. There's something ridiculous about pompous men when they're throwing their weight around. Sid had floored him and he was now trying to process that and work out how to recover some sense of authority. He decided to take it out on me instead.

'You can leave now. I have family business to discuss with my sister so, go, get in your car and disappear.'

'Nope. Sorry, can't do. Orders are orders.' I gave him full on sarcastic bog-Irish, wondering if he was always like this.

'What orders? I thought you were supposed to be the boyfriend. Anyway, whatever you are, be a good little boy and fuck off otherwise I may have to put you out myself.'

It didn't help that now I did laugh at him. Arrogant, self-righteous arsehole that he clearly was. Seb and Josh cut from the same cloth apparently, both so far up themselves it is a wonder that they could see anything without a torch.

'Oh, please go right ahead, Mr Fielding.' I stepped slightly closer and glared back into his indignant fury. He backed away just enough, a flicker of uncertainty in that moment.

Someone else knocked at the door, now that must be Tom. Sid was venting her fury in the kitchen with something metallic; I doubted she would have heard it, so I went instead. Josh turned on his heel and went towards the kitchen.

'Sorry that took longer than I thought.' Tom stood on the step. 'Who else is here? That's a hire car, isn't it?'

'Joshua has just turned up, hissing and spitting. He was trying to throw me out when you knocked.'

'Josh! No, he's not like that. He can be forthright but never heavy,' Tom looked puzzled. 'Oh well, nowt as queer as families.' He shrugged, easy with Josh's sudden and full-on arrival it seemed.

'I expect that's what it's all about. Let's take this outside and leave them to continue the squabbling for a moment.' I steered Tom back to the courtyard, figuring that Sid was probably more than capable of handling her own brother. We went over and stood by my car.

'Suffolk have passed information that an as yet unnamed male has been asking of the whereabouts of Sid. This unnamed male has been quite forceful in trying to obtain information. DCI Moore believes that Sid needs moving so that she's less easy to track down, at least until we know more. Do you know what that means?' his level gaze gave nothing away.

'Is this to be immediate?' my mind was working ahead, knowing where I could take her.

'I'm told that would be prudent.'

'Is there anything more, any more detail? Possible likely identity of this unnamed male? Motive? Location? Anything at all?' I asked, sometimes my information varied from that the police held, anything was useful now.

Tom shook his head. 'No, nothing more, but we're working on the basis that it's connected to the other four murders, although as yet there's no direct evidence. We've no real idea how far this has gone but I'm thinking that you probably know the form better than I do. All these years, Jake and I still don't know who you really are.'

I ignored his unspoken question and stood for a moment, thinking. There was sudden shouting! Shouting from inside the house - I was back in at speed.

Chapter Thirty-Two

'LET GO OF ME! JOSH! FOR FUCKS SAKE LET GO OF ME!' Sid was shouting and there was fear in her voice.

I ran into the kitchen in time to see Josh holding her up against the cupboards, one hand holding both of hers together behind her head. He had his back to me, legs spread as he tried to hang on to her and then drew back his free hand as if to slap her. Brother or not, I was in there then.

'JAKE!' she screamed as she tried to pull away from his grip.

Josh span around releasing her quickly and swung that hand, now a fist, at me, his eyes black with fury. I was already in range, one hand to easily block him and another hand on his shoulder combined with a nifty, but excruciating, little move that dropped him instantly. He writhed on the floor roaring as if I'd stabbed him; I must confess that, at that moment, I hadn't thought of making it a pain free drop for him. Tom stepped in behind.

'Need some help?'

'Sort him out, would you?'

I stepped around Josh to go to Sid. Recovering, Josh made another lunge for me from the floor, went for my leg, I felt his fingers closing around my ankle. In his other hand he was now holding the knife Sid had been using.

This was rapidly becoming something it shouldn't and there wasn't enough room in here for all of us as well as Josh's aggression. I needed to stop him once and for all. At speed I dropped my weight back away from him, kicked the knife hard out of his hand and released my ankle then, before he'd chance to blink, became someone else just for him - someone much, much more scary. No time left anymore for being nice to Sid's brother.

I launched a very fast strike with the back of my right fist direct to his face, using my left fist to balance it, intensified and combined both moves with a full volume kiai, tremendously loud in this small space. I stopped the strike millimetres from his face, at the point when he must have thought, with complete certainty, that I was actually going to hit him and hit him very, very hard. He froze, eyes tight shut, breath sharply inhaled, waiting. Time seemed to stop just long enough for him to realise that although I hadn't hit him, he was probably now the one in danger. I bent down, listened to his panting breath and whispered very quietly into the air beside his ear.

'Back up, Mr Fielding, next time you raise even an eyebrow to your sister, I won't be so understanding.'

I straightened up immediately and left him lying on the floor with only his pride hurt, leaving it to Tom to drag him out. Sid stared at us all there, rigid and wide eyed for a moment, uncomprehending of exactly what had gone on. I led her through to the next room, shutting the door behind us.

There had been a smell about Josh when I'd leaned down to him, for all his front with the knife, he'd been clearly well out of his depth and I'd scared him more than he would ever want to admit. He was obviously not a man used to front lines, he didn't have the balls for it (or the bladder control) however much he shouted and postured.

'It's ok, Sid. Tom will calm him down. Are you ok, did he hurt you?'

'I've never ever known him so angry, never! Fuck! He was going to hit me… Why? Why did he do that?' she was pale with shock, disbelief and fear, all rolled into one. 'He told me to get you to leave! That I wasn't to keep seeing you! Shouting like he can tell me what to do! Told him to bugger off. He just lost it!'

A soft knock at the door and Tom appeared again.

'Is everything ok? Josh is now outside but I can't get much that makes sense from him. I'm going to take him off for a while, let him calm down.'

I was actually pleased that it was Tom that had come with Moore's instructions. If it had been Moore himself, Josh would be heading into custody now and I might be on the list for a verbal slap myself.

'That's a good idea, thanks, Tom. I think we'll just carry on here as planned.'

'Understood, I'll let Moore know,' he went to leave and then turned back. 'Good call, Jake, that was beginning to get surprisingly messy. It appears that he may need more than just a clean pair of trousers now,' he smiled loosely, turned on his heel and left.

'Sid, come on, I think you need a change of scenery tonight. Get your stuff and pack a suitcase for Finn.'

Holding her face with my hands, I rubbed away her tears with my thumbs.

'Get enough for a few days, ok?'

'Um…ok… What about the food, I haven't finished cooking?'

'Leave that. Chuck it all in the fridge; you can save it for later.' I wanted her out of here now, just in case anyone else turned up, 'We can get something on the way.'

'Are we going now? Why can't we wait until the morning?'

She was thinking this through too much and I didn't want to say anything more until I had her somewhere not so obvious.

'Jake, what are you not telling me?'

She stepped back away, cautious again. 'I'm not going anywhere until you tell me. I'm sure you'll have noticed that I'm having a complicated day. Aside from that, my brother comes here freaking out, Tom is all cloak and dagger, you become seriously terrifying and then expect me to just ignore it all, to pack a bag and just go with you. There's too much going on and this is becoming a bit too dramatic, even for my world. I have a life, I'm supposed to be riding on Friday and Saturday and I really don't have time to be swanning off without a very good reason. So, can you give me a very good reason?'

'Someone is trying to find you, someone who appears not to have your best interests in mind. I need to get you to a safe place, I am now officially instructed to get you to a safe place as we don't have time to hang about,' I lifted her chin, 'is that a good enough reason?'

I watched a range of emotions flit over her face. She could argue, many did, she could go in any direction now – I hoped she wouldn't.

'Yep, Dr Steel, that'll do for now as a very good reason. Give me five and I'll be ready to go. Are you sure about Finn?'

'Of course, we can't go without the Jedi.' I grinned and she laughed.

'You see, to me, this is terrifying, a life threatening situation and yet you... *you* can still make me laugh. My world is usually ordered and a little dull, what have you done to it?'

'This is what I do best, ma'am, it's what I'm trained for. Have I ever mentioned my certificates?'

****

As soon as she went upstairs to pack, I touched some numbers into my phone. The phone responded by asking me to speak a name; I gave the first name on my list and instantly it was ringing. Curtain up, here we go.

'Hello?' a man's voice answered, gravelly deep.

'John.'

'Jake? Jake is that you?' his voice went up an octave.

'Yep, John, it's me.'

157

'Bloody hell, it's good to hear you! It has been too long! Is this business or pleasure?'

'Bit of both. Are you up for house guests?'

'When?'

'Tonight, actually it will probably be early hours, five hours or so from now.'

'Can I ask who?'

'Me and someone else.' Deliberately obtuse I know.

'You know that you're always welcome. I'll get Cath to sort it.'

'Thanks, I'm sorry to spring this on you.'

'No, it's a pleasure. I look forward to your infrequent visits, so does Cath. Manda will be in the bath for the rest of the night now, beautifying herself in case she can finally catch your eye!'

'John, this is sensitive.'

'Oh, right. You aren't here then?'

'That's correct. And… hmm, how to put this… it is also personal.'

'How exciting! Can't wait now.' I could hear the pleasure in his voice. 'So who's the someone else? I'm thinking that I probably need to know if I'm asking Cath for one bedroom or two?'

'Details later so don't ask but one room will be fine.'

'Jake! Jake Steel! You sly dog! I'd better let Manda down gently, she'll be in her room for a week and I'll get no sense from her.'

My uncle, John Steel, worth his weight in gold as an all-round top man but also as a sometime provider of safe houses as required. His company was always good.

'Your someone else. Is it a serious someone? Do I need to be extra nice?'

'That's classified, John, need to know and all that. You don't at the moment - need to know that is.'

'Well, well. Soon, Jake, soon then. I may stay up, keep me posted.'

He was incorrigible; I could picture him, sitting in the chair by the Aga, a large whisky in a glass on the warming plate beside him. I disconnected and turned to Sid who had come back with a bag.

'Are you ready? Got all that you need?'

'Think so, I travel light anyway. Finn has his overnight bag and his light sabre for emergencies,' her eyes flashed, 'is there anything else?'

'Nope, just you now. You may need to turn that burn down though as

I'm having trouble ordering my thoughts.'

Keep it light, let her feel like this is an adventure not survival.

She laughed and shook her head. 'Come on, dude, let's rock and roll.'

Locked up the house, set the alarms and checked the outbuildings were secure. Too late, I remembered that the Land Rover was still at the yard; it would just have to stay there for now. I shadowed Sid the whole time and Finn galloped about headlessly not at all sure what was going on.

'Someone will keep an eye on the house whilst you aren't here. Try not to worry about anything for a bit.' I opened the back door for Finn and put her bags into the boot. 'Let's go.'

Chapter Thirty-Three

As we drove, the phone rang in my pocket automatically interrupting the music playing, without looking at Sid I answered.

'Go ahead,' my reply picked up by the car's discreet microphones.

'Tarvos?' a voice that could have been anyone, of any age. 'Available for an update?'

Tarvos; I shared the name with a very distant and very small moon that mooched around the orbit of Saturn, appropriately hanging on the dark side and rarely seen.

'You're on speaker and I'm not alone.'

A brief pause whilst checking occurred. They double checked with themselves over everything.

'Confirm company is the target?' the voice, now speaking Mandarin, asked.

'Correct.' I answered, also in Mandarin, thinking I wasn't going to mention the Jedi on the back seat, reckoned he wouldn't talk out of turn. I glanced at Sid, these kinds of phone conversations tended to sound worse than they were, the language thing was going to make it even more confusing for her.

'We have a positive ID on the unnamed male.'

'And?'

'He's a known defective.'

A nasty bastard then.

'Assume all safe house precautions.'

'Everything is already in place.'

'At all times, Tarvos, backup available as required.'

I looked across to her again; she was staring with wide eyes as if she no longer knew who I was. The line disconnected and the music began to play again softly in the darkness as we sped along. I felt her eyes burning into me.

'That was more than a bit surreal. What language was that? What's going on? Is this what you talked about before? Is this covert work? Is that what this is about?' she rattled out a string of breathless questions.

'Mandarin, but it's not nearly as exciting as it sounds. The heart of this is that we've four murders and intelligence that you've been directly threatened. So, as there is a very real reason to believe that you may be in danger, I'm simply taking you out of range.'

She sighed and looked out the window into the darkness.

'It's strange but the man I know is a professor of languages who's been asked to help the police investigating some horrible murders. But, after what happened at home and now…are you fluent in Mandarin?' she turned to look at me, 'I don't doubt you, Jake, but I think now is the time to tell me a little bit more.'

I watched the road for a moment, thinking. This was another of those times when the words loaded up ready to roll; she was simply far too important, I would have to go with my gut on this.

'You're right, of course. You knew about a covert role independent of the police but now you're finding out that there's a little more to that work than you expected. But before I go into all that, I need you to understand, to really know that you're very special to me and that fact alone constantly astounds me. Sometimes I can't believe the truth of it and wonder if I'm going to eventually wake up on a mountain somewhere with a rock on my head, only to find out this has all been a concussion related hallucination.'

She reached over and touched my hand. I'd been right to go with instinct. To come away with me like this, after all that had happened to her and regardless of what she felt, it was a brave move.

'I'm sure you know that within the horse racing industry there are some global big players, with wallets stuffed so full they could wipe out a third world country's debt with their small change. Occasionally, the moves those particular players make can affect infrastructures as huge as governments. That kind of wealth can bring, even inadvertently, an element of corruption with it.

'Imagine then, that there's a covert international authority within the Thoroughbred world, not one that anyone will ever hear about, but imagine that such a body exists and that it might be triggered into motion when something occurs that needs sorting out. Loosely, that's what I do. It's my job to make sure that everyone is playing fair and being nice. I do actually have a doctorate in languages but I was head hunted, it isn't something you can apply for and it is considered unusual for someone my age to hold the position that I do. I have… certain skills and abilities that made me of interest. For example, I speak ten languages fluently, can get by in about six more but that's probably not my real skill. My role isn't widely known, DCI Moore does know now but only out of necessity; Tom doesn't.

'And so, although I'm yet to be completely up to speed on what's known, my covert role was already triggered with regard to you by Gabriel Wallace's death. The situation has alerted this authority, let's call it the bloodstock police, and the wheels are turning. That is why you're sitting in a car with me instead of sleeping in your bed. And that's also one of the reasons why I was a little heavy with your brother.'

'If we were at home now, I very much doubt we'd be sleeping,' she kept her face deadpan and then let out one of her radiant smiles, 'so where are we going exactly?'

'Still Newmarket. It's the last place anyone would look, essentially straight into the lion's den and often you can't see what's right under your nose. We're going to stay for a day or so with my uncle, John; he has a small private stud and he's helped me out before. He used to be part of the same team as me, but he's now semi-retired. He has a wife, Cath, she's a blast, you'll like her and then there's my cousin Manda who would be about nineteen, still living at home. Cath and John obviously know what I do but Manda thinks I'm employed by the Garda.'

'Am I still going to be able to ride on Friday and Saturday? Is that still possible?'

'I hope so, sometimes matters are resolved very quickly. The fact that we're here means that there'll already be a massive amount going on behind the scenes. I've moved someone before and then found that it was all sorted after one night. I can't guarantee that, of course. The safe houses we use are all over the world, we activate them as we need, appropriate to situation and the target.'

'Do you move people often?'

'Not really. Sometimes it isn't that kind of issue. But I've never had to do this with someone like you; usually it's very dull, no interaction, all sunglasses and dark suits. This is much more fun,' I grinned at her; 'Good job you like your sports exciting!'

She rolled her eyes. 'I do hope you are taking this seriously, Dr Steel or will I need to wake the Jedi for back up?'

'No, let him catch up on his beauty sleep. Are you hungry? I feel an M5 sandwich urge and at least the coffee is good at the services.'

****

We arrived at the outskirts of Newmarket at about two in the morning. Sid had slept on and off as I drove, eventually off the motorway and on through quiet lanes until we got to the stud. I pulled up to the entrance and called John.

Huge and very solid gates swung open automatically, I drove through and watched them close again through the rear view mirror. The road wound on through trees with post and rail fencing on either side, not much else was visible in the dark, until we got to the main house. The tarmac road became a gravel drive and the tyres of the car scrunched around to the front door. Lights were on, we'd been waited up for.

'Sid?' I touched her arm, 'wake up, we're here. Are you ready to meet some of the Steel clan? John's side of the family will make me look very staid.'

I got out and went around to her door, letting Finn out at the same time. He bounded off, peeing up everything he could find as he went. Sid stretched like a cat, I caught her around her waist and pulled her in close. A light came on and the big front door opened, letting out a rectangle of orange light onto the gravel. Finn appeared again, barking.

'Come in, come in!' A shadow in the doorway, instantly blinded by the light, we could only make out an outline. 'Oh, who are you? And you're very handsome, aren't you?' Finn had hurtled into the house as if he lived there.

'Hello Cath, long time and all that. Thanks for putting up and waiting up; you could have just left the key under the mat.' I walked to the door, taking Sid with me by the hand.

'Is that the recommended security procedures they teach these days? It's all softly, softly and must respect their rights. I say shoot the bastards or castrate them or both!' The shadow laughed loudly at its own cleverness.

'Cath! You don't change, do you? Have you and John been on the shorts all night? Cath, this is Sid, Sid, Cath.' I walked in through to the hall.

Cath, visible now, blue jeans and a red sweatshirt with Keep Calm, Kick Butt emblazoned across the front; she was in her late-fifties but looked younger. Full face of makeup even at this time of the night and spiked blonde hair, as aunts go, she was one of a kind.

'Sid, it is a pleasure,' she hugged Sid as if she'd known her for years and then launched herself at me.

'Jake, look at you! Don't you just get more gorgeous with each passing year? He's just too delicious, isn't he, Sid?'

I covered my eyes with one hand and groaned. 'Take no notice, she's not too tightly wrapped, it's a family trait.' I took Sid's hand again and pulled her through the hall. 'Where's the main man then? Have you locked him in the cupboard again?'

I let my voice become louder, waiting for John to respond. Finn bounded on ahead, no doubt thinking this was a huge adventure, down the long hall to the kitchen at the back of the house.

'Jake, I hear you! Come on boy, let's see you!' his gravelly voice boomed out. 'Blimey who's this? Hello mate, don't let Cath see you, she's a soft touch for your sort.'

I went into the kitchen and there was John exactly as I'd imagined, sitting in his chair by the Aga, a glass full of whisky or something similar on the warming plate. He wore a Harley Davidson t-shirt with black jeans, his dark hair tousled as if he'd just woken up. Strong, capable, with a sense of humour that made him the life and soul of any party. When I was younger he'd always made me think rock star and I still held that view of him now. Finn was sitting beside the chair, a hairy paw on John's lap.

'Don't get up, lazy bastard, we'll see ourselves in.'

He slapped his legs laughing loudly. A longstanding joke but John was paralysed from the waist down and spent his time now in a wheelchair.

'You're the bastard yourself for not coming to see me nearly enough. Come here and bend down so that I can give you a head butt!' he reached up, hugging me hard instead. 'So show her then, where is she?'

'John, this is Sid Fielding, Sid, John Steel.' I introduced them, sitting back down at the broad kitchen table and stretching out my legs.

'Sid... Now you look familiar, Sid – don't tell me, it'll come. Yes, you're Sid Fielding, jockey. I'm right, aren't I?' he grinned up at her.

'Yes, in one. Thank you, I'm flattered, not many people recognise me.'

Cath came in, stood behind the chair and put her hands on John's shoulders. He touched her hand in an easy gesture of affection.

'So, is the kettle going on?' I asked.

'Kettle! Jake! Don't use that dreadful word. We've polished the coal and ironed the cat so get the glasses, Cath; this is a celebration not a meeting of the WI.' John turned his attention to Sid again, 'So what did you do to Jake to make him see sense? I've been telling him to get a decent woman, or even an indecent one, for years but he never listens to me so it seems you've got him sorted at last!'

'John! Let the girl be. Sid, go sit with Jake otherwise John will be flirting with you all night, what's left of it now.' Cath spoke, her back to us, head in a cupboard.

John's eyes sparkled as Sid came and sat down, sliding her hand into mine as she did so. Coming here, whether I was running or not, always felt like coming home and coming here with Sid seemed very easy.

'So Jake, aside from bringing a gorgeous woman into our house and a gift for Cath, what have you been up to?'

Cath had a serious obsession with lurchers; Finn was the gift to which he referred. She was in-between rescue dogs as the last lurcher, a big brindle dog, didn't make old bones and she was still reconciling herself to the loss.

'You can't keep the dog as he's part of my team, cut backs you see, lurchers can feed themselves, no hefty expense claims.'

'Right,' said Cath, 'we've wine, whisky, brandy, beer and...' she held her hand sideways to her mouth as if telling a secret, '...coffee, tea or council pop.'

'I'd love a coffee but for John, I'll do a small whisky with it. Sid? Just to translate, council pop is actually water.'

'I'll have the same, thanks, black.'

'Black! You need more calories! Thankfully I no longer need to worry about watching my weight. I don't even need to worry now if I get a bit tipsy, can't exactly fall over anymore.'

'You can't ride half a side of any horse! Falling over is the least of your worries as you give me the devil of a job if you have too much to drink! Do you know that I've taken to going to bed with a stick to beat sense into him!' she stared at us wide eyed as if she was scared by this thought.

It was the early hours of the morning and they were still on fine form.

'See, what did I tell you? Load of nutters,' I squeezed Sid's hand.

'Jake, so come on — what's the story. Its safe as Manda's out staying overnight with a friend from college,' John wheeled closer to the table; 'Stop me if I'm digging where I shouldn't.'

Cath turned from putting the kettle on and narrowed her eyes at him.

'John Steel, pull your horns in.'

'Jake... come on lad... tell an old man the word on the street,' he ignored her.

'Sid's up to speed but there's not much to tell as yet. We've four murders, one you will certainly have heard of. In addition, an unknown is seeking Sid, been reported here and elsewhere. Threats have been made and we've come here to go to ground for a few days. I'll sniff around and see who knows what. Have you heard anything out of the ordinary?'

'No, not directly, let me think on that though. There's been something going down about Gabriel that might prove a route to try first,' he looked pensive for a moment, the Steel mental search engine had kicked in. 'How significant is this?'

'At all times.' I said.

'Oh,' his face fell and then he smiled broadly. 'You really do get all the fun. I used to get some dry old crusty and you get something delicious of your own instead. I thought you'd be hanging off a mountain somewhere.'

'No, I got Dartmoor instead. That's where Sid's from, she rides for David Flint.'

'How do you find him, Sid? I knew him some years ago.'

'He's ok, a tendency to like the sound of his own voice if he can roar at people, but other than that he's fine really. He trains consistently, some good horses, nothing world beating. I'm riding one of his, if all this calms down, on Saturday at Exeter that's if he's still allowed to have runners.'

'I noticed you're down to ride at Fontwell on Friday as well.'

'Yes, for Mr Carter. Don't know who's madder, the trainer or the owner!' she laughed. 'The trainer is someone I could take your stick to Cath, but the horse… the horse is worth all the hassle.'

I sat at ease now knowing she was safe within these walls, feeling the tiredness from the journey rushing up to greet me as I tipped the small glass of whisky into black coffee.

The kitchen had been unchanged for years, the heart of the house with a big back door which led out into a boot room and then the main yard. The room was kept constantly warm by the Aga, clothes drying perpetually above it on a rack. Scrubbed wood worktops which were liberally littered with books, papers, assorted bits of leather and the usual collection of mystery horse objects. On the far wall, a collection of photographs, horses in every shape and form, doing everything that horses do, interspersed with rosettes, trophies and betting slips that won. There were people too, family from all over the globe in a variety of poses; snapshots of gatherings and new arrivals. Extended was a good term for their side of the Steel clan.

Sid spoke, 'Cath, can you point me in the direction for the loo?'

'Down the hall, just to the left and I usually tell visitors to close their eyes when they go in, Sid, particularly if they're of a delicate disposition,' she winked but didn't explain further. Sid looked puzzled as she left the room.

'Is it as it was?' I had to ask.

'Even better now! You have a look later. We had the builders in couple of weeks ago and one of them was in there for hours!' she grinned broadly. 'Funny thing was he always came out looking a little dazed!'

'Jake,' John interrupted, 'how much trouble is this? I'm getting a bad feeling about Sid.'

'I don't know but I'll keep you up to speed because I'll almost certainly need your help. You probably know more than I do at the moment.'

I tried not to worry him. Gwil was dead and John was in his wheelchair because of jobs that went wrong, we never talked about it but not everyone came quietly.

'And what about you and the jockey? Looks like you've landed on your feet,' he raised his eyebrows. 'What came first, the job or the girl?'

'Mmm…can't remember, it just sort of happened.' I tried to keep it vague and looked down at my cup; I didn't enjoy this kind of personal scrutiny or those kind of questions.

Cath was studying me closely, her eyes penetrating. 'Jake… Jake, if I'm not mistaken you look like a man in love. Halle-bloody-lujah! After all this time! I'm so pleased for you. She's gorgeous too,' she reached across the table to touch my hand. 'Hold onto to it, Jake, you can never have too much love, however you stumble upon it.'

Sid walked back in, a smile twitched on her lips.

'Well?' Cath was eager to know. 'What do you think of our privy?'

Sid laughed - a lot - tears ran. 'I've never seen anything quite so liberating in all my life! Where did you get some of those pictures, they're hilarious!'

'Years and years of collecting! We've a reputation for having the filthiest toilet in the country, so to speak!'

I knew that the walls of that room were papered in cartoons of what was essentially horse porn. It was an acquired taste but it always caused a great deal of interest.

'Right, you two, let's show you to your room otherwise there will be no point in going to bed. Jake, get the bags, I'll take Sid up.'

I took Finn out, checked my messages of which there were none. The wheels of this kind of job turned constantly so no news was definitely good news. Back in with the bags and upstairs with Finn leading the way.

Chapter Thirty-Four

'Are you ok? This is quite a big step from where you were yesterday morning; it does seem to have gathered speed somehow.'

Sid was sitting on the edge of the bed staring at her feet when I came back with Finn.

I'm ok, at least I think so. This whole scene is so weird its good, if you can understand me.'

I lay back onto the bed, pulling her with me, stroking the strands of hair that fell in front of her ears.

'There's a lot more to you than meets the eye, isn't there?' she whispered.

'I could say the same about you. You're dealing with this all as if you've done it before.'

'Am I? I certainly haven't done anything like this before. Blimey, its like something from a film, I'm not even sure I knew that people like you really existed. What made you choose this as a career?'

I looked away. 'Oh, this and that.'

'Aha, an incomplete answer,' she touched my face with one finger, turning me back towards her. 'You don't have to tell me.'

'There isn't much to tell. Same old story: teenage lad heading into a bad place, at risk of getting lost and someone showed him an alternative. It was luck mainly, nothing more.'

'You said that you were headhunted - that you have abilities that made you of interest? Aside from the languages, what do you mean by abilities?'

I was being gently probed; she was checking me out again, getting details that would confirm that she was safe. Answers, everyone wanted answers. I wasn't sure I had the right ones to give.

'I know why you're asking and I'm not deliberately evading, but my whole life has been shrouded in secrecy for so long, it has become intrinsic to who I am.'

'There must be more. You strike me as a brain rather than brawn man, even though your brawn is stunning.'

'I'm impervious to flattery.'

'Your answers contract the closer I get,' she kissed me gently. 'Let's change the subject, it's too late or too early for unnecessary cross examinations. Tell me about Luci instead.'

'Ah... Luci is... actually I don't know where to begin with her either. I have to be careful what I say, she always seems to know. I'd have to say that she's a lot like you - reckless, dramatic, impetuous...'

She pushed away, sat astride me and narrowed her eyes. 'I hope that those are all compliments or will I be asking the aunt for the stick!' she slipped into a very good Irish accent for the last few words. I laughed.

'Sid, when I think what you've been through since yesterday morning, I'm truly surprised by you. Where do you find your strength? How are you coping with all of this really?'

She lay back on the bed beside me with a sigh and I turned onto my side so that I could look at her. Leaning forward and pushing one hand up under my shirt to lay flat on my chest, hot against my skin, she kissed me with her fingers locked in my hair, holding me and moulding her body to mine down its full length. Slightly out of breath she moved back and looked directly into my soul with that sea blue of hers.

'Simply because of you; you make it possible for me to cope. Even though you tell me next to nothing, you've never let me down. You have empathy, understanding, strength. Getting me here, knowing that I needed to be here, knowing all the right things to do and say so that I can cope. Loving, not judging and just being the most incredible person I've ever met. That is why. The only one who's strong in this is you.'

She wrapped one leg over mine, pressing herself into me, the heat from her body rioting about on my skin. I leaned over, kissing her neck, under her jaw, that soft skin behind her ear, the smell of her, the taste of her, I was losing myself. I'd nothing further to say out loud and thankfully Finn slept through it all.

****

It was light outside when I woke. I lay still for a while, just thinking about the situation that we were in. Sid was literally wrapped around me, I pushed the quilt away a little, the heat from her intense. My arm under her neck lying against her back and, as if of their own accord, my fingertips found those long scars. It was so hard to believe that a man could have done that to her, done that to her and she'd thought it love. I found that I was imagining how it might have been for her just after that had happened, wondering how she dealt with the wounds, the pain, the fear. I still couldn't relate the person that had gone through that with this woman that lay here with me.

This woman who could make someone like me laugh, who could lift my mood with one flash of her eyes. This woman who could surprise daily with her words, her thoughts, her take on life. She could drag me along, locked with her into some exquisite free fall time after time and then come back full of glowing mischief and start it all over again. How could that person have been beaten and attacked and dominated in every way and, yet, still remained whole?

She had. Sid had.

This was the magical creature that lay here, clinging with soft skin; it was her breath against my neck, the curve of her shape stretched over mine. I think I fell in love with her all over again that morning.

Chapter Thirty-Five

It was Finn who woke her, his wet nose against her legs. His need to be taken outside was greater, he thought, than any earth shattering musings on my part. He simply couldn't understand why I wouldn't move her. I was patently awake and he had needs; so did I but I still wasn't going to wake her, have her unpeel herself and move away, not just yet. But Finn had no patience with such sentiment, he needed to go out and someone should shift themselves and sort it for him. He was very forward with his nose, not a move I would have tried but, when you're a dog, these things aren't frowned on in the same way. She jumped, I probably would have done too, a moment of disorientation and then realisation.

'Finn, bugger off and lie down, there's a good chap,' she lay back against my chest, closing her eyes again with a soft sigh.

I looked at him silently saying, well good try, you gave it your best, just cross your paws you'll be fine. I swear he narrowed his eyes and then he barked a single don't-you-bloody-dare-ignore-me demand bark with a capital B. She opened her eyes, lifting her face and resting her chin on her hands.

'Finn needs his morning lamppost,' I said, 'and he thinks Jedis need much more attention that he's getting. I'll take him if you like — do you want tea or coffee?'

'What a cup of tea here in bed, is such luxury allowed?'

She was adorable this morning, all blurred edges. I can't think of anyone I've ever known that I could say that about.

'On rare occasions I believe it's permitted. Come on, unpeel yourself, Yoda will be having a spiritual crisis on the carpet otherwise. You stay here and I'll see to room service.' I rolled her over to free myself, she held on so that I was almost on top of her, immediately arching into me, wrapping hands around my neck. 'Sid, you're impossible to resist almost all of the time, don't make this any more difficult.'

'I never knew you were such a grouch in the mornings,' she tutted. 'Ok, go, make Yoda happy,' she grinned. 'Such a treat not waking up until its light, it feels very decadent.'

'We didn't get here until two-ish, a lie in was almost bound to happen; especially as I don't recall you going straight to sleep.' Rummaging around in my bag for clean clothes, I got dressed.

She leaned over the side of the bed and picked up my t-shirt from where it had ended up last night, this morning, whatever it was called; putting it on and pulling it straight over the tops of her legs, she went over to the window.

'Is it ok to look out? How much are we hiding?' she looked apprehensive.

'You're ok, the windows are like yours, you can't see in.' I went over to stand behind her and kissed her neck. 'That looks better on you than me.'

'That's simply because you're already unfairly gorgeous and the rest of us plain Janes need all the moments we can get. Now where's my cup of tea?'

I went with a joyous lurcher, he thundered down the stairs and into the kitchen, skidding through a handbrake turn by the back door and then piling out to check in with the new day. Kettle on, I went in search of John.

'Want anything from the kettle?' I asked when I found him at his desk.

'Coffee, none of that instant crap though, is there any news?' he span his chair so that he faced me. His hair still making him look slightly surprised, but the Harley Davidson shirt had been replaced by a black retro style Space Invaders one.

'Just checking in now, dog's gone out is that ok? Can he cause any trouble?'

'No, shouldn't think so. Cath will spot him and keep him entertained.'

I went back to the kitchen and rang in.

'Tarvos for an update.'

'One moment please, Sir.'

Another voice. 'Tarvos? The danger has been identified and located. It will be removed by close of play today.'

'Is there any other news?'

'Check your messages by other means. Intelligence has been updated.'

So someone knew something, this was getting more like it. I badly needed answers for Sid, for myself and to keep her safe, regardless of the update.

I took in John's coffee, left Finn to introduce himself to all outside and, with tea, went back to Sid.

A little while later, we were alone in the kitchen, trying to organise some breakfast with the distraction of some very juvenile giggling. She was sitting on the work top with a piece of toast between two fingers, instructing me on the fine art of butter spreading, or lack of it, for jockeys who struggled with their weight. It had reached a point of ridiculous silliness and she was almost incapacitated with laughter, I'd told her that she was just too childish for words and she'd trapped me with her legs. Things had gone from bad to verging on the indecent then and in the middle of all this, Manda stalked into the kitchen with two of her friends. I wasn't sure who felt worse.

Manda, my cousin, at nineteen, was young and impressionable. She glared as if she'd caught me doing something unspeakably horrendous, stared at Sid as if she was the devil incarnate and then strode stiffly on out of the kitchen with her friends trotting behind her. Sid and I dissolved again into helpless laughter.

'Stop! Sid, will you stop now! You're going to get me into such trouble! Everyone here thinks I'm some super controlled, cool copper who's never had a day of fun in his life! We've shattered all Manda's illusions — she may need counselling!'

'Jake, have you no idea? She's going to want you now, mark my words, you'll have to lock doors!' she hiss-whispered and then pulled me into her, kissing me hard with quite unnecessary passion.

'Bloody hell, get a bucket of water!' Cath stood in the doorway with one boot off and the other in the boot jack, her face full of delight at us.

'Hello,' I smiled at her, Sid, head down on my shoulder, was praying to the time gods that that hadn't just happened. However, I work on the basis that its best to just brazen it out if you can't escape. 'Have you found an errant lurcher who thinks he's on some 18-30 rabbit and hare holiday?'

'Oh yes, he's a treasure, I'll happily adopt him at any time,' she put the kettle onto the Aga. 'Sid, please don't worry; Manda, however, may not see it the same.'

'Ah, Manda… Cath, Manda has already come in, with a couple of friends. I don't think she likes me very much anymore.' I had to forewarn, which is forearmed so they say. 'We're going to head into John's office, low profile and all that.'

I took Sid and went to John; he seemed delighted to see her. She found a corner and sat down, listening to him telling her about a betting scam he was working on. Our work wasn't really known by anyone not directly employed by it and having Sid here with me was necessary but unnerving. Perhaps, without having to directly tell her, she'd get those answers she sought.

'Sid, usually you'd just have to sit around in a room somewhere twiddling your thumbs and being bored but safe as all good damsels in distress should be; but as it is you, do you want to hang out in here with us? I can't guarantee you won't be bored but it might be slightly more interesting than staring at walls or watching daytime tv.'

'Of course I want to stay here. I'll sit and observe what you do to earn a crust. It will be much, much more entertaining than whatever is on television, I suspect.'

Sitting at the far desk, I connected a headpiece bluetooth to my phone and rang Moore.

'Steel, thank God! I need you to look over something quickly. Online, usual procedures, can you access now as we speak?'

'Yes. One moment.' I pressed mute on the receiver.

'John, can I have access for police intelligence?'

He nodded, typed something into a keyboard and the screen in front blinked a password box. I typed in a code and another screen appeared; I spoke back into the headpiece.

'On line.'

Instantly text appeared; a detailed report of an investigation from Drugs. The source of the particular batch of ketamine that Alan Wozniak had in his system was now identified. A veterinary practice was named, further details of the partners there and then a list of people who had provided funding for a new and technically cutting edge equine hospital.

Two details stood out. One of the partners had already been under surveillance for possible supply of controlled drugs, although ultimately nothing had been proven at the time and, second, the company who'd donated the most money, in terms of millions, was owned by Seb Fielding. Sid's vociferous big brother.

That was what I needed, a good place to start and Sid's brothers were a good place to start but then, in truth, I'd known that for a while.

Chapter Thirty-Six

'Connections?' Moore asked as the screen went blank, all the details gone.

'Yes, two.' I stared at nothing and recalled information to my mind, seeking further details from that which I already knew.

'First, partner at hospital listed was under obs for supply, no further action at time. Check records against Jones and Partners, number 10057826750, chief investigating officer at the time was DSI Griggs, investigation paused. Secondly, investor of 9.8 mill, please note name — company owned by significant connection.'

'Who?'

'I'll have to send that.' That was the downside of Sid being here, I'd have to watch what I said.

'Good. All ok?'

'Yes to all.'

'Keep safe.'

He was gone. I scanned through the details of the documents I'd just seen; my mind has a thing for what might be called unnecessary detail and, try as I might, I've never been able to suppress its quirks. I could visualise data as if I was seeing it and read it back, checking details even a long time after I'd seen the original. This ability was another one of the reasons that I came to the attention of my current employers in the first place. Conversations, faces, details, once seen or heard however briefly, they just stayed there in my memory waiting for the day when I could use them. Now this new data — was this coincidence or was it a connection? Cross referencing with anything else I knew, nothing stood out clearly, I had to find out more.

'John, can I use the system again for a bit?'

'Of course, go ahead.'

Cath came in with a tray of cups, biscuits and Finn. Sid blushed as she took a mug of tea.

'Don't worry, Sid. That quite made my day,' Cath spoke softly, a whisper over John and I working but John heard it.

'What's this? What made your day?' he was all attention now, eyes bright.

'Oh John, you weren't supposed to hear. It was nothing, just Sid and Jake in the kitchen, umm…expressing themselves' she stood next to him, wide eyes willing him to drop it. 'It's embarrassing Sid so let's leave it, shall we?'

'Why do I miss everything?' he stared at me and then Sid.

'John,' Sid said clearly, 'it was a kiss ok, nothing more. A slightly more than should be out in the daylight kiss but that's all. No heaving and panting, no body parts, just a kiss,' she grinned and I had to laugh. That was just so Sid. I could have kissed her again at that moment.

'Ah, to be young and in love. We used to be like that, didn't we?' John reached up for Cath's hand.

She bent down to him and whispered, 'We still are John - we just can't manage work tops anymore!'

I went back to the screen, digging, searching for clarity. So, was Seb's involvement with the veterinary practice purely coincidental? He had horses in training and horses at stud, he had money and he was likely to invest in such resources, wasn't he? I rang another contact, this time at Weatherbys, a huge organisation that managed the data involved with Thoroughbreds, from racing through breeding to banking, they did it all.

'Sylvia Freeman's extension please.' I used my Irish accent to its full extent.

'One moment, may I ask who is calling?'

'Tarvos.'

'One moment, Mr Tarvos.'

Smooth, efficient, well-oiled cogs that usually turned without friction.

'Pedigrees, Sylvia Freeman speaking.'

'Sylvie! Lovely to hear your voice as always!'

'Tarvos! My favourite Irishman! How are you?'

'Good, very good now I'm speaking to you.' I glanced up at Sid, watching with one raised eyebrow.

'I need some pedigree information, Sylvie and, as you are my favourite person for such matters, will you help me?' I pressed a small button on the headset as I spoke, there was a slight buzz and then nothing. Our conversation was now scrambled, unintelligible to anyone who might have been trying to pry. Such a system relied on both callers having the necessary equipment which, of course, Sylvie did.

'Tarvos, for you anything. What kind of information?'

'List of horses owned, entirely or in part, racing and breeding, global, corporate and/or personal.'

'Bloody hell! You don't want much do you?'

'Only one name, Sylvie, so don't be going under the desk! Get a valium down yer, slug of gin girl and you'll be right!'

'As if! You know perfectly well I don't touch valium until 6pm and it's far too late in the day for gin.'

'Ah, Sylvie darling, remember I know the contents of your desk drawer. Can you do it?'

'Yes, of course I can. Name please?'

'I need to advise on line.'

'Ok. Hold the line and I'll open the front door for you.'

She was gone for a moment, I stared at the blank screen and then, hey presto, full access to all of Weatherbys' databases.

'Are you in?'

'I sure am. Ready?'

'Go ahead.'

I typed in Sebastian Fielding and waited. Within milliseconds, the screen was active with listings; there were a lot, some in entirety, some barely passing through, a leg or part of a leg. Sebastian Fielding had fingers in many pies. I was quite surprised at the volume of ownership changes though; he was buying and selling regularly. Internationally, he'd interests in all the major racing and breeding centres: Australia, Japan, America, France and, of course, Dubai.

It was his Dubai involvement that interested me the most; knowing what I did now this seemed like a top location to start with. I typed my request for more detail on this country and Sylvie accessed that, guiding me through, opening doors with keys that I'd never hold. Old fashioned pen and paper, I wrote in code: names, people and horses, races and places. Cogs turned and I sensed a pattern emerging.

'Sylvie, you're amazing, can we just work another name through?'

'You said one name! I've not got all day, even for you.'

'Please? I'll bring doughnuts.'

'Oh, go on then. Show me the name.'

I typed in Joshua Fielding. Again a mass of listings, here in the UK and spread wide all over the world. Dubai, let's look at Dubai again. Now I saw the pattern. This was much, much bigger than I could have imagined. But I still didn't know what had upset the balance - this had been ticking along for some time, what made it slide over the edge and into action now?

'Sylvie darling, you're an absolute treasure. I simply wouldn't be able to survive without you. I owe you doughnuts, possibly a box full, with pink icing. Thank you for all your help.'

'Tarvos, be good and stay safe. Come and see me when you're next about. You do my street cred so much good.' Bubbly Sylvie, an all round top girl.

The screen went blank and the line dead, Sylvia Freeman was gone. Another shadowy figure who did something a whole lot more than anyone could ever know. We were everywhere and anywhere, normal and every day, ordinary and often in lowly roles. But it was from the ordinary that the bright lights came. Sylvia Freeman, mid-sixties, looked in person like a storybook granny, twin set and pearls, very staid, very conservative; but she had the mind of a computer and a method of abstract thinking that extracted critical information from the innocuous. She was one of kind.

Sid was still watching, eyes flashing. 'Is this what you do all day, flirt and chat girls up with all that blarney? Pink icing, Jake Steel, pink icing indeed!'

'Um... yes that is modern policing for you. Actually Sylvie was John's bestest first so I have him to thank for the way she is.' I pointed accusingly at John.

John looked up from his screen smiling, 'Want to see a photo of our Sylvie, so as you can see what you're up against?'

Sid nodded, looking back with narrowed eyes.

'Here she is.' John turned his screen slightly, sipping at his coffee as he did so. Sid stood and peered, a broad smile appearing on her face.

Cath came back again, holding the door as she peered around it. 'Jake, can I take Sid out to the paddocks, everyone is on the yards and she's probably finding your work tedious?'

I could tell Cath was desperate to get details; she wanted to know what Sid was about.

'Sid?'

'Yes, love to but is it ok?'

'Cath, usual precautions please and take the radio.' I mentally ran through every possible new risk, now I knew what I did. But I was grateful, in a way, that she wouldn't be in the room as I wanted to ask John's advice.

'Great!' Cath grinned. 'Come on, Sid. Back soon boys; don't swing the lead whilst we're gone. Jake, don't let John get a cork out else you'll get nothing done!'

Sid wouldn't look like Sid when she went to see the horses; Cath was very good at changing people's appearances at the drop of a hat. I'd passed as a woman because of her, been introduced to someone I worked for and he didn't recognise me. I'd faith in Cath's skills and regularly copied her techniques myself when jobs required me to be someone else. Using a radio was quicker and more reliable than phones on the stud and we used an obscure channel, changing it using a code every time we spoke. Even if we were compromised, by the time someone had found the right channel we were gone again. I watched Sid go until she was out of sight.

'John, can we talk? I need some direction.'

'Of course, come round.' He pushed his chair back, shutting the door as I did so, pad and pen, mind full of Sylvie's treasure and the original translation.

I sat facing him and told him what I thought I knew. Once I'd finished he turned immediately back to his keyboard and began typing furiously. Over his shoulder, I watched the pieces come together into a visual form. It was frighteningly complete.

'This is much more than even you can manage even at this stage by yourself,' he looked up, somehow looking older all of a sudden.

'I get what you're saying but I've been working on this for weeks, its still too soon to call in assistance. Let's just poke a fresh stick at it and see what happens, then we'll call in backup.'

If I was right there was a way to find out what had upset the balance, if I could do that there was a good chance we'd get all the players in one hit. The risk always with such operations was that their intelligence, their shadow people, were often as good as ours. A hint of trouble and they would scatter to the four corners of the planet and it would take years to round them up again.

'I sent a cyber-mole with its pockets stuffed full of clickbait, it has caused interesting repercussions.'

John stared. 'I hope it was very, very discreet as hacking is still frowned upon in civilised parts. Many a wrist is being quite sharply slapped for that sort of digging.'

Hacking into people's computer systems for the purpose of gaining intelligence isn't considered to be acceptable behaviour in many parts of the world. Strangely, the Brits are perhaps the most tolerant, it'd been said that such tolerance could have been based on ignorance but, regardless, this was now a world where many a cyber-criminal sat and caused chaos anonymously.

People pretend to be shocked, but the reality is that the majority of the public are far too trusting of the internet, easily providing an endless stream of personal information. The stereotypical image of the hacker only being a spotty lad in his bedroom with the curtains drawn couldn't be further from the truth — it was big business now. Bespoke malware could be designed to fit almost every need, the dark web rife with both spy and malware. All law enforcement agencies use hacking to gain intelligence, they'll deploy any trick to expose cybercriminals. It isn't strictly a case of everything's fair in love and war, but you can't hope to stop a fight if you won't get into the ring.

Hacking from my point of view was just another tool in the box. I didn't go digging for dirt, in fact, mostly I went in to be noticed. I wanted the odd alarm bell to ring, the re-assessing and re-grouping that often occurred when a system thought it was being hacked was often more beneficial than actually hacking it. If someone had something to hide, the possibility of my presence could cause visible panic. Often they ran straight to check on the safe thereby revealing the location of their most precious secrets.

My recent mole had certainly caused a great deal of twitching within several of the companies owned by both Sebastian and Joshua Fielding. Someone had got excited enough to include Sid in their shady deals and that wasn't nice. But, just now, I needed to sit back and wait patiently to see if they'd lead me to the treasure whilst keeping Sid out of range of misfires. On the way to the treasure, I hoped I'd also find a murderer or murderers.

The radio interrupted us.

'Go to ground, we've an unexpected visitor. Coming in the back way,' Cath's voice quiet and calm.

Gathering my paperwork and phone, I slipped out the door and up the stairs. Cath appeared with Sid a minute later, her friends wouldn't have recognised her at first glance.

'Sorry guys, mare owner who thinks he can just turn up when he feels like it. I am right, Jake, that you aren't here?'

'Yes. Is it someone who knows me?'

'Yes, harmless but might say if he saw you. Lay low I'll let you know when he's gone.'

Sid exhaled deeply, pulling off a brunette wig and luminous padded coat as she flopped back on the bed, back to being Sid instead of Essex wag.

'This is exhausting! How do you do this? I wouldn't know if I was coming or going,' she ran her fingers through her hair. 'I've no idea where Finn is. Do you think he's ok?'

'He'll be fine; Cath will make sure of it.' I smiled at her. 'Still having fun though?'

'Oh yes, very much so!'

My phone vibrated at just that moment.

'Identified person has been apprehended and removed. Safe house precaution is considered no longer necessary.' Italian today rather than Mandarin, I went with it.

I disconnected from that call, voice dialled another in English.

'DCI Moore.'

'We have progress and I'm advised that the safe house precaution could be lifted.'

'Are you coming back?'

'No, not yet but on line covert access is requested.'

I needed to pass this by Moore without rattling too many other cages, the fact that this owner had turned up was going to slow me down as I couldn't go back to John's office just yet. If I could pass this using my laptop we could at least carry on as I wasn't anywhere near ready to relax on Sid's protection just yet.

'I can arrange covert on line for 11.15.'

I glanced at my watch, it was five to eleven. The line was dead again.

'What's on now?' Sid sat on the bed, hugging her knees, watching all that I did.

'Just dotting the 'i's' and crossing the 't's'. All very dull, won't be long. But the good news is that the man we were worrying about has been detained.' I connected the laptop to the mobile phone, sitting on the floor facing her, I hoped I could keep the screen private. At 11.15 the mobile vibrated.

I sent the message I'd spent my waiting time typing. It detailed what I knew about Sebastian and Joshua Fielding; it detailed their interests with an oil cartel in Dubai, their possible involvement with a known drug gang that operated from China, all the way and right through to horses in training with David Flint who weren't what they were supposed to be. It also detailed that on Sebastian's bank statements were payments to a bank account that was held, in a roundabout way, by a certain Alan Wozniak – our body number two. Both Alan and John Wozniak were being paid to pretend to be each other and to look the other way when Flint's lorry was carrying more than just horses and hay. Marcus Williams was both business partner and drinking buddy of Sebastian Fielding. As an operation it was beautifully engineered, but I still didn't know why the dynamic had changed. I knew that Marcus Williams was a crook, assumed that John and Alan Wozniak had stuck their noses somewhere they shouldn't – but why kill them? Why kill Gabriel Wallace?

'Big can of worms.' Moore whistled through his teeth down the phone. 'Permission to provoke?'

Moore was in charge of the local murder investigations, I could go over him but better not to. I might need him more than he needed me.

'Do you need permission? I think not.'

'I'm sitting on this for a day or so.'

'That's not prudent.'

'With respect, I'm not always known for my prudence.'

'Go carefully then,' he sighed, 'and I don't want to know about anything that isn't legal.'

Blank screen and dead line. It was on. I would go and see who I could irritate sufficiently so that they'd come out into the open. I smiled to myself; sometimes this was just too boys own to be taken seriously.

Sid was lying on the bed, her chin on her hands, watching intently. 'You like this don't you?'

I shut down the laptop, disconnected the phone and slid it all into a messenger bag.

'You get to go racing and I probably also get to come and watch you.'

She smiled broadly, sea blue glinting.

'Do we have time to finish what we started a little while ago, or is this a chuck it all in the fridge and go moment?'

I tugged her off the bed and onto the floor, she shrieked with laughter.

'I think we need to go back through the menu in some detail before I could possibly answer that!'

Chapter Thirty-Seven

'A moment,' I said, 'I'll be back in a moment.'

As we were heading back into the kitchen my phone rang so I went back into the hallway leaving Sid to be introduced more formally to Manda. Manda still looked like she'd stepped in something unpleasant; I hoped she was going to be nice.

'Go ahead.'

'Just to advise JF is likely to be in your area for a few days, are you aware of any reasons why?'

It had been discovered that Josh was hanging around, which would mean a likely repeat encounter when Sid and I returned.

'Target is riding. That would be the most likely reason.'

'SF is flying to Hong Kong. Both are now under surveillance.'

Seb was obviously off to stick fingers in one of his many pies. I wished I knew what he was up to.

I went back to the kitchen to see how the snarling was coming on. John and Cath were back to the previous night's verbal sparring and, under the table, stretched out in canine casualness was Finn, blissed out post rabbit chasing.

'So, Jake, how long are you staying?' Cath enquired.

'Just one more night and then we need to go. I've got to annoy John this afternoon with some stuff and then I'm done.'

'Am I to back you, Sid? Are you likely to take a place at Fontwell or Exeter?' John asked.

'Each way maybe. The runner at Exeter may surprise but that's just because I made the mistake of telling its owner it would only ever win a race inside a greyhound!' she sniggered and John laughed.

I turned to her, 'You really need to learn to be more honest with your appraisals, Sid. All this girlie fluffiness will do you no good.'

'Fluffy! Fluffy! I hope you're taking notes. I may only ride racehorses but you could learn a lot from me!' she sparked fire straight back.

'Come on, John, let's go do some serious stuff. Thanks for lunch, Cath.'

I was being lined up for a fall, I could sense it and running away seemed a wise plan. Sid stayed with the others and I was glad I didn't have to listen to them. Shutting the door, I sat down near to John's desk.

'Ok, I have police support as well now to see who I can flush out but there's still too many unanswered questions. Do you know anything specific about Gabriel Wallace? His murder is clearly a hot topic but is there any local background I might not have heard?'

'Not much, he was good at keeping his private life very firmly sealed. I do know that he was a nasty piece on occasion, supposed to be a bit rough with his women but that may have just been talk.'

'It isn't... It's hugely sensitive but Sid was, for the want of a better word, groomed by him when she was sixteen. For all that I've done and seen, this kind of thing is so much easier to deal with when it concerns someone you don't know... she was raped when she was sixteen, many times. She has extensive scars and is lucky to have survived him.'

'Bloody hell,' John looked as shocked as he sounded. 'Why?'

'It seems that was how he was, what he liked. I don't know if it was anything deeper than that. We both know rape has nothing to do with sex. Maybe he just had a dom thing.'

'Ok, let's see if we can find out.' John span his chair and together we began to search.

'Why does this keep coming back to Sebastian and Joshua? Jake, I'm getting their names all the time,' he looked at me pointedly, 'and they have serious friends.'

'I know, I do know. But my biggest advantage is that they seem to have completely underestimated me. Arrogance makes them blind and, right now, they can't see past their first impressions even though I had to give Joshua a glimpse of the truth.'

'I'm having a thought, could be off the wall, but just suppose that Gabriel Wallace did what he did to Sid to threaten, blackmail or intimidate maybe. That's something I've heard about him before but it was never followed up. What if he did that to intimidate the brothers or maybe even Sid herself? Could this go back way further than we think? Do you think either of the brothers could murder?'

'Who knows? Everyone has it in them as you well know, it just takes the right provocation. These men... perhaps either could because they're volatile, pompous and arrogant. In itself none of those attributes is enough, but the circles they move in, the people they know, their world is all about influence and string pulling; corruption and power are heady bedmates. That said, Joshua pissed himself after two minutes in my presence and I wasn't even trying to spook him so I'm not convinced that they'd have wielded the weapon themselves but they sure as hell knew a man who could. Would Gabriel have continuously raped just to intimidate the brothers? Intimidate Sid maybe, get whatever he got from it. Otherwise that would infer that they knew. Fuck... that just doesn't bear thinking about. Do you think they knew what he was doing to her?'

I felt sick. If that was true then I was going to find it hard to understand what kind of men they were, or what kind of trouble they'd got themselves into.

Was I now too close to this to be objective? Was my relationship with Sid...the depth of it... was it going to obstruct my judgement? Who knew? I sure as hell didn't, but right now there was no chance I was going step aside and allow someone else to take control. John interrupted my thoughts.

'Look, I'm going to see what else I can find out about Gabriel Wallace. You're staying tonight, aren't you?'

'That's another thing I need to ask your help with. I want to go and talk to someone in town. Can you keep Sid company whilst I'm gone?'

'Yes, of course.'

'She's likely to get jumpy so don't let her out of your sight.' I knew her bravado was all top show, pinned there with a surprisingly sincere smile to reassure all but me.

'Don't worry, I'll look after her.'

'I expect to be no more than two hours, if I'm significantly longer than that, well...' I left it unsaid.

'When?'

'Six or thereabouts. I'm hoping to bump into someone specific.'

'Keep your head down. There's all sorts about in town at the moment, you could get spotted.'

I laughed and shook my head, 'No, that's one thing that won't happen. Can I borrow a car?'

'Yes, take Cath's Volvo, but be nice to it,' he punched me lightly on the arm. 'You will remember to stay safe; it's a tough world beyond these gates, full of wicked bastards, stay well clear of them, won't you?'

***

In the kitchen a major girly gossip was occurring, amidst much laughter. Even Manda looked happy.

'Sid, can I take you away for a bit?'

'Of course. Do I need an umbrella?' she grinned broadly.

Cath looked out the window, puzzled. A blue winter sky, dry and clear, bright flat light shone back.

I tutted. 'You're very wicked and it's just as well I take you away before you tarnish the reputation of these fine women with your debauchery.' I gave her Edwardian acidity.

'Quite so, good sir. I'll just pop for my corset!'

'Sid! Out now!' I slapped my hand over my eyes. 'Sorry, Cath, Manda, I often have to go back and apologise for her.'

Cath laughed, entertained by the foolishness.

'Jake, it's going to be very dull when you two leave again. Even your dog is good sport.'

'Come on, Sid, find a coat and let's go out. You clearly need to cool down after all this messing about.'

I didn't actually want her to think about this too much, glad that, on the surface, she looked like she was enjoying being here — it was much easier to deal with someone who wasn't trembling at every noise.

'Is it safe to go out?' she whispered when we were away from the kitchen.

That's always a hard decision, the one minute when the change of status occurs, when you come out of hiding. We were relying on intelligence, who knew what and whether that information was current and correct. I had to have trust in those that were constantly checking, reviewing and advising. Before I'd become involved myself in this type of work, I would never ever have suspected how much went on in the back rooms of this world.

'Yes, I think so as no one should be out on the stud for an hour. Let's take Finn and talk.'

So we walked, out across the stud, past groups of well-bred yearlings, mares heavy with foals; immaculate yards, all pristine fencing and perfect paddocks. The typical Newmarket stud farm. Every detail considered, the horses kept in consummate luxury. Yes, the staffing was expensive, security and maintenance costs high but these horses had the potential to make millions; just another well-oiled cog in the global machine that is the Thoroughbred industry.

****

I wanted to know more about the stud that Sid's parents had run, all those years ago, I was still mulling over what John had said. Did this really stem from something that began a long time ago? She told me about the horses that her family had bred, mentioned one or two colts that had gone on to stand at stud and done very well for themselves. These colts had been syndicated, divided into shares, some shares sold, some retained, when they retired from racing.

Stallions, like fine art, could be considered a significant investment as, once they had runners on the track, their value could rocket. A stallion that was a winner himself and then produced winners of important races, group races like the Derby, could virtually name his commercial stud fee.

As with all highly sought commodities, it's all about supply and demand. If there's too much of something, its value tends to drop, restrict availability and suddenly everyone wants one. The breeding of Thoroughbreds is strictly controlled to stop the market being flooded with too many offspring from one individual for example, which isn't good for the breed itself or the commercial value of such progeny. Those produced for racing have to be conceived by natural means, an actual mating, no embryo transfer, no artificial insemination, although both methods are common in the rest of the horse world.

Although that's not to say that it doesn't go on. Some stallions tire after three or four matings a day, seven days a week at the peak of the breeding season and young stallions that have recently come out of training can find it hard to switch on a libido that has been effectively trained out of them. There are many reasons why other, less scrupulous, methods may be used. I knew all of this, there'd been cases of high profile mistaken parentage in the past, perhaps because illegal insemination had been messed up, possibly intentionally or possibly not. But in recent times this had been made almost obsolete by routine DNA testing and micro-chipping of all produce as youngsters.

However, even in today's tightened elite market, top of the range stallions still proved to be worthy of big player investment. I wondered if that was the turning point for the Fielding brothers.

Finn was charging about, as lurchers do, all legs with brain disengaged. He would be exhausted later, definitely a sprinter rather than a stayer. We made our way slowly back to the house, stopping to look at a paddock full of last year's colt foals, like a group of lads on a street corner, all innuendo and sniggering.

As we went back to the house, the phone rang again.

'Hong Kong contact is confirming SF's detainment at the airport. Looks like he was carrying suspicious cargo.'

Fuck! Seb had been arrested; suspicious cargo could mean anything but was most likely drugs. He must have upset someone important and that stank of a setup, a deliberate way to hold him out of the picture for a while. The whole situation was beginning to gain speed. I hoped I'd be ready when it arrived. I started to worry that Sid knew nothing, when it kicked off it was going to hit her hard. Not for the first time, I wished for a little of Gwil's wisdom so that I'd know what move to make next.

Chapter Thirty-Eight

'Who was the person following me? Was it someone I know?'

She propped herself up on her elbow as we lay together, watching lengthening shadows as the afternoon aged.

'I don't know as yet, perhaps there'll be an update later. Sobering to think but this is just one case in thousands that are currently on going all over the world.'

'Do you know why? Why those men were killed? It seems crazy that someone just gets up one day and thinks today is the day to kill. I can't understand why someone would do that. What makes someone decide to be a killer?'

'There are few rules in that world, mental anarchy is rife. People who take lives do for so many reasons, some perhaps could be thought of as justifiable, such as to defend or protect; others to intimidate, to wield or gain power, to make someone else behave in a certain way. Sometimes murder is committed as the final act in a long line of desperate measures, when there simply seems to be no alternative available. Then, of course, there is the simply because someone can.'

'There's no chance that any of the men that were killed, that any of them might have been accidents, just an honest accident that resulted in their death? That must happen sometimes?'

'Yes, of course it happens, tragedy and misfortune, Fate calling in its loans. Accidents do happen and lives are lost. Good people and bad if you want to go down that line. But the men you mentioned were definitely murdered; it's always one of the first facts to establish when a body is discovered. None of them could have suffered the injuries that took their lives by accidental means.' I thought of pulped heads, no, there was no element of doubt about the cause of death.

As we were in the moment, I told her about her brothers' not so pleasant business interests, trying to keep it factual and unemotional. She listened calmly and when I'd said all that I could, there was silence, her eyes searched me — for the truth, for my opinion, for answers I didn't have.

'Are they murderers? My brothers. Have they killed people?'

'In truth, I don't know. There's no evidence to say that they have or haven't. The question to ask is always why? Why would either of them feel the need to behave like that? You know them both better than anyone else, did you know about the things that they were involved in?'

'No, but strangely, I'm not surprised. Seb has always been controlling, he liked to play the head of the household, long before he became it by seniority but never by respect. Josh is different, we aren't close but I've never seen the side of him that came out the other day, when he was so aggressive. I didn't think him capable of being like that, especially not with me,' she shut her eyes for a moment as if that memory caused her pain. 'I still can't get that out of my mind. In a way he reminded me, in that moment, of Gabriel.'

I put my arms around her. 'Josh is frightened, actually I think they're both frightened. Perhaps they've overstepped the mark, pushed too hard or simply got it wrong. Some of the people they're involved with are really nasty and they don't like to lose face. It's one aspect of what I'm working on at the moment along with the why — always to find out why. To encourage disclosure, direct or indirect, I intend to push them gently, just enough to get a reaction.'

'Jake, I know that this is your world and I've every faith in you, but this is scary. I'm scared by all of this. What if you got hurt?'

I watched her eyes change, the rain clouds scudding across.

'I know its selfish but I simply can't lose you now.'

'And you won't. Sid, this is hard for you I do know that, talk to Cath if you like, she's been there with John. She has a good philosophy about this crazy world. But this is what I do, I need to be part of the hidden machine that helps not hurts, it is part of who I am. I never imagined that I'd ever have someone like you, feel the way I do about you. But this is part of my life too.'

She put her face down into my neck, I could feel her warm breath against my shoulder, feel her fingers softly stroking my hair.

'I've just had a thought,' she said and sat up suddenly.

'And?'

'Alex. We really ought to find him. If Seb and Josh have brought trouble on themselves, enough to affect me, Alex may be in danger too.'

I had so hoped she'd think about Alexander, whatever my feelings for her, I knew for sure now that she was with me on this.

'Light speed thought contained within such beauty. It's a wonder that I can keep myself under control around you.'

'I think you manage it very well, control and timing and all that.' She laughed, that musical little sound that made my heart reach out to her, want to draw her in and keep her with me always.

****

Back with John, I outlined briefly my need to go and pick something up from the local police station. When I said that I was going alone, something flickered over Sid's face and was gone again. Just go with it, I thought, don't ask. I slipped away going upstairs to change so, as I'd assured John, there was no chance I'd be recognised.

Driving into Newmarket, I turned right on the high street and carried on past Tattersalls, winding roads lined with horse walks for the endless strings of morning racehorses. I arrived eventually in the car park of a snooker club.

John Wozniak had a membership card for this particular snooker club, it had been in his wallet when he'd died. Strange fact that, for a middle aged man who lived in Devon.

Chapter Thirty-Nine

I put on a baseball cap and pulled up the hood of my sweatshirt, out the car, adopt the walk and not many would now know me. Yet another of the skills my employer liked so much: the chameleon, anything anywhere. It was all about subtlety. Disguises only worked if you changed everything, people could be recognised even if not fully seen by the way they moved, little mannerisms that made them who they were. When I went out as someone else, I became someone else in every sense.

I bought a beer at the bar and went to sit at the back of the hall. The snooker club was often busy, a place for the local stable lads (both male and female) to come after work. The presence of air bases in nearby Lakenheath and Mildenhall meant that off duty servicemen tended to hang out there too. That was a draw for the girls, the local lads tending to be short and skinny as a rule.

I saw a face I recognised, playing snooker with someone I didn't. There was an air of unfinished business about them, sitting between like a chaperone, a tension that seemed to relate to something other than snooker.

The one I did know, Danny Flemming, stable lad for Ed Dunlop now but had been up north with Mick Channon, was the one I'd hoped to bump into. Danny was almost always here in the evening, although it had been a long time since I'd been in. I was working on the basis that if he was in town he'd stick to the same routine. Wiry bloke about thirty-five years old, thick gold earring in his left ear, handy with his fists from what I remember but only when he'd had a few. Danny had been known to be the person to go and see if you liked a bit of blow, cannabis of the skunk variety usually and that was how we'd met a few years previously, officially that is. He offered me ganja so I offered him handcuffs.

On the far side of their table, taking his shot, was the tall man I didn't know. Short black-brown hair, military cut, eyes that looked half-closed with heavy lids. His whole body radiated a kind of lazy tension, as if he was buzzing but too tired to deal with it right now. He played well, sinking ball after ball. Danny's anxiety increased every time a ball dropped into a pocket. They didn't speak to each at all.

I made a show of checking my phone, looking to the door and back down at the beer bottle in my hands getting impatient. Danny and the tall guy finished their game, put down their cues and went towards the bar. Tall guy peeled off and went into the gents through a grubby door. After a minute, Danny followed him. I finished my beer and went too.

'You're a dirty little scrote!' Tall guy had Danny by the throat up against the wall, hissing into his face. He'd obviously already swung a punch as Danny was bleeding profusely from his nose and lip. Tall guy turned as I walked in, letting Danny slide back down to the floor.

'What are you looking at? Do you want some too? Hey, do you?'

American accent, red hot fury, tall guy wasn't a happy bunny.

'Not from you, mate, you aren't my type.' I leaned back against the door so no-one else was going to walk in on us easily.

'Come here and say that again, come on! Come on!' he stepped towards me, fists balled, stiff legged, bristling with all that aggression he'd been suppressing outside. I wondered what Danny had done to deserve a hostile yank in his face.

Danny moved away to the sinks, taking himself out of the fight and leaving it to me to finish it. Cheers, mate, thanks very much. Tall guy was standing right in front of me now, burning eyes, tight face, legs slightly spread. From his expression, he clearly thought I was going to be a walkover.

'Not so big now, are you? Not so full of yourself now! Come on then! Come on! Let's have it.'

He furious beyond reason, temper well and truly lost. He raised his fist and hit himself on the chest, he did it twice like a penitent Jesuit. It seemed to increase his aggression though, not provide spiritual release.

It was just too primate and, without much thought for the consequences, I laughed, which, to be fair to him, would have pissed me off too. He lost it good and proper then, reached out to grab me from where I leaned. I don't expect he saw the strikes that floored him, I only hit him a few times as I did want him sorted quickly, time was getting on. Danny took a step or two back until he was up against the corner of the room, his hands held up pleadingly.

'Leave me out of it…all right…I haven't seen nothing.'

He was pale, blood from his nose smeared over his face where he'd wiped it nervously.

'I don't have a problem with you, Danny.'

I rolled the American into a semi-upright position against the urinal. He sagged to one side, breathing noisily through an open mouth. He simply looked drunk, a common sight some nights here, people would shuffle round and ignore him. He'd wake up later with a monster headache and probably wonder what happened.

'How... how do you know my name?' Danny was more anxious not less. 'I don't want no trouble.'

'I'm not here to cause you trouble, seems you brought that on yourself. What did you do to deserve a slap?'

'Nothing.'

'Come on, he might be a bit of a dick but you don't normally hit someone unless they've done something, or you at least think they might have done something.'

'His girl, he thinks I did his girl.' Danny stammered his way into a confession.

'What do you mean 'did'? Hit her?'

'No! Shit no! You're getting it all wrong. He thinks I gave her one. She works on the same yard, we went racing together, had a laugh and he thinks it was something more.'

Danny had a certain charm, I could imagine what he meant by had a laugh.

'I didn't know he was going to start a fight. Just a chat he said, didn't know he was going to turn on me in the john.'

'How's business, Danny?'

He'd never recognise me even though I'd nicked him before.

'Business...? Don't... know... what you mean.'

He was stammering again, desperately trying to work out who I was.

'Yes, you do, Danny, you know exactly what I mean.'

'Who the hell are you? Like I said, I don't want no trouble.'

'Danny, I want a bit of information, nothing more than that. Can you tell me what you know about the driver who works for David Flint. Do you know him, Danny? He comes here sometimes.'

Shot in the dark but worth a punt, it was a small world after all.

'John? Is that who you mean, John...Wozniak...that him?'

Danny was trying to assist now, anything to avoid what the tall guy got.

'That's the man. What do you know about him?'

'Who are you? Police?'

'No. Just a friend who's helped you out this evening. Tell me about John – what do you know about him?'

'Nothing much. He'd come in here now and then, big fat bloke he was, belly on him and a mouth too. Talked big about everything, been there and done it, know what I mean?'

I nodded, waiting for him to carry on.

'He always had a story, dropped names like it was going out of fashion. He'd done it all had John, said he'd got contacts. Contacts!' he snorted, warming to his role of information provider. 'Said he and half a dozen jocks were doing a scam, earning him thousands. But it was all talk, he didn't look like a guy who had thousands.'

Danny was regaining confidence and his information was drying up.

'How often do you see him here?' I kept trying for a bit more but the moment was over.

'Look, I don't spend time with him if I can avoid it. Like I said, he talks out his arse. Time I was on me way,' he edged away from the sink and stood looking hopeful as if I should just go now and let him escape. 'Tell you one thing though, you ain't the first that asked after him. He must have upset someone else because a monster of a man came here looking for him a week or so ago. I wouldn't have wanted to meet *him* anywhere.'

That was interesting.

'Did you know the monster?'

Danny shook his head. 'No, never seen him before. Looked like a mentalist though, like the kind of guy that gets paid for giving someone a fright.'

Perhaps Danny's monster man had found his quarry after all - in the back of the horse lorry at Ashfield.

At that moment we were interrupted by the arrival of two short and skinnies wanting to use the facilities, definitely time to go. They looked at the two of us, Danny with his bleeding face, to me and then to the guy on the floor who was grunting now as he started to come round.

'Pissed?' asked one lad. I nodded. He shrugged and stepped casually over the American to use the urinal as if bodies on the floor in the early evening were to be expected.

'Cheers, mate,' I said to Danny like we were good friends. 'See you around.'

Danny, off the hook now, exhaled slowly and waited, watching until I turned for the door. I could sense his need to bolt as soon as he thought it was safe to do so. Someone else would have to sort out the American.

So John Wozniak was a talker, a teller of tales here too; nice to have it confirmed. Didn't tell me much though, only that someone professional had probably taken him out. Contract killings, surprisingly easy to arrange and a real bugger to get a conviction on. A professional was unlikely to have pulped his brother though.

I drove back to John and Cath's, parked the car and let myself in, I could hear Sid talking from the other room. I got as far as the bottom of the stairs when she came out, heading for the loo. I froze, shit, caught.

Chapter Forty

'Who are you? What are you doing?' she immediately backed up, 'Cath? Cath!'

'Sid,' I said softly. She didn't hear or wasn't listening. Clearly she didn't recognise me at all.

'CATH!' she screamed and turned to run back into the kitchen.

'What? Sid, what is it?' Cath came to the doorway, Sid grabbed her.

'Sid,' I tried again, moving to face them both.

Cath peered at me in the half dark of the hallway and then laughed loudly.

Sid looked from me to Cath, back and forth between us, me still standing like a naughty child at the foot of the stairs. I moved towards her.

'Jake?'

'Yes, it's me.'

She walked one step closer and then fear became anger, it often does.

'You're an utter bastard! What the fuck are you doing? Why do you look like that? Where have you been? For fucks sake, Jake, you scared the shit out of me!' she stood there as if uncertain of what to do next.

As moments go it wasn't great; timing and all that. But before I could say anything further she pulled away from Cath, pushed past and went into the downstairs privy, slamming the door hard behind her. Cath and I looked at each other.

'That went well then.'

'Mmm.'

'Go on, sort yourself out, I'll make Sid a stiff drink and then she can make herself feel better by calling you a bastard a few more times.'

Back upstairs, cap and hoodie off. I took out the contacts, putting them back into the case with the others; a whole range of colours to suit almost every occasion. I slid them back into a pocket on the side of my kit bag, removed the jewellery, washed off the small scar by my ear and changed my clothes back to something more me again. Sid stayed away — that probably wasn't good.

I sat and looked at my bag of tricks; wigs, contacts, makeup, tongs and straighteners, you name it and I probably had it. I used special effects cosmetics that produced a speedy and, at a distance, convincing result. If I was going to replicate a disguise day after day, I kept it as simple as possible.

It was easy to forget something and there is nothing more disconcerting than having a scar that moves.

Scars were always good, birthmarks too and tattoos. Visible marks that people would remember, often they saw the mark and not a lot else, if they tried to remember the rest of me it wasn't so clear. Ears and hands, someone once said, look at ears and hands as they're almost impossible to disguise. I get over that with prosthetics, wigs, hats and pockets, gloves as a last resort as they immediately start making it look like you've just done a bank.

After tonight Danny, if asked, would say I was probably street gang. Ask the right questions and he might say I was black and that I carried a knife. Funny how the memory works, selectively providing false memories from subtle cues, I suggest and the other person's brain does the rest. It helps too that often they're either wanting to kill me or, wanting to know I won't kill them.

I've sat in front of people who are completely certain that they'd recognise me anywhere, but it's not that easy. Context is also a fooler. Meeting someone in an incongruous place is disorientating. You might recognise the face but can't remember the name, it's only later that you realise it was someone you knew.

It's relatively easy to trick someone into believing that you're someone else if you're confident and I am which means I can stay operational in a range of situations for longer, means that I don't make people suspicious and, to be honest, means I stay alive. As I was folding up the clothing into my bag, Sid appeared in the doorway. I turned, tried a smile and got a small one in return.

'I'm sorry.' It seemed inadequate but it was the truth.

'Why didn't you tell me? Bloody hell... No... I'm the one who should be sorry, you're working and I'm here because you're working, it's wrong of me to say that.' There was that sparkle in her eyes that meant that tears weren't far away. 'You fooled me completely. I thought I'd know you anywhere but I didn't know it was you there in the hall.'

'Cath wasn't much help, was she?'

'No, none at all. But then she's used to this and I'm not. It scares me. Its like I've entered another world entirely, you're doing stuff day to day that I didn't know even happened.'

'Well, that means we're doing a good job. Seriously though, I know this is hard. I don't expect you planned on a quick trip to Newmarket to hang out with a load of crazies.'

'Talk to me, Jake, tell me what you do and then I won't feel so lost.'

'You're not lost, you're strong and resilient. I'm here with you. I'm here for you. And Sid, don't forget the most important bit of all.'

'What's that?'

With one finger I tipped her face up and kissed her gently. 'Don't forget that I love you.'

****

John was on top form, he told such stories and Cath, a delight as always, the perfect foil to him. Manda came and went, not staying but going out with her friends for the evening. At what I hoped was the right time, I told John that Sid had mentioned finding Alexander.

'I know where he is, or at least I know where he was a few days ago. I have a feeling he might be a bit of a...um...er... wanderer.'

Sid didn't seem at all surprised that John had already been tracking her brother.

'That's very diplomatic of you, John, but he's been troubled for a long time, even as a child he seemed to carry the weight of the world. He lost his job a year or so ago, I don't know the detail because he was always very secretive about his work. I'm sure it was PTSD but I don't know if he was ever formally diagnosed,' she looked almost as if she felt she was betraying him in some way by talking like this. 'You know he is, or was, an addict. I'm never too sure what he'll be until he turns up again.'

'Yes, I know that,' John said warmly, not judging. 'I believe that he may be on the straight at the moment, perhaps he's found a way through again.'

'Why PTSD? Was he military?' I asked, wondering how I could fit interviewing him in with getting back to Dartmoor.

'No, well, indirectly I suppose he was. Before he became really ill, he worked for Reuters as a photo journalist. I expect he witnessed some horrendous stuff over the years,' she sighed heavily. 'He only comes to see me now when he needs help, I wish he'd come more but it seems he only remembers me when he's at rock bottom.'

'As I understand it, he was receiving proper medical assistance about six months ago,' John said. 'I'm not sure why in particular but at least it seems he does now have a formal diagnosis.'

'Which is?' Sid asked.

'Schizophrenia, I believe.'

'Shit! I just knew it was something more,' she was clearly shocked. 'He seemed so sure that it was just coming off the drugs that made him so messed up. The last time he came to see me he was struggling. He was on some sedatives but they just made him sleep. He slept for days without really waking at all, but then he does get really tired and run down sometimes. Schizophrenia though, that's a bit heavy.'

'It can be managed, he'll be able to access good care if he wants it,' John said, 'what was his state of mind like when you last saw him?'

'Pretty good, aside from being exhausted. But that doesn't mean anything because he's immensely insular. He's made superficial an art form, no-one gets the real Alex anymore. I asked him to come by more often but he won't, I know he won't. All I can do is wait and then give him bed and board when he does turn up.'

My phone interrupted our conversation, 'John, can I use your office?'

'Yes, of course, help yourself.' John waved me away.

Through the door, I answered the phone. 'Go ahead.' Let's try Arabic tonight. Switching languages often helped me to problem solve, sharpened my thoughts and quickened my responses.

'Hong Kong contact has confirmed SF's possession of a controlled drug at customs check. It is denied strenuously, he's detained awaiting consular assistance.' Arabic was fine and dandy apparently.

'A plant?' I couldn't imagine Seb being so naive, but stupidly arrogant as he was, he may have been the ideal target for someone to plant drugs on.

'It is likely considering his reputation.'

'Any news on the detainee in UK?'

'Yes, on line update available. Arrested and charged but unrelated to this job.'

'What's the word on the street?'

I went back and beckoned to John. He wheeled himself in and accessed the information on his computer.

'There are many variables, some of which are decoys for certain. We would recommend that you proceed with extreme caution, as usual, and keep the risk of contact to a minimum.'

I'd heard of this man, he'd be working for someone else as he was contract, not interested in anything himself but money. But who was he working for to be searching for Sid? Was he the monster of a man that

Danny had mentioned? I mused for a moment.

'Request increased resources.'

I had to err on the side of caution, contract stalkers were hard to handle and there may be more than one. I reread through the details about the man who had been arrested. He'd been found in Seb's London house, I wondered if Seb had been happy about him staying or whether he was being leaned on to accommodate.

'Why? Is more known than we're aware of?' Instant suspicion, but I didn't want to call it in yet, I still needed more information.

'No, no specifics as yet. Believe the target is still at risk. Request support.'

Asking for bodyguard backup would be expected as its almost impossible to watch someone 24/7 without imprisoning them.

'Anyone in particular?'

'Is Pan available?'

Pan or, to use his real name, Bill, was now my post-Gwil choice; we worked well together and had done so many times.

'We'll discuss and contact you again.'

I'd wait whilst they tracked Bill and asked him if he wanted to be involved. It was his choice, we could always turn down work of this nature, but I doubted that he would. John was waiting for me to fill him in, I did so as languages weren't his specialism.

'Does Sid know everything?'

'Mostly yes, I've kept the Gabriel factor out of it for obvious reasons and she doesn't yet know about Seb's detainment in China. There's no point in opening wounds unnecessarily.'

'Bill's a good choice but he's going to stand out down your way. You won't be able to hide him.'

'That's where you're wrong, its got quite cosmopolitan down there now, he'll blend right in,' I said. 'Besides if they're going to have decoys, then so can we.' My phone vibrated again.

'Pan is good to go. Collect Stansted at 0900 tomorrow.'

I turned to John. 'Bill is coming to play, we pick him up at Stansted in the morning. We can do that on the way home.'

'Well that's that side of things sorted. I'm still waiting on a bit more information from someone for you but I'll let you have my results in a day.'

'And I'm going to try and track Alexander, see what he knows. That can be done through open police channels as he's a known connection of Sid's.'

'Right then, let's go and get some more drink in these glasses. Can't have talk of this being a dry house.'

Chapter Forty-One - Alyosha

And I will flay the flesh from their bones and strip them bare for angels to eat.

I took to checking in on you, Zosima. I knew that the brothers had horses there, not the horses they were supposed to be but then, what the hell, who worries about such trivialities when you're already up to your neck in shit, it flowed in their veins now. I watched you. You were safe in a way, with me there to watch over you, to take out those who sought to hurt you. I protected you from a distance.

Marcus Williams, remember him. Shifty guy, liked to think he moved in the real world, I could've told him not to bother, but who was I to talk? I got talking to him in the pub, he didn't know who I was, I'm master of being no-one, a master now of murder and madness. We talked about David Flint, as you would, he was into racehorses and Flint's the only yard for miles. He was into shit with the brothers as well (small world) just another user. Even so, he was fine until he mentioned you, Zosima, mentioned you and laughed about what he'd like to do to you. Imagine that? He had to go, of course. He was easy, too easy. I took him out, took his grinning, lecherous face off. It was too easy, far too easy. And most importantly, I didn't mind at all. I became like the brothers in that moment, I could take out anyone now and it didn't matter. In that moment I became Death. I'd already had a practice run in Scotland so I gave him a sky burial, how very buddhist of me, the eagles told me how to do it and so I left him, in the woods. I didn't know about the boar, didn't know that they would eat him and then leave him around for the police to find...

The gloves hid the bandages and the bandages hid the sign of his holiness. The stigmata was still there, a bit scabby but there was no doubt at all as to what it was. It made Alyosha feel pure unadulterated joy when he thought about it.

There was nothing he couldn't do, nothing now to stop him from becoming one with the eagles, becoming one *of* the eagles.

Just think of it! To truly be a dakini, a sky dancer, a holy angel. And he would be, he would be all three. The holy trinity: father, son and holy ghost.

The eagles had moved in with him now, it made it easier, they said. Easier because matters were gathering pace and it was almost time to go and rescue Zosima. He'd been silly, very silly, in thinking that she'd abandoned him. Of course she hadn't, she would never do such a thing. She was being held against her will, being held by the green eyed man he'd seen before.

The cat, but not a fireside cat, the green eyed panther with the cloak of death. Alyosha knew him, knew where he lived and just what to bait the trap with. The death panther was no match for the holy ones and the holy ones would save Zosima. He knew this because they had told him so.

Chapter Forty-Two

Stansted was quiet as airports go and it was easy to spot Bill in the privacy of the section used by airport police. But then, today, it would have been easy to spot Bill in any crowd. I pointed him out on the monitors and Sid stared with frank horror.

'I'm glad he's your friend because that man would terrify me otherwise!'

Bill was about six five and built like the proverbial muscle outhouse with skin like wet ink. Today, he looked like a Bronx gangster, all hair, jewellery and piercings; strutting, totally in character towards us. He blew it all though when he spoke with a broad Birmingham accent.

'Been too long, bro! Too long!' he grinned, turning to look intently at Sid.

He was far too loud, broad brummie vibrating across arrivals, people turned and stared. Not one person there could have missed him — exactly as he planned, even if he had my toes curling.

'Any trouble with your flight?' I asked as we went back to the car, I'd be amazed if he got through unscathed, I could sense that latex gloves were drawn.

'Nah, aside from the usual with customs, but then, perhaps I do ask for it looking like this,' he held out his hands and laughed loudly, producing a dramatic twirl. 'I mean what's not to like here? Sid, I'm a babe, aren't I?'

'Don't answer that, he's quite shocking if you give in to him.'

Bill laughed loudly again, eyes so black but lit with the fire of his personality. He was almost always teasing and laughing, I liked him all the more for that.

We caught up on work and life in general as I drove back to Dartmoor. Bill had been told about Gwil and began to relay it to Sid. I interrupted, asked him to stop, time and place, neither was right. Bill shrugged, made a face and they both sniggered together like kids. Long journey but, strangely, as I pulled up the rough track to Sid's house, it did feel a bit like coming home.

'Cool pad, Sid!' Bill was checking out the house, making himself at home with his own tour of the place. I watched him checking out the rooms and the view but knew he was risk assessing, security checking and making mental notes as he did so.

'Now, where's the best place for accommodation round here?' Bill sat with a cup of coffee steaming in his hands. Finn was back in position on the sofa, all the excitement of the last few days proving too much for him.

I looked at Sid. 'Bill could stay in my flat. Is that ok for you?'

'Of course!' she was clearly pleased. 'I'm sure that you both have plans and stuff to sort out, so I'll cook for you. Do you need to take Bill to the flat first?'

'That would be good, but you have to come too, I'm afraid, I'm not going to leave you here at the moment,' I said, not wishing to frighten but not wanting her to be complacent either.

'We need to talk about what's necessary and what isn't. You're racing tomorrow and Saturday. The sister factor we can't change without good cause, it will only arouse suspicion. I'm very aware that we don't need added complications but we'll just have to roll with it at the moment. Bill and I will fill any gaps in the same way when you're racing, we'll be everywhere except in the changing rooms. All of those rooms are restricted access so none of the great unwashed should be hanging about without being tagged. If there's a hint of intelligence regarding a plant among the racecourse staff then we'll cover that too.'

'The sister is coming? Here?' Bill stared at me.

I nodded. 'Yes, of course, at high speed I'd imagine.'

'Racecourse? Where?' He changed the subject immediately.

'Fontwell tomorrow, Exeter Saturday.'

'Shame it isn't the other way round, make for less travelling tomorrow as I'm likely to have monumental jet lag at some point. I've just come from Hong Kong via Kentucky; long job, long story, no fun. But ok, I'm familiar with both courses, neither should pose unnecessary risks,' he pulled out his phone and began typing in notes.

'At least I won't miss you on the racecourse, Bill, you'll be able to see over us all,' Sid said.

'You'd be surprised, by tomorrow Bill could be anything and he might be very easy to miss. He's quite changeable for a fat lad.'

'Watch your step, Spider! I could take you down from here!' Bill retorted.

'Before this gets out of hand, let's go see the flat. I need to pick up some gear and check in at the police station as well, pass it by Moore. Ok with all of that?' I stood, stretching as I did so, easing out the sore muscles from so much driving.

'Let's go then.' Sid stood and picked up her coat. 'This is such fun getting to hang out with the big boys! I feel like I'm in an action movie!'

'Bring it on, girl, but if he's the leading man it's going to be a budget 'b' movie! You know the type; they call it artistic, which is lovee speak for a pile of crap,' he winked at her and I kicked him on the shin as he passed.

I left her in the car with Bill, buzzing myself in at the police station and going straight to CID. Trev was pleased to see me but then immediately not pleased that I wasn't staying.

'I've another job on at the moment Trev, can't talk about it now. Besides you do have Tom.'

'Yes, but he's far too serious for my liking. So get on with it, Jake, finish whatever it is you have to do and come back, it isn't the same without you to take the piss out off and even Sally is pining.'

I knocked on Moore's door and went in on his bark, closing it behind me.

'Any updates?'

I told him all that was new and that I was working with Bill, requesting permission for him to use the flat.

'How long before we reach a resolution, do you think?' he pursed his lips, tenting his fingers against his chin.

'Hard to tell. I'd like to speak to Alexander Fielding as soon as possible. Could we bring him in here?'

'Possibly. What's his last known location?'

'I'll have to send you more precise details later. He's known to be a bit of a loner, possibly still an addict. He's recently been diagnosed as schizophrenic but is self managing according to Sid. Ex photographer from Reuters so he'll know the form. He's possibly been at a buddhist retreat but I don't have the personal manpower to track him and he may not be connected to any of this. However, as a matter of urgency, I'd like to get a feel for him, especially the way the other two brothers are behaving, he may be at risk.'

'Agreed. I'll do what I can this end.'

'Sid is still under protection, she's racing as planned. I'll be monitoring with Bill. Any idea where Joshua is?'

'Hotel in Exeter as far as I know, but ask Tom, he'll be up to speed with any recent change of status. I don't envisage a problem with him at the moment; Tom did tell me what went on, don't worry about how that was dealt with, there were more than enough reasons to justify it, if necessary.

Tom also tells me that Joshua is currently too busy running, or more truthfully saving, his empire from his hotel room to come out and cause much trouble. I'm waiting to find out more about the nature of what he's struggling with, but I've a feeling that it will turn out that Joshua Fielding may have been extravagantly creative with his accounting.'

Joshua's financial woes had come to a head recently when his own personal set of trading accounts went to the IRS quite by accident attached, apparently, to a piece of computer malware. Can't for the life of me work out how that happened. In the ensuing melee, someone took the time to compare the audited accounts filed in accordance with the law and this set, his personal set, which, strangely, bore no relation to the first. Let's call it karma.

'Back up is available if requested but we need to keep this tight, Jake. No leaking of information for any of us.'

'I can work independently if you prefer.'

'No, that isn't necessary but please keep your head down. I don't want any injuries and the men the Fieldings are involved with are likely to fight first and ask later.'

I smiled. 'I often prefer it that way myself.'

He raised his eyebrows, shaking his head slowly as if I'd yet to learn how to behave.

'How's Sid? Is she coping with all of this?'

'She's strong.'

'It has worked out for the best perhaps. I'm pleased for her that she has you on her side, perhaps you can help her where others could not. Tom's working lates, I'll ask him to ring and discuss Joshua. I take it that you'll be going to see David Flint now?'

'Yes, I need him on side so that Sid can carry on until this is resolved.'

I wasn't looking forward to arguing with David Flint and that is how it would end up.

'We've no further updates as yet on Marcus Williams or the Wozniak twins and, to make a shit job worse, the surveillance at the yard is proving fruitless. Tom will tell you what we know. However we have, thanks to Trev's visit to the Taylors, Wozniak's neighbour, unearthed a significant cannabis network. I'm frankly amazed that no-one knew about it before. Some cautions for possession have been connected with the lads at the racing yard, nothing of any great volume but enough to make things even more uncomfortable for Mr Flint. Use that, if you wish, to your advantage.'

'Thank you.'

'Where will I find you?'

'By phone. Be aware that I'll move Sid again immediately without consultation if any increased activity is suspected.' I would let him make what he wanted of that.

'Understood. Keep me posted.'

I left his office and went to have a brief chat with Trev which consisted mainly of station gossip and nothing of real value. Without lingering I was soon out the door and back to the car.

'Right, let's go to David's. If you're to continue as normal we need him on side especially as one of us will be hanging around. Sid, listen because this is important, he's likely to get angry. Please don't worry about anything that may or may not go on when we talk to him as I do want him to be pissed, I will push him. Are you ready?'

Chapter Forty-Three

David Flint wasn't accommodating. I rang him, checking he was at the yard and to make sure he knew we were coming. He was all defensive aggression, gesturing us into the office as if herding cattle and slamming the door hard. Bill lent against it as if slightly bored already by all these histrionics.

'What the bloody hell do you mean by all this? You clear off for two days, not a word direct to me and then swan back in with bloody minders! For Christ's sake, Sid, this is not on!' he singled out Sid. She stared at him, blue ice, unbowed by his tirade.

I quickly had enough. 'Mr Flint, this is a police matter and, regardless of your petty complaints, Miss Fielding is under our protection, you need to be able to deal with it. One of us will be here when she's working, if it wasn't necessary for her to ride for you she wouldn't be here at all. I'd ask you to calm down and behave in a more appropriate manner.'

Loading the sarcasm, I knew that it would piss him off. David Flint was first on my new list to be poked with a stick.

'DON'T YOU FUCKING TELL ME HOW TO BEHAVE!'

He stood inches away and roared into my face. I sensed a soapbox moment brewing and it came.

'You people come here and harass me on a daily basis, stop my staff from working, interfere with my business and then tell me that I'm to have some dickhead lounging around whilst I'm trying to train horses!' he sneered. I stifled a yawn. 'Let me talk to your senior officer, let *him* tell me that I have to put up with you!'

'Mr Flint, I am the senior officer you wish to speak to.' I stepped forward into his space, thinking that he was protesting far too much. 'And I'm telling you that this is how it will be, you can deal with or not, it is happening.'

'Who is your keeper, boy?'

He clearly thought he still had a say in this. With an exaggerated sigh, I gave him the station number, he was put through to Moore and he roared at him too, screaming obscenities down the phone.

Bill and Sid went back outside to the car. I waited as Flint was obviously being told that I really was the senior officer on this job, he slammed his phone down on the desk with impotent rage.

'So,' he spat out words, 'I'm told that I have to do what you tell me — how someone like you can be in charge beggars belief! So I'll now take this over all your heads and then you'll see that I don't have to stand cap in hand to you! I have influential friends that will make your superiors jump!'

I waited whilst he rummaged through the drawers of his desk looking for his influential friends phone numbers no doubt. He was getting angrier with every moment so I kept a small half smile on my face, letting it wind him up until I thought he might self-combust. I hoped he wasn't going to produce a weapon as that would be unfortunate… for him, not me.

'Mr Flint, I strongly suggest that you pay attention now,' I said quietly. He carried on hauling out drawers, but it was all bluster; he was listening.

'Why the hell should I listen to anything that you say! You come in here throwing your weight around and telling me what I should do!'

What made me smile was that he was the only one throwing his weight around. This was a frightened man; strange there seemed to be a lot of them all of a sudden. Regardless of his motivation, I was still thinking oh go on, just try it, I would so love to put you on your arse. He was a bit too much 'do you know who I am' for my taste, but each to their own.

He was standing inches away; I smiled at him broadly. Just enough provocation to push him over the edge. I saw it coming, the tension ravaging his face changed ever so slightly and, with tight white knuckles, up came his fist with the force of his fury behind it. Bingo! I caught it in one hand, rotated his wrist and pushed it away with seemingly no effort. The result was that he hit the floor hard instantly yelping, legs gone from underneath him. I bent my knees, crouched down beside him and spoke very quietly.

'Mr Flint, you will listen now and you will co-operate. I could have your licence revoked with immediate effect if I was to make official what I know about you personally and about what is going on here. There's a drugs issue known, that much is already in the public domain, but, in addition we have… let's pick just one example for now and what should we call it… serious irregularities? Yes, that will cover it. Serious irregularities with the documentation for the horses in training under your name. Of course that would mean that there is fraud along with tax evasion and I believe the VAT man would be very interested in some of the more blue sky aspects of your work. You're small time, Mr Flint, don't think that you're anything other than that. Don't mess about with me, I'm really not someone you want to growl at.'

I watched his face drain of colour, waited whilst he took it all in and then tried to work out a way to proceed. I carried on.

'I think we could say that this conversation is concluded. Miss Fielding will be at work as normal in the morning, she will have protection that won't get in the way of any of her duties or your business. In the afternoon she'll ride at Fontwell as arranged if the horse is fit to run. On Saturday the same will happen and she'll ride for you at Exeter. This protection will be in place for as long as it is necessary, respect it, don't put her at unnecessary risk; keep your head down do your job, let us do ours.'

He sat, his breathing loud and wheezy in the stillness.

'I would like to stand up.'

I straightened my legs, standing beside him. 'Go ahead.'

He got up awkwardly from the floor and then sat heavily in the chair by the desk.

'This is a bloody mess; I could do without all this now.' He put his head in his hands.

'This protection won't have an impact on your business Mr Flint; it is to do with Miss Fielding not you. I suggest that you take some time to calm down and then get on with what you have to do.'

'Are you going to report me for the horses' paperwork?'

He looked up; a flicker of fear crossed his face that had a whole lot more to do with his influential friends than anything he thought I could do.

'Not at this time as I'm sure that you'll have a thorough spring clean over the next couple of days.'

He nodded and then spoke again with false humility.

'Thank you, Dr Steel, I've been under considerable strain recently, with John's murder and the bones on my land. I apologise unreservedly for my earlier actions, I behaved badly, it was crass and impolite of me. I'll do whatever you want to help Sid.'

Big turnaround. Not. He was going to be on the phone the minute we left, there would a scrabble to tidy up and then I'd have to look over my shoulder. If I wasn't mistaken, the drums were already sounding out an early warning. What stood out the most was that not once had he questioned why I was there, he clearly knew a lot more than he was letting on.

****

We dropped into the flat on the way back, showing Bill the range of luxurious comforts he could expect there, of which, obviously, there were none; stowed a change of gear in the boot of the car and went back to Sid's house. I left her to turn on her phone, still sitting on the table, which she'd turned off when we went to Newmarket, a stream of messages pinged in loudly. I went back to Bill, taking him a beer and firing up my laptop.

'Must say it, Spider, never expected you to fall for anyone,' Bill glanced sideways at me. 'There's me thinking that you'd all your emotions removed when you took up trying to be Jackie Chan.'

'Don't take the piss, Bill. Just because I'm better than you at just about everything, doesn't mean you have to get nasty.'

'Whatever. You'd better find a really good hidey hole for when Sophie turns up.'

'Its Luci at the moment. Luci Pasun,' I said without looking up from the computer.

'Luci who?' Bill was working through it. 'Fuck, that's cheap. Who thought that would be a good idea?'

Bill had a brilliant mind, we quickly moved on away from Luci/Sophie to our current problem. As far as I was concerned it was much more interesting.

As we sat, shifting through ideas, Sid came back. I glanced up and immediately saw that something was wrong, she handed me her phone as if it was poisonous, holding it away from her body with the tips of her fingers.

'Listen to the messages, fifth or sixth now, I've deleted a whole load as I dealt with them, but just listen to it.'

She looked down, lost and small again. I really hated this, what this was doing to her.

'Come here, come and sit with me.' I held out my hands, she looked across at Bill. 'Bill can handle us, he's a grown up. Come on.'

Bill was now seeing how fragile this all was beneath that 'feel the fear and do it anyway' exterior of hers; he didn't know the half of it.

He played through the messages left, the first one an owner wanting to book her to ride, the second the trainer of the horse for that owner asking the same, third someone disconnected before leaving a message, fourth the same as the third and then the fifth, a foreign accent could have been fake or real.

'Message for Sid Fielding, tell your brother that if he doesn't start to do as he's told, people like you will get hurt — very badly hurt. Don't disregard this message; he has until this evening to respond. We will be watching.'

Bill and I looked at each other.

'Sid, this can't happen. We're here to keep you safe, I'll keep you safe and so will Bill. There are other people as well as us working on this, nothing ever stops and we will find these men.'

'Which brother do you think?' Bill asked. I shrugged, who could know?

We played the rest of the messages, transcribing and transferring them direct as data files. Bill set up a trace on message number five, we should soon know where the call was made from and, if we were very lucky, by whom.

If the brother was Sebastian, he was now in a Hong Kong jail on drugs charges, perhaps because he hadn't done what he was told fast enough. If it was Joshua, he was supposed to be in a hotel in Exeter, keeping America turning with his business prowess, or lack of it. Alexander was lurking somewhere unknown and remained unknowable at the moment. Either way, if the brother had done or hadn't done what they'd been asked to do, someone might be coming for Sid. Someone, in addition now to the detained contract killer.

My phone vibrated, 'Jake, Tom, the DCI asked me to call you with an update.'

'Go ahead.'

'Josh is staying at the Royal Lion in Cowell Street; he plans to stay for a week. He has a private jet on standby at the city airport and a linked plane at Heathrow, we know that he also has a heli in this country. I don't know whether he has that on standby as well but I'm working on the assumption that he probably has. After he met with Sid on Tuesday I spent some time with him. He's a man on the edge, he seems to have some considerable worries, he wasn't forthcoming but I'm sure that someone is leaning on him. He's jumpy and volatile, aggressive one minute and little boy vulnerable the next. He freaked when he found out about Sebastian being arrested. I sense an empire that's crumbling but he won't talk about what's going on, not even a hint. He's not the same man that I knew, or thought I knew. He's being watched as he could become anything at the moment, uniform from city are loitering but I don't think he'll approach Sid, it seems to have gone beyond that. I've warned him to leave her alone in any case. I'll check in when I come on duty later and update you if anything changes.'

'Thanks Tom.' I felt myself thawing towards him slightly.

So Josh was cracking under the strain of more than his dodgy accounting. Was he the brother that had to do whatever it was?

Bill's phone pinged, he studied it.

'Message five was made early hours of this morning, the call was made from Penzance, Cornwall, the number was traceable. Someone has been to see, the phone is listed as belonging to a Mr Jack Cowan. Sadly he's ninety in the shade and doesn't know which way is up. The phone's been hacked.'

I sighed deeply, more dead ends, more questions and few answers.

'Sid, come on, let's find something to eat in that kitchen of yours. Let's get some music on and show Bill a good time. Are you up for it?' I nudged her gently.

'Go on then, just to stop you from making a mess.' Her voice was too quiet.

'Bill, Sid lives on half a cornflake once a week but hopefully we'll be able to produce something worthy of a red-blooded male. You choose some music, cracking sound system here.'

'It's one cornflake twice a week actually,' Sid sniffed and smiled but it was a ghost of her usual. I know, I thought to her, I know how frightening this all is.

'Come on, wench, kitchen now.'

I went with her into the kitchen and pushed the door closed.

'This is a bad time, a hard time, but it'll get better. I'll keep you safe, keep you safe with me.' I whispered the words into her hair.

'Don't leave me, I can't do this alone.'

'I'm here; you don't have to do anything alone,' I kissed her fiercely. 'Except maybe ride those horses as that would scare the bejesus out of me.'

She laughed a little, 'Sometimes you're very silly.'

Bill came into the kitchen. 'Someone's phone is ringing. Whose is this?'

He held out my mobile, I checked the number – Luci.

I let go of Sid and answered the phone with a fake smile in my voice, 'Luci.'

'JAKE baby!' a voice screamed, top volume, down the phone, I held it away from my ear with a grimace and Sid laughed out loud.

'G'day! Are you ready for the weekend of your dreams? I've very good news, I've got a lift to Ashfield with a friend whose granny lives in the town! How cool is that? I can't wait to see you again in the flesh. It has been how long?'

'A year, maybe eighteen months,' I opened the fridge door as I talked to her, half listening and half hunting out food. She was coming, I couldn't stop it but that didn't mean I had to pay attention to her.

'Jake, why don't you ever read your email? I sent you photos! Go have a look now, I'll tell you who's who.'

'What right now?' I held the phone against my shoulder, both hands in the freezer sorting through the mystery packages there.

'For me, go on, I'll tell you everything else.'

I sighed, food hunting would obviously have to wait. I fetched a laptop, placing it on the worktop next to Sid, opened my email and there they were, several messages from Luci, with photos.

There was Luci, looking just as I remembered, only now sporting a deep bronze tan. Spikey, mouse brown hair with sun bleached streaks. Petite, skinny and, in these photos, wearing few clothes. Luci on the beach, Luci at some party; she was chattering away ten to the dozen on the phone, I gave up trying to show interest. I opened the next batch, Luci riding, Luci on the gallops – Sid poked me, giving me a wide eyed why didn't you tell me face. I gave her a puzzled look; she slapped her forehead with her hand and pointed again at the photos; Luci riding on the gallops, riding a racehorse - nope, still not getting it?

'Slow down, one minute, just give me a minute.' I muted the receiver on the phone. 'What?'

'Only the clear fact that your sister rides racehorses, which, Jake, you completely and utterly failed to tell me!' she looked astounded. 'How could you not tell me she worked with racehorses?'

'Um, it never came up? I don't know why, does it matter?' I was puzzled as to why this was important.

'Do you know you're such a bloody bloke sometimes, Steel,' she said with exasperation.

'Yes, yes, Luci I'm still here,' I rolled my eyes at Sid who was flicking through the photos herself, glancing at me every now and then as if I'd deliberately kept a major secret from her.

Bill fetched a beer from the fridge and wandered back out again. I leaned back against Sid, still listening to Luci. She was relaying a long story about some guy at the airport in Darwin who'd picked up her bag by mistake and then turned out to be English, she'd gone for coffee with him and the rest was history. I was slow to catch up, only half listening as I was now watching Sid as she was looking at the photos, she felt my gaze and turned her head, sticking out her tongue childishly. I carried on listening vaguely to Luci's life story to date until Sid pointed again to the screen. Luci and a bloke, Luci and a bloke who obviously knew her very well.

'Who's the guy?' I took a long look at that photo. Luci and the bloke, whose hands were where they shouldn't be in public, laughing up at the camera.

'Jake! Don't you listen to anything! I've been telling you about him for the last ten minutes! That's Ben – whose granny just happens to live in Ashfield, remember? Oh forget it! You'll meet him tomorrow. He's gorgeous and I'm a teeny weeny bit in love with him, so you'd best be nice, no being an officious arse, ok?'

So now I knew all I needed to know about her cover and the bloke she was going to turn up with. She was good, I had to give her that. But she was relying on me playing along assuming that I wouldn't risk blowing it whilst the wider situation remained so volatile. I'd done this countless times but, right now, it felt like nothing more nor less than an unforgivable betrayal.

'Sleep well or at least conserve some energy! I'll see you tomorrow and be ready for a party, ok?'

'I don't do partying, I'm far too sensible.'

'You're not and you will, for me you will. You always end up doing what I tell you to so cut out the middle man and just say yes,' she said and hung up.

I exhaled slowly, talking to her always made me feel like a whirlwind had been through. I looked again in more detail at the photos; at her smiling back at me in that moment of frozen time. Words slipped into my thoughts unbidden, *lulled in these flowers with dances and delight; And there the snake throws her enamelled skin, weed wide enough to wrap a fairy in.*

Chapter Forty-Four

In the dark the next morning Bill dropped me at the yard with Sid, I kept out of the way in the shadows as she went back to doing what she did best. I watched her constantly, studied the interaction between the lads there, the constant banter as they worked, getting the horses ready for exercise. Two of the lads were Irish, I listened to them talking and found that I'd missed the sound of their accent, that soft lilt to their words. It was the sound of my childhood, the sound of my roots.

'So there was this feller sitting at the bar...'

A joke was coming, it was part of the life here, so early that most would still be yawning but here they were, fully charged already, laughing and joking as if they'd just popped in from the pub. Regardless of the fact that there had been three murders very recently, there was still an energy here, a buzz; I could easily see why some people found this way of life addictive.

'...He had this little wooden box with him, all ornate like it had something precious init so I had to ask how he'd come by it...'

Saddles and bridles were being fetched, horses tacked up; Jim, David Flint's head lad was sorting who was riding what.

'He lifts from the box a little grand piano and then a little man, suit and tails, the full works, sets them on the bar and then the little man begins to play...'

Sid passed by, I was hidden in the early morning gloom of the buildings and I wondered if she knew I was there. She seemed jumpy but that was only to be expected all things considered.

'...And the lad said, 'I'm not so sure that she wasn't hard of hearing cos I ended up with this twelve inch pianist!'

There was raucous laughter and then the clatter of metal shoes on tarmac as the horses were brought from their stables, riders on board and off they went across to the gallops. I skulked in the dark places and watched Sid. Once at the bottom of the field, they broke as a group from a warming, long active walk into a steady trot, round and round in the gloom. David Flint appeared in his Land Rover, issuing instructions for who would do what work and with whom. Different pairings formed and then moved to the bottom of the gallop, jumping away into a steady canter up the slope, once at the top they turned and walked back down again. The pattern continued and I stayed hidden, watching Sid.

The morning passed, Sid spent time in the office with David; she rode four lots of work in the end and throughout I stayed hidden. At just after 11.30, she emerged from the tack room with a small holdall and walked towards the car park. I followed her and then, as she stopped and scanned the concreted area, walked up to her from behind the replacement horse lorry. She jumped a mile.

'Shit! Jake! Bloody hell! You nearly stopped my heart!'

She held her hand to her chest and then slapped me lightly across the arm.

'Where the bloody hell have you been all morning? I thought you'd be here, I've been freaking out that something had happened!'

'I've been here, all along. I've watched you all morning.' I stood closer to her, somewhat surprised at the level of fear in her eyes, 'I'm starving now though.'

'Where? Where have you been? I looked everywhere for you. I couldn't see you anywhere!' She was cross, fear for whatever she'd been thinking replaced now with anger.

'Sid, calm down, get in the car and drive.' I took her arm and steered her in the direction of the 'classic' as I'd already checked everything was as it should be.

Grumbling, she got in before turning on me again.

'Where were you really, Jake? Did you pop off for coffee with Bill?'

Right, this needed sorting before we left. I turned in my seat, took both of her hands in mine, tugging her gently towards me.

'You're not supposed to be able to see me all the time. I was watching you. I was almost beside you all morning. When you went to the tack room the first time you walked within inches of me.' I pulled her closer still.

'In brief, I've been with you all morning; riding, with David, on the phone and, yes, once, even with you in the john. And to top it all, I've also had to put up with all the really rubbish jokes that pass for humour here. But I'm starving now, so, Sid, can we please go?'

She stared back at me when I let her hands go and then started the engine, reversing out of the parking space and driving back to her house without saying anything further. Pulling up in the driveway, my car was there, parked sideways to the house. Bill must be about again.

'How did you do it? How did I not know? For fuck's sake, we were out in the open most of the time and still I couldn't see you!'

'Because I'm bloody good at what I do.'

'You're also bloody good at being infuriating.'

'Have faith in me, I do know what I'm doing.'

'I know that. I do know that. But cut me some slack, tell me what to expect, please, and then I won't go off on one,' she reached into the back of the Land Rover to pull out her bag. 'Was the toilet thing necessary or is this a perversion you also haven't told me about?'

'I never do anything that isn't necessary,' I said and then added, in Polish, '*the momentary intoxication with pain is the loop through which the pervert climbs into the minds of ordinary men.*'

She chose to ignore me asking instead, 'Where's Bill?'

I watched him emerge from my car, a very different Bill from yesterday, he'd been waiting for us. This was smart Bill, sharp city suit, crisp linen shirt, bright white against his dark skin and dark eyes. His hair neatly smooth against his head, no gold, no piercings — a world away from yesterday.

'Crikey!' Sid was astounded. 'Is this the same man?' she walked over and grinned up at him. 'Is that you there, Bill? You scrub up well, don't you?'

He smiled, giving her a mock salute. 'At your service ma'am, here at your service.' No more brummie, now more Oxford.

****

She bounced back in; black jeans now, black gilet over black long sleeved t-shirt. Picking an apple from the bowl, she stole a bite from my sandwich, switching on the kettle and lifting down the coffee pot.

'How much gear do you take racing with you, Sid?' Bill asked, finding out what was normal for her so that he'd recognise when it wasn't.

'Not a lot nowadays as I've a valet at the racecourse who already has my saddle. The lad with the horse will have the colours.'

'One bag?'

'Yep, I'll show you.'

A text from Luci arrived on the phone. *Flight delayed. What time will u b back later?*

I typed a reply. *7ish.*

Meet you in pub then?

Ok. Ring u later.

I didn't really want to be sucked into a night at the pub, but I'd go with it at the moment.

'We're on our own for racing, Luci's flight is delayed.' I passed coffee to Sid and Bill, sliding Finn to one side to be able to sit down. 'So what else do we need to know?'

'Sid has told me the general routine for her at the course. One ride today and then back home again, bit more involved if it wins or is placed, or if we have to factor in a fall. I can work with all of that. I take it that you'll be somewhere and nowhere throughout, Jake?'

I nodded, 'Lurking, as always. That's something else we need to discuss at another time.'

Sid tutted loudly. 'Bill, he was bloody invisible this morning and then nearly killed me by jumping out in the car park. I was already worrying about where he was and then he almost finished me off appearing from nowhere.'

'It was nothing like that,' I said, 'I don't do jumping out as a rule.'

Bill laughed, tipping his head at Sid. 'Oh girl, don't let him mess with your head, he's a bugger for that! But don't worry if you can't see him, its when you can that something big will be going down. He's known as the spider to his friends and you'll know why if you ever have the misfortune of seeing him in action.'

I was about to shut him up but was stopped by a message on my phone.

AF with GW pm. Query involvement. Tracking and bringing in.

Why would Alexander go to Newmarket to see Gabriel? Why go all that way and what for?

'Sid, did Alexander know Gabriel well?' I showed the text to Bill.

'Alex? I'd have to say no, not that well, he didn't hang out with him like Seb and Josh did when we were younger. In recent times I doubt it would have changed and surely I'd have known if he was going to the races or in Newmarket. I'm almost certain he'd have got in touch.'

'He's going to be traced and questioned by the police now. He was seen with Gabriel a few hours before he was killed. Alexander may know who killed him or why he was killed.'

'Poor Alex. He's not going to be happy but I expect he'll know nothing at all. Still, at least if you lot can track him down I'll know he's safe. Can I see him, when he has done what he has to for you? He doesn't answer his phone but he may have changed his number.'

'He's only being questioned, he's not in trouble as far as I know, but he may know things that could help us a great deal.'

'I hope he'll see it that way,' she shrugged, gathering up empty cups. 'Come on then, let's go in case the traffic is bad.'

'How do you get to the races usually?' Bill was still checking. 'Do you have another vehicle as that old rust bucket and the bike in the shed wouldn't get you there.'

I could've warned him but I wasn't quick enough. Sid drew herself up to all of her five foot four and gave him ice blue eyes.

'That rust bucket,' her voice loaded and precise, 'is a classic Series Land Rover. It has more character and more personality in one head lamp than most people do in the whole of their bodies! You and I will fall out very, very badly, Bill, if you're rude about my Land Rover.'

Bill held up both hands, mock scared face. 'Whoa! Back up, Sid. I give in! I'm grovelling. I'd no idea it was that special, I now stand corrected.'

I added softly. 'Riot helmet and stab vest at all times when the classic is mentioned. Sorry, mate, should have forewarned.'

'Are you sure we're up for the job? Just us?' He was hamming it up.

'Yea, don't worry. She's all bark and no bite most of the time!' I kept my eyes on her as he laughed, knowing this was dangerous territory.

'Don't push it! Behave now or I'll unchain Yoda.' She pushed a sleeping lurcher who briefly opened his eyes, wagged his tail twice and went promptly back to sleep. 'Well, maybe not.'

Bill stood, I could feel him preparing as if he was about to start a race himself.

'Let's go then.'

Chapter Forty-Five

Fontwell Park racecourse on a cold and damp Friday afternoon was just as I remembered it. Bill walked with Sid and stayed by her side whilst I remained hidden, just watching. He played the bodyguard routine to perfection and that alone would get the right people twitching. That is if they were there.

As I slipped down behind the stands I saw someone else, someone I recognised, also trying to remain unseen. I moved around silently until I was right behind him. A small weasel of a man, cheap suit and tie, shoes a few sizes too big as if he'd found them somewhere and a fake race pass flicking from his lapel on a short piece of coloured cord. He leant against a concrete pillar as if trying to be brave enough to peer around it. I lightly touched his shoulder.

'Hello, Skunk,' I whispered close to his ear; my accent would mark me as an Ulsterman. His reaction was dramatic, I was glad I'd hold of him. He panicked in a big way, knees shaking, a little whimper escaped his lips.

'Mick! Jesus, Mick! How you do that!' He knew who I was straight away, gabbling away in a stage whisper. He tried instinctively to turn and face me, I kept him held away.

'What're you doing here? Is something going down?'

Skunk, otherwise known as Tobias Miller, small time pickpocket and general busybody. He'd been a sometime resident of virtually every correctional establishment in the country since he was a baby; a dyed in the wool old school villain. Skunk simply because he often stank.

To me he was a supplier of good information, finding him here meant that I'd learn a lot in a short space of time without having to do the legwork myself and he'd give this information freely because he was absolutely terrified of me. At some point in the dim and distant past he'd got the wrong end of the stick and now truly believed that I'd all the mental balance and self-control of Freddie Krueger's more deranged brother. I'd never been challenged by him, but I did just enough to keep him secure in the belief that I'd do bad things to him if he crossed me and, perhaps more importantly, I always paid him well. He called me Mick purely because he thought it more respectful than Paddy. Meeting him was a little shining light of good fortune. I squeezed his shoulder with my fingers, pinching a nerve point, he whimpered again.

'Ah, Mick, don't hurt me. I ain't done nothing to you, I never would,' he cringed away, I reduced the pressure just enough to let him stay standing.

'So what's on Skunk? Who are you running from?'

'No-one! I ain't running from no-one. Just having a look, just a quick look to see who's about.'

He was shaking and he'd bolt the minute I let him go.

'Who's here that shouldn't be? What do you know?'

'Usual terms, Mick? Usual terms for a friend?'

'There's always payment for good news, you know that.'

'Supposed to be some drug thing going down, Mick, I don't know who set it up, but there's supposed to be some Chinese here today,' he kept his voice to a whisper. 'You must know that, you're part of that scene. Did you set it up, Mick? I ain't told no-one else, I swear. I'm only here to pick pockets, that's all and to keep my ear to the ground always for good blokes like you is.'

'What else? What else do you know?' I increased the pressure on two fingers only.

'Nothing! I swear it, Mick! I know nothing else,' he whined a little. 'All I know is that one of the jocks here's supposed to have a marker on them. Drugs marker. See I don't understand it, I thought they was tested, but maybe not often enough.'

I latched onto that little snippet.

'Which jock, Skunk? Think hard and tell me which jock has a marker?'

'I don't know, I really don't. I only heard a first name, nothing else.'

'Name, Skunk. Give me the name.'

'Sid, Mick, Sid Fielding, but I ain't heard it right 'cos she's a Fielding and all and they don't mess with the Fieldings. But maybe it's her, 'cos she's got a sitter today so someone's got to know something.'

Word was getting out, the contract stalker had friends, the foreign voicemail perhaps, or someone completely different.

'Top pocket, Skunk, a pleasure as always,' I whispered into the air, let go of his shoulder and was gone.

He span round, too late and too slow, he couldn't see me from where I watched him, still deep in the shadows. I stayed watching as he dipped two fingers into his jacket pocket and pulled out a little roll of notes, fifty quid, it was our agreed price for good news. I kept an eye on him for a while, to see where he went when he left his hiding place. He was a highly skilled pickpocket, joking his way through the crowd, apologising with great humour to everyone he bumped into as he fleeced them.

It was wrong on so many levels, but he never pushed his luck so, mostly, I turned a blind eye. He hadn't the first idea who I really was, to my knowledge he'd never seen me and would never recognise me even if he had. I tried him out every now and then, walked up to him as myself, even asked him a question once and he never sussed me. I slipped away again, still in the shadows and watching.

Mr Carter, the trainer of the horse Sid was riding, had a small yard on the Welsh borders. He looked like a farmer going to market, Sunday suit and overcoat; he smiled with few teeth at Sid, giving her instructions in the paddock. The owner, a lady who had overdone the fake fur, tottered on high heels, obviously believing the dress code at Fontwell to be along the lines of Ascot on Ladies Day. The horse, however, was just as Sid had said, probably worth the pain.

A smartly dressed girl led round a statuesque chestnut gelding, oozing very blue bloodlines and an aloof air as he walked around the paddock with the gait of a lion. Long easy strides that ate the ground, a serious looking horse that must have had the chance of a place, if not of winning, if it's jumping was up to scratch.

'Jockeys please mount.' A dislocated voice rang out over the loudspeakers.

Mr Carter legged Sid up onto the horse in one quick movement. The girl at his head walked around the paddock once more and then went out the gate to the course with the other runners. Goggles down, short stirrups, legs tucked underneath, gloved hands – Sid could have been anyone now. I watched as the horse was released, watched the sudden surge of power as it jumped forward into its stride. She was small against so much horse, balanced and tight. She'd give him a good ride, he'd enjoy himself with her. I smiled to myself, knowing I always did.

There were fifteen runners all making their way down to the start, just over three miles in front of them, solid steeplechase fences to jump on the way round. This was the vulnerable time. This was the time when neither I nor Bill could be close enough to her, we could only stand and watch with everyone else. The race began and I concentrated on listening to the commentator, reeling out a constant string of who was where, who fell, who dropped back, and who surged forward. As I listened I moved about from one hidden vantage point to the next, scanned the people; who wasn't watching the race, who was somewhere they shouldn't be, who looked simply out of place. There were so many factors to this. I saw nothing untoward but that didn't mean that it wasn't there, especially now I had Skunk's news.

The last half mile of the race, runners thinned down to six in contention, the others were tiring and tailing off. The commentator was speaking fast, his voice more energetic, more enthusiastic, as the race was in the closing stages. Sid was lying fifth and gaining ground. They came back into sight, powering over the last fence and on to the finish line, tired horses running their hearts out, jockeys pushing and urging for just that little bit more.

'Photo. Photo.'

It'd been as close as it looked; Sid's horse had run on, stretching its long neck, gaining ground with every stride, catching the horse that had been leading. Everyone now waited for official confirmation.

'The result of race number five on the card today is first number twelve, second number eight, third number four and fourth number fourteen. Distances a head, one length, and a distance.'

The loud disembodied voice rang out over the speakers. Sid was beaten by the nod of a head into second place.

Her horse was led into the enclosure next to the winner, she jumped off and began to undo the saddle, talking all the time to the trainer and owner, replaying the race for them. The owner looked pleased, her face alive with delight, fake fur quivering with her animated actions. Mr Carter looked pleased too but I watched how Sid kept moving as he got closer, keeping herself out of range of him all the time. I wondered if he suffered with overly familiar hands. Photographs were taken to record the event for posterity, for mantelpieces and scrapbooks and then Sid made her way back to be weighed in, disappearing again from view.

As I watched, still scanning the activity there, I saw something that was somewhere it shouldn't be. A person, a man, waiting by one of the bookies perhaps just placing a bet or collecting winnings, very innocent he looked the part, behaved as one would expect. But this man wasn't part of this scene, he was someone I knew from somewhere else; this man I would class as a danger. He was a runner who'd previously worked for the Chinese. Might have just been a coincidence that he was here but now, with Skunk's information still ringing in my ears, I was taking no chances. Back into the hidden places, on the phone to Bill.

'What's up?' his voice soft into my ear through a very discreet little microphone.

'Assume immediate increased threat.'

'Understood.'

I watched him go in through the door of the Weighing Room; he'd remove Sid through whatever back doors he could find.

'Weighed in. Weighed in.'

The voice again over the speakers, the riders were all weighed in, the result of the race now stood, a surge of activity around the bookies as people collected winnings, it seemed the horse that won had been favourite.

My man moved casually through the crowd going up to Mr Carter, the trainer, as if just to congratulate him, smiles and happy gestures. He was talking to the lady owner and she was all teeth and eyelashes. He cupped her elbow in his hand and steered her off towards the bar. He'd no doubt now be finding out all about my favourite jockey.

Chapter Forty-Six

Out through all the back routes, I arrived at the same time as Bill and Sid, quick security check of the car then out the gates. I thanked the gods that the traffic was still light.

Pulling over at the first lay-by, I said, 'Bill, you drive, I'm going to do some finding out.'

'Budge up, Sid,' I got in the back with her. Her face and hands were still muddy; she'd been removed pretty quickly thanks to Bill, just time to get changed but not showered.

'I take it you've been enjoying some lurking this afternoon?'

'Mmm, I've been skulking in the all the best places today.'

'What was the hurry afterwards, did the rozzers turn up?'

I laughed. 'Something like that and now I'll try to find out why.'

We sped along, joining the dual carriageway; phone calls, endless phone calls and still no answers. Bill made my borrowed car look good as I concentrated on trying to work out what was what. Sid fell asleep, curled up against my shoulder and looking irresistible with mud flecks still on her face.

'I bumped into an old friend today, Bill,' I said quietly. 'Do you remember Skunk?'

'Indeed I do. Who'd forget that particular brand of body odour?' Bill glanced in the mirror, 'was he as full of delight at meeting you as usual?'

'Of course, I always have a positive effect on him.'

'A positive laxative effect maybe!' Bill snorted loudly. Sid stirred briefly and then went back to sleep again.

'Your presence wasn't unnoticed. It seems that Sid is reported to have a drugs marker on her, but interestingly the word is that one doesn't mess with the Fieldings. Have you heard that before?'

'Only very recently and not here, in Hong Kong actually, I've just done a job out there and it was mentioned. I didn't made the connection until last night.'

'I wonder what started all that off? Something bigger than it seems is going down. I wish I could work out who's pushing it close to the edge.' I looked back down to Sid, sleeping so peacefully.

'Jake,' Bill said, his voice still quiet and calm. 'We've been friended.'

Oh bollocks... We were being followed.

'Ok, I'm on it. Get a number if you can.' Ice in my blood; this wasn't good, not in this car.

I got back on the phone.

'Travelling west bound on M27 about to join A31, being tailed, have target in the car. Apprehend tail as a matter of urgency.'

I listened as I was asked for an exact location and the speed we were travelling at, answering quickly and updating with the registration number of the car as Bill relayed it. He picked up speed, weaving his way through traffic calmly, my heart was pounding; Sid slept on, oblivious to the danger. A blue light appeared on the other carriageway as a marked car sped past, I hoped that we wouldn't encounter a driver that was either asleep or not paying attention. Bill flashed lights at every car that got in the way, going round if they didn't move, ignoring the hand gestures his driving elicited. All the while the car behind got closer.

'If they're not stopped soon, I'm going to get off this road and try and lose them. Do you agree?' Bill was worried. Bill worried about small matters like guns, guns fired from cars at speed. I worried about such things too.

'Whatever you think is best, you're driving.' I kept my head down and let him get on with it.

A roundabout was coming up and we'd a decision to make. Coming off would possibly make it harder for them to stay with us, but it also made it hard for help to reach us. Roundabouts, the car slew from side to side, all the while the tail ever closer, ever faster... I wanted to see that blue flashing light, I wanted to see that very badly, we were sat in the equivalent of a burning house waiting for the fire brigade and now I really needed them to arrive.

At last, lights appearing at speed behind us and confirmation on my phone that help was here. Bill slowed a little even so we were still well over hundred and twenty miles an hour on the straights; this was definitely not the road for it.

Five minutes later and it was as if it had never been. Bill slowed to nearer a legal speed and grinned at me through the mirror.

'I love a fun filled day, don't you, Spider?'

'I'm not sure I like your kind of fun.'

Looking down at Sid still sleeping, I wondered if I should even tell her what she'd missed out on.

'You need a better car, mate.'

'Probably, but that was a top piece of driving, I'm surprised you still had it in you.'

'Like riding a bike or sex, so they tell me!' he grinned back.

'What's like sex?' Sid was awake again, stretching her arms out and sitting up. 'Where are we?'

'An hour away now perhaps a bit less. You sleep like the dead,' I said; she often told me the same.

She lifted my arm and wriggled in, curling her legs up on the seat.

'Are you up for meeting Luci tonight? Do you think you've the energy for her, she's very, very tiring and that's just having to listen to her, don't let her ever talk you into going dancing.' I reached for her hand and rubbed mud from her fingers. 'You may need to wash first though, I've heard the splatter look is so last year.'

As events had heated up a bit, we checked the house before we went in. Finn was a wagging worm of a lurcher, all chattering teeth and excited woofing. He'd lots to say about being left home alone in the dark in the winter, without even the fire lit for his comfort.

'Are you going to join us this evening, Bill?' Sid asked as she passed him coffee.

'Don't know, what's the plan?' Bill looked at me.

'Umm, don't think there's anything as useful as a plan. Say pub with Luci and whoever he is and then back here?' I was making it up as I went along. 'But one or other of us will need to be about throughout, just in case.'

'Yep, back here is fine.' Sid nodded.

'In that case, I'm going back to the sumptuous flat that used to be yours, these heels are killing me and I need to put my party dress on.'

Bill seemed to inhale his coffee and stood, pouting and strutting, Sid laughed; Bill being Bill was very entertaining.

'Right, I'm off, see you in the pub later. I'll take the bat car, Jake, is that ok with you?'

'Of course, consider it yours.'

He left before I could tell him that the car would need dumping.

'I like Bill. I like Bill big time. He's a lot of fun and you were right, he's my kind of bloke,' she reached up, wrapping her hands around my neck. 'As are you, absolutely my kind of bloke.'

Leaning into me, slipping my jacket off my shoulders so that it just dropped to the floor, she held me by the hand, leading me towards the stairs.

'Just one moment,' I stopped her and quickly removed the hidden wiring that I was wearing, putting it down on the small table. 'I've a feeling we ought to keep this between ourselves.'

****

I sent Luci a text enquiring of her whereabouts; she was already at the pub apparently, waiting. I sensed a tapping foot and thought we'd better hurry along. Quickly checking in, I was informed by those that were up to speed that the tail was a stolen car, the occupants included the man from the racecourse and, due to all sorts of complicated procedural issues, most of which were almost certainly made up, the occupants were going to be detained for a few days. I really needed to find out if one was the voicemail threat or someone else entirely, but I was glad that it wasn't my big pile of paperwork and that it bought me time to find out why. Always to find out why. Tonight was now more about Sid and Luci, much more down to earth, much easier to deal with... mostly.

Chapter Forty-Seven

We took the classic to the pub, with Finn riding shotgun. Bill was a big distraction to many in that not so sleepy place, when he turned up the pub became something else entirely, it's a wonder we didn't get a raid. So much for low profile. They won't forget him for a while.

Luci hit me in a roaring, squealing cloud of arms and legs, literally wrapping herself around me as I walked in the door.

'Yer a bum, yer a punk!' she squealed, eyes shining, broadest bog-Irish.

'Yer an auld whore,' I replied, same accent but a lot quieter.

Sid stepped back, eyes wide at this over excited woman. It didn't take long for her to recover. The first part of the night was really set by that tone. Ben, the boyfriend, was obviously well briefed and coped with her exuberance, further enhanced by meeting Sid. We left the pub, piling back into the classic, with Bill bringing up the rear. I half wondered if we might have been asked to leave if we hadn't already decided to do so. Back at Sid's house, Bill kept everyone entertained whilst I checked the lay of the land.

The five of us in that living room, hard to think there were only five, it did feel like so much more, six, of course, if we include the Jedi master. Bill was deep in conversation with Ben, I tried not to go there with those names; Sid was being quizzed about horses by Luci, or maybe it was the other way around and Finn was upside down, asleep, oblivious. I sloped off to find out what was going on in the wider world, speaking to John to get his stone turning update and that alone was enlightening. I passed on Skunk's little gem at the same time.

It seemed that Gabriel Wallace was consistently a very nasty piece of work but in the nicest possible way. He managed to ingratiate himself with everyone who was useful and those people thought nothing but good about him. Then, there was another side; the side that worked effectively with people who had different needs. He made himself available to these people, lulled them, just as he'd done to Sid. He was helpful, perhaps overly so and then, just when people thought they knew him, he became someone else. He became the person from your worst nightmare. But by this time, he knew what he shouldn't and he utilised that knowledge in ways that no normal human being would.

Of course, none of this was reported because the kind of things he knew weren't those that people wished to be aired, even if they'd been brave enough to stand up to him. I was certain now that Seb and Josh had an arrangement with Gabriel and that the price for such an arrangement was Sid. I sat for a long time just dealing with the reality of that.

I thought of what she was to me, replayed all of my most special memories of her to date, laced with all that I now felt. I couldn't comprehend what it would take for a brother to put his sister in that position. What Seb and Josh were involved in was going to have to justify that in some way; it was hard to imagine where that place might be. And as the unknown in all of this, what was Alexander about? What did Alexander know of this? Did Alexander know any of this?

Alexander Fielding was evading questioning in the way that meant that Alexander Fielding had gone to ground — he was hiding. That meant two things: Alexander did know something and he was probably afraid of that knowledge.

So bleak, so dark. I stood, hands in pockets and walked to the window that faced out onto the moor. I thought of the whys in all of this, staring at nothing through the glass. A movement from behind, I blinked back from where I was — Sid.

I turned to her, caught still wondering how she got to be the magical creature she was; literally a phoenix rising from all the damage, from all the nightmares, from the bed of pain and torture she'd lain in. I was truly in love with her. It hit me suddenly; the enormity of what I felt for her. I finally understood, like a religious experience it almost shook me to my knees.

'Penny for them?' she put her arms around my waist.

'I was just thinking how much I love you. And, by that, I don't mean just thinking as in any superficial sense, I've realised what that truly means. Enlightened I am, without the assistance of our Jedi, I got there all by myself. Not bad for a bloke.'

I sensed someone else come in and then gently melt away again, wondered if it was Bill or Luci; Sid, in this particular moment, that was all I wanted, just her. From there I had another epiphany.

Sid had become my Achilles heel. She'd become something I would die for.

'Are you ok? Jake? Are you all right?'

She was intently peering into my face. I blinked a few times, shutting out those thoughts again.

'Of course, you're here.'

'You were a million miles away for a moment. Is stuff I don't need to know going down?' she was still looking at me, concerned now, with whatever was going on in my head.

'Just dusting through memories.' I hugged her, a big bear hug, inhaling deeply into her neck. 'Come on or I'll be accused, yet again, of being antisocial. But remember one thing always, I really love you.'

'And I really love you too, Jake,' she spoke with such a gentle voice, touched my face so tenderly that, out of the blue, I felt a sudden prickle of emotion behind my eyes.

'So, is there more beer?' I fought back on the unexpected emotion and went with activity instead. 'I was thinking as Bill has made it a night of bad behaviour we really should toast your photo finish. Do you like Luci by the way?'

'Oh yes, I can't imagine anyone not liking her and she's been very informative.'

To distract I scooped her up suddenly, squealing, into my arms and took her back in with everyone else, via the kitchen to collect celebratory beer. Bill caught my eye, a question on his face, I nodded and he blinked slowly. He knew now, tomorrow we would start putting some of this right.

****

'Are you going to tell me about you and Sid?'

When I went into the kitchen to make coffee, Luci was immediately coming to help. I was effectively cornered and she wasn't going to let it drop until she'd said her piece.

She leant back against the fridge door, one ankle crossed against the other casually, her arms folded. I remembered that look.

'I shouldn't think so. Shift yourself, I need the milk.' I decided to stare her down.

'No, not until you tell me what the score is,' she uncrossed her legs and stood immoveable and in the way.

'Ok, I'll manage with black then,' I turned away to pour the boiling water into the pot.

'Oh, come on, you have to tell me.'

'What do you want to know?'

'Are you in love with her? Is this serious? There's obviously something major going on between you two but what is it really? Are you making this part of the job?'

'Do you really think that's my style?' Rounding on her, I was suddenly furious about that statement. What did she take me for?

A slow smile creased her eyes. Why did I feel like I'd just walked into a trap?

'Well, that told me more than I thought it would. So you are in love with her. Actually I don't know why I'm even asking, its plain to see.'

'You're not covering your obvious attraction to Ben and I'm not giving you the twenty questions thing about him?' I bit back on the words that would have escalated the situation, that wouldn't help.

She tutted with exasperation. 'What is it with you? Always so closed off, always so difficult, why can't you stop fighting me and be nice.'

'I'm always nice to you, much more than you deserve so don't try to take me apart. You don't need to know everything about everything; life has few surprises as it is, let some of them be.' Those words stung and I began to wonder why I was being so defensive.

'Ok, ok, back up a bit. I'm only looking out for you. I need to know that you're ok.'

I sighed, running a hand through my hair, deeply uncomfortable with this level of questioning.

'Just to make you happy, Sid's a major part of my life at the moment and, yes, I hope she stays that way.'

'Thank you. Oh, look at you! How do you manage to be both infuriating and utterly gorgeous at the same time?' she grinned, 'Come on, make that coffee.'

I went back and sat next to Sid who was yawning loudly.

'Are you racing tomorrow, Sid?' Luci asked.

'Yes, supposed to be. Two rides at Exeter, but both novices so I might not survive, a hurdle and a chase.'

'We'll see you there then. I'll ring and let you know what time tomorrow but it won't be early.' Luci took hold of Ben's hand; I watched the look that passed between them. 'Bill, can we get a lift back with you? We ought to make a move before Granny locks us out.'

Bill stood, stretching himself to his impressive full height. 'Yes, of course, I need to go and get some beauty sleep if I'm going to be formidable tomorrow as well.'

'And what will you be coming as? Actually don't tell me, I don't want to spoil the surprise,' Sid laughed. 'Bill the chameleon; makes you sound like a super hero.'

'Who says I'm not!' he sparked back.

'You'd best go to bed, Bill, you're starting to ramble with lack of sleep,' I said. 'Take the bat car and don't forget to look out for villains.'

He gave a mock salute. And then there were two and a comatose dog.

'I'm so tired,' Sid yawned again and stretched herself out, 'I might just sleep here tonight.'

I picked her up and carried her upstairs; she was asleep before I eased her onto the bed. Covering her with the quilt, I went back downstairs to collect my kit and phone, returning to sit cross legged on the bed beside her.

I wasn't going to let Luci spook me so I hauled my mind back to matters in hand, let's start again with the brothers. Sebastian still in Hong Kong, Joshua, on the edge in Exeter and Alexander, underground somewhere, probably shaking. I had a drugs connection, connections to influential oil movers in Dubai, a vet dishing out ketamine and possibly also LSD to whoever would pay and a dodgy national hunt trainer on Dartmoor. Holding that strange mix together were the four brutal murders: Marcus Williams, warned off racehorse owner, small time crook; Alan Wozniak, identical twin of John, passing himself off as his brother and losing his life possibly because of that; John Wozniak, drunk horse-box driver, possible paedo, possible supplier and then, last but most definitely not least, the infamous Gabriel Wallace.

All of these people, dead or alive, orbited erratically around Sid. I glanced across to her, sleeping so soundly, her face softened by whatever she dreamt about.

I really needed to find out why this had suddenly begun. Needed to find out what made it all begin in the first place, way back whenever. Who was pulling the strings and making the puppets jump? But for that matter, who were the puppets? Was it the Fielding brothers? Was it the people who'd been murdered for not doing what they were told? Loose ends, dead ends — there were far too many of both. I'd still got a pile of bodies and no real clarity as to who had played Death for them. I pulled out the translation that had been the start of all of this and wished, yet again, that Gwil had been a bit more transparent with his clues.

Chapter Forty-Eight

I worked on quietly tapping questions and getting answers, not necessarily the right ones but answers nonetheless. Sadly, they just made the whole puzzle become more complicated. With a metaphorical pin, let's pick a ring leader, a possible puppet master - let's look at what he thinks is private.

Pulling together some software, I crafted a little probe that disappeared off deep into cyberspace pretending to be an update from the backup server that Sebastian Fielding used personally. In its binary sheepskin, it knocked on the front door and got welcomed in. Surprising how easy that could be if you knew the right disguise to wear.

Its all about logic and algorithms.

However convoluted the route, there was always a way through. Sometimes I piggy backed another program, limpet like and unseen, getting access straight to the heart of the beast. Spyware was challenged all the time but almost always there was a hole to dive down; I followed it in and ended up staring at the mad hatter's tea party at its most insane moment. When I removed the probe I let it cause havoc, blowing the main system, shattering the sick and twisted web that Seb had woven, corrupting data into a jumbled mess of codes that would be frankly impossible to unpick. Like a nuclear bomb, the resulting outpouring of virus laden damage reverberated back, taking out his servers as well.

Didn't matter, I'd got copies of everything that had been there. Coming back out, I swept the trail, conscientiously tidying up behind myself so no-one could track me. It helped that I'd first hacked an obscure server located somewhere in Zimbabwe and conducted my business through them. Hacking the hackers, they took me hidden deep as payload with their malware. I could hear the alarms sounding as I made my retreat. Sebastian's people would be having a meltdown now, exaggerated by the fact that main man himself was sweating incommunicado in an Asian jail. As Josh was already suffering, it only seemed fair to share the pain. Keep it in the family as it were.

At about three Sid woke up, she came back to consciousness from some dark place, struggled her way through and, with a sudden gasping breath, opened her eyes. She leapt back away, disorientated and unsure as to who I was for a moment.

'Sid, it's me, it's only me.' I whispered.

'Crikey, it's been a while since I had that kind of dream.'

'Funny thing sleep, your mind does crazy stuff with memories.'

'I don't remember going to bed only that I was really tired. I almost fell asleep on the sofa.'

'I know. I carried you but you were asleep before I got to the top of the stairs.'

She sat up, 'You carried me?'

'Yes. You were after whippets so I thought it was best to get you off the rug before you found one.'

'I can't believe you carried me but, perhaps more importantly, that I let you.'

'I wouldn't worry, you were obviously so overcome with my chivalry you fell instantly asleep.'

She looked around noticing now the tablet and phones, scattered sheets of paper with my scribbling on.

'Have you not slept at all?'

'No, not yet,' I shook my head. 'I'm trying to solve a puzzle; I don't always sleep when I'm trying to do that.'

'What puzzle — murders or my safety?'

'Bit of both. Finding out why all this is going on and keeping you safe whilst I do it.'

'Can I help at all? I'm never going to go back to sleep now.'

'Ok, but I probably need to tell you some more things first.' I eased her closer and kissed her, small trust me kisses. 'Sid, some of what I should tell you isn't easy to say. I want you to stop me if its more than you want to hear.'

Those eyes, sea blue depths that could be both sunlit pools or unfathomably deep — they held me, locked me to them.

'Can I ask you something first? And you can say no, I'll understand.'

'Ask away.'

'How dangerous are you? I know you and Bill mess about all the time, but there's a lot more to you both, isn't there?'

'Dangerous! That's a very strong word,' I raised my eyebrows as if what she had asked was surprising. In many ways it was.

'Bill's told me a little, not actual detail but enough that it made me think a bit more.'

'Sid, don't go there,' I wondered what Bill had said. 'I think you've probably worked out that the martial art thing is a bit more than just a hobby, but dangerous, no, that's not my scene.'

'I'm still just trying to understand.'

'It's just like policing really. The covert stuff is more involved but the heart of its just the same. You never really know what will walk in the door or how you'll deal with it. It's all about being prepared and being sharp, staying one step ahead. Reading the signs which are always there for the finding and not being too macho about it all. Keeping it humble. Keeping it real.'

There was no doubt that this was all so much harder to explain. There was also no doubt that this job was a dangerous one, but me personally dangerous? No, I didn't think so, but, then again, I suppose that would really depend on who was asking.

'Jake Steel, you may already know this, but I love you and because of that, I'm going to get up and make us some coffee. Stay right there, I'll be back.'

With coffee, we sat together and I told her what I knew, recapped on the stuff I'd already said and added some of the tough stuff, Gabriel Wallace for example, I'd class him as tough stuff for her to deal with. I still left out the payment bit though.

'It was him, dreaming of him, that was what woke me up. I'm getting better at dealing with all of that, maybe because it has been discussed so much recently, maybe because he's dead, or maybe just because you've shown me a whole new world that I didn't know was there.'

'Sid, I really need to speak to Alexander. Can you think of anywhere that he might be? Somewhere perhaps that you remember from childhood; a special place where he might like to be if he was scared? Sometimes, when people are in real trouble, they go back to those places, physically as well as mentally.'

She shook her head.

'He's such a strange one. There were times when I thought I'd got him sussed and then he'd become someone completely different and I'd be lost again. When we were young he was such fun, always laughing, always being silly. I loved that.' That memory was clearly strong.

'When our parents died he became mute. It was a terrible time and he just shut down. He actually didn't start talking properly again until his late teens but he was impossible to be around when I was dealing with Gabriel. I needed him then but I couldn't tell him or anyone what was going on so perhaps it was my fault, my silence, that made him leave, maybe I shut him out along with everyone else then.'

I knew that she'd had to do that, just to get by and it'd been her way of dealing with the trauma. It was a tragedy that Alexander hadn't known, maybe, just maybe, he might have been able to help. Ah yes, the beauty of hindsight, life was rarely that cut and dried.

'I can't believe you let me sleep through a car chase though!' she'd listened, open mouthed to what she'd missed at the racecourse and afterwards. 'Why didn't you wake me up?'

'I would have done if it'd been necessary. Sometimes those kind of situations get out of hand very quickly and, even to Bill and me, there's an element of fuck. You've enough of that particular element in your life already.'

'You're a good man, aren't you?' she turned so that she was facing me. 'You do all the right things.'

'Not always. I've made some phenomenal mistakes, really screwed up and done stuff for all the wrong reasons.'

'Well, you're doing all the right things now. I simply couldn't comprehend any of this without you. As heroes go, you're right there on the top of the pile.'

'One thing I'm definitely not and that's a hero. I'm good at my job, I like being good at my job and that's about it. But, if I can keep you safe as well then I'll be happy. In that regard, I'm very easy to please.'

'Will you tell me something else?' she slid her hand up my sleeve to my bicep. 'Under here is a discreet little tattoo in French, what does it mean?'

'It might not make any sense but it's meant as a reminder to myself, when I'm getting out of hand.'

'And?'

'It says, 'On ne voit bien qu'avec le coeur. L'essentiel est invisible pour les yeux', which means, 'It is only with the heart that one can see rightly; what is essential is invisible to the eye.'

'That is unbelievably apt,' she murmured.

'Mmm, it seems to get more so as time goes by.'

My mind was wandering as she was touching my leg, stroking the seam of my jeans making my skin tingle. No power to resist at all when it came to her.

Chapter Forty-Nine

Bill knocked the door at about ten to six. We were in the kitchen, trying to sort out the residual carnage from last night and avoid starting anything else that we'd no time for. She was deliberately getting in the way, accidentally, of course.

'Sid, behave! You've to go to work in a minute. We've not got time for any of that and anyway you'll wear me out with all the overtime,' I grabbed her hands and put them back by her sides. 'You're bad, very bad. Go wash your mind with soap and put your boots on!'

'I love it when you get all assertive!'

I covered my face and groaned, 'Sid! Girl, is there something in the water here? Its like being back at station! Go get ready for work or call in sick and then we can talk about whatever you like!'

Bill was on first watch this morning, his turn to be me. He was dressed like a shadow too, all black and so completely covered that his eyes looked almost disembodied in the gloom of the doorway.

'Your car needs changing this morning, Spider,' he smiled, a Cheshire cat smile against the darkness.

'Yep, I'm already planning its replacement. Poor little car, it's never known such speed!' I thought for a moment, 'What do you want to do?'

'Can we borrow from the station? Preferably unmarked.'

'I can but ask. Do you want to use mine to get you to the yard now?'

'Not really, we'll end up with cars in the wrong place ,' he was thinking out loud, working out the safest way to proceed.

'Don't take any chances, anyone could be anywhere at the moment, especially as I've been causing fires all night.' I thought some more. 'For speed, what if you both go on the bike and I'll take the car to the station, swop it for an unmarked, meet you at the yard?'

'Mmm, that'll work. But will she ride pillion without arguing?' Bill looked apprehensive. 'I imagine she might not want me being in charge of her bike.'

'Probably, but no reason why you couldn't be the pillion for such a short run.'

'Not sensible, I'm hardly a lightweight.'

'She handles that bike better than most blokes I know, Bill. Don't be put off by her size, she's more than capable.'

Sid walked back in. 'Who's she? The cat's mother?'

'No, the tiger who should keep her claws sheathed.' I turned and found a white lie to tell her. 'Want to take Bill on your bike to the yard? The bat car has developed a fault and I need to change it for a panda, not literally though, they tend to attract attention — something to do with all that bamboo.'

'I wonder about your mind sometimes,' Bill shook his head.

'I wouldn't, Bill; there's often not much normal going on there, you might find it frightening!' Sid giggled.

'Ok, Miss Lightning and Mr Droll, go take the big bike to work but try and resist off roading on the way. I'll meet you there as soon as.'

Bill went to see if he could find a spare helmet that fitted whilst I started worrying about letting Sid off on her own.

'Take no chances, let Bill do what he does. I'll be with you as soon as I can. This is deadly serious now, Sid, no more joking, these guys don't do pretend. No risks and tell Bill if anything looks out of the ordinary. Anything at all. Ok?'

'I know. I'll go straight there. You won't be long anyway, will you?'

'No, quick as and I'll let you know when I'm there this time,' I held her away to ensure I'd her full attention. 'Would you do something extra for me?'

'Yes, if I can.'

I slid up the sleeve of her jacket placing a plain chain, like a bracelet, around her wrist.

'Within the clasp of this is a tracker, it means that I can find out where you are. Now, don't freak out,' she was growing paler by the second, 'call it nothing more than me indulging myself, ok?'

'How does it work?' she examined it closely.

'The link there on the side of the catch, that contains a tiny responder. If you press both sides of it, like this, then it activates and starts sending out a signal. It won't work unless both sides are pressed simultaneously so there isn't any real risk of it being set off accidentally. The signal from it can be picked up by a mobile phone if you happen to know all the codes and have the right software. But you don't have to turn it on if you don't want to.'

'What if I lose it? It doesn't look very sturdy for someone like me.'

'Unlikely under your sleeve, but if it gets lost then it does,' I shrugged,

'I'm probably just being overly protective anyhow. Bill is the best of the best but don't ever tell him I told you so.'

Bill returned with a helmet wedged on and they left, the bike's throaty roar loud all the way down the lane. I spent five minutes doing a quick bit of puzzling and updated work whilst looking through Sebastian's mess once more, then took Finn, locked up and got in the car.

It refused to start, point blank refused. No response as I turned the key. I popped the bonnet and peered inside. Skin instantly prickling cold, the leads to the battery had been cut, cleanly severed twice with something sharp and laid out over the engine was a long string of fabric squares - prayer flags - buddhist prayer flags. I was back in the house in two strides, Finn close behind.

Voice dialled the station, got a car to go to the yard to alert Sid and Bill and sent a message to Moore. Disconnected that call and rang Bill on his mobile. No answer. No...! Fuck! No! Rang him again — still no answer, I wondered if he could hear it over the engine, perhaps he hadn't put the headpiece on. I paced the house, up and down, ice in my bones, rang again, still no answer. Rang Sid's mobile and heard it ringing from the kitchen. There it was still sitting on the work top. I stared at it, black in its case, forlorn and abandoned on the granite surface.

I tried to think calmly, tried not to let panic surge. Sid...please, no...not Sid.

Stop! Stop!

Think.

This situation could simply be something and nothing. Sid could safely be at the yard now, be calm, just wait. Stay, wait.

Could be someone outside waiting for me to go out again - the someone who'd cut the battery leads. What was the significance of the flags? Fuck! Fuck! What was I missing? I scanned for a memory of anything unusual? What had I seen when I went to the car? Was there anything there that shouldn't have been?

Sid.

My thoughts rushed back to her. I had to know she was safe then I'd laugh about my overreaction.

Now.

I had to know.

Right now.

Then I'd deal with the someone outside issue.

I rang covert, no news but they took the update. I rang Bill again — no answer. I disconnected, ran my hands through my hair, swearing internally all the time. I felt a trickle of sweat on my hands, no... This wasn't happening. Sid was ok. She was safe. My teeth gritted, she had to be ok, had to be safe.

Somehow, from somewhere I couldn't rationalise – I knew - I just knew that she wasn't.

HE SPENT HIS TIME HERE, IN A MIST

Chapter Fifty

I looked through the windows then opened the front door just enough to check the porch area immediately outside, easing the door closed again when my phone rang. I looked at the number, it was the police.

'Jake, its Tom. We've a problem… its Bill and Sid. Moore's on the way to pick you up.'

'Tom! What's happened?' I hissed at him down the phone.

'Stay calm but it looks like Bill's been assaulted. He's still unconscious. He's been found alone on the track...' Tom's voice, so slow, so matter of fact but he wasn't telling me what I needed to know.

'Sid? Tom! Where the fuck is Sid?'

'Sid wasn't there. She isn't at the yard. We've reason to believe she's gone, or been taken. I've got a priority team going to search the immediate area. Stay where you are, wait for Moore.'

No! No! NO! I couldn't process this. Frozen in one spot, staring at the wall, my heart pounding so hard, breath rattling in my throat, acid ice in my blood and terrible pressure in my chest; a weight pushing, pressing me down so hard I could feel my knees shake.

They had Sid.

They, whoever they were, they had her.

The people who had murdered, who had beaten to an unrecognisable pulp grown men, what would they do to Sid?

The voicemail message 'people like you will get hurt…'

They had Sid.

I was on my knees in her kitchen, my head bowed to the floor. I said I'd keep her safe. I promised I'd keep her safe. I'd caused this…poking sticks at demons, they'd bitten back now…they'd taken Sid….

My vision tunnelled, the world was spiralling, collapsing around me in the roar of my own blood surging.

They had Sid.

'Jake? Jake?' Tom's voice calling out down the phone, I ignored it, lost in a profound pit of despair. My mind, gibbering, ran over all the graphic 'what ifs'. I saw a snapshot of every murder I'd ever attended, saw splatters of blood, strewn body parts, pulped heads. I saw a lone child's shoe in the middle of a road; more powerful and brutal than all the blood because of what it symbolised. A sick slideshow, faster and faster powered through, images piled up one after the other; sounds, screams of pain, screams of terror, wailing like twisted whale song, distorted with the intensity of this pain. I hauled back; roared at myself to stop it, STOP THAT, don't even let those thoughts come in!

I was back up on my feet, cut off Tom on the phone and grabbed the nearest thing; a china bowl with flowers painted around the side. Threw it as hard as I could against the wall, it exploded into pieces like gunshot with the force of my throw and I roared out all my impotent rage with it.

I'd failed her.

Failed to keep her safe.

I'd let them take her.

I threw a coffee cup from the sink against the wall, it showered porcelain splinters and left over coffee dripped darkly brown, like old blood spilling down the white wall. I reached back for another...

'Steel... Jake... Stop that,' said a calm voice from close behind. 'Stop that and listen.'

****

I span around defensively, in position to attack instantly. DCI Moore was standing there in the doorway, close enough to flatten him in one stride, he locked onto my glare.

'Stop breaking up this place. Get yourself under control, calm down, breathe a bit. Then we can go and get her back.'

A distant far away echo of a question to myself that asked how he got in, then the memory of the phone ringing as I was checking the porch – I must have left the door open.... Shit, that wasn't a good move. What if hadn't been Moore?

He spoke calmly, so controlled, I felt myself fighting to return, I felt strength come back in over the blackness. I needed action, I needed to do this. I'd simply go and get her back again. Of course. How hard could it be?

'We're all over this. The quicker we get going, the quicker we'll find her. Come now, come on. My car is just outside,' he touched my arm and I went with him. Finn trotted along at my heels, locking the door of the house and pocketing the key, I opened the back door of Moore's car and let Finn get in without thinking to ask. Only one good thing, if there was someone still waiting and watching outside, they let us be for now.

'Where's Bill?' My voice sounded hollow against the steady hum of the quiet engine after a seeming eternity of managing nothing more than breathing.

'In an ambulance, thankfully he's conscious now but concussed. He can't tell us anything at the moment. It all presents as if they were ambushed. He was certainly hit very hard; he may have a skull fracture.' Moore spoke with a matter of fact tone, telling it how it was. 'Someone came by, must have been just after it happened, found Bill alone in the road, he called a 999. There was no one else there.'

I couldn't manage any more words. My emotions were in tatters, everything seemed so far away and I was clinging on, clinging by bloodied fingertips, to reality. All my training gone, Mr Kick Ass Confident was a million miles away and still running off into the distance. I spiralled again with rampant thoughts. One minute I wanted to kill those bastards. If they hurt her I'd track them down and kill them one by one, without a doubt. In the next, I wanted to curl up and let go, if they'd killed her, I'd do that, without a doubt. In desperation, I clung onto the anger like a life raft.

The car pulled up on a grass verge at the end of the track. This was where it had happened. I looked at the skid marks from the bike's tyres, looked at the flattened grass, the pieces of light lens, indicator lens flashing orange sparkles in the early morning light. The bike had crashed. Numb and to the bone cold, I looked at the pool of drying blood on the tarmac, dark red against the grey stones.

People already working, finding the clues, more cars arriving, road closures already set up; the microscopic search for answers and evidence began.

'The blood is Bill's. That's where Bill was. There was another vehicle here, parked along there,' he pointed to a small lay-by. 'Forensics are onto it, we'll trace it.'

We got back in the car, went to the racing yard. Moore strode up to David Flint, his face a mask of calm. He led him into the office, I stayed sitting in the car and tried to hold myself together. My phone vibrated softly in my pocket.

'Go ahead.' My voice came from somewhere else as I was back roaring again and breaking plates inside myself. I was replaying saying good bye to her, replaying her smiling, laughing, kissing me. It was tearing something within, ripping me apart with vicious teeth. I clenched my fist to contain it, gripped the phone so hard I heard the plastic casing creak.

'Its John.'

I tensed as if his words could cause yet more pain, I wasn't sure I could talk to him. He was too close, too close to all of this. I swallowed hard.

'I'm doing everything I can here. I'll help you find her, I promise. We can sort this out. Be strong. I'm here, I'm helping too.'

'John…' I could manage nothing more, I sounded as broken as I felt.

'Don't worry, I'm here. I'll ring you later. Know that we're here for you.' I heard his voice break slightly as he disconnected.

I sat, immobile, frozen like I was nothing more than stone. Emotions rioting uncontrollably underneath that rigid skin, I held them at bay with some part of me - I don't know how, I felt as brittle as those plates I'd thrown. One small thing and I'd fracture into a thousand pieces to explode against the hard wall of this unbelievable pain. The noise in my head was like a hold down, just like once, when I'd been surfing, I'd met a wave wrong and got forced down under the water, held for as long as it took to fill my sinuses with salt water and make me think seriously about drowning.

And I was now.

I was drowning in this, in wave after wave of un-surfable agony.

Where was my stone zone now? Where was my full on, think straight, get in there and get this sorted courage? Not here, nowhere to be seen now …

Moore came back from Flint's office. David Flint now knew that Sid had been taken, that she wouldn't be riding today at Exeter, he'd been told to keep it to himself. Part of me wondered if he'd had a hand in making her disappear. A greater part was glad that I didn't have to deal with him, because if he'd spoken as if to infer that it was awfully inconvenient of her to do such a thing, I think I would have torn his face off with my bare hands.

Back to the station, into the office and the searching carried on. I sat, staring at nothing. Finn slept and I stared, then, suddenly as if pulled up by invisible strings, I stood. Action, I needed action to force myself through this. I'd go and find Joshua, see if he knew anything.

Moore walked out of his room, his face said it all, 'Jake, Joshua Fielding has just been found dead in his hotel room. He's been shot. It looks like murder. Time of death about two and a half hours ago, but we're working on room service records only at the moment.'

His voice soft and steady filtered in past my internal screaming. About an hour and a half before Sid was taken. Someone could have killed him and then come for her, it was doable from Exeter in that time. I sat heavily again, my head in my hands.

'I know what you're thinking and I have to say that if they were going to simply kill her, they'd have done it on scene. Why take her and the bike away if she was just to be killed? Why leave Bill and not Sid? They, whoever they are, haven't moved any of the other bodies, just left them where they fell. I'm not sure if that makes this better or worse. But, at this time, I'm certain that she's still alive, Jake and we'll get her back, don't doubt that for a second.'

His voice washed over, like those waves, that sea that hushed in and out and held me down. I breathed with it, concentrated on managing that, in and out, just like those waves. I needed to start thinking, needed to solve this puzzle. Solve this puzzle and find Sid. Whether she was dead or alive, I had to find her.

'Where's Alexander? He's the only unknown now. Sebastian is in prison, Joshua is dead and that just leaves Alexander,' I reached to find some rational thought. Pushed away the terrible pain of Sid and covered her roughly with the rug of my job. I hauled Mr Kick Ass Confident from the cupboard, gave him a bloody good slap and set him back on his feet. 'I'm going to see Bill.'

'Ok, good plan. Stay with it, you can do this, take Trevor.'

'I need a car.' I stood again.

'Ok, I'll arrange that. You call him in.'

I rang Trev, told him to shift his arse. He did. Fifteen minutes later he was there and, shortly afterwards, so was the car. As I went towards the door of the office Tom walked in with Trev behind him.

'Jake. Good to see you and I'm glad you're able to be here,' Tom reached out one hand, caught the look on my face and pulled it back again. 'Is there anything new?'

I shook my head, willing him to move out of the way, I knew words weren't there, not sensible words in any case.

'We've some positive leads already, everyone on duty is out and asking, everyone is on this,' he paused, looked away, to somewhere above and behind me, I stared at him – felt it coming, knew he had to ask it and knew just how hard it probably was for him to do so. 'Jake, do you think that there's any chance that she's involved? That she's run rather than been taken? Do you think she could have assaulted Bill or caused the crash deliberately? There's no sign of her bike, of her... Jake, did she arrange to meet someone there and then have help to escape?'

For a millionth of a second I let that question find its way in. It was the self-same question I would have asked if I was on the outside of this. Tom, playing devil's advocate, he had to ask it — he was right to do so. But, within me a surge of naked anger, his eyes on mine, calm and open. I knew he was doing his job, just doing his job.

But I still hit him.

Chapter Fifty-One

A light speed strike that came from somewhere instinctive, not a strike I'd thought about. A silent snap of one hand; it channelled out and made contact with Tom's face. He flew backwards against my desk as if I'd bodily thrown him; there was a crashing noise of upset furniture, of files carried with him to the floor, of Trev's swearing exclamation. I hadn't moved my feet at all, just launched that strike and then stood there as if it'd been someone else. Moore appeared at speed from his room, Trev stood close by, wide eyed and open mouthed. Tom lay sprawled on the floor, out of it for a long moment and then he moved to sit up, putting his hand to his face and an ice-cold gaze on me.

'WHAT THE FUCK IS GOING ON!' Moore shouted. 'We've a serious situation here so why are you scrapping like schoolboys?'

He looked from Tom on the floor to me and then to Trev, working it out in his mind.

'DS Sorrell, get the fuck up off the floor and tidy this place up! One thing that might have been good for you to remember is timing. Charging in with your mouth in gear before your brain is likely to get you what you just got! Get up now and get on with it!' he roared down at Tom, sitting in the mess that was once my desk.

'And you, Steel,' he rounded on me, moved so that he was millimetres from my face. 'If you ever lay a finger in anger on anyone else here, for whatever reason, under whatever provocation you will wish you'd never set eyes on me. Back up right now, ensure that you're fully under control and then FUCK OFF OUT OF HERE AND DO YOUR BLOODY JOB!'

He shouted, military power voice straight into my face but I let it wash over. He was pushing deliberately, putting himself in range for the same as I gave Tom, testing before he let me leave. But I was back now and I wouldn't allow that to happen again.

'Jake, come on, let's go,' Trev said and went to the door. I turned and went with him, Finn trotting to heel beside me as if that was what he always did.

'How did you do that? That was so quick, looked just like a touch and yet he literally flew across the room! How is that done?' Trev chattered away as we walked down to the car park. 'Fuck that really was something else - hope I'm never on the wrong side of you.'

He looked over and whatever he saw shut him up instantly. I was glad for his silence but I shouldn't have done that to Tom, not then, not at any time. Finn jumped in on the back seat; I let Trev drive and got out the phone. First call Luci.

'Bloody hell it's too early, what's going on?' she spoke with a muffled voice.

'Sid has been abducted, Bill is in hospital. I'm not going to be about later, keep your ear to the ground and let me know if you hear anything at all.'

'Fucking hell! Are you ok? Are you hurt?' she was loud now down the phone.

'No. I wasn't there. Just do as I ask. I can't talk now.' I disconnected.

I rang John again, straight into Irish, willing him to keep up as Trev was sitting right next to me. I rang covert and found that they still had no news, nothing new apart from the fact that they had intelligence that Joshua was a contract killing.

Another vicious sabre stab of grief.

If that was the case, Sid wouldn't stand a chance. If that was the case, it might be better if she was already dead. Buddhist prayer flags. Where did they fit?

I rang one of my pet squeakers. Roared violently into him until he cracked and told me, yes, contract, the word was a contract was laying traps for the Fielding brothers. Big shit - don't get caught up in it - really bad dudes…

Part of me, somewhere deeply hidden, fractured terminally with an audible snap and released a wall of acid fire that crippled me, stole the air from my lungs and the beat from my heart. Already dead. Internally I writhed through that realisation, acceptance hung above me like the proverbial sword. A voice in my head, issuing venomous commands. Fall on it, fall on it, you selfish bastard. You brought this on her. You deserve all that you get.

Trev, just drove, said nothing, kept his eyes front and drove. He glanced at me a couple of times and then left me well alone. That was wise.

Leaving Finn in the car, I walked fast up the hospital steps in search of Bill, Trev trotted beside me. Through long corridors and swinging doors, I tried A & E first, yes, he's here, in a side room but you can't go in. I flashed my card, yes I can, yes I fucking well can, so just step aside and let me otherwise I'll just go right through you.

It's amazing how much can be said with just your eyes, the poor nurse moved, quickly. When I thought of eyes, I tried not to think about sea blue depths, tried not to hear that musical laugh, tried not to smell her on my clothes. That was a black place, a very black place and absolutely no help to me now. Trev stayed and apologised for my appalling behaviour to the nurse, did his very best to constantly remind me that I didn't need to be a shit to get this done, whatever was going on.

Bill, big Bill, stretched out on the hospital bed, his eyes closed.

'Bill? Hey, how are you doing?' I whispered.

He opened his eyes and winced against the light.

'Jake...' he croaked, 'I'm so sorry; there was nothing I could do to stop him. It was a planned ambush. I was out before I knew it,' he licked at dry lips. 'Any news?'

I shook my head. 'Nothing. I'll kill whoever has done this though.'

He smiled weakly, 'No, you won't, but you'll find her, I know you will. Go and get her back, Jake, you love her too much to let her get lost.'

I looked away quickly, out the side window, squeezed my eyes tightly together and forced emotion away. So brittle, one small thing and I'll be a million pieces on the floor. Suddenly a thought rushed in.

'Bill, you said him, you couldn't stop him and that it was a planned ambush. Do you remember anything more?'

'I didn't even know it was a him! Where does this stuff come from? A minute, let me think, one minute. Yes! A man, scruffy, looked like a homeless, green van like a furniture van, small though, I saw the back of it, double doors, not a roller. Right, get someone here to take this all down.'

He edged his way up the bed onto the pillows, wincing all the way. I went back out and down the corridor, pulled out my phone and called Moore.

Hang in there, Sid, I'm coming.

Hang in there.

Alive...I hissed to myself through gritted teeth...please be alive...

I heard my words to her, 'because I'm good at what I do.' Now was the time to prove that.

Trevor and I left the hospital armed with all Bill could remember. Driving now, I flicked on the lights and sirens and hurtled out through the traffic, my thoughts sharpened as pieces of the puzzle slotted into random combinations, clicking into place or being discarded. I drove back to the place that it had happened. Trev and I stood on the verge surrounded by forensics and blue and white don't cross markers. Trev said nothing, tried very hard not to get under my feet and to jump whenever I told him to.

Forensics had found a wire. A thin strand of wire stretched across the track, invisible in the dark and set at just the right height to take Bill off the bike. Sid, in the front, would have ridden right under it oblivious. How did the attackers know Bill and Sid would take the bike? Was that just a punt? Or were we manipulated into doing so somehow? Either way, the ambush was well planned, too well planned.

Trev and I got back in the car, went to Sid's house. My car remained in the courtyard, bonnet still up — a silent, immobile traitor. Police and forensics around it. If it had started, if it had stopped itself from being nobbled, Sid might still be here. I couldn't look at it, wanted to torch it and watch it burn.

To the front door, key in, step into the house. Another tsunami wave of loss hit, nearly drove me down onto my knees again; she was so here still I could smell her, hear her, taste her in the very air. I walked stiffly, with that agonising pain snapping at my heels, and pulled out the drawer of OS maps, hauling them all out and taking them back to the table.

'Right, Trev, you know this area better than me, tell me where to start looking for someone who might be hiding? We know the suspect looks like a homeless man; let's start with a place where a homeless man might hang out.' I flung open the first map of the moor.

Four hours she'd been gone now. Four whole hours.

We looked at the map and Trev tried to work magic with suggestions. We loaded back into the car and went to them all. Sid wasn't there. She wasn't at any of those places.

Seven hours now.

Seven whole hours.

She could be anywhere. I rang John, rang Moore, plagued them constantly for news; there was nothing, everyone was doing all they could but there was nothing. Exeter was dealing with Joshua's death. No news from traffic, no sightings on the roads, no news from the ports or airports. Nothing. She'd simply disappeared. Gone now, without a single trace to show of where she might have been.

Tracker! For fuck's sake, she was wearing a tracker! With a sudden surge of hope, I accessed the responder, linked it to GPS and...

...nothing. ...not a sound...

The tracker hadn't been activated. Was that because she was safe somewhere? Or was that because she'd had no time to set it? I thought back to Bill on the road. Ambush...no signal...she wouldn't have stood a chance...

But here she was: she was stroking my face, she was telling me a joke and laughing so much she couldn't get out the punch line, she was wound around me in the shower, she was hugging Finn, she was riding, perfectly balanced, galloping over fences. Over and over, like some perverted torture movie, those memories wouldn't be suppressed, they tore through like a physical force, and each one carried a knife.

Those highly skilled in Silat use a unique and distinctive knife called a Keris or Kris. It is razor sharp and, when it is forged, the metal is supposed to be infused with a powerful neurotoxin. It is said that the slightest scratch is fatal. The pain as the toxin enters the body is beyond excruciating. I could imagine that now...I could feel that now...

I have never known such pain.

I tried to breathe through it, tensed myself against the onslaught, clenched my teeth and held my head in my hands. Shut down. Contain this. Hold this, like a bomb, deep inside...

'Jake? Jake? Are you ok?' Trev's voice from beside me in the car.

There was no way I could answer at that moment.

'Look, I'm going to take you back to Sid's house. You can't carry on like this, ring your sister and get her to come.'

He turned the car and all the while silently I was screaming no! NO! KEEP LOOKING! We have to keep looking! But I couldn't risk trying to speak, I was holding on to myself so tightly now, if I spoke, I knew I'd fall apart.

Chapter Fifty-Two

Trev took me back to her house. Trev made phone calls. Moore was suddenly there with Tom, whose face was darkening with one hell of a bruise. I couldn't speak to them, couldn't look at them for more than a quick glance, terrible rage still boiled and with it wave after wave of silent black agony. So wanted to let this out, to really batter the fuck out of something, it took every ounce of willpower I had not to do so, not to lose control again. So I was stuck in that no man's land, holding on to Finn and outwardly still, staring blankly at nothing.

Luci turned up, she got rid of everyone and when we were alone, put her arms tightly around my shoulders. All that pain surged up with her compassion and I could no longer restrain it, it grew relentlessly like the tide coming in until it poured out.

Guilt. It marched in with the agony, arm in arm and cackled. This is your fault - you made this happen - digging where you shouldn't - should have left it - shouldn't have got involved - your fault - you've killed her. Words in my head, sadistic words that poked and gibbered and whipped…

Luci made coffee, placing some steaming blackly in a cup on the table. Finn lay with his head on my lap, not really sleeping, just being, just being there with his canine wisdom. I was lost into a void; a deep, dark and truly terrifying place filled with guilt, grief and loss. She pushed the cup closer, then put it in my hands. It contained a lot of sugar and a lot of brandy or whisky as it made me cough through the first salt sweet mouthful. I drank it all; maybe it would numb this, blunt the knives that ripped and tore whenever I moved. It brought back a minuscule amount of focus; I lifted my head and looked at her.

'Oh God… I'd do anything to make this better for you.'

From granite more than a trace of emotion, I wondered how bad I looked for her to react like that. With tight arms around me again she whispered soft words.

'It's ok, it's ok, you'll get through this. You'll get through this.'

Over and over, like a mantra, like a prayer.

Twelve hours now.

Twelve hours of not knowing.

I needed to do something, to force myself to move; this frozen state might hold the screaming at bay but I needed to force myself through and out the other side.

'I'm going for a run.'

'No! Its dark; you need to be here, just in case. Wait, Jake, please,' she was in front of me instantly, on her knees.

'I need... need to burn this out. I'll take my phone, please understand I need to do this. I'll take Finn.' I looked at her and saw my pain reflected in her eyes.

'If you must, but tell DCI Moore, tell him where you're going. Just think for a moment, what if they need you and you're not here?'

'I'll be an hour, I'll take my phone.' I pulled away and stood, unsteady on my feet. Finn shadowed every movement.

I couldn't go upstairs, couldn't go anywhere near the things that screamed of Sid. I would never make it off the floor, I knew this now, I understood this. So close to the edge. Too close. Holding on by bleeding fingertips alone. The dark, bleak, bottomless drop I was mentally hanging over was petrifying.

I went to the boot room and forced myself to change shoes, my kit bag still there from a lifetime ago, forced myself to lift down the head torch. I didn't look at her things, kept my eyes away from those weapons as they'd slay me, they'd knock me down and take away the minuscule amount of strength I had left.

Voice dialled Moore. 'I'm running, be an hour, have my phone.'

My voice sounded so empty, robotic. Part of me wondered if I should do this. The greater part knew I had to.

'Is your sister there? Let me speak to her for a moment.'

So steady, measured and calm as he always was with this, so long as I wasn't trying to kill someone.

I passed the phone to Luci and sat on the bench to put on trainers, staring at the laces as tying them was suddenly an impossible task. I half listened to what she was saying.

'I know, but it's what he does, maybe it'll help.'

'I understand your concern.'

'Yes, but perhaps it'll bring him back from where he is right now.' Luci understood.

It was a one sided conversation, just listening to what she said and not knowing how Moore replied. I sat there, hugging my knees, trying so hard not to let the memories start all over again. I forced myself to be numb.

Luci handed back the phone, she held my hands and looked into my face.

'Please don't take any risks. If she comes home and you're not here, think about that, please. Go run if you must and then come back, you're needed here, you need to be here, for her, for yourself,' she reached to touch my face with her fingers, just like Sid had done... the pain flooded back, acid...crippling...

I couldn't breathe...my chest...my throat raw, an open wound. I couldn't put into words, especially not to Luci, that there was no coming home now. I had to accept that Sid was gone. Just like I'd done with Gwil. Sid wouldn't be anywhere anymore.

Forced to my feet, I went out past the uniform standing sentry, Finn on my heels. I looked down at his amber eyes, the whole world within them. Yoda, Jedi master, his presence had done it again, held me still whilst the big stuff happened.

I switched on the torch and set off with him loping along, keeping me company and guarding me from the one thing that there was no escape from. It did work for a while, the rhythmic pounding of running; every time my thoughts strayed to her I ran faster, the pain receded with the increased pace, my breathing laboured, my heart breaking invisibly in the dark. I let it go, let that pain pile out, tears flowing in the darkness, I ran on through it all faster and faster. Kept pushing myself, kept pushing and punishing.

Ran on, up the back of the tor, up into the cold, dark night stopped and stood at the very top, buffeted by an ice wind slapping into my body as if it, too, wished to berate. Finn sat with his tongue lolling long. Crouching down I hugged him, cried with him there, on my knees in the blackness simply because I could, because no one was there and Finn never judged me as I judged myself. I was overtaken by debilitating fire. It gripped me, ripped through me... I was destroyed...breathing now impossible without her.

Without her...

I was without her now.... was nothing without her...

Head bowed to the ancient rock panting through the severity of my thoughts; venomous, bladed, bullet laden thoughts that forced their way through, giving themselves barbed birth with no compassion. They crippled and tortured, pinned me to the rock and held me under. I began to think I might let go...

She's dead... I am without her...not just for now...for forever.
Gone.

No. Please. No.

Waves and waves of darkness, I gagged onto cold stone. On my knees, retching onto timeless granite, my whole body shaking as if an invisible being tore into me over and over for letting this come to pass.

Death.

She's dead. Please let it have been quick. Don't let her have known.

A snapshot image of her face, filled with terror, of her hands - those elegant, feminine fingers wound tight in mine, white knuckled muscle memory of all the pain she'd already been through.

She's gone now.

No.

Still.

She's so still. I can almost see her.

Hazy image of her lying on a blanket - words in my head, a quote from somewhere distant - *if I must die, I will encounter darkness as a bride, and hug it in mine arms.* No! No, death should have no part in this play, not her death. Death is not romantic. It is nothing. *...death isn't anything...death is...not... The endless time of never coming back, a gap you can't see, and when the wind blows through it, it makes no sound.*

You lied, told her that you'd keep her safe, told her that you'd keep her safe and then you let her be murdered.

Lies and failures. Its just like Gwil.

For murder, though it have no tongue, will speak...

I picture her again and we're walking on the moor, I can feel her hand in mine and it's so warm. She's speaking but I hear no sound. She lifts her face, the wind catches her hair and takes it gently from her shoulder, a tendril floats momentarily and captivates me, like spun gold in the sunlight. Her face, so heartbreakingly beautiful, the sparkle from her eyes, the upturn of her mouth as she laughs...

How?

How do I come back from this?

What was is no more. She is no more. What we had has passed. Past – been and gone. A relic now to hold in my heart and never more to hold in my hands. Never more to hold her. Never more to feel her soft skin, never to have her next to me, to smell, touch, hear her. She is no longer. Past now.

She is gone.

Finn whined a little and licked my face as I lay crumpled and incapable on the tor. I had nothing left. Nothing at all. Not even for him. I let go with bloodied hands and let myself fall into the dark cavern that yawned wide open.

Time lost meaning. Numb. Nothing else existed in this emptiness. So cold…past shivering but so cold…it didn't matter, nothing mattered now.

My phone pinged with a muffled message alert from my pocket. Curled tightly, foetal-like on that tor, I felt it vibrate against my leg and, somehow, it drew me back. Straightening, I forced rigid fingers to hold it and blinked at the screen. A text message. Tracker coordinates. GPS linking…

I stared at it for a hundred years and then it sunk in.

It was Sid's tracker. Sid. Fuck! Sid!

I stared at the flashing pointer on the screen map.

Scotland.

The tracker was in Scotland…

Chapter Fifty-Three

Stumbling to my feet, willing strength into stiff muscles, I ran. On rubber legs, with burning pain in my joints, I ran down off that tor, throwing myself down the tracks, mud flying, all the way back to Sid's house. Finn ran with me, eating up the ground with his long legs. I flung open the door, forced huge gulps of air back into my lungs and tried to find words. Luci stood in the doorway, wide eyed, silent, waiting. Beside her two uniforms. Why were they here? How long had I been gone? Questions. Leave it now. Not now! Sid. Just find Sid now.

'I know where the tracker is. I know where it is!' I scrubbed at my face and forced myself to act, pulled out the phone and rang John.

'John... a tracker co-ordinate from Sid's unit... on my mobile. Access my unit, extract the data - do it now!' I spoke too fast, in big gulps. Simultaneously a text message pinged but with an unrecognised number, *A here ill need help luv fvr Sx*

Alive! Oh! Please! Alive!

A? Who's A? Alexander! Shit! Alexander is with her! Scotland? Why?

I relayed it to John and then rang Moore. He agreed to everything I asked, told me to wait for back up and disconnected the line.

John rang back, the text had been sent two hours ago - so much for the immediacy of texting. I was already entering coordinates and locating the place where Sid had used the phone with GPS. The tracker matched the phone location. The tracker cursor blinked back from the 3D map not moving. I prayed she was still there. Most of all I prayed that she was still alive.

Back on the phone. Now was the time to pull in contacts. Now was the time to haul them from out of the shadows and make them work for me not the other way around. I needed the kind of assistance that made what I usually did look like child's play and I'd go on my knees to ask for it if necessary. Focus. Breathe. Numbers into the phone and, within seconds, action.

I left the directions with Luci, grabbed my rucksack from the boot room and went to bolt out the door again, Finn still at my side. One of the uniformed constables stepped in front and caught my sleeve.

'Sir...' he stammered nervously. He'd obviously been told to hold me if I came back. 'You have to wait here. I've been ordered to arrest you if you try to leave.'

I stared coldly at his young man's face, watched fear and uncertainty flicker in his eyes. He had his orders.

'If you don't get out of my way immediately I will hurt you very badly.' My voice was harsh and, in that moment, I meant every word. Luci inhaled sharply and half-stepped forward.

'Constable, I'm sorry I don't know your name but just let him go. Forget it please, let him go.' She gently lifted the man's hand from my sleeve and he didn't try to stop her.

I was out the door without another word. Glancing into the police car parked so innocently on the drive way and there were the keys shining at me, left in the ignition. Stupid copper! Who leaves the keys in at anytime, let alone when there's a murderer about? Never mind, I requisitioned it without a second thought, spinning wheels and sliding sideways out of the courtyard, Finn clinging to the upholstery with clawed paws. I drove fast through the narrow moor roads. I didn't give a shit about any order to wait for back up, didn't care about protocol and covert, I simply drove.

Ten miles down the road, I turned off into a large gravel car park beside dark woodland. Forestry Commission signs to both sides, telling me what I could and couldn't do there. Out the car with Finn, locked it and pocketed the keys, strapped on the rucksack.

Focus and breathe. Concentrate. Wait.

A harsh noise from the distance. A mechanical slapping, getting louder and louder. Lights in the air coming closer.

The helicopter landed in the clearing as I clung to Finn with my head bowed, eyes closed to avoid debris from the updraft. The very second it touched down, I threw Finn in through the open doorway and jumped in after him. The heli was off the ground immediately.

Special forces. Exactly the right kind of backup for this kind of job. Those in the shadows had done me proud, but I'd also called in every favour I was ever owed and, even then, would probably never pay off the debt I would now be generating. If this came back to bite me, I'd never see the light of day.

Four pairs of bright eyes shone expectantly from the dark interior and voices spoke robotically through intercoms. I pulled on the helmet that was thrown to me, vaguely strapped Finn onto a seat and took a moment to exhale heavily. It was that time again. Time to rock and roll.

Within minutes we all knew the plan. Time blurred into a smudge of dark airbases, hurried conversations and different helicopters. I followed the line of almost all of the UK on a variety of radar screens, each one taking me closer to the static blinking cursor that was all that I had left of Sid.

On the outskirts of Pitlochry in Perthshire I caught my last ride with Finn. Mountain ranges now and a bitter, ice cold, penetrating wind. Pitch black night all around. The heli took me as close as it was possible to be to the cursor. And that place was close to nothing at all. Not a great place to take a lurcher. Not even a Jedi master.

I AM ASHES WHERE ONCE FIRE BURNED

Chapter Fifty-Four

I watched it leave. Standing alone on hard granite, waving briefly as it lifted up and away, taking with it all the light and leaving me alone in the black void of a winter's night in Scotland. Awareness of the cold was immediate, even in my hastily borrowed mountain kit, it seeped in with wanton fingers. Switching on night vision, I looked down to Finn beside me. He was also wearing someone else's coat, his front legs thrust through the arms, the whole thing belted tight and zipped up along his back. It may have been insane but I'd refused all offers of care for him; rightly or wrongly, to have left him behind now would have felt like leaving part of Sid. Besides he was my wing man and, although somewhat unconventional, you don't leave that kind of man behind as far as I'm concerned.

We stood together on the summit of a mountain called Schiehallion, some three and a half thousand feet up. Hidden in the darkness down below was Loch Rannoch and behind us, over another mountain range lorded over by Ben Lawers, was Loch Tay. Not so far away, in mountain terms, over the bleakness of Rannoch Moor was Glen Coe, otherwise known as the Great Glen. Innocent blood had been spilled all over that ancient place with every sort of battle since time began but, and I said it out loud, it wasn't about to get anymore tonight from those who were mine.

The fact that Schiehallion was close to my own home wasn't lost on me. That Sid had been brought here wouldn't be marked down as sheer coincidence. Someone had a plan and I was clearly part of it. Well, I'm here now so bring it on.

****

Schiehallion has an almost perfect conical shape from its western flank and sits in glorious splendour isolated from the other peaks. As a munro, its popular with daylight walkers, a broad eastern side lends itself to the less hardcore visitor but west was my direction, the steepest side - of course, I wouldn't have expected anything less.

There is a saying up here that if you don't like the weather, then you should just wait a bit. I wasn't about to hang around waiting for anything; winter windows in the weather are about as rare as sighting a real kelpie.

The most immediate concern for me was avoiding injury. The visibility now down to about a metre and, although it was a dry, the mountain summit was covered with frozen snow; there was a good chance that it was due a top up any minute. Slipping almost immediately on sheet ice, I stopped to sort myself some better traction. A fracture or sprain would help no-one now, least of all Sid. Socks off, boots back on and socks on over them - no crampons but much better grip nonetheless. I checked the phone again, the comm signal here was fragile but the GPS receiver was doing its thing. In a place just over eight miles away, as the eagle flies, from where I stood, Sid's tracker still flashed silently luring me in.

A flashing cursor and a delayed text message; not much perhaps to justify such a full on rescue mission. But, invisible here in the blackness, I thought of nothing at all now except getting to that place.

Half running, it was apparent that Finn was going to struggle. Ice had already packed into his paws, pushing the pads apart and sandpapering delicate skin into bleeding splits. With my knife, I fashioned socks for him from my t-shirt, tying them with strips of fabric to keep everything in place. I stroked his head and willed be strong thoughts to him; no delays, Finn, I'm sorry but no delays.

Sliding down the loose scree that littered our descent, we made good time by literally letting it take us with it, leaning bodyweight back and surfing our way down. Delight at how well we were doing was rapidly squashed by the presence of a very swollen river at the base. Too wide to jump, no time to find a way around, I stood facing it and uttered a few swear words at whichever being thought I hadn't had enough for a day or so.

Water is highly dangerous in this kind of place and especially so at this time of year. Clothing freezes almost instantly, the cold itself can cause cardiac arrest and, even ignoring those issues, it was going to delay us. On a normal trip I'd find a way around, especially as I had Finn, but this was anything but a normal trip. Assessing the depth with a long dead branch; too deep to wade through and the current clearly in a hurry to get everything in it to Rannoch. Nothing but a few sticks nearby, not enough wood for a raft. Quick! Think quickly! Wasting time! Come on! I badgered myself with all sorts of thoughts. Make a decision and go with it.

I gathered what small sticks I could find, stripped off everything but my boots, stuffing sticks and clothes into my waterproof rucksack. Without giving him chance to have a point of view, I stripped Finn also, picked him up and held him tight under one arm, hauled my rucksack with the other and ran into the water. It was like running into a wall.

Instinct to survive got me across that water, nothing more or less than something ancient within my bones. I threw Finn onto the far bank as soon as I reached it, dragging myself out as quickly as I could after him. I had about two minutes before I lost the feeling in my hands, no time at all to mess around. Scrabbling to a large rock I pulled out the dry sticks and some cotton wool from my pack. With chattering teeth and a monumental ice headache, I frantically used a small fire starter to ignite a rudimentary fire.

Rubbing the worst of the moisture from my skin, I dressed at speed as the flames grew, swinging my arms around myself in great circles to get the circulation going again. Then, sharing with Finn, I ate two emergency ration bars, high calorie and easy to eat as I rubbed his body in the same way that I'd done mine and zipped him back into his coat. He may never ever forgive me but any apologising would have to wait. As soon as there was feeling back in my fingers, I kicked out the fire and we ran on again. Cold, battered, but still fighting.

Zooming the focus in on the screen, the GPS showed the structure around the tracker again, something like a shieling at the base of the slope I was heading for. Shielings ranged from something as simple as a wall to shelter from the worst of the prevailing wind, to a full building like a bothy. No longer often used, they'd been originally built for shepherds and their like to tend animals grazing away from steadings during the summer months. Sid's tracker was in a shieling - my remaining hope was that she was there too.

****

The shieling turned out to be a derelict barn or sheep shed, the roof half fallen in with freeze dried brambles and elder sticks growing through it. Crumbling stone walls set into the land. I crept closer, did a very quick recce around, desperate not to spook whoever was in there.

I heard a man singing in a wavering voice, he was singing nursery rhymes, Jack and Jill, Humpty Dumpty, Mary had a Little Lamb; he sang them in a loop, repeating them in the same order. Another voice perhaps, I strained to hear it over the singing, but Finn heard it, he leapt from my side and into the building. That had to be Sid in there.

There was sudden shouting from inside but only one voice, a man's voice. I moved forward, eased myself in through the broken door, resting as if asleep against its frame with one hinge gone. More shouting which muffled the noise of me. A slight glow from a torch, a torch with a weak battery on the ground, it was enough: one man waving a gun, an incongruous pile of supermarket carrier bags and then, to the far side of the stone structure, on the floor, Sid.

She was curled up into herself but I could see reflected light flicker from her eyes every now and then. She was alive.

The man had his back to me as Finn danced around his feet and he tried ineffectually to make a grab for him. There was no one else in the building. Where was Alexander?

I hit the man hard from behind, targeting a nerve cluster to the side of his neck. One quick but very hard blow and he was out cold, folding to a heavy heap on the ground. Moving the gun out of range and checking for pulse and breath, both present, I went to Sid. She was staring at the body on the ground with blank eyes that glittered. Crouching, I took hold of her hands.

'Sid, it's me, it's Jake. Sid, can you hear me?'

I rubbed her hands to warm them. Her face was chalk over purple-blue, streaked with filth and the dry tracks of tears.

Please Sid, I willed her, please come back. This is a dangerous place and I need to get you back with me before anyone else comes, before the man on the floor wakes up.

'Sid, it's me, you're safe now. I've come to take you home.'

My voice broke with those words and maybe it was simply that which brought her back.

She blinked as if waking up and stared at me for what seemed like an eternity, watching the emotion that I couldn't stop spill from my eyes. She raised a hand, shaking violently and tried to wipe away a tear.

'Jake?' her voice was hoarse and trembling.

'I'm here. I've come to take you home.'

'Alex…that's Alex…it's only him.'

From somewhere within, she answered the question she knew I needed to ask. That's Alexander? Why is he here?

'Alexander is sleeping, just there, see? Help is coming. Come on, let's get you warm.'

Pitifully under dressed for the climate, her skin felt beyond cold; I took off my jacket putting it on her and pulling my hat down over her ears. Easing the phone out of a pocket, I held her close whilst I checked the screen. The signal was weak, I tried twice to make a call but each failed.

They knew where I was, they would come, there was nothing else to do now but wait. Unlike Sid, I had a more permanent tracker under my skin. A microchip about the size of a grain of rice which meant that I stood a good chance of extraction during those times when I couldn't ask for it myself.

****

The wind picked up, it was still bitterly cold even after I'd got a fire going. Just how long had Alexander thought he was going to remain here? He seemed to have been unprepared for the reality of such a place; whatever he'd had in mind, it seemed surviving wasn't top of his priorities. I shut out those thoughts and stuck with more practical ones.

Fashioning restraints from some rucksack cord, I wrapped him with one of the silver blankets from my pack. His hands were covered in drying blood although he didn't seem to be obviously injured so I bagged him and left him be. When he woke up, a head bag might slow him down a bit.

Wrapping Sid in another blanket, I reclaimed my coat and heated some water for packet soup. It wouldn't be great but it would at least be warming. Then there was nothing but the waiting. With her wrapped in my arms, I sat silently watching Alexander by the light of the flames.

Her first seizure caught me by surprise. The tremors hadn't eased even though she was now hot against me in the blanket. Her pulse stuttered, caught like a caged bird in her wrist, as she arched in waves of violent tremors. Her pupils raged wide, her breathing almost imperceptible... Drugs! Fuck, she'd been drugged. What with! Fuck! What had she been given?

I laid her on her side, wrapped the blanket around her, padded her head and tried to work out what she might have been given. Still no signal on the phone. Fucks sake! Her pulse was now racing, I tried to wake her as the last of the seizures eased. She didn't respond, simply gazed vacantly at nothing with that dead stare and then, as if that wasn't enough, she was sick. Making no attempt to move, vomit gagged out of her, rattling in her throat and nostrils. Fuck! Fuck! I used what was left of my t-shirt to keep her mouth and nose clear, let her body do what it needed and tried to stop it from making anything worse.

Far too many times she rose rigid with shock tremors, far too many times she gagged bile onto the hard packed ground. If Alexander had woken as well, I would probably have hurt him, hurt him a lot.

Eventually, after a lifetime or three, help came. From outside, the unmistakable noise of a heli approaching and then two men, camouflaged and prepared for the unknown; they came slipping in, as insubstantial as vapour. I picked Sid up, carried her out of the doorway until we stood starkly silhouetted by the dazzling light from the helicopter, now hovering high above. A quad bike appeared with a medic on the back, another quad with more help and then a military Land Rover. The whole world seemed to be on the side of the mountain all of a sudden.

More silver blankets and warmth, duly wrapped I sat propped against a quad with Finn on my feet. Military medics were helping Sid, I stayed close and growled at everyone who suggested I might move; more went into the shieling with a stretcher and took Alexander out, still sleeping.

The medics asked a string of questions, I've no idea what I said but they nodded, took notes and then spirited Alexander away. Someone else was crouching in front of me, I looked up and couldn't hide my surprise.

Equally surprised it seemed, the crouching man said, 'Bugger me, Jake, what the hell are you doing here?'

Paul. My friend, Paul Oliver.

He took a long look at me, assessing without jumping to any conclusions, 'Need a lift? Come on now, I'll take you home.'

There were heated conversations about where Sid should be taken. She was stable now but that didn't mean anything I had to say would be listened to. She woke briefly on the stretcher, calling out my name and trying to move against the straps, holding my hand so tightly, like it alone could save her, when they let me close again. Decisions were made and, thankfully, she was coming with me, for now, at least.

I've never been more thankful to simply walk away. I had nothing left and now it was someone else's job to do the stuff that had to be done. To take care of Alexander, start forensics and preliminary reports. I'd nothing left to give that might have been useful. They'd know where to find me.

Sid held onto me in the Land Rover. Finn beside us with a solitary sock still on one paw, big tongue hanging out; he was having such an adventure.

Paul took us to my house as it really was the nearest place to go. I carried Sid in and put her down in the armchair. Then, without much in the way of conscious thought, I lit candles and the fire, the warmth like an embrace compared to the wall of cold we'd left behind. Paul went out briefly and came back with a square shooting bag from which he produced hot coffee in a large thermos, single malt and cake. Cake? I stared at him.

'Best thing for the cold so my missus says,' he smiled, 'cakes not bad either; I think she only puts in one handful of sand now.'

I wanted to smile back but it wouldn't come. I felt dislocated; comfortably numb as the Pink Floyd lyric goes. I couldn't take my eyes off Sid. People in military wear fluttered around her now she was awake once more. They asked all sorts of obscure questions very intently then disappeared. One medic talked softly, checking her over again, asking the questions that had to be asked, apologising often as he took another blood sample and a skin sample from under her nails. She spoke to him in a whisper, yes and no answers; Paul talked to her as well, she said nothing, gazed at me the whole time.

Locked in those sea blue depths that I'd thought I'd lost, I remained somewhere else too. Let the people do what they had to in situations like this, let that happen all around us. But all the time we were silently saying let me look at you, stay with me, don't let me go.

There I was looking for gangsters and drug runners yet it was Alexander that took her; her brother and I never really saw him coming.

Chapter Fifty-Five

A touch on my arm, a man spoke quietly in Cantonese.

'Alexander Fielding is conscious but appears to be suffering from a psychotic episode. He'll be sedated and left to rest for a while longer. He's being moved to a secure unit near Bristol.

'Sidra Fielding is reported unharmed but she's been drugged; very provisionally there appear to be traces of both ketamine and LSD in her blood but its too early to be completely sure. That no real harm has come to her is thanks perhaps to you and the speed with which you reacted, regardless of the fact that you hadn't received full authorisation to do so. We don't have a ballistics report yet, but Mr Fielding had a loaded rifle and a bag full of ammunition with him. There is no evidence at this time of any person other than Mr Fielding being involved with this event.'

There was silence for a moment, I wondered idly if he was checking what was ok to say next, then he continued.

'Job went well, Tarvos, you made the right call. We'll send transport when you are ready, say in twenty-four to forty-eight hours, sooner if required. We have also authorised a medical watch here for Miss Fielding. Take yourself off-line and get some sleep.'

Bloody hell - praise - that was a rare occurrence.

It felt strange after all that had happened in little more than twenty-four hours, for it to be suddenly almost over again and for Sid to be back with me, especially here of all places. People came and went and then, quite suddenly it seemed, but I might not have been paying attention, there was no one but Sid, me and the Jedi master.

I sat down and she climbed into my arms, wrapping herself around me as if she'd returned from somewhere so very far away. We stayed there for what was left of that night, in front of the fire with Finn. Gently and quietly through the dark of the early hours, back together again. I thanked every god that ever was that it had ended and that she was alive.

Woken by stiff and painful muscles dragging me back to consciousness, I went to make coffee finding that someone, probably Paul, had put a small box of fresh groceries on the side in the kitchen. When I came back Finn had eaten all that was left of the cake.

Another day dawned, pink tinged sunlight brought soft shadows into that room. I helped Sid into what I generously called the bathroom, hoping that the bothy might oblige with a decent quantity of hot water. Making a heap of filthy clothes in the sink, I crouched in front of her and washed the mud off as if she was a child. There were bruises; on her legs, back, arms and on one side of her face; on her wrists now clear evidence that she'd been tied or restrained. There was no sign of the tracker, that was gone too now. Lost on the mountain as she had been.

Dressing her warmly in some of my clean clothes, I got changed myself then wrapped her back in a blanket and lay with her on the bed, holding her close in the silence.

****

When I woke again the light was already fading outside. I edged away carefully, she stirred a little but stayed sleeping. My phone clock said 3.30 as in 3.30pm which I couldn't quite believe, the whole day had nearly passed by.

I stared at the bedroom door, knowing that I never shut it and yet here it was, firmly against its frame. Opening the door slowly, I raked my hand through hair that felt exactly as could be expected by the previous twenty-four hours and was met by the heavenly smell of hot food. I padded barefoot to see who was about in my house.

Finn was in his at home pose, legs in the air next to the wood burner which crackled merrily as if happy that someone was finally paying attention to it. I glanced around and there was Mairi, Paul's wife, her back to me, bending down by the little gas oven.

'Hey, Mairi,' I said softly. She yelped and jumped away, nearly throwing the casserole pan she was holding onto the floor.

'Jesus Christ! Jake! Do you just levitate yourself about! You nearly had me in the oven!'

She straightened up, once the casserole pan was safely stowed, oven gloved hand over her chest and blew out a loud breath.

'I hope I wasn't the one to wake you. Paul checked in but as you were asleep he shut the door.'

I smiled, touched by their care.

'I can't believe I've slept so long, Sid's still asleep, I thought it best to leave her to it.'

'Tch. I'm sure that there's nothing you need to be doing and, in case you don't know, there's a couple of soldiers lurking about outside pretending not to be there.'

She gave me a wink.

'Now I see that the cake's all gone, is that a good sign, or did the dog eat it? No matter, there's now a casserole in the oven which will be done in half an hour or in three, whichever you prefer, it'll wait as long as you need.

'How's your girl? How was she last night? Is she ok, not hurt, is she? I'm being told she was kidnapped by her brother; is that right? No one would tell me anything and I don't often get sense from Paul.'

Mairi always talked in a stream of words, I soon learned it was best to just smile and nod and wait for her to finish.

'She's going to be ok, I'm sure of that. Physically she's worn out but, on the whole, unhurt. As for the rest of it, who knows.'

'Is she your woman then?' Mairi said after a long pause whilst she looked intently at me with her bright bead eyes.

'Yes, I suppose you could say that she is,' I thought of something else to add. 'Mairi, ask Paul to be careful around here,' I had to say it, this was far from over. 'Would you do that for me? Just tell him to be extra careful.'

Chapter Fifty-Six

After she'd gone, I lay stretched out on the bed beside Sid, just waiting. I watched her wake about half an hour later, watched the tremendous struggle she went through with whatever she dreamt. That was going to take some healing.

'Jake?' she whispered. 'Is it over?'

I thought of all the words I could use but went with the truth.

'No, I don't think that it is. Don't worry about it at the moment though, rest, get strong again. Let me do the worrying about all the other stuff.'

She half sat up, 'Alex?'

'Still sleeping. He's resting too.'

The worst of this was that we were still only halfway through. Those unanswered questions, the whys, they were all still there. That was what would happen next, to find out about the whys along with the small steps, the little steps to allow for healing, for moving forward and healing. When the missing were found it all began again. It's often forgotten in the jubilation of the reunion, but it is then that the work begins again in earnest. All the skeletons have to be dragged from their cupboards and made to stand up, made to tell their secrets. Often those times can be worse than the original loss. Detective work at that stage was all about finding out what those skeletons had to say and being able to do it in such a way that the truth was known without too much further pain.

I couldn't protect Sid from that kind of pain, it would come out, hand in hand, with the truth.

'Are you hungry? A friend here made us a cake - for Finn,' I smiled. 'Actually she didn't make it for him directly, he just helped himself.'

'Is Finn ok? Where is he?'

'He's here. He's been with me all the time.'

I watched her. She looked dazed, distracted - it was hard to describe. She was a long way from herself.

'He's been riding around in police cars and helicopters like he was born to it.'

'Cars and 'copters?' she was slurring slightly.

'Yes, with soldiers, sirens and blue lights; he'll have had his head turned with such excitement.'

'Blue lights?'

'Yep, he rode shotgun. I'm thinking about getting him a sheriff's badge.'

She tried to speak but the words were gone, her eyes filled with tears. I simply held her in the rumpled bed, keeping her whole just now by physically holding her together.

'Sleep now, Sid, if you can. Go back to sleep, you are safe here.'

Someone was knocking at the door. Ah yes, the unstoppable return to reality. Sighing, I knew I had to get on with it sooner or later.

'I have to answer that. Would you like me to bring you anything - water, tea?'

Holding her away slightly, I was trying to see her eyes.

She pushed me roughly away, sank back onto the bed and pulled a pillow to her chest.

'I'm here. Anything that you need, I'm here. Ok?'

Someone knocked again insistently. I was stuck momentarily; stay with Sid or answer the door? Her eyes were closing again, I went with the door. As soon as I opened it, I was silently handed a phone by someone in full uniform.

In all the time I've been living there, I don't think anyone has ever knocked at the door and certainly no-one has done so to hand me a phone. It was a bit surreal. Especially as the reception was perfect.

'Hello?'

'Jake, Moore. Its good to hear your voice. How are things?' DCI Moore, ever calm with his measured words.

I dragged myself back to answer that question sensibly.

'Uncertain but it's early days yet. I don't know how much she knows, don't know what Alexander said to her, if anything. She's not yet in a place where I can find out. Someone, probably Alexander, has drugged her.'

'From what I hear Alexander Fielding is also still away from us, we're advised to let him be for another day. When are you due back?'

'I'm going to try for tomorrow. It's too basic here for what we need and I'd like to get her back to somewhere more familiar.'

Too basic for what Sid needed right now but not for when I brought her back again and I would, I knew that.

I disconnected from Moore, sat uneasily with Finn for a moment and then stood again, pacing up and down, thinking. My thoughts went to the book that Gwil had sent. There it was still sitting on the low table; The Brothers Karamazov by Dostoyevsky. Why? Why give me that particular work?

I picked it up and flicked through the pages, reading the inscription again: *To Spider, Happy Christmas.* Oh fuck. This book wasn't simply packaging for the codes. How utterly and completely stupid had I been?

The story, considered a Russian classic, was set around the murder of a man. Chief suspects are his sons, of which he has three by his first wife and the key character's name is Alyosha which, of course, is the Russian diminutive for Alexander.

Gwil had known.

Gwil had known, or suspected all along and I'd totally failed to grasp what he'd been trying to tell me. I fetched a knife and began dissecting the book cover. There had to be more.

And there was. Just not anything that was going to immediately help me with Alexander.

Hidden in a way that I might never have found if luck hadn't, for once, been on my side, was a letter. Folded into the actual layers that formed the hard back of the book, was a letter from Gwil.

Spider

There's a time for truth and a time for lies, a time for brevity and one for disguise; I know you've heard that one from me before but its never been more significant. Don't ever think I took the coward's way out lightly. I didn't. It's taken months of agony. Months of indecision.

I had the diagnosis exactly a year ago and I've been fighting it ever since. The odd missed word, the odd absent minded error. I put it down to fatigue; too much work and not enough play. But its got worse, much worse. A week ago I found I'd completely forgotten how to use the kettle and for a whole morning it eluded me. That morning made me realise what I needed to do. I'm writing this, sending this now because, whatever happens, I want you to know that it was my choice. It won't be an accident or anything more sinister, however it looks. It will be me, making the right choice for me.

So, to get to the point, (I digress often, I know and don't call me a dickhead, I'll hear you, wherever I am) I've been looking for Alyosha - you'll need to start with Alyosha too. You will have found the codes and probably translated them by the time you read this but, if not, I'm passing all of this to you because time, for me, has run out. I am no longer safe to continue.

One small request: find the woman called Zosima. Protect her, Spider, shed your stone coat and protect her. I knew her father. Protect her for me.

Burn bright, my friend, always burn bright.

Gwil

A large part of me registered relief that his death hadn't been something he'd no control over, many of us might prefer to have that choice and it made sense. Gwil wasn't a man who would have worn disability well. Would I have told him if it had been me? No, probably not. Although I wished he'd been more expansive and less secretive about the identity of Alyosha. That might have saved a life or two.

Ah, yes, but hindsight is a marvellous thing...

At least I was a step ahead with regard to Zosima; if I was correct, she was currently asleep in my bed and, some time ago, had reduced my stone coat to nothing more than sand and gravel.

On the heels of such a revelation, I knew I had to move Sid tonight, not tomorrow. She really wasn't well enough to stay here and I couldn't hide her with so much still to do. I had to put us both back into the fight. I had to take her back.

We moved her with the helis again. A more civilised approach than before, Finn hopped in and out each time as if he'd been doing it forever. They insisted that we travelled with a medic, but there was nothing else now that could be done. Sid remained asleep throughout, deeply detached from everything. I sat with her, awake but lost somewhere else too most of the time.

In the dark we'd left and in the dark we returned once again. I carried her, still sleeping, placing her on her bed and then because I couldn't think of anything else better to do, lay down beside her. Uniform were outside once more and, by then, sleep was unavoidable.

I woke to daylight, my stomach clearly wishing that I'd eaten some of Mairi's casserole instead of giving it back to Paul. I left Sid, still endlessly sleeping, took myself downstairs for a hot shower and some food. Moore rang as I was eating.

'Glad you are back; can you come into the office, or is it better that I come out to you?'

'Come here if it can't wait. Is there an update?'

'I'll have Bill with me later as he's made of granite apparently and has discharged himself. I'd like now for the three of us to meet up.'

'Ok. When?' I knew that this couldn't be avoided, didn't really want to avoid it, but dominating my thoughts was Sid, still not here, not really.

'Say two?'

'Fine. I'll contact you if there's any change.' I looked at my watch that gave me an hour and a half.

I sat just thinking, the house eerily empty and quiet. Finn lay beside the wood burner, his head on his paws staring at me.

'Come on then, Yoda, come and see if you can work some of your magic on Sid.' I called him and went back up the stairs.

He trotted up in front and jumped up onto the bed, lying down beside Sid. She reached out to him, pulling him close and closing her eyes again. A scrap of faded green fabric showed from underneath her pillow, dislodged as she turned. Without waking she tucked it in her hand under her chin like a child would a special toy, her breathing settling into the rhythm of sleep once more. I looked more closely, recognising it now I could see more, it was my sweat shirt, one she'd once said was more holes than fabric. I slipped away, pulling the door half closed but leaving enough room for the passage of a Jedi, should it be required.

Chapter Fifty-Seven - Alyosha

And I will flay the flesh from their bones and strip them bare for angels to eat.

I was gone then, Zosima, gone away. It was a long time perhaps, I forget often, lose days often, before I came back again. That's when I found out about Marcus and the police being all over David Flint's yard. I hung around, spoke to people to see what was what. John Wozniak was a mine of information, all for a pint or a tab, bit of E, bit of special k, even acid; he went for it all. I keep some, just in case, the brothers have been supplying me so they think I'm still using, still needing - still needing them. John Wozniak was another who said bad things about you. He was another who was easy to kill, easy to lure and kill. Thing was, when I had him there, it occurred to me that he didn't look quite right. Just before I killed him and he's begging, pathetic he was, he's telling me he's John's brother and not John at all. He doesn't have the tattoo he says, I look and sure enough he doesn't. I still beat his sleazy head off though... blood and brains everywhere. Too easy and I still didn't care. John's brother or not, he was now one less to trouble you.

I didn't bother to dismember him, bloody boar would only pull him about and, in truth, he wasn't worthy of the honour. I left him where he fell and it made it much quicker too, strangely enough. So where's John Wozniak, he's next on my list - where's the real John? Over to David Flint's and round to the horse lorry, the place where John conducted all sorts of 'business', so sordid - very sordid all of it. As I arrive two men are leaving, nothing unusual in that, John had all sorts on the go. I wait a while and then go in. Bastard! Bloody bastard! He was only nearly dead already! Kneeling there, throat and wrists slit, blood pouring. He looked at me, Zosima, looked at me whilst making these dreadful gurgling noises. I told him he was a bastard but he probably knew that already. I sat and watched him take his last as it seemed a shame to leave on his own at such a time. Funny thing, I truly think he expected me to help him. Me! Help him? He was another, in with them, up to his neck. I stayed with him for a long time, hours maybe, thinking about him and his brother. Watching his body die. He'd been alive and now he wasn't. I almost wanted to care but, do you know, it just wasn't there anymore. Time passed. It got dull. He was just meat, just a piece of meat: trade him, swop him, use him, didn't matter. So, in the end, I hung him, just like a piece of meat. Let him bleed out slowly just like the carcass he was.

Of course now I absolutely had to take out Gabriel. I'd intended to do that, for a long time, I knew I would one day. And that day came and I did, I killed him, just like the others, beat the fucking supercilious smile of his pretty face. He was surprisingly easy too. I expected a bit of trouble, but I got none. Funny thing was all these men were easy to lure because of you, Zosima. I only had to mention your name and they came as meekly as bulls with rings in their noses.

The nurses moved around him quietly. He could hear them, feel them, smell them. The rustle of bed linen, the scratch of a pen on paper, the squeak of a rubber sole on a polished floor. He knew that they were nurses; you never forgot the smell of a hospital.

Aloysha, Alyosha, the eagles, his special dakini, still whispered to him but their voices were muffled by whatever sedation he'd been given. Sedation that took away control of his body but left his mind running riot with kaleidoscope thoughts, as colourful as the prayer flags that flapped constantly at the shrine of the sky dancers. He took himself back there, lay prostrate at the feet of the eagles and prayed for guidance as to how to proceed.

He knew he'd failed. Failed to do what they'd told him. He couldn't kill Zosima, he'd thought he could, but when she'd been there in front of him, he just couldn't do it. A part of him, a part that wasn't yet holy had stopped him. The dakini soothed, whispered words that made his failure seem smaller than it was. There was still a way to make her safe, to keep her spirit beside him always, to make sure that she never left him alone again. There was still a way but first he had to catch the devil.

Of course, the green eyed panther who had taken her from him, he was the rock that was in the way. He'd met that being before, known him - the one wearing the cloak of death.

He'd rest here and then, when he was a bit stronger and with the help of the dakini, he'd go and have his final fight with the death cloaked devil. He'd draw the light from those shining green eyes, draw what life there was from out of that black soul.

Zosima...

Zosima would be safe then. She'd take the holy journey then. He knew this, was certain of this, because he was marked. It should be clear to all that he, and he alone, wore the stigmata of a higher being.

Chapter Fifty-Eight

I spent the time before Moore arrived just sitting with the original set of codes laid out, staring at nothing in front of the wood burner, grateful for its warmth when inside of me there was little. I listened constantly for sound from upstairs but there was none so I listened for sounds from outside, the slightest noise putting me on edge.

Wood popped and hissed as it burned; a shift, a sigh as the flames ate through. I could hear the water in the pipes as the boiler clicked on automatically. Small insignificant noises of this place, so loud now in the deafening silence of my thoughts. But the more I thought the more the fog descended, my thinking muddled. I struggled to make sense of the simplest facts, things that I thought I knew for certain. Come on, Alyosha, Alexander, whoever you are, let me into your head.

I heard the car and went to the door to avoid them knocking, Finn ignored their arrival thankfully. Moore and Bill got out. Bill, smaller somehow, as if he'd shrunken a little into himself with what had happened. He had a dressing taped to his skull just behind his right ear; that must have been pure luck to not be a fracture. I had a sudden flash of Alan Wozniak and what was left of him after he was murdered…

Bill stood in front of me, 'You look better than I thought you would.' He punched me lightly on the arm, a bloke hug in its way.

'You too, did it knock any sense in, do you think? There wasn't a lot to take out.'

He narrowed his eyes, 'Watch your step, Spider, I might be concussed and have a monumental headache, but I'm still bigger than you.'

I led them into the house, voices lowered so as not to disturb. With coffee we sat and talked through the last few days. There was always this state of gathering and regrouping, don't the military call it de-briefing? It was an act that fulfilled many roles, the sensation of returning to normality was one of them. Note though, the word *sensation*, defined as feeling in one's body; awareness of, or impression and this felt like it was giving me the impression of normality which isn't quite the same as the real thing.

'There is no news at all on the wider situation; it has gone quiet in every quarter since Joshua was killed. Sebastian has managed to get himself consular assistance and it's likely that he'll be deported back here within a day or so. It seems that he isn't as guilty as they first thought. I can only assume that that means that he's got really good legal assistance or simply been kept out of the way for long enough.' Moore sat back, thick fingers tapping his lips.

'If we look at this a different way...' I started to speak and then lost the train of where I was going, I stood and paced for a minute, grasping at slivers of facts as they passed out of range again in my mental fog. '...I had this all earlier, now I'm not so sure.'

'You've had a tough time, you want to be kinder to yourself,' Bill said quietly.

'But that's the problem, there's no more time.' My voice sharp, I ran my hands through my hair in frustration. 'Gwil knew about Alexander and I missed it completely. I've a feeling that this is all going to kick off again any minute and I really don't want to be so badly prepared again. Alexander had a gun and that could have made matters very different.'

'Yes, he had a gun, but he didn't use it,' Moore said. 'We've no evidence to say that he ever intended to. His mental state is such that he may not have even known what it was.'

I stiffened and moved away. 'Nope. You see, with all due respect, I can't go there. How does a man in such an apparent state of psychosis manage to orchestrate such a complex abduction? He managed to be somewhere here, set up an ambush wire for the bike, sabotage the car and then to be in the right place to get Bill and take Sid. He had drugs, a vehicle and a place to go and that place was to my doorstep. He shouldn't have known anything about me. Absolutely none of that speaks of a man who didn't know who he was.' I was adamant now. Alexander held the key. He'd done so all along.

'Ok, ok. Those are fair points. But he's under guard, he's not going anywhere fast.'

Moore was back tracking and I wondered if he was making inane statements to drag me out of the place I was heading - into that mental fog.

'Sid told me that Alexander was alone, that it was only him. I wonder if that was always the case. Who's behind the murders? Alexander alone? It's unlikely but it makes me wonder if he had help and if so, who and why? What was in it for them? We need to speak to him; need to get out of him what he knows.'

'I plan to do that as soon as he's fit. I can't go in there yet, maybe tomorrow I can try again.' Moore sighed and placed his coffee cup on the table with deliberation. 'I need you to push Sid as soon as you can, we have to find out what she knows. There's a chance that Alexander will tell us nothing, he's tremendously unstable that much is certain. Can you talk to her? Will you talk to her about this as soon as possible?'

I walked to the window that looked out onto the moor, let my thoughts run around, willing them to show me the truth, to show me what this was all about.

'Yes, of course, I'll talk to her but, thanks to Alexander, she's been in a very deep k-hole, there's no guarantee she'll remember anything at all.'

I wasn't at all certain that she'd be strong enough to face this new batch of demons anytime soon even if she did remember what had happened to her.

'Just do what you can.' Moore stood, Bill with him. 'I think its time we left you to it. Bill's supposed to be resting too.'

I went with them to the door, 'Thanks, Bill, get well, we still have stuff to do.'

'Don't worry you won't get rid of me that quickly. I'm still digging for you,' he winked. 'Still, one piece of good news is that now you'll want to get a decent car.'

'I'm not going with your idea of a decent car and, besides, there was nothing wrong with the one I had before you got behind the wheel. Your kind of decent won't get round the roads here and, with all that bling, its bound to get nicked.'

DCI Moore looked at us both and raised his eyebrows.

'I'm glad I don't have to work with you two directly, you'd drive me mad. Jake, I'll be back in touch in the morning.' He held his hand out and I took it. 'Don't forget how hard this is for you. You're emotionally involved here, that makes it very different to any other case you've worked on and, as Bill said, be nice to yourself now and then.'

They let themselves out. Hands in pockets, I stared at that closed door for a long time and then putting a still frozen stew into the oven for later, went up to check on Sid, taking the papers with me.

She slept on, but it wasn't a restful sleep anymore, it was one that dragged her through hidden dramas, pulled her shouting sometimes from one place to the next. Finn got up and sloped off downstairs. She clung to my old sweatshirt and cried without waking; begged for help, begged for someone to stop, to go, to never come back, to come back, to never leave. She cried on and on. Those words, those tears tore at me. I forced myself to stay there, to be part of it and be there for when she woke. In the end, she suddenly sat bolt upright, eyes open but blank, screaming for me with terror in her voice.

I tried to hold her, to talk to her, to bring her back but she just screamed all the more. Fought me off with kicks and punches, all the while screaming for me, begging me to come and help her. I waited momentarily until she drew back her arms to hit out again at whoever she thought was there and then caught her, held her firmly, trapped her legs against mine and simply held on. For a few more moments, which felt like hours, she fought against me; so scared, terrified of the thing that held her in her mind.

Holding her through that has to be the hardest thing I've ever had to do.

By degrees, she calmed and became still but I wasn't going to let her go just yet. I felt rage boiling for whoever had done this to her; it wasn't just Alexander. I felt the blackness she was drowning in as I held her close to me.

From losing her and all that went on dealing with that, I realised that I might have her back physically but she wasn't anywhere near home yet, not really. Part of her was in that shieling, part of her back in that place with Gabriel Wallace, or under the horse in the stalls as it struggled through the terror of its fracture. I held her and willed her back to me whole.

I must have eventually fallen asleep because I woke to my face being gently touched, opened my eyes to her looking at me in the gloom of the night; her fingertips tracing the line of my jaw. She leaned forward and kissed me gently.

'Hello sleepyhead,' she said, her voice roughened by all that had happened.

I felt like someone who has sat with a coma victim and then seen them wake after all seemed lost. There was a moment earlier, in all that screaming, when I'd wondered if she might really be gone. That this, whatever she'd been through with Alexander, had been the straw that finally overloaded her and pushed her back into the ashes never more to be reborn.

'Hello you,' I whispered back.

'I'm hungry and really thirsty. Do you think there's anything to eat downstairs?'

'Oh shit,' I winced as I registered her question. 'There was a stew in the oven, I forgot all about it. Shit, bet it's burnt. Want to come and see what damage has been done in your kitchen?'

Something I never knew and that is that a more than semi charcoaled beef stew eaten from a pan with spoons at one in the morning, actually tastes really good and even more so when the pan can go to a Jedi for pre-washing.

Sid was coming back, little by little, returning in every sense and, for what was left of that night, we slept, a proper sleep that did what sleep should.

Chapter Fifty-Nine

And I will flay the flesh from their bones and strip them bare for angels to eat.

Then of course, I had this policeman. I would have to do something about him too. But he's confusing. I watch you with him, Zosima. I watch and you seem happy. He makes me wait, makes me think.

Then the brothers want me. I know what they want; they want to know who is killing. I'm not going anywhere near them, they're very bad men, they'll beat me again, I'm sure of it, and so I'm hiding. They'll send men to track me down, bad men like themselves to beat me and drag me back to them. So I think that before they find me, which they will eventually, however hard I try to hide, I must make sure you are safe. Especially when I know that they are looking for me through you.

When comes to it, I hope I can make you safe. I've struggled with it, Zosima, I'm worried that I won't be able to do it. I've planned it so well. The policeman, I knew that I'd seen him somewhere before. When I'd been at Suileag, he'd been there. He'd been there with his death cloak. I knew he wasn't a not so secret policeman, he was the Devil. I could tell, I could see it in his eyes. I don't forget a face, especially one as striking as his. Ask and you will receive. I followed and went to have a little secret look of my own around his mountain but got seen off by some big bear with a gun. He chased me away and that's when I found the barn. The perfect place, I thought, to use with you as bait for our secret policeman. The perfect place to kill him and then to make you safe.

Aloysha was humming a tune to himself. The nurses had reduced the sedation, plumped his pillows and lifted him up in the bed. He glanced around the room as he hummed, checking out what was where and whether he'd been there before. A dull ache in his hands made him look down. They'd been covered now with neat bandages, brilliant white bandages to hide the brilliance of the holy marks. That wasn't right. The mark of the dakini, the marks given in recognition of who he would become, shouldn't be covered, not ever. To do so was sacrilegious.

He tried lifting one hand only to find that he was tied to the bed frame. Both hands and both feet pinned him to the metal of the bed. And tubes, tubes from him and into him. Once again, they were sucking it out of him and making him less than he was.

He smiled.

He knew what this was now.

And he loved a challenge.

Chapter Sixty

An alarm chirruped at 5.15 and she woke, opening her eyes a moment after I did.

'Don't even think about it,' I whispered. 'You're not going anywhere.'

'Oh, ok,' she said and moved a little closer. 'What'll we do instead? Any ideas?'

I smiled at her, she was definitely on her way home.

Bill arrived at about half nine. He looked so much better than he had the night before, I expect I did as well. Wearing a black beanie hat, perhaps to hide the dressed damage, he took a long look at Sid, sitting cross legged on the sofa, gave a wide smile and bent to hug her.

'How's my favourite jockey today? Aside from looking utterly gorgeous, as always.'

He sat down beside her, folding his legs surprisingly gracefully and ignoring her very vivid bruises.

'Much, much better, Bill. I don't know where the last few days went but I'm much better today. It must be something to do with all the blarney I have to put up with.'

'Do you know, Sid,' I said, 'when all this is over I'm going to take you to Ireland and educate you properly, that'll get your back down.' I waited for the retort that was bound to come.

'Mmm, that a fact. And there's me thinking you were already doing that.'

'Right ok, you win; I'm going to make coffee, some for you, Bill?' I stood and beat a retreat into the kitchen. I heard her laughing and smiled to myself, much more like Sid.

The three of us sat and talked about nothing specific for a while, Finn wandered about, got let out and then immediately wanted to come back in again.

'Can we walk? Can we go outside?' she asked. 'Is it safe? I need some air and Finn needs company so who's up for it?' she stretched her arms up above her head, curving her back like a cat.

I glanced across at Bill and he shrugged, nodding at the same time - nothing like staying on the fence.

'Ok let's do it.' I stood and took the cups back to the kitchen, she came in after me.

'If you're not happy about this, then say so; I don't really mind,' she put her hands around my neck and tipped her chin up for a kiss, curving herself into me.

'Well, we can't always stay inside. Let's go, get some air as there's far too much pigeon shit in here at the moment.'

I was still trying to get over her screaming and yet she was moving on again, brushing off the ashes from yet another reincarnation - extraordinary. That's what she was, extraordinary.

Outside Finn bounded ahead, mad dog legs in top speed circles, it was impossible not to laugh. I wondered if he did it on purpose, just for Sid, just to bring back the light to her eyes.

'Has anyone found my bike yet?' she asked, looking from me to Bill. I shook my head, not as far as I knew, not yet.

'I don't remember much from the crash. I remember Bill falling backwards off the bike and someone in the lane ahead but I'm not sure what happened first. This man, who looked like he was drunk, staggered out in front and he was so close that I thought I'd hit him. I'd seen a van in the lay-by, like a furniture van with its doors open,' she laughed, 'its ridiculous but I was worried about fly tipping! I thought that was what it was doing, fly tipping in the woods!'

She pushed her hand into mine, matching strides as we walked along the rough track.

'I had to slide the bike; it was the only way to avoid hitting the man. He jumped back and then ran at Bill when I was on the ground...on the grass; I got up in time to see him hit Bill.'

She stopped dead.

'He hit you so hard, I watched his arm come up with this long metal bar, like... shiny silver, like a crow bar, he pulled it all the way back behind his shoulder and then... Oh... I'm seeing it all over again... I thought he was coming to help. I thought he was going to you, Bill, to help. You were lying on the ground and instead of helping... he hit you.' Her hand flew up to her mouth and she stumbled away.

'I can hear the... I can hear the noise as he hit you so hard... the noise of his breath...grunting, the blow, the sound as he hit you!' she put her hands over her ears as if to shut out the memory.

Bill gestured with his head back to the house. I reached out and caught her hand.

'Come on, let's go back. It's too cold. It's easier to talk about this stuff at home. Come on. It's hard, I know, but this does have to be talked about. You understand that, don't you?'

'Stay close, I need to know that you are close.'

'I'm here, always here for you.' I tucked her in under my arm and we turned back.

'Why did you fall off, Bill? And why did you take your helmet off?' she asked abruptly as we walked back.

'There was a wire across the track, you rode under it and I got it across the front of the helmet. If we'd been going any faster or if the wire had been set lower, one or other of us might have been killed. As it was, it shattered the visor. I took off the helmet simply because I couldn't see but I was unhurt at that point. You did well, Sid, to slide the bike like that,' he smiled at her.

We walked back then with no more words except to call Finn. Back in the warmth of the house, Bill went to make coffee unasked.

'Is this ok? Me talking like this? I don't know why it's all suddenly there and I need to tell you, need to get it out.'

'If you felt strong enough I could see if the DCI could come, then we could do this formally. Its up to you. You can of course just tell me or Bill now, whatever you want.'

She kissed me, touching my face, 'I love you, Jake. I really love you,' she whispered.

'I know and I love you too.'

'Ring the Inspector and see if he can come.'

Her face was pale and bruised; next to me she felt small and vulnerable; funny how she could appear so frail and yet be so strong.

****

Moore turned up about an hour later alone, full of apologies for the delay. I hadn't expected him to drop everything and was surprised he'd come that quickly, but then I knew what he had to achieve in the day. He shook hands with us all and asked Bill if he would scribe for him, handing him the papers to do so.

'Miss Fielding, I really appreciate you being able to talk to me like this, you've been through quite an ordeal and it's early days. Your brother, Alexander, is still not well enough to speak to us, so being able to take a statement from you now is most helpful,' he smiled and I felt her soften a little. 'This interview will be recorded as well. Are you ok with that?'

She nodded and began by recounting what she'd already told us about the bike crash. Bill scribbled away and Moore simply listened, no questions unless he needed a specific point answered.

'I stood and watched Alex hit Bill. I don't know why I did nothing. Why didn't I try and stop him? Bill, I'm so sorry, I should've helped you.' Tears again.

'I just stood there, everything going through my head, all the things I'd promised, about going straight to the yard and staying safe. I couldn't believe that this was happening, that minutes from leaving home Bill had fallen off the bike. I first thought it was a branch or something that had caught Bill, I'd seen nothing but he's so much taller than me and sits higher still on the pillion seat. I was angry about the man but thought nothing of the danger of him, thought he wasn't a threat, I thought only of stopping for Bill. I made loads of assumptions. All of them wrong.

'The van was there. The drunk...he was Alex. I didn't recognise him... he just looked like a tramp or a drunk. He hit Bill and then he came towards me. I ran... I tried to run away,' she stopped again.

It can sometimes be impossible to escape and that's why people like her, people like any of us, could be trapped in those situations if someone else wanted it to happen badly enough.

'I run all the time, miles and bloody miles over this moor, up the tors and tracks, you name it, I do it. And yet...and yet...I couldn't run away. The man...Alex... he came after me and I couldn't outrun him and he caught me. He grabbed me and pulled me down on the grass. I fell down. I remember grass in my mouth. He held me down on the grass. It was wet...' she stopped again, her heart thumping so loud I could hear it.

She struggled to say something, started and then stopped several times.

'Miss Fielding, do you need to take a break? Some water? Would you like some time with this?' Moore asked gently.

'No...thank you. No, I must say this...must get this out.... When the man, who was Alex but I didn't know that... why didn't I know that? When he held me on the grass, so heavy, so strong... oh... he...'

She looked up and said in a rush, 'I thought he was going to do what Gabriel did... I was so afraid... all those years... I said I'd kill anyone who tried that again and yet... I did nothing. I could do nothing... lay on top of me... held me to the ground in the grass and I could do nothing... so fucking weak, so fucking stupid... all my strong words... all those years and

I thought that was what he was going to do. I froze, I couldn't scream, couldn't fight him... how fucking stupid is that? I'll never... ever... as long as I live forgive myself.'

She dissolved into intense sobbing. I looked up to Moore and shook my head, he nodded.

He said for the recording and to Bill. 'Interview terminated at 11.43am.'

They stood and gestured that they'd leave, I nodded. Moore made a phone me gesture and I nodded again. The heavy front door shut behind them and I stayed just as I was, holding her.

Chapter Sixty-One

'I'm so sorry. How could I have let you down so badly? How could I have been so stupid?'

'Sid, never think that. No one thinks that, especially me. No one could've done more in the situation that you were in. You are my phoenix, remember that - I'll never forget.'

In my arms, she lay looking at me. We had a closeness, that which bound us, through all that black, still here together and, together, they say, there is strength.

'Which is your favourite place in this house? What is your favourite memory of here, the place that you feel most at peace, most content?' I asked softly, trying not to interrupt the mood.'If we're to talk about what happened, where would be the best place to do that? Where would you feel most safe bringing up all those memories?'

'Is this to be just us, or with Bill and the Inspector?'

'This time is just for you and me.'

'One thing first; a cup of tea, that's what I need, a simple cup of tea,' she moved away and laughed suddenly. 'What are we like, aside from a little stroll and a great deal of ridiculous crying, we've spent most of today on the sofa! Should I be keeping you from your serious work like this?'

'Of course, this is my serious work and if they needed me the phone would ring. It's not like they don't know where to find me.'

With that, my phone rang, making us both laugh.

'Ok, you do grown up stuff and I'll make tea.'

I answered the phone.

'Jake. It's me, Luci,' her voice was unexpectedly quiet.

'You ok?'

'I was ringing to ask you the same!' she laughed.

'Yeah, we're getting there.'

'Would you like me to come round later? I'll bring you food, or just come and see you?'

'Ok, what time?'

'Say six thirty, I'll bring food for us all.'

'That sounds good.'

'No worries, it's what big sisters do, you know.'

'Yeah, don't push it, Luci. But, ok, see you later then.'

****

In the end Sid just started talking without any further planning, no special place of safety, just the two of us and, as it turned out, a few gallons of tea. I wished I had the hindsight app along with the crystal ball one; it would save so much heartache. With her permission, I recorded what she said.

'Alex dragged me to the van. I think he must have given me something then, I remember something sharp in my arm and then nothing. I woke again in the dark.

'It was so cold, I couldn't stop my teeth from chattering, couldn't stop shivering. I was lying on a pile of sacks, like old fertiliser bags, all crinkly and plastic, couldn't move without them making such a loud noise.

'He heard me wake up. He stared at me for ages, kept touching my face and just looking at me. I tried to talk to him but he wouldn't answer. He went away again, somewhere out of my sight, I tried to move, tried to sit up but he'd tied me so that I couldn't. It was so unbelievably cold.

'I think I might have gone to sleep again because when I opened my eyes there was a torch shining on all these bags, filled with I don't know what, so many of them,' she laughed. 'I remember thinking that someone must spend far too much time in Tesco.'

I knew. I knew that those bags contained newspaper cuttings and a single pair of cheap shoes. Years of cuttings. Probably everything that had ever been put into print about the Fielding family. From financial reports in business papers for Josh and Seb, to Sid smiling out from the Racing Post, trophies held high. There were also thousands of rolled clippings, like rolls of twenty pound notes held with elastic bands, which just contained the word 'fielding', almost as if Alexander had become fixated with the name and collected it wherever it appeared. Josh and Seb were major share-holders in Tesco, the fact that all the carrier bags bore that logo wasn't lost on me. The shoes had a Fielding connection too, stamped in faded gold italic inside as the style of the shoe. Those shoes had belonged not to a Fielding but actually to a Wozniak, John Wozniak to be precise. I'd wondered where they'd gone. Alexander had taken it all in advance, perhaps in some form of preparation, as the bags had been frozen solid when they'd been recovered from the shieling.

'He released whatever it was he'd tied me with, it wasn't tight, just enough to stop me from sitting up. He still wouldn't talk, just kept looking at me as he rearranged the bags into some order that seemed to matter to him and then went out again. That's when I saw the phone. A mobile phone near the torch. I wondered if it was a trap, like he'd left it there to see if I'd use it.

'I looked at that phone for so long, recited your number over and over in my head. Eventually I summoned some courage from somewhere, reached for it and sent a text, praying that it wasn't out of credit or anything. Once it sent I deleted it and went back to sitting where he'd left me.'

She reached forward to kiss me; a small, just checking kiss, like the squeeze of a hand. To send that text, in the situation that she'd been in, that was as act of real bravery. I knew of many that wouldn't have had the courage to do so. It was also sheer luck that she was physically able to after the drugs he'd given her.

'It was only then that I remembered the tracker bracelet you'd given me. Amazingly it was still there. I set it as you'd shown me and then I began to worry that he might see it and know what it was. I was so scared that you'd find it and not me, so I swallowed it.'

I interrupted her, 'you did what?'

'I swallowed it. If you'd found it and not me, if it fell off somewhere...' she gave me a half-smile.' It seemed like a good idea at the time. Hope I don't have to give it back.'

'It was,' I hugged her, 'it was a very good idea. I'd been wondering where it was.'

'Well, anyway, he came back and he seemed different, more... I'm not sure how to describe him... agitated, on edge? I wondered if he'd gone out to take some drugs because that's how he looked, a bit spaced, a bit out of it. I'd no idea where he went, no real idea how long he was gone. I was still so cold, I couldn't feel my hands or feet. Its funny how you can focus on those insignificant things!'

She held up her hands and examined them closely, checking the marks on her wrists, the bruising vivid purple now. I waited for her to start again.

'Now he began to talk without stopping, to me and to himself. He wasn't making much sense. He kept asking if I remembered when we were children; remembered a horse, a colt that he'd watched being born. He said that Dad told him it would be his horse one day, when he was old enough. I did remember the horse; it was one of the best, went on to be a stallion at stud.

'It was a time when our whole lives seemed to revolve around that horse and what he did. At stud, he did really well too, his first crop of foals were exceptional, maybe because he had some really good mares. That was the same horse that Mum and Dad had gone to see race in France. He was a three year old then and he'd won all his early races easily. I think there'd been interest in France and that was why he went there to race; in any event he always ran in the best company.'

'On the day that he won in France, our parents had a private plane to take them, it was a major deal. I had to go to school, as did Alexander. We hated going on such an important day.

'And that was the day they were killed, in the plane. It crashed into the sea. Alex talked on and on about all of that and then he became very odd, agitated again. He'd start reciting nursery rhymes, always the same ones, over and over, like a stuck record. I was so cold, so afraid of what he was going to do. I wondered if perhaps you hadn't got my text, that I hadn't done the tracker thing right. I wondered if I was too far away to find.'

She pressed her face against my shoulder and I could feel tears yet again. I couldn't stop this, it had to come out.

'He was sitting, rocking on this log, like a big piece of tree trunk; he'd been using it as a seat and now he rocked to and fro, talking to me and then nursery rhymes. He said he knew what Seb and Josh were doing. That they'd told him that they didn't need him, that they had someone else to help them.'

She reached for tissues, blew her nose and wiped her eyes.

'That someone was Gabriel. But Gabriel was a bad man and they'd laughed at him when he'd said so. So he ran away. When he came back he found out that I was seeing Gabriel. He says he came to the house to challenge Seb and Josh, to tell them to leave me out of it. He said that they beat him… hurt him so much he had to go away again…

'It seems that Gabriel had some kind of deal with Josh and Seb, a debt that they owed him. Alex said he's put that right, he's made the people pay for what they did wrong. I know that he wanted to take me away because he believed that I needed to be kept safe — whether that's from you, the man who was looking for me, or from Seb and Josh, I'm not sure. He knew of you, said he'd watched us together.

'He had a gun, he showed it to me like it was something special. That gun was just too terrifying. Then, whilst he was talking, he took this knife from his pocket and began to cut the palms of his hands - just slicing into the flesh! He's hurt himself in the past but I've never had to watch him do it. I thought it would revolt me but it didn't, it just made me feel even more numb. He said that he was going to keep me there and make sure you were out of the way. Then Finn came bounding in.

'I couldn't believe it. Finn is growling and I'm thinking that Alex is going to kill him with his gun or the knife and I'm afraid that this isn't actually Finn at all. And then you're there, suddenly in front of me telling me that Alex is asleep and that I'm safe. Did I dream it?'

She'd done it; she'd told me it all. I stopped the recording.

'You didn't dream it. I couldn't quite believe that you were still alive. That I could simply take you home again.'

She gazed up at me. Silent for an age and then she said, 'And you came all that way for me. You did all that just for me?'

'Of course, all that and more for one such as you.'

Chapter Sixty-Two

She still insisted on wearing my shirt. I offered her another, one that was more presentable, but no, it had to be that one. Like a child with a comfort blanket, a remnant that told me that she was still papering over cracks. Almost more shocking was that my sweat shirt was green, not black.

But what about Alexander? It was highly probable that Alexander was the murderer, it was possible that he'd killed Joshua, Marcus, Alan, John and Gabriel. Had he been the one to stir up his older brothers' business partners? Had he been the one who set Sebastian up? Alexander was clearly a very clever man, he'd managed to put together a highly engineered plan and then he'd waited until everyone walked centre stage for him and then, if I was right, taken them out one by one. He'd missed me though. There was an urgent need to talk to him. But he drifted in and out of whatever fractured state his mind was in, it was anyone's guess as to what he'd be able to reliably recall. Time, it needed time. My gut feeling was that we were still in the game, whether instigated by Alexander or not. I had to assume that there was still a threat.

Bill arrived about half five as Sid was on the phone cancelling immediate riding plans, smoothing feathers with tact and a measure of diplomacy that would hopefully mean that she'd still have the option to ride in the future. I wanted her out of the public eye for a while longer.

He listened to all that she'd told me. We had two situations still. We had whatever Seb and Josh had done, finally coming to a head like an abscess. And then we had Alexander, the one who had remained unknown and whose motive was still, in truth, unknowable. I wondered if the rhyme I'd translated held the key.

'I think we should go to ground again,' Bill said. 'Personally I don't like the fact that you're here with Sid. This place is hard to defend. Its too isolated.'

I nodded, I was thinking the same but I'd come back here to stay in the fight not to surrender.

'I also think you personally should be much more careful. Just because Alexander is secure, it doesn't mean that you're no longer at risk.'

He was right. Sid was my Achilles heel. Maybe that's what I was to her too.

'Ok, I get it. I'll speak to Moore and see if he can interview Alexander in the morning, give him the questions to ask. We'll go to ground again tomorrow but I don't want to charge off with Sid tonight, not unless its imperative, she's nowhere near strong enough for unnecessary drama. I'm not sure that she knows about Joshua as I've not told her and Sebastian will be in custody as soon as he gets back into the UK.'

Back on the phone, I requested safe house status. We'd go, once again take ourselves somewhere where we had more backup, more protection. But I still really wanted to speak to Alexander. He held so many answers.

'What are you two gossiping about?' Sid walked back in, smiling up at Bill and sliding a hand around my waist.

'You, short person, getting you back to normal. I'm missing your dreadful jokes.' Bill shifted back seamlessly into English. 'You're getting slow in your old age, Sid, you need to sharpen yourself up. You'll end up in the shed with the rusty classic otherwise.'

He knew that would be incendiary. She narrowed her eyes and he simply laughed; I sensed a kick in the shin moment was coming.

'You should tread softly around me, big man. I'm known for my ability to restrain half a ton of horseflesh and you wouldn't be that different,' her eyes flashed and he grinned.

'Aw now, Sid, you love me really.'

'That can easily change if you say bad things about my Land Rover. So back up and play nice. The bigger they are, the harder they fall and your ankles look like they might taste nice to Finn.'

I stayed out of the way and watched her spark back at Bill. Finn was only likely to attack an ankle if you tied a live rabbit to it and only then if he was nowhere near a sofa.

'Well, I can't stand here all night playing with you, I've work to do. A decent car is first on my list – I'm off now to collect it.' He left, dropping the front door latch so that it deadlocked behind him.

'What's on?' She knew, I could tell by the look on her face.

'We're going to disappear again for a while; I think we should start by revisiting John and Cath but not to stay this time, we're heading ultimately somewhere else. Are you up for it? I need some assistance and, as a first port of call, it's the easiest place to get it.'

'Ok, I'll go pack a bag and dust off the light sabre again. When do we go?'

'In the morning I think, Luci's coming in a little while. Let's do that first.' I hoped I wasn't pushing my luck.

As soon as Sid went upstairs, I spoke to Moore. Alexander had given Sid both LSD and ketamine, I'd put money on them being identical to the batch found with the Wozniak twins. It explained, in part, her delayed recovery. The visible police presence had been increased in and around the area, lots of eyes now watching for things that were out of place. But we both knew that the best players would never be seen, they were almost impossible to spot unless you were really lucky, often impossible to spot until it was too late.

Sid came back with her bag and I made sure that we'd everything together for a quick exit should one be required. Finn waited to be woken as he didn't want to waste a moment of potential sleeping time with unnecessary action.

We both heard a car pull up outside, flooding the courtyard with light. Luci and Ben arrived in a whirl of energy and laughter, clattering into the kitchen with bags that spoke of them having too much time on their hands.

My phone rang at the same time as another car sped up the drive, stones and gravel flying. I answered it whilst going to see who this was making such an entrance. Sid in the kitchen with Luci and Ben was momentarily oblivious to what was going on.

'Tarvos, quick exit, Alexander Fielding has absconded. He's been gone for possibly just under an hour.' The voice was calm but this was a catastrophic fuck up. Alexander was supposed to be under guard, supposed to be too ill to move by himself.

The car up the drive was Bill, he'd already heard. I let him in as he ran up the steps. We were leaving and now.

'Sid, there's a problem. We need to go right away.'

I ran into the kitchen and spoke over the general laughter, ever the bearer of bad tidings, the ultimate party stopper. Bill took Sid by the arm and picked up our bags.

'Luci, Ben, this is too complicated to explain now. We have to leave immediately; I need you to do the same. Go back to Granny's and keep it low. These are serious people and you don't want to be anywhere near them. Luci, I'll be in touch.'

Another car up the drive, Trev and one other, full uniform in a marked car, a very visible presence.

'Jake, how do you get all the fun? There's shit flying everywhere yet I'm to secure the house and just loiter which mean nothing but dull and boring to me. Meanwhile, you've been here minutes, all hell breaks loose and you get to run off with the girl in the fast car. How is that? How come I always miss out on the action?' Trev, irrepressible as always, full of easy humour; he was enjoying this, whatever he said.

I locked the house, set the alarms and told Trev the code should he need it.

We bolted, straight to the underground burrow again. I landed in the seat as Bill was already gunning the engine. Inside the car was wall to wall high tech encased in leather luxury; warmth and silence except for a radio relaying words to the air in general. Finn sat, shot gun position again, Sid with him. Bill span the car and we left in a spray of gravel and mud.

Chapter Sixty-Three

'Where did you nick this?'

I looked around impressed with our surroundings. A fast response vehicle that obviously spent its time doing very important stuff, it was fully kitted out with all sorts of gadgets.

'Are you sure that you are well enough to be behind the wheel?'

'Authorised use, Spider, you just need to know who to ask and what to ask for. None of this second rate rep's car that you were happy to trundle about in. This is a proper romulan, homeboy,' he grinned his Cheshire cat smile in the darkness. 'Of course I'm well enough, take more than a bang on the head to keep me down and well you know it.'

'What's going on?' Sid asked.

'Alexander has done a bunk. How I don't know, he was supposed to be sedated.'

I wasn't going to tell her just yet that Alexander was probably after me first, along with whoever else felt I needed sorting, but then again, maybe she'd worked that out already. We sped along as fast as we could through high sided lanes until we met the main road where Bill instantly converted the sleek, black car into something else entirely - something with wings. I got back on the phone.

'Jake, I'm updated,' John's voice answered instantly in Welsh, (bloody hell, as if the situation wasn't complicated enough). 'Are you out and about?'

'Yep, at speed.' I struggled with replying in the same tongue, gave it up and shifted to Irish instead, so much easier.

'Rooms required?'

'Correct. Two this time.'

'Bruce or Sheila?'

'Bruce definitely and a big bugger at that!' I laughed. 'Put the kettle on for the usual just after sensible time.'

'Kettle! Kettle! There'll be a cork out, none of that soft stuff!' John snorted. 'By the way, tell the jock I scored each way.'

'Tell her yourself, she's shotgun with the dog.' I disconnected the call and glanced back to Sid, staring out the window as the darkness hurtled past.

The phone rang again instantly. Police.

'This is DS Sorrell and I've some distressing news. PC Brunning has been shot. There was a gunman at Miss Fielding's house.' Tom relayed the news matter of fact, he wasn't alone making this call, I could hear radios chattering in the background.

'How bad?' I felt ice, a slow vice grip. There had been someone there, or nearly there. That could have been us.

'On the way to hospital now, touch and go. Currently he's alive.' Tom made it sound like that status could change at any point.

'Please check on family staying in the town.' I looked across to Bill. He kept his eyes front, concentrating on the driving.

'Trev's been shot, sniper at Sid's house.'

'What? A gun! Someone with a gun at my house? Trev! Is he dead?'

'No, he's on the way to hospital now. We got out just in time it seems.'

'Alex?' she asked in a whisper.

'I don't know, possibly,' I exhaled slowly. 'There may be more than just Alexander, Sid, and I'm currently top of the hit list. There's a good chance that whoever shot Trev thought they were firing at me. They're looking for a policeman after all.'

'No… No… when will this ever stop? How many people have to die? Why? Why is this happening?' There was panic in her voice.

'We'll find out, we're close now. Try not to worry, we're safe here.'

'Jake, I'm going to pull over so you can drive. I want to check in with some of my people. Sid, don't get out, climb over to the front seat, as soon as we stop, quick as, please.' He looked at her through the rear view, she nodded.

Stopping the car in an empty pull-in on the dual carriageway, he was out the door and in the back before Sid had chance to move, I was across the seats just as quick.

'Sorry to hurry you,' I waited, 'there's no tail but you never know.'

Finn sat observing Bill whilst the radio crackled away; a bank of screens across the dashboard and below, information being fed to us constantly, not all applicable, but information just the same. I could tell at a glance what was going on in the police world around us; a mine of information, but none that said if someone with a gun was nearby. Hidden in places you couldn't easily see were other tools of the trade, this car had it all. I sincerely hoped we wouldn't have cause to use any of it.

We met the start of the M5 and traffic got heavier, container HGVs heading back to depots, cars getting in the way. I flashed a few, got the finger from one who then overtook on the inside after braking hard as I came up behind. I sighed and flicked on the lights, it's amazing how that can make everyone suddenly become very pleasant. The car was easy to drive, I was glad Bill had sorted it as I'd never have asked for the real equivalent of a Bond car. It ate the miles without appearing to do anything at all.

'Sid? You ok?' I glanced at her quickly. I knew that she struggling, I could feel it coming off her in waves.

'Thank the gods I got to sort the car,' Bill interjected from the back, trying to lighten the moment. 'Spider here would have us all on pushbikes if he had his way!'

'Back up, what about the mini experience? At least I could get out of the bloody thing!'

I referred to another job we'd done together. Bill had requisitioned a car from some poor lady who just happened to be in the wrong place at the right time, I swear she thought she was being carjacked. Bill hadn't thought about how small those cars were when he dived into the driver's seat. It was like watching a Great Dane getting into a Jack Russell's skin. I laughed as I remembered it – I'd had to pull him out.

'That was an honest heat of the moment mistake and anyone could've done it.'

Bill pretended to sound hurt. I had to recount it all to Sid; I did exaggerate, but only a little. She did laugh, you had to know Bill, but it was still very funny. It went a little way to easing the tension.

We made good time along quieter motorways. Under a bridge and another car sped up behind us from a slip road. I saw them coming and instantly increased speed, alerting Bill, third lane, one fifty, we kept running. Bill pointed to a screen on the dash, Sid read it off, a friend, another police car, the radio crackled with a disembodied voice asking me what I was about. A lively conversation ensued which no doubt entertained a few having a dull night shift.

Eventually those familiar gates came in sight. They swung open as if by magic with one phone call and the car purred down the drive, all pussy cat now after the way it had roared up the motorway. Finn leapt out in joyful abandon as if this was his favourite holiday home and began his liberal watering. Bill unfolded himself from the back seat, it was similar to watching a hot air balloon inflate. Sid, in comparison, stepped out like she'd just got in to come down the drive; I wished I felt the same. Stiff shoulders from driving at speed for so long, my back felt like it had been botoxed. Cath was there to meet and greet, hugging Sid so hard she lifted her from the floor.

'One moment, Jake,' John said, 'I want to speak to Sid first. Come here, girl, give us a hug,' he reached out from his chair and whispered something to her. I didn't hear what he said but knew it had to do with the kidnap, I could tell that from her face. She smiled, kissed him on his cheek and stepped back.

'Now, what have you been doing? You've only been gone a few days so I take it you've been digging where you shouldn't as usual,' he peered around me.

'Bill Adams! Bloody hell Bill! It must be five years!' his face split into the widest grin.

Bill, all teeth now, went over to him. They produced some complicated 'yo yo man' handshake, all thumbs and fists.

'John! I was more than delighted when I knew we were heading here. Last time I saw you, you got me so drunk I woke up in a woman's dress in a lift,' he laughed loudly. 'There was only me in the dress, no sign of any woman! Still don't know how I got there!'

'Jake, Sid, I'm so pleased to see you both.' Cath said, as she came back in. 'I heard, of course I did, how have you managed to come out of it all looking so radiant, Sid? Tough little cookie, aren't you?' she hugged her again, ignoring the bruises. 'I know it's not good news when you bolt here, but I still love having you about.'

'Cath, this is highly active, we have one shot and we'll be gone again in the morning all being well, but, as always, that may change.'

'It's ok I know, John told me,' she smiled like this was all perfectly normal and, for her, it was.

Car parked in the barn, farm jeep parked back in front of the doors, bags in and Finn located. I shut the door and flicked on the perimeter sensors, silent sentinels that would alert us to unexpected company.

Sitting on the settle inside the door, I rang for an update on Trev and everything else. Trev was still in surgery, it had been hours now; a bullet in his spleen, mashed up insides, still touch and go. No one to find at Sid's house, despite extensive searches and still no trace of Alexander.

Alexander had pulled the wool firmly and just how could a man like that, in the mental state he was supposed to be in, manage to slip away unseen and unfound?

****

'News, is there any news?' John asked.

'The constable who was shot is still with us, just. Bullet in his guts, big mess, lots of unpicking and stitching. Otherwise all is too quiet, no sign of anyone. Alexander has melted away to somewhere unknown.'

I sipped on coffee which seemed to have half a pint of whisky in it. Shockingly strong; it went straight to my head.

'Cath, can I do a sandwich or something? We've yet to eat.'

'Of course, but I've already put some bits together for you all.'

She stood and proceeded to unload the fridge onto the table, some bits was an understatement.

John held forth while we ate, reminiscing on old jobs, leaving out the gritty bits and keeping it light and entertaining for Sid. The phone vibrated softly in my pocket.

'Moore. Trev is out of theatre. They are giving it a guarded prognosis, a wait and see for a few days.'

I exhaled slowly, looked down at the table and willed him well again.

'Any other news?'

'It's likely that the shooter was Alexander himself, footprints have been found that match. He was squirrelling away his medication, had it all stashed in the liner of his mattress. Christ, that man can get about quickly! They're frantic at the secure unit, heads have rolled and I'd have dropkicked a few if I was there. Total bloody idiots!' His fury radiated down the phone at such incompetence. 'Keep very low as he's highly volatile and could be anywhere now. A side issue, your sister is safe at granny's house.'

'Understood, thank you, I'll update in the morning.'

'Until tomorrow,' he disconnected abruptly as usual.

I sat saying nothing for a few moments. Sid had a hidden hand on my back, soft against my skin. I smiled at her, warm eyes to mine and turned to the others.

'Trev is out of theatre, still a guarded prognosis. The gunman is almost certainly Alexander and he's non-medicated,' Sid flinched. 'John, can we work on this in the morning, or rather when its light, I think it's morning already.'

'Of course, can you show Bill where he is?' John said, the message in his eyes meant much more, I knew he was trying to shield Sid. I also knew that he wouldn't sleep now; he'd be turning stones to help find Alexander.

I showed Bill his room and then went back to Sid, lurcher in tow. It felt like we'd barely been away, Finn stretched himself instantly on the rug, asleep before his tail stopped wagging.

'I wish I knew,' Sid spoke into the air, a whisper tinged almost with despair.

'Knew what? What Alexander's about?'

'I wish I knew what he wants, what it is that he's trying to protect me from. Where's Seb?' her hand flew up to her mouth, wide eyes to mine, 'Where's Josh? Are they safe...will he go after them?'

'Oh, Sid... This is going to be really hard, I haven't kept this from you deliberately, it happened just before you were taken. Sid, Josh is dead, shot; it's very likely now that Alexander killed him. Seb was arrested in Hong Kong for possession but its possible it was planted on him. He's been deported but remains under arrest.'

She stood stiffly and walked over to the far side of the room.

'Oh fuck... Josh and Seb... Josh dead... murdered... fucking hell...Alex has done this. It makes sense now, all his rambling and all this madness. He thinks this is the way to make the bad men pay,' she leant against a chest of drawers as if she could no longer stand by herself. 'Oh... Oh fuck, fuck, fuck... Jake, Alex thinks that you're a bad man too,' she span around. 'This isn't going to stop until he's killed us all.'

'Perhaps he's not trying to kill now, perhaps he wants to protect.'

'No! No! Don't you get it! If I'm dead then I'm safe. Nothing can hurt me if I'm dead. He won't stop now until we're all dead. Oh Alyosha, my Alyosha, what are you doing?'

Chapter Sixty-Four

'Will you tell me more about yourself now? I need all the distraction I can get.'

She lay beside me, both of us trying to shut out Alexander, Josh and Seb just for a while longer.

'What do you want to know?' I closed my eyes, letting a wave of sleepiness wash in and over. I'd come this far. Now I'd answer her questions.

'Those abilities, the ones that you got you headhunted, you could start there,' she rolled over and I felt her stare without having to see it. No wriggling out of it was going to be allowed. Ok, ok, I owed her this much.

'Probably three abilities marked me of interest, actually there are four. One, a nearly photographic memory that's hard to explain, I sort of just look stuff up in my head, picture it and re-read. Can I use what I see, as in do I understand it? Yes, mostly I do. Languages, you already know about, easy because of the aforementioned fact. Secondly, I'm highly skilled at disguising myself in a variety of situations, you know that already too. Thirdly, a high level of ability with martial arts.'

I opened my eyes and looked at her. She was concentrating hard, looking for the unspoken words, listening not to what I said but what I didn't.

'You've noticed that Bill carries a gun. He almost always does. I, on the other hand, almost never do. I can't stop a bullet, can't stop a bomb but, if I can get within ten to fifteen feet of a serious opponent, I can disarm and/ or disable them. That skill isn't just about violence and aggression, strangely, it's really more to do with physics and bio-mechanics.'

She blinked slowly, 'Explain.'

'It's dull.'

'Not to me. Explain, please. And, for the record, I need all the details,' she smiled, the cat with a paw on its prey.

'Ok, but if you start to glaze over, I'll stop. Make sure you're paying attention, Miss Fielding, and remember, you did ask.'

She countered my attempt to dissuade with her radiant smile, the one she saved for special occasions. I gave up.

'In its truest form, any martial art is simply about neutralising threat as quickly as possible. All are efficient in terms of energy use and, without exception, all are extremely brutal and violent. I have ability in several recognised forms; Bill calls me Spider, something which Gwil started; he's taking the piss of course, but that's why I rarely carry a gun. Karate, in all its forms, is where I began, and then Kendo, Kung Fu, Jujitshu, Taekwondo, Judo and others. Most of those you'll have heard of and possibly know lots of ordinary souls who practise them.

'So, aside from that lot, there are also the lesser known forms, such as Krav Maga, Savate, Eskrima, Muay Thai, Pangrateion and Silat. Lesser known in the UK because they're, to be frank, killing skills; people can get seriously hurt whichever way you go. You wouldn't want to walk into any of them without some level of prior ability. But, in their country of origin, most of the ones I've just mentioned are taught to all, even, in the case of Muay Thai, competitively to children as young as six.

'So, where to start with the more hard-core forms? Krav Maga is my number one, aside from Silat. Like many other art forms, it's a mishmash of several styles, refined and developed to fit the purpose. There are throws that hail from Judo and strikes that have come from Karate, but the disarming is probably more Jujitshu.

'In Krav Maga, there are no real rules. You can use anything, any part of your body, anything that may come to hand, as a weapon. That's where physics and bio-mechanics come in. The force you can generate, for example, just from your leg muscles; a burst of power from those muscles alone can put over three hundred pounds of force into a strike and that's enough to take out a man's windpipe in one go. Most of the moves block and strike simultaneously, defending a range of three sixty degrees which is essential because, unlike the films, there's usually more than one attacker and they rarely wait their turn.

'You've got to be quick for any of this. The normal reaction speed for an adult, on average, around point one five seconds - mine is less than a tenth of that. It's not innate though, I trained for years to get that quick.'

She moved, pulling a pillow under her head and settling back down again.

'Carry on. Don't stop now, this is fascinating.'

'That I doubt, but as it's you... Let's go with a specific example. Think about knives, Sid; perhaps the most common street weapon, but it doesn't have to be something as obvious; you can do a lot of damage with something as ordinary as a set of car keys or even a pen. In fact any sharpish point is potentially lethal. In less than a minute a single stab wound can cause the loss of over four pints of blood, even more if you know where you're stabbing. Defending from an attack means getting control of the situation very, very quickly, it doesn't mean stepping back out of range, it means getting in close.

'A kick is always an effective move. A low kick to the knee, say, using the quad muscle and allowing the hamstring to snap out the power; that can accelerate a simple kick to over thirty miles per hour. Low kicks can be aimed at the femoral nerve which, from experience, hurts like hell, take two or three well aimed kicks and you won't be able to use the leg for a while. High kicks can work as strikes to any part of the upper body. A blow with the shin bone generates the same force as if you used a baseball bat. Dirty but useful in so many situations.

In summary, kicks are best used when there's sufficient distance, strikes when there isn't. A kick is twice as powerful as a punch and something as innocuous as a palm strike, delivered properly can cause cardiac arrest, stopping the heart instantly with the force of a battering ram. It sometimes happens accidentally in rugby games or any contact sport, when you might try to push someone out of the way.

'So to continue with our example, what's more deadly than a knife? Let's go with the gun thing, could be a knife but a gun is more of a threat for obvious reasons. First rule is that it's never worth losing your life over a street fight but, in a combat situation and, for me, most fight situations are classed as combat, then it's different. Say a man, or woman, puts a gun to your chest, you need to get close, twist your body, your core, out of line of fire - twisting at the hips does this. Grab the hand holding the gun by the wrist and pull the attacker forward towards you. Sounds mad, sounds like you ought to be pushing him or her away, but this way off balances them. Once pulled forward, hold their wrist against your chest and you're in control of the gun now. Take hold of the barrel, twist and suddenly, you're the one holding the gun and the whole situation has reversed. Step away, get distance and there isn't a lot the original attacker can do about it.'

'But,' she said, 'that might work for you but I'd have little strength to hold a man like that.'

'That's where the science comes in again. Think about it for a moment. The barrel of the gun is a lever, anyone can use a lever to generate a very high level of force against one point. Aside from that, mostly the attacker wants to hold onto the gun as much as you want to take it, so they hold on tight; twisting the barrel forces the attacker's wrist into a flexed position, a nifty little move as it completely stops the upper arm being used and effectively turns off the power. If you get round to using the muscles of the chest as well, you'll deliver ten times more force into that wrist and bones fracture long before you get to the point of real effort. This method of disarm, if you were skilled in it, would mean that you personally could take a gun from someone as big as Bill without breaking sweat.'

'Ok, but what about fear? I know I'd be terrified if someone was pointing a gun at me.'

'Yes, so was I the first time it happened. Confidence, that's what you need, skill and confidence. You get both from training. But it doesn't matter how skilled you are; if you aren't in the right place mentally, you're going to get hurt. There's a word, *zenshin,* it's a hard word to define but the best I can do is to say it means being constantly aware of potential danger. By constant I mean all the time, wherever you are, even now Sid, even here and now whilst I'm lying here with you. All these skills require a high level of inner balance and I'm not talking tightropes. It's a lot more than just being a nasty bastard, a lot more than just a mindset, a lot more than once a week training - in many ways it is a way of life in all things that you are and all things that you do.'

I sighed deeply, I was starting to sound a bit too 'grasshopper' for my liking.

'And, of course, there are tricks; for example, I try and watch an opponent's eyes if they're trying to attack me and look away if it's the other way around. There's an involuntary reflex which affects the pupil of the eye, it occurs about a hundredth of a second before a move is made. An experienced assailant is looking for that – I always look for that My reaction time means that I can get in first with a block or a strike.

'So, Sid, that's it, that's what makes me flavour of the month with covert agencies.'

'Is that how Gwil became your friend? You don't need to say anything if its still too raw. Bill told me you were very close to him.'

'Yes, I was. He was killed in a solo climbing accident a month before I came to Ashleigh. Its odd but that seems like a long time ago now.'

I couldn't bring myself to tell her the truth, not sure I'd ever tell anyone or, if it would change anything if I did.

'I'll always remember the first time we met though as I punched him full in the face.'

She gasped, 'Why?'

'You might have already noticed but I'm not always the easiest person to be around and, when I was young, I had dickhead on a default setting. But Gwil saw something in me and, even after having to get his nose reset, he stuck around. It took five years before I found out that he'd actually been sent to recruit me. He'd obviously seen something in that furious teenage boy that was worth getting a nose job for,' I exhaled slowly. 'He wasn't just my mentor, Sid, he became my closest friend. He saved my life and I returned the favour, many times. I miss him a great deal.'

She lay silent for a moment, dealing with all that. I waited. She would ask and she did.

'Have you killed?'

'Yes, when there has been no other choice. Yes, I have.'

That was a tough one for her to take on board. Too tough perhaps, but as we were in the zone, let's get the final bit out too.

'Last but not least, the fourth reason. Sid, the fourth reason why I was recruited was that my character, my personality was such - *is* such - that I can kill. I can walk confidently into the full force of conflict and take someone out. But, to put some perspective on that, I'm on the side of the good guys, I want to be part of what helps not hurts. To defend those who are being hurt, or who are in danger. So, to draw this to a close, that's who I am and that's what I do.'

'Bloody hell,' she breathed out the words. 'No wonder you're so complicated. Thank you, now I know.'

'Now you do.'

'I'm glad you're on my side,' she rolled over and kissed me.

'Mmm, so am I.'

I wasn't sure that saying all that made anything better, probably the opposite, too late now, it was done. Another wave of tiredness swamped in so I closed my eyes again and wondered if I could just drift off for a while.

In the back of my mind, I knew that Alexander was still somewhere, biding his time, waiting for us. I tried not to let that thought sneak in too often.

Chapter Sixty-Five

'Jake? Are you awake?'

I looked up from where I'd buried myself against her hair.

'I think so… not sure… I may have lost myself in another reality that's made up of only you.'

She wriggled as I wrapped myself around her and tried to go back to sleep.

'You're very silly sometimes; utterly and completely gorgeous in every way but also silly,' she pushed me away.

'What time is it? It can't be time to wake up yet?' I lay back against the pillow, feeling totally drained.

'Please don't go back to sleep. I need your brain for a minute,' she prodded me with one finger.

'Sid, it's because of what you've done to my body that I need to sleep. My whole being is worn out, the batteries are flat.' I spoke against the cotton of the bedclothes, my eyes firmly shut.

'Jake, this is serious. Please wake up, I need to show you something. Please, I need you to tell me if this is important.' She prodded me again, in the ribs, several times until I moved.

'Ok, I'm awake… just.'

I hauled myself out of the deep syrupy state that tried to pull me back, as attractive as a surf siren calling me into the sea. She was sitting cross legged in front of me, all bright eyes – I couldn't believe she could look so awake. She laughed.

'You look done in! Let me show you something and then you can sleep again '

I leant back against the pillow, tried to pay attention.

'In the post at home was this package. It must have come at some point whilst we'd been away because I'd not noticed it before. Anyhow, its addressed to Alex but its written in his handwriting,' she held up one hand to stop me from interrupting, 'it isn't unusual for him to send me stuff - photographic files usually. He's done it for a long time, thinks its safer to have hard copies of his work somewhere away from where he's living. In case of a fire or whatever. Its good stuff, he didn't get his position with Reuters by pulling strings; before he became so ill, he was really good.

'Anyway, to get to the point, I usually put the packages into a bag of his which he takes on again. Last time he left his bag but he'd not been well; he came, I think, just to sleep.'

'You called him Alyosha last night, why was that?'

'It's a nickname that he's used for years; it's a sort of thing between us, he'd call me Zosima and I'd call him Alyosha. Have you ever read Dostoyevsky? He always said that I was the special one, the one he needed to take care of, hence Zosima. Alex was about the only person I ever knew who read Russian literature for fun as a teenager. Anyway it was a game at first and then, after our parents died, it became symbolic really, a symbol of our closeness. I liked that we had secret words, it made me feel special when not a lot else did.'

All I could think of was Gwil. Gwil knowing about Alyosha and sending the book so that I'd know him too. How could I have missed it? Dostoyevsky had a bit of a thing for villains.

Murder is permissible in the pursuit of higher purpose - Alexander had purpose, Alexander had an agenda.

Or was Alexander truly Aloysha - a Christ figure standing alone in a debauched world?

If that was the case than this was so much more than one man acting out deranged vendettas against 'bad men', this was more along the lines of one man's holy war.

'After Alex had taken me, I can't think of him as Alyosha anymore, that is a name from another time now; anyway after we came back, I put the package in my bag meaning to open it. I forgot about it until just now, remembering woke me up. It isn't photos, it's a notebook.'

She passed a thick, leather bound notebook to me. The cover was cracked and worn, inside the pages were covered with tiny script. Every scrap of paper had been used with writing as well as illustrations sideways down the margins and on both sides of each page. Fucking hell!

It was the original of the notes that had been left with Marcus' body. It was the original of what Gwil had sent.

Line after line of it, page after page, tiny spider scrawl. I switched on another light to look at it more closely. It was mostly written in Tibetan, the language classically taught to buddhists.

'Can you read it?' I asked her. 'Can you understand his code?'

'No, I've never known how it works. Can you?'

'Probably, it's not easy, but I think I can. I've already seen the first few pages, its what brought me to Ashfield in the first place. The rest of this notebook doesn't look as complicated.'

'Why has he done this? He's a spiritual man, a pacifist - always has been. He went to record war photographically because he wanted to help stop it. Ever the humanitarian, he wanted people all over the world to see the damage that was done. His illness is frightening. Not Alex himself, but how it makes him behave. I suppose that's the psychosis but he's gone from being a right on happy smiley vegan to someone who is terrifying.'

'Why Tibet?'

'I don't know why specifically but he talked a lot about visiting buddhist monasteries and learning about sky burials; you know where the birds, vultures I think, are given the bodies of the dead to eat - he did an article on it for the Telegraph. He called the birds, sky dancers, said that was their proper name. I remembered it because it was such a lovely way to think of such a grisly job.'

'Has he mentioned it again recently?'

She shook her head, 'No, not for a long time, that was a conversation from long ago. Do you know what makes someone do this? What starts it off?'

'As far as I know there isn't one single cause. Factors like trauma or drug abuse can tip someone into a psychotic episode but what makes someone schizophrenic in first place is really unclear.'

'Alex was an addict. For a long time, when he was younger. He had all sorts of treatment for it. Is that why?'

I shrugged, who could know.

'I've tried to remember exactly when he began to get ill, when it all became too much for him but there's not one single event that I can recall. Losing our parents was a major trauma but I didn't stay around much after then, I ran off to ride my horses. Then Gabriel came along and everything went downhill. I know I didn't care much about anyone else at that time.

'One thing does keep coming back to me though. It may be nothing and it was a long time ago, when I was still young. I remember that there was talk of a problem with one of the horses. No one talked to me directly about it but I did a lot of listening at doors. I'm not sure why now, probably just because I liked a bit of intrigue as kids do. The horse that everyone was going on about was the colt, remember the one that Alex had a thing for? Apparently he was having trouble with one mare during his first season at stud. Obviously, because of his success on the track, he'd a lot of mares booked to him but he wasn't doing very well. Of course, I didn't pay much attention to all that at the time. But then Alex told me that it would all be ok because they'd given the mare some straws and that would make it better. He'd heard Seb talking to Josh about it, or they'd told him, I'm not sure which. For a long time I thought that the straws held some kind of medicine,' she watched me closely making sure I was still following her. 'It took me a while before I clocked on to what those straws really were.'

The proverbial penny was there on the edge, about to drop and with a sudden raucous ringing of the solution bell in my head, it did. Seb and Josh had been using artificial insemination to get the colt's mares in foal.

The straws that Sid talked about were insemination straws, full of semen that had been illegally obtained. None of that colt's progeny conceived by insemination were eligible for registration as Thoroughbreds for racing. It did go on, for sure and certain, but not on such a scale. The other side to this was that they would have needed help, veterinary help. Inseminating a mare was often pointless unless she was at the point in her cycle when she could conceive, someone had to know what they were doing to predict that. There we were, back full circle to the veterinary hospital that Seb had invested 9.8 million in; the veterinary hospital that was also a supplier of black market ketamine to half the muppets in Newmarket and elsewhere.

I urgently needed to translate the rest of the book and see what else Alexander had to say. Without doubt it would be important.

'That's it! That's what I needed and that could be where all this started,' I pulled her to me and kissed her fiercely. 'You're not just smarter than the average bear, you, Sid, are the love of my life! You're a complete darling!'

I jumped up out of the bed, pulling on some clothes, no time for tiredness now. I sat back down to lace my shoes and turned to look at her as she sat there, just staring at me, her eyes shining bright.

'What?' I stopped. 'What's wrong?'

She shook her head, smiling at me. 'Nothing's wrong, quite the opposite. You just told me I was the love of your life.'

I must have frowned, this was puzzling...yes...and?

'You've never told me that before. You've told me that you are in love with me, but never that I'm the love of your life,' her eyes were shining in that way that meant she was close to tears. 'That means so much.'

I hugged her tight, 'Oh Sid, I'm sorry for all the things I don't say and for all the ridiculous things that I do manage to get out. Frankly, I adore you, love you more than I can possibly ever put into words, you're quite simply the whole world to me, love of my life, my absolute everything,' I kissed her gently. 'Is that right, does that sound right to you?'

'Oh yes, that's perfect and you are perfect, perfect for me. Go, I'll come and make some tea,' she smiled, shining so brightly.

'Put some clothes on first; I'll never be able to think straight if you come like that.' I shot out the door as she threw a pillow after me, thundering down the stairs two at a time before I remembered that everyone else was probably still asleep.

'John?' I stuck my head around the door of his office. There he was, headphones on, beavering away at the keyboard. I touched him lightly on the shoulder and he jumped away.

'Sorry, didn't mean to startle you.'

'Jake, bloody hell, you've just shortened my life by ten years! What are you doing still awake?'

'Sid has just given me this; its Alexander's journal and she's also given me a little gem that may prove to be the first solid explanation behind it all.'

I must have looked as psyched as I felt because John brightened instantly.

'Come on then, man, let's get cooking!'

I sat next to him at the desk and we opened the next Pandora's Box, this time it was that of the intimate thoughts of Alexander Fielding as well as the corrupt dealings of his brothers.

FOR WORDS, LIKE NATURE,
HALF REVEAL AND HALF
CONCEAL THE SOUL WITHIN

Chapter Sixty-Six

And I will flay the flesh from the bones and strip them bare for angels to eat
One had a secret
So he hid it in numbers and gold,
Two had a secret
So he hid it in Uncle Sam and straw,
But then the strange one found the secret
And it made him yellow and cold,
So he gave it to the red dwarf to help him thaw,
But yellow tore the heart and flesh from it
And slew it dead with silvered hooves.

One was Sebastian, he hid his corruption in finance. Two was Joshua, he lived in the states - Uncle Sam, and he'd initiated the use of AI on the mares. Alexander had found out and been abused. Yellow, the colour used in Dostoyevsky's novels to symbolise mental illness. Alexander gave his knowledge to Sid - the red dwarf - Sidra meaning *star* in Latin and red dwarf another name for a small star... Oh, why couldn't I have worked this out sooner!

....yellow tore the heart and flesh....and slew it dead with silvered hooves... the murders; he was telling of the murders.

I worked on, so much easier now I had the key to the code. John worked with me throughout.

The late Joshua Fielding and his brother, Sebastian; two fine upstanding names in the corporate world, men whose businesses stood as global models to be aspired too. It was all smoke and mirrors. Both men would have struggled to lay straight in bed at night.

My cyber-mole had helped to uncover the true nature of these men, as had Gwil's painstaking intelligence before anyone, aside from Marcus, had been killed. My loose ends were finally meshing.

Luxuriating in their millions, they'd sat in ivory towers and screwed over those below them with pitiful contempt. It seemed that there wasn't a deed too low, to base for them to consider. Any form of corruption and they had a finger in it. Once you knew which stone to lift, it was there to be seen. The thing that amazed me the most was that no one had called them to account sooner. It all hinged on greed and blackmail.

Sid came in with tea and the biscuit tin, John sent her straight back out for whisky and coffee, proper coffee mind, none of that instant crap. She went with a smile, fully clothed, thank the gods. When she returned with the proper stuff I pulled her close. John raised his eyes and then looked back to the screen again.

'Sid, this is going to get very messy, put the stab vest on - I am serious. Now, more than ever, I need you to be very strong. You're about to find out some really shitty stuff about Seb and Josh.'

She looked at me for a long time and then said, 'Solve this so we can walk out of here without looking over our shoulders. Solve this so we can walk, run, whatever on the moor or up your mountain without fear and I can ride again without fear,' she touched my face very gently with her fingertips. 'Solve this and give Alex back some peace, set him free from his demons as you've done for me.'

The world could have just been me and her in that moment, condensed from two souls to one, irrevocably bound to each other by something that, to me, seemed almost impossibly pure. All I could think of was how profoundly I loved her.

'Can you go and wake Bill? Would you ask him to come down?'

'Yes, of course,' she slipped from my arms and was gone.

John stared for a painfully long time. I waited for whatever it was he was going to say.

'Jake Steel, I never thought I'd see the day. You've always been so distant, so contained that I worried for you. So good looking - too good looking I always thought. That was your burden from when you were a little boy. A heavy burden as well, though not many would see it that way. The work you chose didn't help, all enforcement and shadows. But to look at you now, with that woman, you've grown beyond measure. I'm so very proud of you,' he smiled, his eyes shining.

Bill arrived yawning and Sid brought another cup, sitting neatly on the chair behind me, legs drawn up, hugging her knees. I translated Alexander's book and dug some more.

All that I'd seen before had been left of centre; I knew that there was something crooked going on through the oil boys in Dubai, but that wasn't really what the Fieldings were about, not where they began. We looked back to the Return of Mares for the colt, the list of mares that had visited Alexander's stallion during his first season at stud. Of sixty-five mares,

Marcus Williams owned five and Gabriel Wallace had been gifted, for winning rides, an interest in two more, both particularly successful race mares having their first seasons at stud. Seb had kept a record and there were others as well, who may have been complicit in the insemination of their mares or who may have known nothing until afterwards and then might have used the disclosure of such information to their advantage. Perhaps they hadn't minded so much, a foal is a foal after all. Perhaps they hadn't minded until someone, probably Gabriel, decided to push his luck and ask for a little bit more.

So what did these brothers stand to lose if their actions were found out? Millions. Tens of millions, that was what they stood to lose in real terms. Each of the horses conceived by insemination ought to be removed from the stud book, become ineligible for racing and, therefore, in many ways, become worthless. There would be a barrage of compensation claims, the litigation would run and run.

They also stood to lose face which is, to some, more important than the millions. Their reputations, their status and standing would be lost. They didn't strike me as the kind of men who would take such matters lying down. Driven, hard-nosed, money makers both of them, they ran their days to a different tune. A shoulder in front of them was something to climb, to tread down on as they surged ever onward, more money pouring in, more backs to climb until they'd reached the very top. Lords of all that they surveyed.

Greed. It is an addiction and there are many forms but, in this case, it was financial greed. They, the brothers and their partners in crime, got a rush from screwing someone over, from stamping on the weak and the vulnerable. Greed looks just like you would expect; an inflated, bloated, amorphous mass that seeks to consume everything in its path until there's nothing left to be had. Different markets had to be tasted, that meant that different people living different lives could also be consumed in this ever needing, ever wanting, desire to always — always - have more. The need, the addiction, began to outweigh the attainment. And still it went on.

But what if they climbed so high, to those lofty heights of the mega wealthy; so visible now at the top of their respective piles, that they drew the attention of others who'd also got there by nefarious means? There are clever people who chose to walk the crooked path, brilliant minds that choose to direct their brilliance to subversive acts instead of for the greater good. Sebastian and Joshua, all big boy bluster, would have been easy pickings for those kind of people. I saw through their false pomposity when I met them, how would they have looked to people whose pie they were taking a slice of?

Enter the drugs now. There's more money in that than almost anything else, except maybe the sale of arms; more corruption, double dealing and back stabbing than in any other aspect of the twisted sub-culture that passes for reality in this oh so civilised world. Sebastian and Joshua would have been lambs to the slaughter. In over their heads before they realised what they were standing in. Drugs came before the human trafficking but they were involved in that too.

The man at Seb's house was up to his waist in trafficking; his was a different kind, not humanitarian, if there is such a thing. He controlled, like Seb did, he pimped - just like Seb did. The man at the racecourse was a decoy, a fall guy in so many ways. It had been his blade that had stolen John's Wozniak last laugh, his blade that had lost patience with John's tall tales. But his blade had acted on someone else's instruction.

But. There it is again. Always a but, hanging around and slipping in just when you've already got enough balls to keep up in the air. Neither the man in the flat or at the racecourse had done the shooting or, for that matter, the pulping. Neither had hung around to do the hanging, if you'd excuse the pun. Some final loose ends, still twisting and contorting looking for their solutions.

I'd put money on it, the solution that is, I could see it clearly now; I just hoped it couldn't see me.

It was Alexander.

It all came back to Alexander. But what had turned him so much? His schizophrenia? His drug abuse? He'd stepped out and not come back, he'd tried once and been beaten for his pains. He'd gone away, tail firmly between his legs, to lick his wounds. To lick his wounds and wait, it seemed, until now. Until now when he'd twisted himself up sufficiently, or straightened himself out, to take a crow bar, it had to be something like that, and batter to death the men associated with the mess his brothers had made. There was still a big why as to what made him bother to take such a stand. But, then with these murders under his belt, he chose to escalate it still further, take a gun, be the one to kill his brother and then abduct his little sister, finishing it all off by shooting Trev. Alexander had an axe to grind and I didn't know why except that he wanted the bad men to pay. I carried on picking out words from the almost illegible scrawl in his notebook.

Sid sat silent but attentive through all of this. Listening to the conversations going on, back and forth between Bill, John and myself; she sat saying nothing just listening. It must have been hard. This was her family we were picking apart, her brothers and yet she said nothing.

Cath came in at about half five and started in surprise at all of us already there. She gestured to Sid and together they went into the kitchen. We carried on picking through the debris.

I wandered out after ten minutes or so for more coffee; Cath was standing hugging Sid tightly at the far end of the room. She silently indicated that I left again. To draw myself back in, I picked up the phone. The drugs connection was still active as was the oil. It seemed that they were surfing along, not directly affecting traffic, just checking it out, seeing who was doing what and when - keeping low.

I knew that Alexander had set off a chain of events by lighting fires under the Fielding brothers, just as I'd done with my cyber mining. Joshua had come, or been sent and Alexander had taken him out. Sebastian ran to see what he could salvage from the Chinese side of his empire and Alexander, or someone else, had planted on him. The detained man, the trafficking pimp, he'd been known to have stayed at Sebastian's London house and that man was also working for Sebastian to find Alexander. He'd chosen to do that by sending his own version of moles to track Sid; he'd assumed, wrongly it turned out, that Sid would know where Alexander was. He thought that if he turned up the heat, Alexander would be exposed. Sid was never directly in danger, it was a ruse to get Alexander out in the open.

Alexander fought back as he'd never done before and he killed. No more the yes man, no more the man who could be beaten into submission. He was the one who called the shots now, or the crow bar, whichever way you chose to look at it.

But Alexander was still absent. No trace, no sight nor sound of him. He was buried deep somewhere and, I had to presume, he wasn't at all well. To make that even worse, he probably still had access to a gun.

A short while later I realised that Sid hadn't come back in and went into the kitchen to find that no-one was there. Back to work but uneasy, it was unlike Sid to go but then again, she was with Cath, wherever Cath was. On impulse I turned on the short wave radio we used on the stud. It crackled into life and I was immediately listening to something that froze me to the spot. Bill's head snapped up from the computer screen, John turned slowly; we all looked at one another in slow motion horror.

Cath and Sid were talking, talking to someone whose voice I struggled to recognise. Cath holding the transmit button down on the radio because we heard it all with no pauses.

'It's ok, I do understand, at least I think I do.' Sid's voice was clear, placating.

'You can't stay here, this stable needs sorting out and the lads will be here soon to turn out,' Cath next, soothing and encouraging.

Nursery rhymes, over and over. That's all we could hear in the background.

Alexander.

Fuck.

Alexander was here.

Chapter Sixty-Seven

'Come on, come with us, come and get some coffee, let's talk about this,' Sid said.

'That's a good idea, come with us back to the house. There's no one else about so we can talk in peace,' Cath again.

More nursery rhymes. Humpty Dumpty…

'Alex? Alex, come on, come and have coffee,' Sid's voice failed to hide her fear. 'Come on, come and have something to eat with Zosima?'

I turned to John. 'Where are they? Which part of the stud? Can we get to them without being seen? Can you stop everyone from coming onto the stud? If the lads turn up for work…'

John looked stunned briefly, 'They could be in one of three yards. Listen some more, be patient, Cath will tell us, she'll know we're listening,' he picked up his phone and touched in numbers, talking again as it rang. 'I've locked the gates; no one can come in easily.'

Bill also on his phone, armed response would be on the way. I abandoned the book and ran upstairs, three at a time, grabbed the wire microphone, paused for a moment then grabbed my bag, hauling out my work vest - the bullet proof. I was out the room at speed, jumping back down the stairs again, Finn appeared from his slumbers and came too. In the office, I fitted the wire, pulled on the vest and threw Bill the control; I was on the way to the door when John spoke again.

'Top yard, pregnant mares, Cath has just said to not mind the mare that box walks. He must be jumpy; he's worried by the noise,' he caught my wrist to stop me. 'I've done what I can to stop anyone arriving on that yard for work. Jake, listen to me. Don't be a hero, not for anyone. Play this by the book. Heroes get their names in stories after they're dead – I need you around and so does Sid.'

Another transmission silenced him.

'For fuck's sake, Alex, a gun is no good to you here. The horses will be frightened, I'm frightened. Come on, it's me, Sid, you know me, come on Alex, take my hand.'

Sid, Sid and Cath with Alexander. And Alexander had a gun.

That was enough, I was out the door. Finn was waiting, hopping from foot to foot, he ran out with me into the gloom.

****

The top yard was surrounded by a copse of trees specifically planted for shelter and it was isolated from the rest of the stud buildings, to reduce the risk of a sick horse infecting anything else on the stud. I ran around the outside of the paddocks, not knowing which part of the barn they'd be in, it opened either end, whichever entrance I chose was a fifty-fifty chance. A small buzz in my ear and Bill spoke to me alone.

'John says that they are at the west end of the barn. Hope you get that, I'm assuming that you can't respond. As soon as armed response is on site I'll be with you. Wait for me, Jake, please.'

I ran on, in along the hedge line, deep in the shadows. Thankfully the paddocks were full of rabbits and Finn quickly left for an early morning hunter gatherer moment. My breath came in short bursts, my legs felt like lead, I was trying to run in jeans and now wet Converse, it was like running with bricks tied to my feet. I arrived at the far end of the barn; Bill spoke again in my ear.

'He's come out of a stable, it sounds like he's walking with Sid, Cath is behind. There's water on the floor, we can hear a splash, perhaps a puddle, one moment...'

It went silent, I waited, heart pounding, breathing settling, adrenalin surging.

Sid, please no, not Sid again.

Angrily, I forced away those thoughts and slipped into the mind set of martial arts; took myself to energy, rebalanced and thought of nothing other than channelling energy. Breathing. Concentrating. Focus. Focus the power. This was just another of those moments I'd spent years training for. Nothing more than a defensive weapon in human form, the weapon that would protect and defend Sid and Cath: the weapon that would take out Alexander.

'...they've stopped, he's talking to Sid, talking one minute, nursery rhymes the next. Cath is still with them but not side by side. Armed response is on site, I'm on the way. Wait for me.'

I crept around the back of the barn. I remembered this place; two parallel lines of stables facing each other, with stores for hay and straw at either side of one end, feed and tack stores at the other. Twenty stables, ten on each side, with pregnant mares waiting to go out into the paddocks for the day. The water points, there were two, one at either end of the barn; either could be leaking. I chose to come in from the east, hay and straw here, it would give me cover. I couldn't risk going further down inside the yard, there was nowhere to hide; the stable lines overlooked an immaculate central aisle, empty and cover free. I carefully climbed up the straw until I could see them; saw the leaking tap at the top of the barn, saw the puddle where it had dripped untended all night. Saw wet footprints leading away from it, showing where they'd walked, like footprints in the sand - transient and passing, soon to evaporate and be lost...

Alexander: head full of dreads, bedraggled and unkempt, big coat, scruffy trainers, holding a gun that looked like a rifle. Sid next to him. Alexander was a big man, or appeared to be in those clothes. I'd just taken him down in the shieling, not really paid much attention to his build. Slightly behind, Cath, hands in her coat pockets, she must be still holding the button down on the hidden radio. They walked slowly heading away from me, stopping every other stride for Alexander to pace and recite rhymes. I slipped back down and ran silently to the other end of the barn.

The tack store was at this end, part of the barn itself; a solid, brick built, windowless room with a heavy door to stop easy theft, something that had happened, even here. I could see from the bright electric light spilling out on the floor that this door was open. I had to hope that the padlock was on the outside as it usually was, open and left hanging with its key in the lock when someone was on the yard.

I crouched down just outside, a mere few feet from where they stood. John came through again into my ear, that must mean that Bill was en route.

'They are by the end of the barn, Sid's asking him to leave the gun again and Cath is agreeing. He's repeating rhymes.'

I knew this because I was feet from them, still hidden, but I could hear them. In a split second Sid would step out onto the concrete right next to me and then Alexander would know I was there. I waited and tried to estimate the distances between them, this was going to be a once only attempt and if I failed someone would get shot. I breathed deeply. Focus, condense, concentrate. I watched Sid's feet step out over the runner that held the metal door of the barn...

Chapter Sixty-Eight

As soon as I saw both of Sid's feet, I launched myself up and around the corner, between her and Alexander. There was momentary shock from them all and, in that millisecond, I assessed who was where. Alexander was further away than I'd thought but I still went for the gun first.

Manic, wide eyed, he swung it up straight at me, the barrel coming up fast level with my chest. Shifting weight, I launched a kick to the barrel, sending the gun pointing up into the roof and releasing a deafening noise as he simultaneously pulled the trigger. A light fitting crashed down striking Cath, she fell back against the wall, sliding down to her knees. The horses in the barn were instantly panicking, the sound of hooves banging and kicking against wood and stone.

Time slowed, all movement was exaggerated in those short seconds and I focussed on Alexander only - everything else would have to wait. I shut out the noise, shut out Cath bleeding, shut out Sid, somewhere behind me. The world became simply Alexander, the gun and me.

The rifle was still following through the force of my kick, arcing backwards with Alexander holding tightly to it with one hand. At its furthest point, he pulled it back underarm towards me again, re-balancing his weight, launching forward using the energy from my kick to bring it back around again. Super sensitive to all of his movements, it was obvious that Alexander was skilled; deep down in his bones, he had ability with this kind of fight and that high speed thought actually gave me a fleeting, perverse moment of satisfaction. I could now up my game.

Still not quite close enough, I struck down across his wrist with the rigid side of my hand as he tried to lift the gun. Full force powered that move. Small bones shattered, cracked and popped, I heard them, not unlike walking on fallen autumn acorns. His grip released involuntarily, fractured bones absorbed my strike, fingers outstretched automatically as if in an autonomic plea for help sending the gun across towards me as if he'd meant to offer it. I took hold of its long barrel. His side was exposed by the follow through of his body, cringing with the searing pain in his wrist and determination to retain the gun; a novice move on his part. A kick followed the strike, so quick it could have been one movement not two, massive torque generated by rotation of my hips, same principle that cracks a whip, the quicker the rotation the faster the kick. A fluid kick to his ribs using my shin bone, not polite but effective - same amount of force as if I'd used a crow bar - how apt.

He span around, bent over, clutching his wrist and side, the noise of his breathing a rattling, gagging wheeze and then reared up, heroically or stupidly, raising his left hand to attempt an attack. Keep moving, keep the energy flowing, keep the power coming. I rolled on the balls of my feet, struck him across the shoulder with the butt of the rifle he'd so kindly given me and followed through with an elbow strike to his jaw. Metal, such as the butt of a gun, doesn't deform like human bone so every bit of force flowed from my strike into his shoulder. The elbow strike was just less than fracture force, one hundred and eighty-four pounds and his jaw would shatter. Blood spattered in an arc of crimson from his mouth and nose as I fired another kick to his chest compressing the air both in and around him.

Pushing now, pushing him with my attack back towards the wall by the store; upright again he kept with me, appearing to be waiting for the next move, his eyes black and glassy. He reeked of danger, stank of a person too far gone to be treated with any allowances; head back as he held me with a stupefied stare. His throat exposed; one of the most vulnerable areas of the body, only seventy-six pounds of compression can cause total collapse of the larynx - that's less force that it takes to crumple a beer can with one hand. I could easily. But I didn't. Any second now and he'll explode from this catatonic suspension, he might be fighting back but it was as if on an automatic response; adrenalin must be coursing through and he was probably oblivious as to just how much pain his body was in.

Constantly aware of everything around me, I never left his eyes, waiting for that explosion. I knew with just one false move he would kill me, there was no doubt. In his apocalyptic thoughts he fully intended to kill me and then, too close was Sid, too close was Cath. No back up yet but then I'd also been asked to wait for them. Yeah, right, like that was going to happen in reality.

I kept pushing, herding him to the place I wanted him to be. His left hand shot out, fingers stiff, tightly fixed to inflict pain; I blocked him instinctively, pushed away the blow with my forearm, loudly breaking three of his stiffened fingers as I did so. He tried again with a low kick, I blocked it deliberately hitting nerve clusters in his leg. He kept coming, kept trying, shuffling from one side to the other as he sought to stay focussed. He was in position now, he'd put himself right where I wanted him, it was time I stopped indulging him.

I knew my speed would catch him defenceless, I also knew with absolute certainly I could kill him with one move, just one quick strike with my bare hand and he'd be gone. He might see a blur and then his death would be with him, perhaps he was already seeing nothing more than that. But, even with that knowledge sitting primed and straining to be unleashed, I knew that wasn't how this should end. The ability to kill, so very much part of what I was about but here, now, I knew that I could disarm, disable and contain.

I had options.

I don't do killing if I still have options.

One free hand, one holding a gun, channelling and concentrating inner energy, whippy full strikes one after the other, hammered home with a tremendous kiai that came from somewhere else purely to disorientate. I struck him hard in the face, one strike after the other; then instantly shifting weight again, leapt and kicked him twice in the middle of his chest with enough force to stop his breath. I wanted him to go backwards, directed his passage with my choice of strikes, felling him like a tall tree in a forest. Nowhere near quick enough he'd simply no time to defend and he was lifted up off his feet, thrown backwards in an arc with his arms cartwheeling and his spine curving impossibly with the kinetic force of my strikes and kicks. I used just enough to knock him out, pulled the rest back out of the way so there wasn't enough to kill. He kept falling backwards into the tack store and, as soon as he was clear of the frame, I hauled the door closed and locked it in one movement. The heavy door, metal lined, should hold him. I'd disarmed, disabled and now also contained.

I snapped a look to one side - Cath crouched against the wall, bleeding from a head wound and surrounded by a shattered plastic light fitting but safe now. I span again; the other way was Sid, outside, shocked hands up to her face, unhurt, safe - both safe now. Less than three minutes from my arrival in the barn, time drawn out by the severity of the moment. It was done now. All done now. I inhaled deeply, stood taller, stopped the ready for action crouch and it was then that he shot me.

Through the air vent right there in the wall by the side of the door.

He fired a clean shot.

If you can call being hit by a sawn off at close range a clean shot.

HE HAS BEEN REBORN AS AN IDEA, SOMETHING INTENDED - COMPLETE

Chapter Sixty-Nine

I went down instantly. Cath was there in a heartbeat, blood still running down her face, grabbing my shoulders and hauling me out of range of anything more. Pain arced up as I forced myself to swallow back a roar of agony. In a flash, Bill appeared at the end of the barn, bodily lifting Sid, screaming, away out of sight. Cath above, holding my hand as I slumped against the wall and breathed out the pain, shut it out from my body and refused to accept it. From outside, over the noise of frantic horses thundering around in stables, there was the sound of cars skidding to fast stops on loose gravel, distant sirens hurtled towards the barn, car doors slammed and booted feet hurried.

Sid came running back in from the far end of the barn; she must have run from Bill and around the outside. She threw herself onto the hard yard beside me. I looked from her to Cath and then down my body. Blood pooled, a spreading red puddle from the mess that once was my leg, pain hurled in.

Cath on the radio, talking to John, telling him what had happened and it was Cath who fashioned a tourniquet from a lead rope. I concentrated on Sid and breathing out the waves of crippling fire that flowed from my leg. Sid was safe; safe by me… nothing else mattered now.

Alexander continued to let off what cartridges he had left, out through the vent and into the walls whilst I worried about ricochet. I should have known he'd have another gun, wished I'd decided to hit him harder as it was clear now that I was actually the one who'd made the novice mistake. He pounded at the door with fists, kicks and eventually with an empty gun, I wondered how he was finding the strength to do that with fractures but was glad for the thief who'd come, just once, and prompted the reinforcing of all the store doors. To stop people getting in, not necessarily to stop them getting out. Oh well, shit happens, if he gets out now, we may well be stuffed. I could have laughed if I wasn't too busy filling the yard with my blood.

Sid clung, Cath hovered and, outside, I knew Bill was with the people who could sort this out. We were all waiting. Did he have any ammunition left? We all listened and waited.

More blue lights and sirens. The world, it seemed, continued to turn up outside the barn in a noisy haze of cars and lights. Meanwhile far too much blood pooled around me, a puddle of viscous red that darkened and grew as I watched it, slowly seeped into the cracks in the concrete. I was losing focus. The light was smudging, blurring... Sid held on. She stayed with me, talking constantly in a low whisper and I fixed my consciousness, such as it was, to her words.

Shouting! Sudden shouting from nearby! Bill and armed response took charge, took down the store door in a deafening volley of intimidation and commands. A chaos ensued, just part of what they had to do to subdue someone like Alexander. It was all noise, just wave after wave of noise: horses, police, cars, boots running on stone, hooves banging on timber walls and concrete.

'All clear! All clear!'

A final shout. Alexander was held. It was over. That part of this was over.

It was my turn now.

Paramedics beside me talking in quiet voices as one placed an Entonox mask over my mouth and nose, another cut through my jeans, cut off my boots; someone by my feet mopping up the bleeding. A disembodied voice telling me it was inserting a cannula, connecting me for fluids but first injecting morphine for the pain... what pain? I came back from somewhere momentarily as it flooded back armed with razor wire. Oh, yes, that pain... The morphine washed coldly into my vein and effectively trampled over the burning acid fire. I refused to let go of Sid's hand until it tugged me away leaving only vivid dreams of blood rivers that continually poured from monstrous gaping wounds.

I woke briefly in the ambulance, Sid was still there so I let myself wander off again into the pain free blackness. When I woke the next time it was dark outside, soft electric light revealed that I was now in a hospital bed; an angled window to one side of my bed reflected street lights and moving car head lights from outside. My lower left leg was now encased in a complicated Meccano-like frame on both sides with tidy looking stitching from ankle to knee; the foot swollen and slightly smeared in places with dried blood.

However, consciousness came hand in hand with monumental discomfort. I tried to turn unsuccessfully onto my side but stopped short because it really hurt, as in a wave of breath stealing, red fire, sweating, swearing hurt. But now I could see that, in the chair beside me, Sid slept curled like a cat, resting against one arm with her golden blonde spun silk over the folded cushion of my green shirt. I studied her for a long moment and wondered how long she'd been there, how long she'd slept whilst I'd been off somewhere else in anaesthetic absence.

I lay back against the pillows again and my leg settled to a dull throb but a good dull throb, the kind that speaks of healing. Part of me registered profound relief as I'd wondered if I might lose the leg after all that blood and mess back on the concrete yard. I looked across to Sid again and so wanted to touch her, got my hand half way out and then, quite unexpectedly, wandered off again slipping back into the arms of a deep, dark sleep.

It was some time before I next became aware, the sunlight streaming through the window beside me as I turned my head, blinking against the brightness. Sid was there still, awake now and leaning with her elbows on the bed.

'Hello, dude, you sleep like the dead,' those eyes, that sea blue reminding me of waves and mountain skies.

'Hello you. How's tricks?' I replied, my voice croaky and dry.

'Fine and dandy now,' she leaned forward and kissed me gently. Without a thought for all the tubes, I put my arms around her and tried to pull her across onto the bed, I wasn't really looking for gentle at that moment. She giggled.

'Better obviously, you're obviously feeling better!' she pushed away from me as the door abruptly opened and a young male doctor walked in with Bill hot on his heels. I noticed that I also had a guard outside. That was interesting. I saw that it was a uniformed and armed guard before the door swung closed again.

'Well, Spider, put the molly down, medic's here. Its good to see you with your eyes open. You'd win medals for sleeping.' Bill was sporting a very impressive black eye.

The doctor came over with cool fingers feeling for a pulse and looked intently at me.

'How do you feel, Dr Steel?' he let my wrist go and wandered to the bottom of the bed to check the chart that lurked there, consulting something like an iPad at the same time.

'Fine, I feel fine,' I replied as he studied my paper progress, a 'too much to do, too little time' air about him.

'Quick update now that you are back with us again. You suffered a gunshot wound to your lower left leg. You have a complex fracture to your tibia and fibula, both fractures were reset, plated and pined with surgery and are now immobilised with an external fixator… the framework that you can see. The gun shot was messy, they nearly always are, but, lucky for you, there is minimal muscle damage, the bone took it all. You've had pain relief, I've written you up for more four hourly and you're on a course of antibiotics to deal with any infection. You're strong, very fit and will, no doubt, heal quickly. I suggest a provisional discharge for the end of next week, that will be five to seven days from today, assuming that you aren't going home alone,' his diction clipped and precise, he looked across to Sid.

'No, he won't be alone,' she smiled at him, her radiant smile. I watched him visibly melt.

'Good, good, Sid. I'll leave him in your capable hands then,' he said it as if he wished he could be in my place, 'I'll keep an eye out and have a fiver on you next time you're riding.' Then he winked at her and I instantly bristled, pushing up on my elbows and glaring. Bets were one thing, winking was something else entirely.

Bill laughed as only Bill could. The doctor coloured and left quickly. I felt much better immediately.

'Why's there a tooled up outside?' I asked, reaching out a hand for Sid at the same time.

'He's here just in case,' he grinned, 'be a bugger if you get shot again, but at least you're in the right place now! It's a lot less messy.'

'Is anything new known?' I wondered if there was a threat still present from quarters other than Alexander. 'How's Cath – she was hurt, or did I just imagine that? And Alexander, how's Alexander?'

Bill shook his head, making eye contact for too long. 'Thankfully Cath only had a superficial wound, sticking plaster worthy but nothing more, she remains at full speed as always. Alexander is, at last, sedated and secure.'

'Cracking shiner,' I had to mention it, it would've been rude otherwise. Sid flushed beetroot and began intently examining my hand.

'Impressive, isn't it,' he touched his face gently.

'So was it Alexander or have you been somewhere you shouldn't?' I stared at him, something was on that he wasn't telling me.

'All right! All right!' Sid said sharply. 'It was me ok, I'm not proud of it, I've grovelled - a lot.'

I was stunned. 'You did that? To Bill? What with?'

'My fist.' She still wasn't looking at me.

'Why?' I was surprised, mainly because no-one I'd ever known had planted one on Bill and also because I'd never known Sid react physically whatever the provocation. He smiled at her and that just made it worse.

'Right, tell me this minute what you did to warrant a punch like that.'

'Steady up, Spider, don't be doing yourself a mischief,' he grinned broadly. 'I was the stupid one, ok, and the moral of the story is: don't carry off your best mate's girlfriend when he's just been shot and expect her to stay with you just because you tell her too. Well, at least not without body armour!'

'Well, well, Sid, you looking for a new career?' I squeezed her hand.

'I'm so ashamed. It was just that he took me away and I...I couldn't bear it, whatever was going on...you'd just been shot for fuck's sake!' she kept her eyes down. I lifted her hand and kissed her fingers simply because I couldn't reach anywhere else.

Chapter Seventy

Healing was, as always, tedious and there were several more days of lying around which were only bearable because of Sid. She disappeared briefly and came back armed with tedium busting equipment and her own brand of company which was now my favourite kind.

During the time that I'd apparently slept like the dead, she'd become part of the fixtures and fittings. The nurses, doctors, cleaners, physios; they all now knew her by her first name. People came, edging past Mr Serious on the door, wanting to discuss horses and betting as she sat, often cross legged, at the bottom of the bed, holding court with all and sundry who just seemed to be passing by. Cath came with John and Luci was still around, no doubt she'd be on the way to Newmarket as soon as I was discharged. My parents had been informed and I was to phone them. In a day or so, I probably would.

I was off line but I carried on translating the notebook with only occasional raised eyebrows if it got too raucous down by my feet. Sid had been messing with my music and now my phone had several new playlists that I listened to during the times that she was made to leave. Staring out of the window, often in the dark, listening whilst lost in thought; just waiting for her to come back again. One morning, when it was still far too early, I rang home and spoke to my parents at great length for the first time in years.

Those days passed and, one morning, the door guard vanished swiftly followed by my discharge. They gave me crutches, showed me how to use them and posted me out the door - with a huge sigh of relief I'd imagine, Sid and Bill were a big presence on anyone's ward.

Nothing had stopped whilst I was sleeping; it had all carried on, gathering information like moss on those stones. Alexander had been hard to subdue but it had happened and he was secure again. I'd battered him a bit; cracked his jaw, broken his wrist, collar bone, some fingers and several ribs but he was healing, on the surface. People waited for him to start talking but he remained silent, alert now but silent. Conversely, Sebastian was singing at the top of his voice, requesting witness protection if he told all that he knew and it was anyone's guess where that would end up.

John had DCI Moore as a constant phone companion. Trev was recovering slowly, every day getting stronger and Tom was filling gaps. Sid's bike had been found, partially burned at the bottom of a disused quarry, along with the helmets and the furniture van. It was hoped that the bike was salvageable but whether Sid would still want it was another matter. Everyone sought information; everyone sought the truth in this mess.

Luci and Ben arrived shortly after the sleek black car had decanted me into the real world once more. The kitchen buzzed with noise and laughter; Finn stared in frank horror at such frivolity and clearly yearned for his quiet sofa whereas Cath and John revelled in it, corks popped and glasses chinked. I sat, or rather stretched myself on cushions on the bench and watched it all unfold. Sid stayed close by, I noticed that the more holes than fabric shirt had put in an appearance again but I made no reference to it.

Like Finn, part of me yearned for peace and quiet, for my mountain and some normality as well as the ability to walk without pain. I knew I'd been lucky, very lucky to have come away as unscathed as I had; Trev was going to have a long journey back from where he was. But, it was a known flaw of mine, being ill, being injured made me even more irritable and impatient. I was a dreadful invalid, immediately desperate to escape the constraints placed on me by the need to heal.

I watched John and knew that I should be ashamed of my poor humour. John was never going to get up and run, never going to climb anymore, never going to cling by his fingertips to a rock face. Time I put myself back in my box and got on with it.

'Let's go do some thinking. Do you mind if I drag Bill with us, Sid, I need his brain. Bill, want to come? Can't have you enjoying yourself too much now that Luci is here.' My voice betrayed me, my frustration clear in it for all to hear. Bill had been deep in conversation with Ben.

'Some of us haven't stopped working, Spider, so just because you've been lounging about and sleeping, don't assume that everyone else has.'

He held my stare as if to say, go on then, make something of it you grumpy shit. I tried to laugh, but it wasn't there.

I swore most of the way up the stairs, getting angrier with each agonising step, wishing I'd not discarded the crutches somewhere too far away to easily fetch. I eventually arrived and dropped myself unceremoniously on the bed, drawing my good leg underneath but any sense of humour had also been left, like the crutches, too far away to easily find. Bill looked at me with barely concealed laughter, his chest quivering as he tried to hold it in.

'Bill, I'm not in the fucking humour for any comments, ok?'

'This is just too good an opportunity to miss! You're being such an arse, come on lighten up a bit, will you?' he let out that laughter, thumping the bed with his hand, which did nothing but send more red fire up me. 'All this bad temper just cos you can't go dancing!'

Sid looked away, I could see her mouth twitching. I was obviously on my own with this.

'Bill,' I swallowed hard to conceal the pain, 'pass the laptop, then you can go back to taking the piss and I'll do some work.' They weren't making me feel any better.

Bill picked up my bag, sliding it across and said, 'When you've remembered that you're actually a good bloke and not a dickhead, I'll tell you what I've just found out. In the meantime, I'll go and make coffee for us. Sid, please make him see sense otherwise I'm going home.'

'I can't believe you,' Sid said as he left. 'You're a bear with a sore head and after all that's gone on. Come on, play nice, I don't like grumpy Jake very much, he's not nearly as much fun.'

'I hate this, ok? I'm really bad at being ill.' I was still cross.

'I know, but you aren't ill. You've a badly broken leg that's all. It'll get better. It's not affected your brain or any other part of your body as far as I know.'

She smiled, pushed the door closed and lifted the laptop onto the floor then gently eased herself astride me, holding her weight on her knees, putting soft hands onto my chest.

'They've all been doing absolutely everything to make this right again. Let them do this now, let them do the running about as you would want to do for them. But be nice about it, I'm not exactly having a ball but I'm with you and I like it very much on planet Jake. It doesn't rain often and the scenery is gorgeous.'

She bent and kissed me, barely touching at first and then letting her body sink against mine. I held her tight, wound fingers into her hair, breathed her in, indulging in her passion. I hoped making coffee would take a long time but, sadly, it didn't. Bill knocked the door briefly and then just walked in; Sid took a moment to let me go.

'I think you'll find Mr Grumpy has been replaced by Mr Tolerable now,' she prodded me lightly in the ribs. 'Get on with it then; start the world turning again.'

Bill sat back down. 'It is likely that Ben is the one who told Alexander where we were.'

I was shocked, 'How? Does Ben know Alexander?'

'No, nothing like that, he said he was talking to Luci whilst waiting in the queue at the petrol station in Ashfield. He asked her if you and Sid had gone to Newmarket to see John. She didn't reply because her attention was taken by this scruffy guy nearby; she thought she recognised him. Ben says as soon as he'd said it, the man walked out.'

And as simple as that was just how this kind of thing happened, how someone's cover was blown. An innocent passing remark that fell on fertile ground, words in the right place at the right time. I wondered if that was how he'd found about me too.

'Has anything else been reported?'

'It was on the local news, in as much as a shooting incident at unspecified stud farm, alleged security guy got accidentally shot by unknown poacher burglar. All disguised by the powers that be. No one except us will know what really happened. It's yesterday news.'

'Has Alexander had anything to say?'

Bill looked at me and then Sid and back again.

'I've not said anything about this yet, I was waiting for you to be here again. Alexander is demanding that he sees you, Sid, says that he'll only talk to you and then he'll give a statement. He won't be pushed, they've tried, he just does the reciting endlessly and they get nowhere.'

'Where is he?' I asked.

'Secure hospital, sectioned and guarded. Properly this time I understand.'

I thought about it for a moment and then asked Sid, 'What do you think?'

She turned away, standing to go and look out of the window. This would be yet another tough decision for her.

'I don't want to talk to him. I'm not going through all that again and, in any case, he needs to remember that he kidnapped and drugged me, shot Trev and then, as if all that wasn't bad enough, came here and shot the most important person in my life,' she kept her face turned away. 'Can he call it like this? Can he issue such demands?'

'No, not really, but he can refuse to talk and he probably knows that we can't force him. If he stays silent then we'll have to find out what he was about another way. It can be done, it's just more time consuming,' Bill said, then added, 'You don't have to do anything you don't want to, Sid. If you talked to him, you wouldn't be alone and it would be strictly controlled.'

'Can I think about it? Can I have some time? Is that ok?'

She came back to the bed, sitting lightly down and sliding herself closer, wrapping her fingers into my shirt and reaching for my hand, eyes averted.

'Yes, of course, of course you can,' Bill smiled, took the pressure off immediately.

We talked some more but kept it loose, more on what her diary was like for the next few weeks and what was happening in Ashfield. She went back downstairs to feed Finn, but probably more to give herself a break from Bill and I.

'I didn't know what had happened to Sid in the past, not until after she was taken, when we tried to get that statement. I don't think she's up to talking to him now, you know her better than I do but, in my opinion, she's wafer thin. She was hanging by threads when you were in theatre, blames herself for you being shot. To be frank, I thought we were going to need help for her too,' he blinked slowly. 'She has continued to give me every indication that she's too close to the edge.'

I knew exactly what he was saying, it was there, clear for all to see.

'I know. When she came back from Scotland, she took a long time to come back into herself. You know that Alexander had given her acid and ket, which might explain it although only in part. But, and it's a big risky but, she's been dealing with this for years so I wonder if she might actually find it strengthening to finally get answers. We need to know and so does she. Alexander has been in a place that has left him with no alternative but to start killing people. It may be purely his lack of mental balance, or it may be something else. I haven't yet finished his notebook and we all need to know if there's a something else.'

Bill remained silent but cogs were whirring.

'You're right. Talk, see what she thinks, I'm going to go back into the office with the paperwork. Start from the beginning once again,' he rubbed at his face with both hands, 'I could do with a decent night's sleep too.'

'I recommend whatever it was they gave me in hospital, it certainly did the trick.'

'Oh yes, you slept for almost a solid twenty-four hours without stirring at all, you must have been running on empty for a while,' he grinned, black eyes glinting. 'Expect that has more to do with entertaining Sid though rather than working.'

'I wouldn't have the first idea what you mean, Bill. I'm asleep by nine every night, cup of cocoa as my only companion.'

'Yep, that's what I thought!' he laughed again, a big Bill laugh which was cut short when Luci bounded into the room.

'Jake! Now don't tell me to go away. I want to see my little bro and finally get the chance to talk to him,' she flopped heavily on the bed making me wince as a fire coursed up my leg. 'Oops! Sorry, I was trying to be careful.'

'Try a bit harder then!'

I shuffled more towards the middle of the bed, taking myself out of range.

Bill stood, 'I'm going to do some reading, see you later.' He turned to Luci and said, 'Be nice, be a good big sister now and no scrapping.'

She glared at his back as he left and then proceeded to talk non-stop about how unlucky I was to get shot by a poacher.

'Sophie,' I interrupted her, 'shut the door and shut up, its time we talked without pretence.' I sounded as irritated as I felt.

Chapter Seventy-One

'Tarvos, I know this isn't ideal but someone has to keep an eye on you.'

'Bollocks. We both know that you came to check up. Did you think you'd find me incapable of doing my job because of the rumours about Sid?'

She glared at me, 'Hardly rumours but, as usual, I've covered your arse, mate, so cut the self-righteous holier than thou routine. You'd have been pulled if it wasn't for me.'

'Covered my arse! Don't flatter yourself!' I swallowed back fury. 'Does that include getting me shot?'

She was no more my sister than Bill was, the similarity in our looks had been a gift to my employers and she'd played the role several times before. Our relationship was an odd one, we were sometimes as close as we appeared but she'd always been much more mercenary than I was. A promotion of sorts had moved her emphasis more to admin; she monitored now, monitored people like Bill and I, made sure we didn't get too big for our boots or, perhaps more importantly, didn't get sucked in too deep in the worlds we hid ourselves in. There were going to be no double standards on her watch. I liked her but I didn't trust her, it had always been clear that her loyalties lay elsewhere.

'If you played it by the book, that wouldn't have happened,' she fixed me with ice eyes, shifting blame back without a second thought.

'I don't get paid for playing it by the book.'

'No, but there are expectations, Tarvos. I never thought you'd be the one to get hauled up for fucking the payroll.'

I laughed loudly and wondered if she was being deliberately ridiculous. 'Oh, get a grip. You're starting to sound like you think you're missing out. Sid isn't payroll, she never was and you know it.'

'Ok,' she held her hands in a gesture of surrender, 'that was underhand, I apologise, but look at it from my side, someone had to check as you've never played it like this before.'

'And I'm not playing it now.'

She arched an eyebrow, 'What's that supposed to mean?'

'Whatever you want it too.' Bloody hell, the subtext became clear; she cared - no - more than that. Shit. And I'd never noticed how much.

'Are you intending to resign?' The trump card, revealed surprisingly early. A knee jerk defensive reaction to the fact that I finally understood. A blade thrust in to warn me off from drawing further attention to her weakness.

Perhaps believing she'd stalled me, she carried on, 'I'll give you the talk, Tarvos. I'll tell you what I've been instructed to say and you'll do me the favour of at least looking like you're listening. Let's begin with unprofessional, tut, taking advantage, double tut, where will this lead? Whilst you're off-line they ask that you think about the situation sensibly.

'They ask that you check the stats for just how many people in your position have any form of medium, let alone long-term relationship. You're critical as a team member, a key player indeed and they want you to think, to really think, how your days will feel when you aren't hanging out of a helicopter or speaking in tongues, or doing any of the stuff you usually do and consider perfectly normal. Pan has tried on your behalf to assure them that your relationship with Sid predated the Fielding investigation. Of course they know better. Of course they do, they know just about everything. Villain or good guy, they still pick and probe at every loose thread.'

'Is that it?' I smiled, probably owed her more but I was never going to lie down and take a kicking fuelled by scorn. 'Well, you go tick your boxes and return your forms and, for the record, I hadn't planned on resigning but you can report that I'll give it some thought if you like,' I paused and then said softly, 'I wasn't looking, Sophie and, if it helps, I didn't know.'

I held her gaze and saw the minuscule flicker she failed to hide as my words hit home. Poor little wolf, I thought, you always had a chink in your sheepskin and actually it gives me no pleasure to point it out. I'd let her file her report and deal with whatever fallout it produced, right now though, I'd still got an investigation to finish.

'Do your family know that you're injured?' she changed the subject, indirectly acknowledging and moving on.

'I've spoken to them. I rang when I was in hospital and had a much extended chat which was the first in a long time,' I said. 'And yes, I told them about Sid, so there's no drama there either.'

I rubbed my eyes, a wave of tiredness rushed over from nowhere. I found that I was yawning, the weight of my leg getting heavier even though it was on the bed.

'Whatever you think I'm here to do a job, not cause trouble,' she said and stood, 'I'll go, leave you to sleep for a bit. Should I ask Sid to come up?'

'Don't worry, she knows where I am.' I was fighting to stay awake. 'What about Ben? All this picking at me, does Ben know who you really are?'

She sighed loudly, 'Not your business, Tarvos, but the difference there is that Ben's nothing to do with work and he isn't under my protection.'

'Well, well. People in glass houses,' I yawned again, 'kettles and pots. Sorry, I'm going to have to sleep, can't keep my eyes open.'

I heard the door close but I didn't sleep immediately just lay for a while thinking about the situation; Sophie was right, I couldn't avoid it for much longer. I fell asleep trying to work out which direction I ought to choose and how, or indeed if, to tell Sid that Luci wasn't who she thought she was.

****

The trouble with pain killers, anaesthetics, surgery and healing is that it all tends to hang around for far too long. My eyes closed and I was woken only briefly by Sid as she curled in beside me, I wrapped her in my arms and went straight back to sleep again.

'Jake?' Bill's whisper woke me some time later; it was dark in the room, light from the landing seeping in through the now half open door. 'You awake?'

'Bill. What time is it?' I moved slowly, Sid was still wrapped around me.

'Five-thirty,' he shifted languages. 'I'm afraid I have bad news. Alexander attempted suicide about an hour ago. He was successful.'

'Fuck,' I replied in English.

'Indeed.'

'How?'

'I don't know but he found a way to beat the system before, didn't he.'

'Bugger... as if this wasn't complicated enough'.

'Just wanted to let you know,' Bill moved back to the doorway 'Catch up with you in a bit.'

I lay there once he'd gone listening to Sid's gentle breathing, knowing how much I'd missed her just being there when I was in the hospital. I moved so that I could see her in the gloom, lifted my hand to touch her face, she smiled in her sleep and murmured my name. There was now an unremitting throb from my leg, it pulsed like it was a separate living thing, healing bone around metal plates, metal plates that held together shattered bone blown apart by Alexander's sawn off.

Regardless of the pain, I stroked her face with my fingers indulging in the feel of her, so impossibly soft under my touch. She lay still, half smiling now and then but still not opening her eyes, I kept it up until her mouth twitched into a broad smile and she spoke.

'Jake. Hello Jake. I'm awake, really I am.'

She kept her eyes closed, sighed and wrapped herself tighter against my side, stretching one arm over me.

I moved again, bent to kiss her, not letting up until she opened her eyes.

'Do you know that even if you're a relentless pain in the arse it's so good to have you back again. I've missed you so very much,' she said with a smile, blinking away tiredness.

'I've just heard some bad news, Sid, very bad news,' I wasn't sure how to word it.

'Alyosha is gone, isn't he? Alyosha has gone and he's taken Alex with him.'

'Yes. A little while ago.'

'I did think he might try.'

'I don't know anything else, only that it has happened.'

'In a way I'm relieved. Aloysha was way too fragile for this life. He always had been.'

She was right, in so many ways it may have been a welcome release for such a troubled man. Even though he'd taken Sid, murdered several times and tried to take me out, I couldn't help but feel that he was the real victim here.

I went to sit up and was stopped immediately by a searing pain that flooded up to my hip. Sid was watching me intently.

'How much do you hurt? Please answer me completely truthfully.'

'Quite a lot, I think I should stick with the resting and crutches.'

'You've about four plates holding those bones together along with numerous screws. You've an entry wound that's a mangled mess of muscle fibre, all of which was further damaged with bone fragments as a zillion of those pesky little pellets passed through and, if that wasn't enough, you've also got an exit wound that looks like a small bomb went off under your skin. If you don't treat it well you'll take ages to heal, you'll get scar tissue and, most importantly, I'm working on a promise that I'll get taken to Ireland. You've a ticking deadline now, dude,' she flashed me with blue fire. 'So sit stay there, I'll go get some pain relief and the crutches. You're going to be good now and no biting anyone's head off.'

I felt railroaded but I couldn't argue. I sat and waited, took the pain relief and made it all the way downstairs to the office without making anything worse.

'Bill?' Sid asked. 'I'd like to see Alex, can you set it up? Can you make it happen?'

He nodded. 'I'll ask but do nothing, commit to nothing until I've checked with you first, ok?'

She hadn't said anything to me but I'd go with whatever she wanted. We needed closure, she needed to go home, back to some sort of normality again. We all needed that. She was very tightly strung; I could feel the trembling from where she stood so very close to the edge.

'Now someone please tell me something funny, I don't want to end up in tears yet again.'

John jumped in with the story of how Bill ended up drunk in a lift wearing a dress. We moved to the kitchen as no work was going to get done just then and, in the end, they drank far more than was necessary, especially John, who was hilarious but very drunk. Sid and I made excuses and hobbled off, me not her, to face the Everest climb to upstairs. That had an element of farce about it too.

****

Daylight woke us. My leg was thankfully much better behaved but I was now faced with the daily inconvenience of having Meccano as a constant companion.

Finn had been out and about with his surrogate aunt for hours and was sleeping off his excesses under the kitchen table, waking briefly for a crust of toast. Refuelled and armed with coffee I went into John's office, finding him with Bill, already hard at work. They'd set up a place for me to sit with half a leg of scaffolding so I sat and got on the phone to Moore.

Trev was now in a side room on a surgical ward, the usual day to day petty crimes were still happening, relentlessly life went on. David Flint was apparently getting increasingly twitchy and, for some strange reason, had lost some horses from his yard. The arrival of an unexpected VAT Inspector had done nothing to still his twitches. What with that, evidence of illegal immigrants using his lorry and the Wozniak drugs involvement, even the racing authorities had stirred themselves from liquid lunches to stare at him over half-moon glasses, shuffling licences with old boy grunts. Moore and I smiled to each other down phone lines, what goes round and all that. He said the word good bye to me on the phone for possibly the first time ever. Updates were promised, to come as soon as they were available on both sides.

Bill was in conversation with someone who could help Sid see Alexander and John was typing away.

'Message for you, Jake. Came in a day or so ago but not urgent. Go on line and I'll send it over,' John said, without looking up.

I turned back to the screens and logged in. It was from Sylvie Freeman, the blue rinse and twin set laser mind at Weatherbys. I read through the brief note and picked up the phone. She'd found quite a list from the very first two seasons at stud for Alexander's stallion and, perhaps even more interestingly, for another stallion that had been under similar syndicate ownership but at a different farm. The full names and details now on the lists, not all but too many for chance, would've made any police station start putting out extra seats. Looking at the names, I'd say that, aside from illegal conception which, to be fair, we already knew about and wasn't life threatening in its own right, only by default; there was also a fair bit of money laundering going on.

The passage of large sums from one place to the next in payment for goods supplied so no crime there - on the face of it. But. Always there was a but. That particular money had been got by dubious means, secreted perhaps from the people who rightfully owned it and certainly secreted from the powers that be at Her Maj.'s Revenue and Customs. It was fraud money, drugs money, blackmail money and it was sliding around pretending to be something else entirely. I promised Sylvie a visit and a large box of doughnuts; she told me I'd already promised both things. I thought for a while and suggested poteen, she laughed and told me just to come and see her.

Chapter Seventy-Two

And I will flay the flesh from their bones and strip them bare for angels to eat

At Sid's request, I was reading the translated contents of Alexander's notebook to her. It had been harrowing. Now, in the last few pages, which became almost a direct letter, she was getting the answers to the mystery that he'd been.

Who is that man to you? Who really is the man that you're with? The policeman. What is he to you? He's not who he seems to be. Do you know that, Zosima? He's not strictly a policeman. He's not strictly anything that can be defined.

Perceptive, astute; that little summary, considering the time when it had been written, was surprising. I let it go without comment.

He'd actually sent the notebook around the time that he'd abducted her. Why? Because he thought he'd fail or did he send it as a form of confession, to be found after the event?

He'd intended to kill Sid, to kill her to keep her safe and out of danger forever. Just as she'd said he would. Even with the implication of that fact, all I could think now was what a waste; what a waste of him and all that he might have been.

'He keeps saying he wanted to protect me, why not protect himself? Why didn't he just stay away? He could have stayed gone, made a new life and kept himself safe, its what I did eventually. Why did he feel he had to come back and protect me?'

'There's still a little more, ok to carry on?' I had the advantage of knowing the answer to her question. It wasn't easy knowledge to hold.

'Yes, go on, whatever he's written, don't leave anything out.'

Seb and Josh and what they did - don't push me, I can't write this. I see it but I can't write it. I've never said it, not once, not ever. I see it every day since it happened. I can't write it. I see it. It is the reason I don't want to sleep, it is printed on my eyes, I see it all the time. Reflections of it, the ghost of it and it stalks me.

I came to see you, Zosima, all those years ago. I came to the house. I had a present for your sixteenth birthday. It was late, your birthday had been and gone but I'd taken a long time to pluck up the courage to come. They, Seb and Josh, wouldn't let me see you, so I always had to sneak around. I came in the back way, through the garden and crept in the kitchen door...

Alexander's lettering became large, violent looking scrawl, the pen had dug into the paper as he'd written it. Even in coded form it read like a shout.

Gabriel. Oh Zosima! Gabriel happened! Gabriel Wallace and you. Gabriel had you in the kitchen. There was blood from your face. From everywhere! There was blood and terror and pain and force!

Silently, Sid curled herself tight beside me, 'Go on,' she hissed the words through clenched teeth. 'Don't stop, go on.'

Alexander's words must have tumbled out of his pen thick and fast, the dam breached and out it all flowed. But he bled those words, each one torture, each one must have caused him tremendous pain. I, in turn, spoke it, made it real, gave it life with those out loud words.

He did that to you. I watched, frozen, it was rape, assault, pain, terror, force and I raged. I jumped up to help you, I wanted to kill that bastard, might have done it too, but Josh got to me first. He was hiding, guarding the back door, so no one came in. I didn't know he was there, I hadn't seen him. He knew, Zosima! For fuck's sake... he knew! Seb too! In the other room making sure no one came the other way. That's who they were. That's who they are! They gave you to him. You were payment. But even Gabriel didn't have to do that, he didn't have to do that to you! I tried to help, Josh wouldn't let me. He beat me, Zosima, I couldn't walk, he threw me out the door dragged me to the bushes and left me. When I could stand again, it was hours later and you were no longer there. There was no Zosima, no Gabriel, no blood, no pain, no terror left to see there anymore, just kitchen cupboards and shiny floors. But it was there... it tainted the air... it hung like curtains... spectral entrails in that house, touching my face and ripping me apart. When I came to see you, after, you wouldn't talk to me, about anything. You hated me. I couldn't protect you. I couldn't save you. I failed you. I failed myself. Bastards. Oh Zosima. It wasn't just happening to you... That would have been bad enough but, Zosima... You must have worked it out by now #me too.... #balance ton porc

The only one of your brothers who could have helped and I could not. That is why. It has taken me this long to shake them off, taken me this long to get strong enough and they are never going to get away with hurting either of us again. It won't happen again, Zosima. Cross my heart and hope to ride a National winner...

If there's any truth behind reincarnation, I hoped that Alexander really would get his lifetime as a sky dancer as, in so many ways, he deserved it.

****

We arrived with Sid, pale and trembling, at the place where Alexander was. He'd yet to be removed from the secure unit, so we stood outside in corridors waiting for checks and double checks; there were going to be no heads rolling here for anyone to drop kick out of doors. Heartless institutionalised corridors painted in gone-off white, far too cold a shade to call it anything glamorous like magnolia; plastic chairs and echoing floors. This was a place with purpose and that purpose wasn't entertaining visitors, rather more for discouraging them from having the audacity to visit. It was devoid of most things; pictures of bubonic plague might have lightened the atmosphere.

Cold, clinical and utterly silent; Sid became paler. I felt a landslide occurring on that fragile edge she stood on. She was shaking, in great waves, it couldn't be ignored.

'Are you ok with this? We can leave if this is too much,' I tipped her chin to look at her eyes.

'I can do this, I must,' she said it like she was trying to persuade herself as much as me. 'Don't go, not for a second, stay right there.'

'Think phoenix, imagine it and take strength,' I smoothed her hair back over her shoulders and repeated, 'phoenix, ok?'

When we saw him, I was somewhat surprised; he was no longer the bowed, shabby, tramp of a man with dreads. Uncovered to his chest, he was muscular in the way that spoke of considerable training. He had short, light brown hair that may have been blonde when he was a child. A handsome face if it wasn't still so haunted and touched with purple-yellow bruising from when we'd last met. He was clearly kin to Sid, he'd a lot of her in his face, much more so than either Seb or Joshua had. I realised that I'd actually seen the core of this man on that morning in the barn, when he'd fought back against me so bravely.

Sid broke the silence. She still clung, as if I was the rope that stopped the slide, but her voice was clear.

'Alex, my dear sweet Alyosha, I'm so sorry that I wasn't there for you. There to help you before this all got too hard. Wherever you are, know that I forgive you and that I loved you so much. I will always love you, Alyosha. Be at peace and fly high. I know that you're finally where you always wanted to be - truly are a sky dancer now...,' her voice broke and she turned her face into my chest.

After a while she dried her eyes and we left that place, Sid and me with Bill. Out, cleansed in a way, leaving horrors behind and back into the real world again. Bill went outside first, holding open the door for us, letting in bright winter sunlight and fresh air. A shaft of that sunlight caught on the brass door handle and shot a fire halo around Sid, reflecting across her hair and shoulders, making her look as if she had golden wings.

She was my phoenix, of course, with golden sunlight wings.

Epilogue

All of us were now making those kind of plans that would enable a return to what was classed as normal life. A case would be put together by the police for the coroner, for the prosecutions that had to follow and a line would eventually be drawn under this investigation.

I was going to be out of action for a few weeks but then even that would pass and I'd carry on pretty much as before. Undeniably, so much had happened and it seemed like a lifetime, someone else's lifetime, since I'd wandered into the station at Ashfield. I wouldn't go back as the job there was done. Once I was healed there'd be another job and another place to be. It had begun with a mountain and wild boar.

A mountain, wild boar and sea blue glinting like the sun on small waves.

Sid said very little more about Alexander, she didn't want to see Sebastian and wanted nothing to do with arrangements for anyone's funeral. She seemed to be coping but I was never too sure how much was lurking, out of sight for the moment but still prowling around, waiting.

What did I know? I knew that Alexander had destroyed the Sid that was, yet another incarnation was in the offing. I knew that she'd lost everything, her past nothing more than a manipulation. Everything had changed; for her, for me, for us - deep down, it had all shifted.

The newspapers weren't helpful. It was there, the Fielding downfall, in full and lurid detail *sub judice* notwithstanding, a pile of still warm bones to be gnawed at. Everyone who was anyone, it seemed, had something to say about it from disbelief to the downright vicious. A slavering pack of media hyenas stalked, yipping after every new morsel that was revealed. It was gossip gluttony for the sake of it.

I sensed Sid's gradual withdrawal back behind the defensive walls she'd spent years making, precipitated by the media frenzy. I wondered if she'd decide to withdraw from me too. But, then again, maybe I should be the one to make that decision. As Tommy would say, mountain mist was never meant to be held after all.

Cath called from the hallway, 'Jake, post for you. Irish postmark.'

I hobbled out and took it from her, putting it in my pocket unopened. Then, after going into the office with none of that instant crap for Bill and John, I precariously balanced two cups and made for the stairs.

The room was empty but the shower running so I simply sat on the bed and waited for her.

My next big move was ready to be played and it was important, so critically important, that I got it right. To be totally frank, I was very afraid mainly because I'd no idea whether it was the right thing to do or not. There were no certainties now.

Can I give it up? Can I really? Can I walk away now if I had to?

Change; I had to make the change. For her, whatever I felt, I had to do this.

She appeared from the bathroom, towel drying her hair.

'Hello,' she stopped and looked at me, her face paled. 'What? What's happened? Bloody hell, Jake, you look like something really bad is going down.'

'Sid, come here, please, sit here with me.' I held out my hand.

'Please. Tell me. This looks major.'

Those eyes; deep sea blue that had mesmerised me right from the start.

I exhaled slowly. Mentally kicked myself and realised my mouth had gone dry, words sat stalled and unable to be spoken. I stood, hobbled to the door and whistled for Finn. He came at top speed, tongue hanging out of his happy, laughing lurcher face.

'Jake, please will you talk to me?' Sid stayed sitting, ashen faced.

Come on! I gave myself another kick. Do it or don't do it, but do something otherwise she's going to freak out.

'Sid…' I managed her name and nothing else. I glanced down to Finn, legs in the air, rubbing his back in doggie ecstasy against the long pile of the rug and laughter wanted to bubble up in me from somewhere. Such a silly Jedi master; it was as if he was clowning just for me, deliberately taking the mick out of my ridiculous drama.

'Sid…' I started again.

'Yes? Fucking hell, spit it out!' she moved so that she was kneeling on the bed, clutching her towel in tight hands. 'You're really scaring me.'

That kicked the words back in. 'Sid, no, please don't be scared, please just hear me out.'

I sat again. Breathe, Jake, just breathe. This was it.

She held up one hand, palm flat. 'Enough! Stop. Please stop. Before you do or say anything further I need to give you something,' she stood and went over to her jacket, hanging up on the back of the door, took out an envelope from the inside pocket.

'This was meant for when we got back to Dartmoor but, now... oh Jake, how do you do this? Why can only you do this to me? Right now... oh fuck... you'd better open it. It can't wait now.'

Even Finn was frozen on the rug, eyes up to us both as if we were in danger. I wondered if we were.

She handed me the plain white envelope. An innocent white envelope, nothing sinister about it, but reading her now, seeing confusion and apprehension, even fear written all over her, I felt another brief flicker of what I'd felt when she was taken. Nothing was certain.

I opened the envelope and eased out what was inside, slowly turning it over to see the front. It was a photograph. A black and white photograph of the tor behind her house. I glanced at her but she was frozen again, unfathomable eyes on me. I read what was written on the back.

Those lines that I before have writ do lie....

...Love is a babe; then might I not say so; To give full growth to that which still doth grow.

Shakespeare. A sonnet.

And then the words she'd written that almost stopped the pulse in me.

Jake, because every day my love for you grows; you are love, life, strength, sanity - my absolute everything. Marry me? Please. Will you marry me?

Stunned, I looked up at her, couldn't quite believe it. From my pocket I took out the package sent from Ireland, slipped it out of its padded envelope and placed it into her hand closing her fingers around it. As our fingers touched I knew instantly that she truly thought I'd come to her with nothing more to say than good bye.

'Sid, you've always had this way of taking my very best lines,' I unwrapped her fingers from the little box that she held and opened the lid. A ring sat prettily within, sapphire blue, a colour so close to her eyes. 'This was my grandmother's and I was trying to ask you the very same question.'

Without words, locked in her eyes, I placed the ring on her third finger, there on her left hand and it fitted as if it had been made for her alone. I took her in my arms and kissed her as if my life depended on it.

And it did. Now it did.

Quotation Reference

1. Lulled in these flowers with dances and delights... A Midsummers Night Dream; Shakespeare, 1595.

2. The momentary intoxication with pain... The Face of Violence; Jacob Bronowski, 1954.

3. He spent his time here in a mist; John Cleveland 1647.

4. If I must die, I will encounter darkness as a bride... Measure for Measure; Shakespeare, 1604.

5. Death isn't anything... Rosencrantz and Guildenstern Are Dead; Tom Stoppard, 1967.

6. For murder, thou it have no tongue... Hamlet; Shakespeare, 1601.

7. I am ashes where once a fire burned. Byron, 1823.

8. For words, like nature, half reveal and half conceal... Tennyson, 1850.

9. He has been reborn as an idea, something intended... W.B. Yeats, 1914.

10. Those lines that I before have writ... Sonnet CXV; Shakespeare.

30074982R00214

Printed in Poland
by Amazon Fulfillment
Poland Sp. z o.o., Wrocław